THE AMULET

THE AMULET

A Novel of Horror

by

A. R. Morlan

THE BORGO PRESS

An Imprint of Wildside Press LLC

MMIX

FIRST WILDSIDE EDITION

CONTENTS

DEDICATION

(1988)

In memory of

LITTLE GUY
(1983-1989)

More than a cat, you were family—
More than a friend, you were the child of my heart.

(2009)

This reprint edition of *The Amulet* is dedicated
with all of my thanks and respect to:

ARDATH MAYHAR

Who not only sought out a new home for my novel, but
took it upon herself to scan the text, and submit it for me
to a new publisher. For that task, she has all my gratitude
and unending admiration. She is truly a class act, and a
generous human being. Without her, this book would have
remained forever *Cancelled*, and eventually forgotten—
she made it come alive again. Thanks, Ardath: I can never
repay you for all you've done for me, and for my work!

FOREWORD

This novel was written during a twenty-two-day stretch back in January of 1989; while I usually write short fiction that quickly, I'd never done anything this long that fast; but I was working under a do-or-die deadline. My written-first novel, *Dark Journey* (that wasn't actually the title I wanted, but that's another story; from now on, I'll just call that first novel *Dark Journey*, or *DJ* for short), had already been accepted for publication as a hardcover (which is yet *another* story, since it was dumped out as a tightly-spaced paperback less than a year after this novel was published), but my publisher had a small problem.

DJ was a very long, complex book which they supposedly wanted to release with some degree of care, but it was considered an unlikely "first" novel; so they wanted me to put out a shorter, somewhat less complicated novel, albeit using some of the same characters that would be utilized in the second, more ambitious novel, in order to generate readership for the "second" book. And so I was told that, before a contract could be issued, I had to write a second "first" novel. *DJ* had taken me about seven years to write, and that didn't include the final drafts I did *after* I actually did get the contract, which should tell you a little something about how my novel-writing vs. short-fiction writing creative process operated.

I'm fairly proficient at writing short fiction, but the long works give me more trouble. *DJ* had taken years to reach a cohesive linear narrative, so suddenly I was faced with a choice—either come up with a second novel which could be written *fast*, or I'd lose my chance at being published by that particular house. My then-agent wanted me to jump ship and try the book elsewhere, but I had a problem—since I am probably one of the world's worst typists (a fact my editor later confirmed when she screamed at me over the phone, "You're the worst fucking typist in the whole god-damn universe!" a couple of years later), and computer illiterate on top of that, thanks to some learning disabilities which also prevented me from learning how to drive, etc., I was dependent on my editor's then-husband to actually get the book submitted in disk format to the publisher.

He'd ordered an Atari word processor and a different-brand printer for me from some computer company out East; and since the printer he ordered never worked right with the word processor, I was dependent on him to turn my diskettes into printed copy. And he told me that if I jumped ship with the book, he would not help me print out my disks—and since the system he used was obscure, and my typing skills were so awful, I'd have to pay a great deal of money up front to have my typed version of *DJ* turned into a submissable text, something even my agent would have to charge me for. And since I was hurting for money, I was trapped. But…my editor's husband came up with a solution to my novel problem on his own….

A year or so earlier, I'd published a short story in *The Horror Show* magazine called "Night Skirt," which was set in Ewerton, my fictionalized version of my own residence in Wisconsin (the setting of most of the stories I'd already had published, in the magazine my book-editor's husband also edited); and that story concerned a magical black skirt with dark, evil powers which falls into the hands of a most unpleasant little girl, on whom I'd based on my equally unpleasant and actually rather evil grandmother (who acted like a child until her death years later). The story was brief and pretty much self-contained, but the book-editor's husband thought it might work as a Foreword for a present-day story.

Since I was faced with many years spent writing *DJ* going down the drain if I didn't come up with a new novel, I reluctantly agreed that I'd try and come up with something based on my "Night Skirt" story. Only, I was soon told by the editor at the book publishing house that I could not use a skirt *per se*—the art department there simply could not find with a way to make a skirt scary. So I had a choice—I could turn the skirt into a ring or a bracelet of some sort. Which could be hidden *in* the skirt, initially, so I could still cannibalize most of the short story to act as the novel's prologue. I decided to use the bracelet, since I thought a scarab ring was just too darned clichéd (I'd also been told to make it a beetle-based ornament to provide a good cover image). And then I had a few days to create a rough outline and submit that. The editor wasn't crazy about it, but thought I could punch it up later—and so I finally got my contract.

That was December of 1988, and by the next month, I was writing a novel I'd never dreamed I'd be writing, using an infernal word processor I'd only employed once before to transcribe a previously-typed piece onto. I soon learned that the WP's rather bizarre system of self-filing each disk wasn't conducive to my style of writing (that is, looking at what I'd written a page or two earlier, then going on to the next section)—as each of the three banks within each file filled, it was impossible to scan backwards to, say, the beginning of the first or second file while filling up the second or third. So I had to guesstimate what I'd written about several pages earlier, and try to keep it all in my head as I worked.

If time hadn't been an issue, I would have written it on the typewriter instead, and then transcribed it into the WP; but I'd been told that writing directly into a WP was so much "easier" and sup-posedly enhanced the creative process—well, perhaps for most people, but not for me. This novel was the first—and last—thing that I ever wrote on a word processor. Which I'll admit wasn't a real computer, but the experience working with that blasted machine and its clunky software was enough to sour me on all non-typewriters for life. Within five years I'd sold the thing to Ardath Mayhar and her late husband Joe, who ran a used computer shop, along with the printer I'd never been able to use (and which, I later found out, was so thoroughly incompatible with the Atari machine that it would have never been recommended by anyone who sold computers, no matter what the fellow who ordered it for me said).

So…writing this novel wasn't the most naturally creative proc-ess of my writing career. Surprisingly, a number of people have liked it—once it was published, something my book editor wasn't thrilled to see happen, since she never did like the book, and only ended up putting it out because she had missed the accept-or-reject deadline once I sent the diskettes to her husband. Even though the book was cancelled from reprint status within a year of its release (along with *DJ*, which was summarily canceled immediately after the first sales statement arrived), it did earn back its advance plus some royalties. I have no idea to this day if all the copies of both books which had been sent to stores sold out, or if the rest were pulped. No one there seemed to know what happened with the two novels after my editor was fired a few years later—save that the rights ultimately reverted back to me.

Although the genesis of this novel was not the most pleasant creative experience I've ever had, the end result seemed to please a lot of folks, and it did eventually emerge as a serviceable prequel to *DJ*. I made every effort to produce an interesting read.

I ended up dipping into my own family history, so some of the events in this book were inspired by real (and deadly) occurrences. A brother-in-law of my maternal grandmother actually did kill his mother with an axe—this happened in the late 1930s in the Chicago area. No one knows why, and the man was never tried, just shipped off to the state mental hospital. Neighbors heard his mother calling the man's name, and shortly afterward, he was seen wandering around with the bloody axe still in hand. He wasn't a blood relative of mine, just a stray leaf on the family tree, but that didn't stop my "father" (aka the Deadbeat Sperm Donor) from getting it into his pea-brain that the man was somehow a blood-relative of my mother, and therefore had tainted her (and by inference, me) with "killer" blood.

Lucy Minor is based on my maternal grandmother in virtually all ways save for being an only child (even though she *did* act like one), having a living grandparent to bond with, and, of course, her choice of a real-life mate (my maternal grandfather wasn't much of a catch—he was born blind with prenatal cataracts, remained legally blind as an adult, became an alcoholic, and had only a fourth-grade education). My grandmother was pretty much the Poster Child for Back Alley Abortion—one of those people the world said would have been much better off without her having graced it with her presence. She destroyed her only child's life, and she destroyed mine; and I know if I'd had a child, she would have destroyed that kid's life too. It was simply in her nature. Out of the ten children her parents had raised (five died in childhood), she was the one whom they feared and disliked the most.

I don't know why she was the way she was; all I know is that virtually everyone who came in contact with her ended up disliking her—or using her for what they could get out of her, then dumping her. She was a flirting machine: if she saw a man, she felt compelled to flirt with him, be he married, underaged, or openly not interested.

The "real" Lucy Minor was far more evil, frightening, and dangerous than my fictional creation could ever be on her own. To this day, I still have nightmares about her, even though she's been dead for many years. I wasn't even able to write about the worst of what she did to us; for that bit of information, check out my short story "Powder" in the *Smothered Dolls* anthology.

I do know one thing: if I were writing this novel today, I'd add one more quote at the beginning of the book, something which hadn't been written back in 1989. In a seventh-season episode of his show *The X-Files*, creator/writer Chris Carter had one of his characters say this about his blighted background: "A big ugly dog lifted its leg on my family tree."

So...consider that added to this novel. It sums things up better than I could.

There's an old, old saying that starts off "The sins of the fathers..." which Anna Sudek came to know by heart; but the past sins in her family were far stranger—and far more pervasive—than anything most people might encounter in their lives. A long-ago theft of something more dangerous than financially precious, a mysterious death by axe, and—worst of all, a grandmother who continues to cast her manipulative spell over the life of her only granddaughter—these are the sins that are continually visited upon this young woman.

But once she learns the nature of the first sin, and figures out a way to fight its insidious powers, Anna realizes that she might have a chance to combat the forces in her life which threaten to destroy not only her, but those who come between Anna and her malign blood relatives.

—A. R. Morlan
July 2007

PROLOGUE

PRAGUE, BOHEMIA, LATE OCTOBER 1880

NIGHT SKIRT

Chill wind scattered blown leaves along the lamp-lit cobbled street outside Karel Nezval's diamond-paned front parlor window. An occasional clawed leaf raked the window glass with a faintly chitinous sound, disturbing Nezval's sensitive ears. He paused to rub the shell-curled surface of his left ear as he read his archaeologist friend's latest letter, which had arrived simultaneously with a small wooden box carefully wrapped in oiled paper and thin but incredibly strong twine, said box also sent by his boyhood friend.

Shifting his slightly protruding, yet deeply hooded brown eyes away from the fine feathery tracery of Josef's penned words, the glass manufacturer (and armchair Egyptologist, a holdover from his student days in Berlin) glanced at the opened wooden box, which rested on the small, round cherry wood table near the hissing and sputtering fireplace. The box itself was propped up slightly, the upper end resting on the box lid, so that Nezval could better view the small treasure Josef Zeyerhad so recently freed from Egypt's sandy soil. The deep yellow-gold and green basalt surfaces of the object were warmly illuminated by the red and orange tongues of flame in the fluttering fire. Nezval leaned across the left arm of his chair and squinted as he admired his unexpected gift from Josef—the delicate, almost impossibly fine detailing, especially on such a small piece of jewelry; the way the scales on the lower half seemed to strain *through* the oily-smooth skin of the thing, as if originating from within the gold, and not merely molded or incised upon it.

"Beautiful," Karel Nezval whispered, his tongue darting out to almost touch the deep indentation of flesh under his lower lip, before he reluctantly returned his gaze to Josef's letter:

...most unusual sort. As you see, the end with the serpent head is not fashioned of red stone, paste, or jasper at all, as is fitting for a symbol of the snake goddess Isis. I do not know for certain, nor do I wish to know, dear Karel, what the maker of this amulet had in mind when he cast the serpent in gold, but according to the *hekau* inscribed on the underbelly (what I have been able to translate of them), he was seeking power greater than that of a scarab alone, yet not necessarily the customary one of a serpent's head-to protect the deceased from the bites of the snakes in the underworld. Instead, he sought *deviating* powers, whose range and intensity are most intriguing, albeit thoroughly atavistic, and most genuine, as I myself can attest.

This is why I have sent the amulet to you for safekeeping—the natives in our camp fear it, with good reason, and those of us in charge of the excavation respect it mightily. But it has proven too much of a temptation for us, dear Karel, which is why I have entrusted it in your care. I implore you to heed the warning enclosed in the box, and written at the beginning of this letter: do *not* touch the amulet with your bare hands, or with gloves, unless they are of asbestos. Use the tongs provided in the box, or tweezers, if you have them.

Please heed me in this, Karel. One man, a native worker, died as a result of the power of this piece. We killed him out of necessity, before he killed us and demolished the entire dig. The *hekau* inscribed on the amulet (and, I suspect strongly, amplified by more "words of power" uttered *over* the amulet upon completion) are, as far as I can tell from a limited translation, most detailed and specific, with the most malicious of intentions.

Imagination fails when I attempt to envision the master plan of this object's maker. One of my colleagues, Herr Dobbershutz, has surmised that the maker of the amulet introduced quicksilver or some similar alloy in the casting of the gold, and added the ground up bodies of a real scarab beetle and a serpent to the crucible. Upon witnessing the unfortunate state in which our native man met his demise, I find myself in agreement with Herr Dobbershutz. Words of power alone do not account for what happened when that fellow held the amulet.

Dear Karel, if you can further decipher the *hekau* on this amulet, please do so. But, I implore you, remain cautious in all your contact with it. I knew not where else to send this *entity*, to keep it in safe, sober hands. I hope that by removing the piece from the land of its origin, I have somehow negated even a small fraction of its powers.

Karel Nezval let out a soft, barking laugh as Josef's letter spiraled to the lush carpet below with a dry flutter of stiff rag paper. After poking the logs behind the grate until they sent upsputtering points of light, like a miniature meteor shower inst the sooty bricks of his fireplace, the owner of the third largest glass-making factory in all of Austria-Hungary rubbed palms together with a dry snicking sound and said aloud, not caring if his cowed servants heard him or not, "Poor Josef—always acting like a hysterical woman. Even as a boy...and now as a man, if 'man' I dare call you, my friend.

"A native lackey goes on a rampage, and my poor Josef is shaking in his drawers, blaming a trinket of gold alloy. Josef will believe me when I tell him that I simply *had* to dispose of the amulet, for his own safety. He would never dream of asking me where or how, or impose on me to show him the contents of my safe. Trusting, unquestioning Josef—"

"You called for me, sir?"

Summoned by the sound of her employer's voice, Nezval's parlor maid now stood in the doorway, her reddish-brown upswept hair a blaze of burnished copper in the fireplace's still low-burning light. After giving his excelsior-bedded golden treasure a final, longing glance (*later, later, I will discover what Josef was so intimidated by*, he thought), Nezval turned his attention to the young woman waiting next to the opened door, admiring the swells and valleys of her as-yet-unused body under the prim white aproned black uniform, the metallic gleam of her coiled reddish hair, until he hit upon the best mode of attack, of getting the most service for the money he paid the girl. He said nonchalantly, in a tone that belied the growing tumescence in his lower regions, the eager anticipation tingling in his hands, his lips, "Yes, Anna, the fire needs tending," then waited, his insides already aflame, until the tall, buxom maid had crossed the parlor, with a gentle sighing swish of black wool brushing against starchy petticoats below, on her way to the fireplace. And when she had her back turned to him, Karel Nezval was able to shut and lock the thick oak parlor door, unnoticed by his obedient parlor maid.

OCTOBER 1931

Lucy's bare feet made soft slapping sounds on the dusty plank floor as she made her way down the upstairs hallway, heading for the staircase. Her cotton nightgown brushed against her calves, almost making her giggle, but she curled her lower lip between her teeth and bit down hard, telling herself, *Gramma doesn't giggle when her night skirt brushes her legs—she just lets it trail out like twilight, all dark and deep and wide behind her.* Lucy always tried to be like her grandmother, even though her blue serge middy skirt only came down to her knees, and the blue wasn't blue enough—not that rich, plum-like blue-black of Gramma's night skirt, with the star-like twinkle of lacy petticoat peeping out from under the thick rolled hem when she walked.

Gramma had been everything to Lucy, for all of her six and a half years on earth, just as Lucy was everything to her mother's mother. Ever since Gramma's big house with the gingerbread trim on the roof overhang and big curved porch was taken away by the county (Mother said it was all President Hoover's fault, "For getting us in this mess," but Lucy didn't think that her Gramma even *knew* the president), Gramma had lived in Lucy's house.

Downstairs, because climbing the stairs was too hard for a woman with too-white hair and soft, puffy, dotted arms, and teeth that could pop out of her mouth. But Gramma's age wasn't the only reason she slept downstairs. Lucy wasn't supposed to know any of this, but like maiden Aunt Dora said, little pitchers have big ears, and Lucy couldn't *help* it if her room was next to Mother and Daddy's.

"Couldn't she live somewhere *else—anywhere* else?" Mother had said to Daddy many a time after Gramma swept into their house and settled down in the sewing room off the kitchen, And Daddy's answer was always the same: "She's your mother, you're her daughter, and you happen to be an only child. Where else is she *supposed* to go?"

And Mother's answer was always the same, too. Never answering Daddy, she'd almost sigh, "I wish Lucy hadn't attached herself to her like a barnacle on a barge. It isn't *healthy*."

"Your mother did all right by you—you turned out swell. Why shouldn't Lucy be fine?"

There was always a pause there, as if Mother wanted to say more, but couldn't or wouldn't. Then: "But those were different times. When I was small *every* mother wore long swishing skirts and tucked lace hankies in their sleeves. It's 1931—she shouldn't be dressing like that. And don't tell me I should buy her a dollar cotton pongee dress from Sears and burn her old things. Oh, I know that's what you were thinking, *and* it wouldn't work. My mother has worn a long black skirt for *ages*—since before Poppa died. And I do believe she will *die* in that awful thing. What's that Lucy's taken to calling it—night skirt? Some such silliness—and *she* fosters it. I won't stand for it, the way she addles poor Lucy's mind. It's bad enough *we're* old—"

"Old? I feel pretty fit for—"

"Fifty. And I am forty-five. Perhaps having a baby so late wasn't the ideal thing to do—after all, my mother is in her seventies."

"Oh, you worry too much," Daddy would always end up saying, before turning over in bed and making the old spring mattress creak and groan like a withered tree in a thunderstorm.

Lucy could almost feel her mother's anger seething out of her, through the wallpaper and plaster of the wall between their bedrooms, and into her. She imagined her mother's displeasure as something cold-bright and pulsing, like the full moon swimming in a foggy sky.

Arid as she lay in her too-short bed, her feet poking through the white enameled spindles at the bottom, Lucy wondered if Gramma could feel Mother's seeping anger dripping down on her, through the floor to the sewing room below. Gramma often told Lucy that grandmothers have a way of knowing all sorts of things. And since Lucy's other grandmother and both her grandfathers died back in 1918, during the influenza epidemic, Lucy took her Gramma's word for it.

After all, Gramma wore the night skirt with the star-sparkling white petticoats, while Lucy's mother only wore a rayon slip under short cotton and pongee dresses. And didn't Gramma sit Lucy down on her big lap and whisper in her ear that short dresses were bad—that they weren't *special,* like the rippling soft and oh-so-dark-it-sucked-in-the-light night skirt?

Once, Lucy had tried tying her winter coat around her waist, using the sleeves like apron ties to keep it around her body. But even though the coat was blue-black wool, it just wasn't the same as Gramma's night skirt. The ripple of the material wasn't there, and neither were the other things. Hadn't Gramma laughed when she had seen Lucy strutting around in her thick, ersatz skirt?

Bending over to scoop Lucy up in her plump arms, she'd whispered in the girl's ear, "Is my Lucy trying to wear a night skirt? Oh, Lucy, Pumpkin, Gramma's night skirt is very special—not for little girls. Oh no, no, no." But when Gramma said, "No, no, no," it didn't sound like it did when *Mother* said it (as Lucy *slapped* down the uncarpeted stairs, her small mouth twisted like she'd just tried to eat a peeled lemon), oh no, not at *all*....

And hadn't Gramma *shown* Lucy how special her long blue-black-purple skirt could be? There was that time in the front yard, in winter (the most special, *secret* time, when Lucy swore on her heart and hoped to die that she wouldn't tell Mother or Daddy what she'd seen), and the other time, when Lucy had scooted along the floor while Gramma was napping she'd lifted up the hem of the night skirt and curled up in a little ball under the heavy fabric.

As she made her way down the stairs in the darkness of evening toward Gramma's room, Lucy remembered how she had been able to see only a faint haze of light, like trying to look through the stacks of screen windows resting against the house, the day Daddy changed the windows in early summer. But the more she'd looked, the better she could see—only through the cloth of the night skirt, things looked different. Colors changed, and the shapes of things, too. At first, Lucy hadn't recognized Mother at all, for seen through that night-dark fabric, Mother was a horned, angled creature, all hard surfaces and spikes.

That was when Lucy whimpered, and Gramma nudged her out from under the night skirt and had Lucy on her lap before Mother could open her thick lips to scold or complain. But Lucy saw the look in her mother's hazel eyes, and almost imagined the horns again. And for many a night after that,

Mother told Daddy in the half hour or so before sleep overtook them that she ought to take Gramma's "damned skirt" out and burn it—just toss it on the trash heap and *incinerate* it. Lucy wondered why Mother didn't suggest giving the skirt to the woman who came around every week, but every time Mother mentioned it, all she seemed to think of was destroying it.

Lucy was careful not to make the treads squeak as she went down the stairs, even though she could hear the loose flutter and harsh *blap-blap-blap* of her parents snoring above. She held onto the big thick railing that was almost level with her shoulders, her slightly damp palm sticking in places to somewhat gummy old varnish of the oak rail. Down below, moonlight came through the shaded and curtained windows in hazy patches, just the way the light had been filtered through Gramma's night skirt, only different, too. It was hard for Lucy to put into words, but the mind-picture came easily enough along with other pictures, from other times with Gramma. Like last winter.

Reaching the cool first floor, her bare toes feeling cautiously for any sharp things like gravel or splinters on the varnished wood surface, Lucy slowly made her way, hands outstretched, toward Gramma's room. As she did so, the memory of another walk, this time over snow and cold cement, came back to her.

Gramma said she didn't like going outside in the snow—she might slip and fall and break her brittle bones—but Lucy's birthday was coming up next week, and Daddy had forgotten to mail the invitations for her party when he had left the house that morning. Mother was busy ironing clothes, making puffs of whitish steam come up with a hot fabric smell off the ironing board set up in the kitchen, so Lucy begged and begged until Gramma said she'd walk down the street with Lucy to the mailbox, and drop the tiny stamped envelopes into the slot that Lucy couldn't reach herself.

But Lucy could tell that Gramma wasn't too keen on the idea, even though she said nothing to Lucy as she held her hand, which poked out of the fur trim on her winter coat. Lucy was so happy to have her invitations mailed that at first she thought Gramma would get over being upset.

And maybe Gramma would have been just fine, but Lucy shook her hand loose from Gramma's kid-gloved grip and began walking backwards, like Vernilla Nemmitz in school did at recess time. Gramma began to cluck and scold softly, telling Lucy, "Oh, Pumpkin, little ladies don't walk like that!" But Lucy was thinking that come Monday she'd show old "I'm in-the-second-grade" Vernilla what *she* could do, and then she looked down at her faint footprints in the sugary dusting of snow, and her grandmother's, and stopped in her tracks, one tiny gloved hand *pointing,* just pointing down at what she saw.

That was when Gramma reached out and took her hand and steered Lucy back to the house, leaning down every once in a while to whisper something fast and quiet to the little girl, until Lucy began to nod in awareness. Near the front porch, Lucy solemnly crossed her heart and hoped to die rather than tell anyone, even

Vernilla Nemmitz at school, what she'd seen in the fast-melting snow.

Other grandchildren might have been scared after seeing what Lucy had seen, but she loved her Gramma, and the deep, pitch-black secrets of the night skirt, and in return for promising never, *never* to tell, Gramma had made a promise to Lucy, too.

Her breath billowing out in small, semitransparent white clouds before her gently sagging face, Gramma had whispered with soft popping clicks of her false teeth, "Someday, my little Pumpkin, *you'll* get to wear the night skirt, too—not your mother, but *you.* Your mother doesn't understand—not like *you,* my girl."

And even though Lucy really didn't understand *everything* just yet, she'd nodded in agreement. A few weeks later, she'd tried making her own night skirt out of her coat, making Gramma laugh. *That* was when she'd said the night skirt wasn't for little girls-at least, not yet.

But as Lucy made her way toward the doorway of Gramma's room, now keeping her arms at her sides so she wouldn't knock over Mother's bric-a-brac stand with a thump and a crunch and a delicate shatter, she told herself that now she *could* wear the night skirt, that Gramma surely understood, even if she wasn't alive anymore.

Lucy had been what the neighbors called a "brave little girl" when the doctor came out of Gramma's bedroom-cum-sewing room that afternoon, closing his black leather bag with a snapping-fingernails *click* that made almost everyone in the parlor jump in place and twitch their closed mouths before they cast their eyes to the floor and began to pat Mother on the back with gentle hands. Even without being told, Lucy knew what had happened, and without needing to ask, she'd known that the night skirt was now hers.

Gramma had said so, hadn't she?

For on that day, Lucy had seen footprints that weren't always footprints trailing out behind Gramma, even though she had been careful not to step on the snow if she could help it, instead searching out the bare spots on the cold cement...but in some places there was nothing *but* snow, and in others, Lucy had seen the rounded arches of hooves, the four-toed round pads of cat paws, only really big, and the thin skitterings of bird claws, and here and there a regular shoe print, but *only* here and there.

All the funny tracks in the snow trailed out behind Gramma's wonderful, terrible, oh-so-thick-and-dark night skirt, dusted here and there by the sweep of the trailing skirt, but not obliterated.

And Lucy had been a good girl, keeping the secret she'd exed into her breast with trembling fingers. And without being told she'd kept secret what she'd seen *through* the night skirt—that angular place that wasn't Gramma's room anymore, with that homed, strange thing that was but wasn't her mother.

When Gramma had nudged her out from under there, Lucy had felt sharp claws at her back, poking through the wool jersey of her dress, and the lashing curl of a tail whip around her arm, but she hadn't told about *that,* either. For even if she hadn't liked her Gramma, and had run screaming for her mother, begging her to look, Gramma would have had normal feet tucked in normal dark stockings and sensible leather shoes, for that was part of the mystery of the night skirt, that keeper of the dark, and all that crept or crawled or prowled under cover of darkness.

The mystery and *magic* of the wonderful night skirt, and of the secrets that Gramma promised to tell Lucy, "later, when you're a big girl and can wear the real night skirt," only "later" was *now*, and Lucy was a big girl, almost *seven*, so she figured that that was big enough to wear the night skirt. To use it, like Gramma had *used* it.

For hadn't the men from the county who took away Gramma's house gotten all tumbled and broken when their Ford went into that ditch last fall? True, Gramma's big fancy house was sold by then, to those nasty Parks people, but hadn't Gramma had a big smile on her weathered face while she rocked after hearing the news about the car accident from Daddy?

Even though Mother and some of the ladies from the neighborhood had come into Gramma's room and washed her, before setting the damp cloths on her now slack face and folded hands, they hadn't taken away the night skirt. They hadn't thrown it on the trash heap and burned it to a cinder, like Mother kept saying she wanted to do, even though the skirt was Lucy's now.

Maybe Mother didn't want the other ladies to see her do a mean thing like that, Lucy said to herself as she paused at the closed door of Gramma's room. That her Gramma was dead didn't bother Lucy much, at least not in the way it might have bothered other little girls who loved their grandmothers. Because her Gramma had told her things—oh, *lots* of good stuff—when Mother wasn't listening. And even though Gramma had been caught by surprise when the mean men from the county took away her house, and hadn't been able to make the night skirt work for her then, she'd still gotten something called *revenge* on them all. And she had chuckled and hugged Lucy tight when she had said that, and all Lucy could think was, *When* I *get the night skirt. first I'm gonna show old Vernilla some really fancy walking, and then I'll....*

THE AMULET, BY A. R. MORLAN * 21

But up until yesterday, when Gramma's lower tummy got to feeling had, and Mother all but tore the night skirt off her, saying it was so she could get a nightgown on Gramma (but Lucy knew what her mother was *really* thinking when she pulled the skirt off the protesting old woman), Lucy had always thought of "*and* then" as being a long, long time away. Like next year, or *longer*.

Rut when Lucy had heard Gramma's whimpers from under the closed door, while Daddy rang for the doctor, then the neighbors, Lucy had realized that the time of the night skirt flapping and flowing and dragging around *her* legs had come at last.

And as much as losing Gramma hurt, Lucy was all antsy inside during the rest of the evening, until the time when she beard her parents' last faint words coming through the wall ("And first thing tomorrow, that *skirt* goes out the door, you hear me, Alvin?" "Uh-huh....") and then only raspy breathing. And now, she had her small finger wrapped around the doorknob, the metal cool and just the faintest bit greasy. Slowly she turned the knob until the door swung inward, into darkness even deeper and thicker and softer than the night skirt itself.

Gramma was in there, in the almost solid blackness. Lying on her bed, a drying cloth over her face and hands, even though it wasn't nearly warm enough to start worrying about that sort of thing yet. Lucy was glad that Mr. Byrne and Mr. Reish were both down with the grippe. Otherwise, the two undertakers might have come and taken Gramma away, and mother might have tossed the night skirt into the backyard trash bin, where any *animal* might have slithered or crawled into it—and Lucy didn't want to think about what might happen *then!*

Her eyes were more accustomed to the dark now. She could faintly see the two pale places where the damp hankies rested on her Gramma's face and hands. Which meant that if the bed was *there*, the rocker where Mother had placed the folded night skirt had to be right *here*.

Like a slumbering animal awakened by the gentle, loving touch of its owner, the night skirt *rippled* under Lucy's small fingers. Darker than the surrounding darkness, the night skirt felt as warm to Lucy as if her Gramma had just removed it only moments before.

Feeling for the opening with her hands, Lucy opened up the waistband. After tucking her nightgown around her legs (it would make a good, if makeshift, slip), Lucy stepped into the night skirt, rolling the fabric up and up, until the skirt's hem dusted her insteps. After patting the seat of the rocker, Lucy found Gramma's belt and tightened the stiff strip of fabric around her waist, her arms hampered by the thick roll of excess cloth scrunched up under her arm-pits. But Lucy didn't mind that at all; as Gramma told her, she was going to be taller *someday*.

Relishing the heavy swish of fabric around her thin legs as she walked, Lucy paused by her Gramma's bed, whispering, "I'll come and make you better in a little while—after I come back from *their* room. Then we'll play, okay, Gramma?" After giving the still hands and face a cloth-screened pat, Lucy left the room, heading for the staircase.

The cloth of the night skirt made a faint, susurrus noise that *almost* masked the delicate *click-click* of claws and scrabbling *scritch* of talons as Lucy made her determined way across the carpetless floorboards. But as she mounted the first stair tread, her skirt brushed against the next step up, and even the muted swish of the fabric couldn't cover the thump of something hard coming in contact with soft wood.

Lucy bent down and felt the hem of the night skirt, feeding the rolled material through her damp hands until something long and hard and bumpy slid through her fingers. As she probed the bunched fabric, the hard shape moved, first rippling, then curling in on itself as the little girl smiled in the moonlight-splashed darkness and whispered, *"Gotcha."*

Tongue pressed between her tiny teeth, Lucy worked the heavy thing toward the sewn edge of the hem, where the stitches were...and where the threads finally broke. And as Lucy extracted the oily-warm thing from the hem of the night skirt, the belt around her waist came undone, letting the night skirt drop to a cold, musty heap on the floor. Stepping out of the skirt, the special thing trapped in her sweating palm, Lucy felt nothing but limp nubby cloth under her feet...nothing more. The skirt no longer rippled, nor did it suck in the darkness anymore.

But the coiled object in her hand was warm, *writhing*, as she stroked it with a tiny, short-nailed finger. She thought, *I am a big girl now. I know the night skirt's secret, and nobody had to tell me, either.*

The tiny entity curled in her palm made Lucy feel fizzy-funny inside, like her insides were all jumbled up, but it was such a *nice* feeling, too. And then, realizing that what she was going to do to Mother and Daddy could wait awhile, she hurried back to her Gramma's room, her vision suddenly *different* in the gloom, thinking, *Now we both can have some fun. I want Gramma to watch me when I get them upstairs.*

In her excitement, Lucy didn't notice as her wing tips brushed Mother's bric-a-brac shelf. Small china and glass things shivered and chattered in dumb anticipation on the polished mahogany shelf, waking Lucy's mother in her room upstairs.

PART ONE

THE YAHOOS

By what I could discover, the Yahoos appear to be the most unteachable of all animals, their capacities never reaching higher than to draw or carry burdens. Yet I am of the opinion, this defect ariseth chiefly from a perverse, restive disposition. For they are cunning, malicious, treacherous, and revengeful. They are strong and hardy, but of a cowardly spirit, and by consequence insolent, abject, and cruel.

—JONATHAN SWIFT,
Gulliver's Travels

When the stars threw down their spears,
And water'd heaven with their tears,
Did he smile his work to see?
Did he who made the Lamb make thee?

—WILLIAM BLAKE,
"The Tyger"

CHAPTER ONE

MONDAY, OCTOBER 19, 1987

ONE—Anna (1)

Clawed leaves skittered before Anna Sudek's sneakered feet as she walked down Ewert Avenue, crossing from the shabby residential section into the business district. The brittle oak, maple, and elm leaves thinned as Anna passed the first of the rough-siding and shake-shingle-roofed businesses on the left hand side of the street. Soon, she found herself walking down a dimly lamp lit, cracked, and pitted cement sidewalk as queasily luminescent and lightly pocked as the thin vestiges of the last quarter moon above her.

Despite their now dead state, Anna missed the rustling of the wind blown leaves. Ewert Avenue at 2:30 in the morning was a hollow, wind-sucking discarded bottle of a place, a length of quiet emptiness enclosed by the overhangs of two- and three-story brick and frame offices and stores. The comparative silence was broken only by the lonely, rusty scree of the illuminated revolving clock/ thermometer mounted on the corner of the tan brick Savings and Loan building. The bright yellow dots against black numerals indicated that the temperature was a brisk thirty degrees, but Anna knew that the wind chill made it much colder.

Over at the intersection of Ewert and First Avenue West, a Mountain Dew can clunked against the sewer grating; the sound was overloud, tinny, ringing in the predawn quietude.

Kneeling down to pick up the empty pop can, Anna saw movement out of the corner of her eye—a chunk of darkness, breaking free of the dimly lit alley behind her side of the street—and huddled against the flaking yellow-painted sloping curb, bottle-bug green can clenched in her gloved fingers, until the moving darkness resolved itself into a brisk-walking sneakered figure clad in a navy pea coat and layered babushkas.

Anna saw just how tense she'd been when she dropped the can into her plastic mesh bag—the swirling red and green Mountain Dew logo was crushed beyond legibility. As she continued down the avenue, now walking in the middle of the street, Anna scolded herself. *Great going. Now I'm freaking out over old lady Campbell. If some yahoo creep bastard came up behind me, I'd roll over and spread 'em wide without being asked to.*

In the distance, Anna could hear Mrs. Campbell opening one of the Dumpsters in back of the Ewerton Bakery. "Shit," she muttered. Usually Anna made it to the bakery first, especially on Monday mornings. Sunday night was when they threw out the last of the left-over pastries and stale bread, and sometimes the paper tubes of hardened decorating frosting Ma liked so much. As Anna neared the bakery, the sounds of Mrs. Campbell rooting around in the Dumpster, ripping open white plastic bags of crumb-encrusted baking parchment and bent foil baking pans, became clearer.

Anna made a diagonal shift to the east, toward the IGA which had its own in-store bakery. While it didn't usually throw out as many baked goods, there was a chance that she'd at least find a frosting tube or two. *Anything to get Ma out of her mood*, Anna told herself with an unconscious frown, as she reached Wisconsin Street, where the large brick-fronted supermarket was located. It was close to Sixth Avenue East—only a block from the law enforcement building.

Not that the cops or sheriff's deputies were any problem (they were long used to seeing one of the Sudek women—occasionally both of them—out dumpster diving, and some of the friendlier officers even honked and waved in passing, but Anna never really felt comfortable with the thought that Ewerton's finest were watching her grub around in Dumpsters for lid-popped jars of pasta sauce, or half-rotted tomatoes and onions. She had gone to school with too many of them, and it galled her to think that they were secretly smirking at her in the wire mesh and crackling radio confines of their cop cars, no doubt thinking over their steaming Styrofoam cups of coffee from the café over on Third Avenue West, *Looking for Granny's body, Sudek?*

Anna didn't think her supposition was paranoia; she'd heard that taunt over and over during her twenty-nine years—in the sandbox at Ewerton Elementary, as she searched her locker for a missing Algebra B book, and as she surreptitiously peered in an EHS trash can in search of almost-blank notebooks tossed out at semester's end. And several of the nitwits who'd uttered those words had become deputies, patrolmen, and meter maids since graduation. Ma had heard the same jibes, but she had been able to laugh them off.

Setting down her black mesh bag next to the first dented and paint-flaking white dumpster behind the IGA, Anna thought as she raised the cracked and misshapen black plastic lid, with the embossed clench-fisted gorilla logo on it, *I wonder if Ma had that sonic-boom laugh when she was at EHS...if she only knew that the more they hurt her the louder she gets.* Ripping open the first plastic garbage bag after feeling the outlines of baking pans inside, Anna extracted the foil pans, faintly slimy with cold, moist cake residue. Bending down, so that she was hidden from view just in case any early worker opened the loading doors, Anna pulled the plaid shopping bag out of her mesh bag, and pushed the first two inside. Ma may have liked the old baked goods the IGA pitched, but Anna thought the pans were more valuable. Washed and cut into strips, then stuffed into her scavenged cans, they added weight to her weekly load of aluminum—sometimes as much as an extra two pounds.

And that extra dollar or eighty cents of can money (depending on the going price per pound) often meant two more cans of food for the cats. Ma kept threatening to throw both of them out the door, but then she'd get over her latest rage and go on a cat food-buying binge, using the money they'd earmarked for their own food.

Having put the pans in her plaid bag, Anna stood up and leaned over the Dumpster again, pulling out pans, a few Mountain Dew and Diet Coke cans, and a clear plastic bag of raw, pale yellow sweet dough. (She'd fry that off for the birds, come winter.) But there was nothing else edible in the bag—not even so much as a wrinkled bit of parchment dotted with cookie crumbs.

"Shit," Anna muttered as she felt the rest of the bags on both sides of the Dumpster. They contained only regular trash. After fighting the town's stray cats for the contents of Ewerton's Dumpsters on a daily basis for the past seven years (and doing it catch as catch can during her high school and college years), Anna had developed a feel for what was worth scavenging and what wasn't worth the effort of ripping open the slippery plastic bags. Even through gloves or mittens, her blunt fingertips (her peeling, brittle nails kept short thanks to a combination of a mediocre diet and two part-time cleaning jobs) knew what was packed into Dumpster bags. Anna supposed that in a half-assed way, her ability was a talent, no doubt inherited from her mother, who had been doing much the same thing ever since her father had taken off back in 1960.

And the old lady could have helped us out even then, Anna reminded herself as she softly lowered the wobbly plastic Dumpster lid and bent down to pick up her two bags. When she was about to straighten up, she saw moving beams of light cross her sneakered instep, then wash up over her knees

Praying that it wasn't an IGA employee (once, a little putz of a stock boy had caught her grabbing some thawed pizzas out of a Dumpster full of once-frozen vegetables after the store had had that power failure in the frozen food section; he'd chased her for half a block, shouting, "Bring those back, thief! Scum! That's store property!" but she did get even with the four-eyed blond squirt when she put a negative comment about him in the customer suggestion box inside the store, after she'd learned what his name was), Anna defiantly stood her ground and stared at the source of the headlights.

A blue horizontal-striped white car with the rectangular gumball machine on top. Sheriff's patrol—just what she needed. Terry Von Kemp was on duty every other Monday—Terry of the swinging greasy bangs and the open-lipped grin. Even before he rolled down the driver's side window, Ann knew what was coming.

"You lookin' for Granny, Sudek? After all this time, I'd think you could smell her out."

"Weren't you paying any attention in biology, Terry? Bodies decay down to bone in a few weeks—less, if the weather's right. I figure fifty-some years would be enough to do it, no?" Anna shivered in her denim jacket, glad that it was a size too big for her. As familiar as the old jibe was, hearing it when she was trapped between a pair of Dumpsters and an idling patrol car, at three-something in the morning, was enough to set her teeth to rattling and her muscles to quivering. And being pinned in the glow of Terry's high beams, like a moth, was unsettling, even if Terry *was* all threat and no action. He could always say the car just happened to accelerate.

Terry mulled that over, then said, "I don't remember nothing like that in Mr. Naughton's class. Maybe you're thinkin' of some art-fart course you took in *college*. Murder One, or—"

"That sounds more like something you would've taken in cop school—or is that joke about the law enforcement departments out here true?" Nonchalantly Anna leaned against the Dumpster, planning the streets she would use going home to miss Terry on his usual patrol route, while Terry took his time nibbling that bait. Finally, the line jerked.

"What joke?"

"That they wait outside the school for delinquent boys in Wales with a stack of sheriff and police force applications?"

In the light of the car Terry's face went red, and as he leaned over to do something with the ignition, Anna took off in a northwest direction, running over the abandoned spur tracks. She hit Seventh Avenue, then ran east to Dean Avenue, parallel to Ewert Avenue, her full bags banging and clanking against her a thighs, until she had to stop, gasping for breath. Damning that case of bronchitis she'd had as a child (her lung capacity was so low she hadn't even been able to resuscitate Resusi Anne dummies in freshman health class), Anna wheezed her way down Dean Avenue, forcing herself to keep up the pace. Detour or not, she had to be home by four, and home was half a mile away.

In the distance, she heard Mrs. Campbell drop another Dumpster lid. The old bat acted like she owned the town, not caring who heard her, or whether or not anyone saw her. *Maybe it doesn't matter when her late husband was one of the City Crew workers...no little stock-boy fucker would dare call her "Scum!"*

Not that Arlene Campbell had ever done anything to Anna. Why, Anna now supposed that the old woman had actually meant to be friendly when she'd first seen Anna Dumpster diving several years back, and said, "I see you walk alone, too." But at the time, Anna had simply ignored her and turned down a side street, unsure of how to react. And these days, when they'd approach the same Dumpster from different directions, the most Mrs. Campbell would do was diplomatically mutter, "Age before beauty," or some such nice-but-barbed admonition, prior to planting herself in front of the Dumpster, hogging the bags within. But nevertheless, Anna detested the old bat.

I'm taking out everything Ma's mother ever did to me on Mrs. Campbell, the college psychology professor voice in Anna's head told her, but the college-grad-with-two-menial-jobs voice told the other voice, *Mind your own fucking business, okay?*

Anna's labored breath was ragged enough to be clearly audible over the crunchy scrabble of the leaves she was dragging her feet through. She glanced up at the occasional lit windows in the houses on either side of the street. The ones with the unlined curtains drawn or the flimsy shades pulled only captured her attention for a few seconds; she couldn't see much more than tantalizing strips of flowered wallpaper; angled ceilings, an occasional headboard, or closet door hung with empty padded hangers. But some windows were uncovered, the light within spilling out in warm squares and rectangles across the frost-nipped lawns and crack-veined gray sidewalks beyond.

Anna's pace slowed as much as legally possible without being labeled a Peeping Tom as she looked into those windows, telling herself that if a woman went around showing everything she owned, people couldn't really be blamed for looking, could they? For Anna, the same thing applied when it came to window-peeping. After all, who but a show-off would light up the inside of his or her house like a Christmas tree, and leave the drapes or shades up? It was as if those people were saying to Anna, Look, garbage picker, at the things you won't ever have, no matter how many castoffs you grub out of Dumpsters and garbage cans.

And despite the imagined insult implied by the showy, well-lit windows, Anna willingly went along with it, eagerly looked at what others apparently sought to rub her face in, for it was the only way she could keep herself sane—keep herself from getting like her mother, who thought that the world was limited and bleak as the four walls that surrounded her come the end of each working day.

Her sneakered feet shuffling through light mounds of frost-backed leaves, and moving lightly over the ribbons of dried dead grass bisecting the slabs of concrete below, Anna stared at walnut Colonial living room ensembles; at plump, plaid sofas surmounted by grouped picture frames in artful configurations; at tasteful ceramic ginger-jar lamps positioned next to daring open staircases; at kitchens whose appliances all matched, the refrigerators bearing all-one-theme sets of magnets; at wall-mounted collector's plates and full sets of old fine china in big dark wood cabinets. The people in those lit rooms acted as if they were oblivious to the street beyond.

Anna had seen things that would have gotten her arrested if one of the cops been driving past just as she had her head turned in the direction of some of the homes. The people who performed those acts in the spotlight seemed to taunt her: We *can* do what we wish, and no one will ask us where the skeletons of *our* great-grand-mothers are buried.

Anna knew her peeping was wrong, despite the apparent invitation to look that the bare glass presented. But she also knew that these people could be wrong, too, calling out things she and her Ma already knew, already wondered about themselves, though no answer was to be forthcoming, even after the passing of fifty years and more. Anna never knew if they'd taunted the old lady; *she* wouldn't admit the sky was blue if you held her eyelids open with pliers and forced her to stare up at the heavens, let alone admit to Anna or her mother that she, too, had been greeted almost daily with that rote cry.

At any rate, if any of the cop cars ever were to stop her, Anna had the perfect retort ready: "Just looking for Granny, Sir."

TWO—First Kill

Arlene Campbell let the Dumpster lid slam down, aware of the racket she made, but regally beyond it. With a sense of humor most of the citizens of Ewerton would have found astonishing, considering the image they had of her as a spare old crone in ratty head scarves and cheap Sears running shoes, Arlene privately dubbed herself duchess of the Dumpsters, queen of Ewert Avenue, the dowager of debris.

True, if any of the lowlifes who cruised the streets, party-hardying and tossing full beer cans out passenger windows whenever a squad car rolled past in the other direction, were ever to call her any such name, Arlene Campbell wouldn't hesitate to take down their license numbers and phone in a complaint after she had walked home. But nothing of the sort ever happened.

Sometimes, Arlene wondered if it was the ghost of her Don that kept the hoods' mouths shut—Don, with his steel brush butch, and his BB-shot eyes surmounting jowls that flapped like an old woman's breasts. "Old tittie cheeks," his co-workers used to call him; Arlene had heard them, but never had the heart—or sheer courage—to repeat the sentiment in Don's presence. Bad enough that those fellows had to work under him.

And Arlene remembered how he'd bark and bitch at the kids who spent the summers painting the curbs and crossing lines of Ewerton's asphalt-and-gravel patched streets yellow, some of the same kids who spent their Friday and Saturday nights whooping it up in the shoddy over-the-store apartments on Wisconsin and Ewert, with the whores who lived there, and then cruised the streets for hours afterward, shouting and slamming on the brakes ten feet after the stop signs.

If they can make all that noise and nothing is done, I can drop the Dumpster lids. Arlene thought as she started for the IGA. When she saw the white squad car slowing down by the Dumpsters, she hesitated. She'd seen the Von Kemp boy's rather small head and narrow shoulders in silhouette as the car had passed her earlier that morning. She knew that Sheriff Sawyer only kept him on because he was somehow very distantly related to Stu Sawyer's wife Val, but nepotism wasn't enough to forgive idiocy, in Arlene's opinion.

Arlene ducked into a shadow between two scabby, silver street lamps and watched the squad car stop, its lights on that Sudek girl, the one Arlene had tried to make friendly conversation with years ago, only to be rebuffed, not that she actually held it against the child. Arlene Campbell had lived long enough in Ewerton to know how it could warp the perceptions of those less favored in the townspeople's eyes. Faintly, from a distance, she heard garbled voices, and caught the word "Granny."

That nonsense again. The Alvin Miner case had been the talk of Ewerton's lowlife population for much too long—ever since Arlene could remember. The silly questions the other children had asked little Lucy ever since it happened (the questions little Arlene Weiss herself had asked, even though old Arlene Campbell conveniently forgot uttering them), and kept on asking long after Lucy wasn't so little anymore.

"Where's Granny?"

"What happened to Granny?"

"Seen Granny lately?"

"Find some more of Granny anywhere?"

Childish, spiteful questions that remained unanswered, and thus kept curiosity alive and thriving, especially among those who refused to give up puerile curiosity. *Morbid* curiosity, some might call it.

Not wanting to listen, even at a distance, to what that Von Kemp trash was saying to the Sudek girl, Arlene walked back Wisconsin Street and began peering in the piles of boxes behind the businesses there, in hopes of finding something as good as the cast-off boot trees she'd picked up behind Happy Step Shoes, or the big box of dress patterns she'd found behind the clothing and fabric store on Fourth Avenue East this past summer.

Nothing.

From its nest somewhere above the novelty secondhand store an owl hooted—a low, reverberating sound that almost always made Arlene lose control of her bladder for a few dribbling seconds. *Silly, it's only a bird—a dumb animal. How much harm is it going to do you? Have to watch out for the two-footed beasts,* she thought, getting out of the alley and crossing over to Ewert Avenue.

Still no luck. Banging down lid after lid, Arlene found herself walking to the point where Seventh Avenue West and East met in one long, unbroken street, close to the new ugly law enforcement building and the rusted railroad tracks beyond. Past the abandoned Soo Line tracks (oh, North Central used them on occasion, but Arlene didn't consider a train made up of an engine and two boxcars really *using* the tracks) was the Sash and Door to the west, and a smallish patch of woods bisected with the fairground road directly north.

Kids used those woods for drinking, and what came after. And that meant cans. Arlene usually left those to the Sudek girl (payment for letting Arlene have first pick of the bakery), but she knew for a fact that the Sudek girl never ventured into the woods, or anywhere beyond the railroad tracks, after daylight saving time ended. *If I were her age, and had a bosom like hers, I wouldn't go in the woods now, either. But who wants a flat old biddy—Don Campbell's old biddy, at that?*

There wasn't much light out this way. The last street lamp was a block behind her, and even though the law enforcement building (police, sheriff, and jail) was lit in the front, the building was facing away from the woods, so Arlene fumbled the little flashlight scavenged last summer from behind Norm Hibbing's novelty shop out of her jacket pocket and thumbed it on.

The small batteries inside offered only a rancid circle of light, but combined with the faint moonlight above, Arlene could see well enough to move forward without tripping. As she crossed the slanting railroad tracks, something emerged from the woods to her left—something dark and small and scissors-legged, with eyes that flared green-gold when it passed through her flashlight's weak beam.

A cat, she began to think, until a minor but disturbing point crossed her mind. *Eyes are in the wrong place—at least, one is.* But by the time she'd realized what was wrong, the animal—cat, skunk, small dog, whatever—was gone, lost in the high grass near the abandoned depot to the northeast.

Arlene told herself she was too old, too tough, and too practical to be letting herself get all riled up over a silly *animal,* and kept on walking forward, into the woods, casting her flashlight about as she moved. The sallow beam picked up the glint of a Coors can—no, two Coors cans—and the shed skin of a rubber beneath. Arlene recoiled as her fingers brushed against the slightly sticky pinkish latex, still faintly body-moist. Through the twist-limbed trees, most still adorned with withered leaves, she could see the streetlights on Ewert Hill to the east, where all the fancy old houses were. Few people lived out that way anymore, but the fact that there were houses and lights beyond gave her a mild sense of security. And the law building behind her helped, too.

Aiming her light downward, reading the play of shadow and flickering light with all the intensity of a palmist studying a client's hand, Arlene looked beyond the shadows cast by the fallen leaves, to the deeper places below—places where things dropped became things lost, waiting to be found.

The woods were only a couple of blocks long where they were bisected by the road, but to Arlene's left they were much deeper, thicker, and noisier. She could hear subtle rustlings—snaps and low squelching sounds she hoped were animal in origin. She had no idea how some pair of lovebirds might react to being discovered out here, in mid-thrust, as it were. *Maybe it's some of those boors who drive up and down my street at midnight, waking me up when I'd rather sleep,* she thought petulantly, like the Arlene Weiss of old. A deliciously nasty thought came to her, nurtured by too many years lived under Don's callused thumb: Suppose she were to sneak up on a couple and shine them like a pair of deer?

Her ribbed rubbery soles searching out secure footing below, Arlene followed the direction of the almost inaudible squelching, taking care not to let her bags make too much noise as they grazed the lower branches of the trees that surrounded her. For a second, the thought that she was close to the place the where the strange animal had emerged from the woods made her pause, but the prospect of having some harmless fun, of turning the tables on at least two of those little shits who broke her sleep many a night, kept her going. And that cat, dog, or whatever had flitted by so quickly that the odd shine could have been *anything*—a tag—

(But I didn't see any collar on it—)

She was sixty, after all, even if Dr. Isham said she didn't need glasses. Old eyes play funny tricks, especially in the dark.

But it wasn't quite as dark now. Even though the sun wasn't due to come up for hours, there was a faint rim of half luminescence lying low across the horizon behind her, silhouetting the random trees and houses with cut-paper sharpness. Even the places where her flashlight beam didn't touch, Arlene could half-see shapes, near-colors...and that soft, almost strangled little squelching sound was louder.

Much louder, as in almost on top of her, yet Arlene detected no movement, no breathing, heavy or otherwise. Running her pale tongue over her rough lips, she slowly panned her flashlight in a half-circle before her. Nothing but tree trunks, fallen branches, leaves, an old shoe...two shoes—filled with stockinged feet, toes up, but tilted away from each other in a bottomless "v".

Gripping her bags in her left hand until her swollen knuckles protested, Arlene trained her right hand toward the legs attached to the feet. Tight jeans, the paint 'em on your body kind, with zippered ankles. Hands, resting on the thighs, dirt-rimmed nails peering out from chipped paint over the moons. Blackish streaks on the tops of the hands—a liquid shimmering black that turned another color altogether when Arlene's light hit them. The saffron beam jiggled a little as it played over the slumped torso; the metallic threads running through the cheap, tight sweater; the forward-lolling head with the jagged, moving, leaking parts in the bleach-blond hair—the parts no comb had made in that frizzled curtain of curls.

The torn furrows in her flesh dripped blood, producing a most unpleasant squelching sound.

THREE—Ma

"Shit."

Anna paused in the doorway between the living room and the dining room, bags in one hand, her house keys in the other. Before her, the dining room table was as it had been when she had gotten up that morning, as it had been when she and Ma had gone to bed at seven the night before. Anna's beige mug rested next to the two-day-old newspaper Ma had found at her FmHA job, their two place mats askew near the middle. Ma's purse sitting open near the place opposite to where Anna sat. The only difference was that Ma was sitting at her usual place, the kitchen door, her thin arms crossed, pointy elbows resting on the edge of the table. From Ma's tone of voice alone, Anna could guess that the older woman wasn't over last night's funk, but as if to bring the point home to Anna, her mother's face was scrunched up like a tear-crumpled Kleenex, all creases between her eyes, around her thin-lipped mouth, and under her wobbling chin.

Not bothering to actually look at Anna, or acknowledge her presence, Ma repeated, *"Shit. Shit, shit, shit!"*

Uncertain what to do, Anna just stood there, trying out scenarios in her mind. *If I ask her what's wrong, she'll say, "You." or "Everything." but if I ignore her, she'll start raging that I never pay attention to her. If I try and make breakfast myself, she'll start in on how I'm not doing this or that right, or how I waste water filling the coffee pot, or something. Christ, she's had all morning to think of something that I'm bound to do wrong. But if I just stand here, she'll—*

Anna's mother got up with a flurry of pink flannel and jerking limbs. She and Anna were within five pounds of the same weight, but she managed to make her pounds look and act smaller, swifter, the way a horse seems leaner and thinner than a cow, even if they're the same size. Ma stomped into the kitchen. Through the open doorway to the basement below, Anna heard the floor joists protest uselessly. Over the whine and pop of the floor, Anna gradually made out words. Her mother was mumbling just loud enough to taunt, without making herself completely clear.

"...control...always trying to live my life through me...won't work this time...she wants her little Anna, she can have her...old bitch."

Anna didn't realize she'd lost her grip on her bags until they fell to the floor with a muted thump. Instinctively, she tried to make herself as insignificant as Ma always told her that was, but Ma was already storming back into the dining room, eyes blazing behind her oversized wire-rimmed glasses, wisps of permed, pale-blonde hair shaking around her heart-shaped face, the furrow between her eyes as lethal as a sharpened dagger.

"Goddamn fuckin' clumsy *bitch*."

Anna knew that the challenge had been given—she either had to take what was coming, or try to stand up for herself. Dammit, I *stood up to that Von Kemp yahoo, and he was armed and in a car that could've rammed me. She's only got her tongue.*

"What's wrong?" Neutral enough, Anna hoped, as she dimly wondered where the cats were.

"What's *wrong?*" Ma mocked Anna, making her voice higher and more nasal, in scathing imitation of her child. She jabbed at the air, the table, and Anna with one pink-nailed forefinger as she shouted, "*That's* what's wrong—look at the damned *table!*"

Anna looked. She had to move her head to see what Ma was talking about. At the right angle, the shine of the overhead light picked up a faint sheen of moisture on one of the plastic place mats. Ma's place mat—the one that didn't have a white smeared streak where a portion of the stylized pattern of farm fields and a far-off house and barn had rubbed off. As Ma sputtered, "Look what *your* damned cat did," Anna realized what had happened, and cursed herself for not taking the time to push the cats into her bedroom before she had left the house that morning. Mouth, their female tiger cat, had a bladder problem. Sometimes, when she was excited or upset, she dribbled. And Mouth was wont to climb on the furniture, including the table. *But I couldn't put her in the bedroom—Bruiser doesn't get along with her. And if I put Mouth in the bathroom and shut the door, Ma yells because she's not sure if I'm in there or what, and Ma doesn't want the cats in her room.*

Anna made a break for the kitchen, mumbling, "I'll go wipe it up," but Ma blocked her way, lean arms crossed, elbows pointing out like the narrow ends of billy clubs. Anna backed up, intending to circle the table and edge into the kitchen behind Ma, but when she was halfway around the table Ma shifted position to further block her way. Shaking, Anna tried to squeeze past Ma anyhow, but her big bust got in the way, for Anna couldn't press her right arm close enough to her body. When the elbow of her jacket grazed Ma's pink nightgown, Ma pushed her into the small easy chair that sat near the opposite side of the kitchen doorway.

As her face hit the rounded back of the chair, hard, Anna told herself, *Don't cry out, for Chrissakes—she'll only get angrier. My god, what has happened to us? We were actually happy here, just a couple of years ago.*

"Get up and clean off that table."

Later on, Anna wasn't sure if it was the tone of Ma's voice—more metallic than usual—or the cumulative effect of having that same voice shout out so many orders, curses, and insults over the past two years, the years of the old lady—

("I wanted a *daughter,* a human *being,* not you!" "You clumsy *moose,* can't you do anything without—" "You're *just like* the old lady, just fuckin' *like her—and* her crazy old man—")

—but whatever it was, something in Anna snapped.

"No *way.*" Pressing herself into the chair, the cat dander on the throw tickling her nose, Anna looked up at her mother, whose forehead furrow grew impossibly black and deep, like a widening cleft in her very skull. Ma glared down at Anna.

"No, *what?*" One good thing, Ma wasn't ripping skin off her lips, or tearing strips of skin off the sides of her fingernails, hurting herself in a seething rage that often boiled over to splatter her daughter. Anna slowly shifted until she had her feet on the floor and one hand stationed on the left armrest before saying, "I'm not cleaning up something you could have cleaned yourself. You know Mouth has accidents. A little cat pee won't hurt anything."

"Yes it will!" Ma pounded the table with her fist, shouting, "It hurts *me!* I'm sick of always cleaning up after the fucking cat! Isn't it enough I had to pick up after the old lady almost all my life? Now it's pick up after *them!* Not when I'm picking *garbage* to eat while they—" she pointed in the direction of Anna's room "eat fancy fucking cat food!"

"But they eat garbage, too. That beef from when they get done grinding at—"

"Screw that! That's not what I'm talking about!"

"What are you talking about, then? We just don't always find cat food, that's all—"

"Fuck finding the cat food!" Ma bellowed, kicking at Anna's legs with her house-slippered bare feet, unconsciously mimicking the actions of her own mother when Ma was a girl. Ma's thin toes hung far enough out of the yellow scuffs for the bones of her toes to connect ringingly with Anna's tibia, but Ma didn't feel the connection, for she kept on screaming, "Can't you *understand* I'm *tired* of it all? Tired of waking up to find *cat piss* on the fucking *table,* tired of going *garbage picking,* tired of playing nursemaid and *playmate* to that crazy old lady, tired of listening to the old lady ask why her little *Anna* won't come see her, just *tired* of it *all!*"

Anna didn't know what to say. She never did know what to say when Ma started on an "I'm tired" tirade. It wasn't as if Ma was the only one suffering in the house; at least she'd been married once, and had had a kid, which was enough to make her less of an object of ridicule. Anna was twenty-nine and had never so much as dated, or even been able to pay a guy to take her someplace. Not that there was any guy poor enough in town to need to accept date money from someone like Anna Sudek, descendant of the embarrassment of Ewerton. And after years of going without male companionship, Anna no longer wanted it or needed it—it was simply easier to give up the search without ever having really begun it in the first place. Even if it meant not being able to sweet-talk any of her former classmates into hiring her now.

Ma above all should have realized just how damned hard it would be for Anna to get anything more than menial jobs, despite her degree. No jobs would be forthcoming to Anna Sudek, any more than they were forthcoming for her mother, Tina Miner Sudek.

It was as if what had happened fifty-some years ago had occurred yesterday. People who had actually been there were mostly gone, but the memory lingered on, thanks to the oft-told tales. And with the memory came the smoldering rage that someone had dared to give Ewerton a bad name, had dared to do something embarrassing—and that the Miner-Sudek clan still had the audacity to remain in town.

Not that Anna and her mother actually wanted to remain in Ewerton. While free to go in one sense, they were chained in other, less obvious ways. Lack of money, for starters. Ma had managed to break free of town when she was a teenager—had made it all the way to neighboring Wright County, in fact—but her divorce had sent her scuttling back home, Anna in tow, to the bitter sanctity of the old lady's house, to be her unpaid slave. And when things got to be too much there, she and Anna had pooled the money Anna had earned doing work study in college (said education paid for by Uncle Sam, thanks to Anna's unacknowledged-at-EHS intelligence, and ability to supplement her grant with scholarships) with the little money she had, and moved halfway across town, to this ticky-tacky house on Wilkerson Avenue, close to the smelly paper mill.

When Ma and Anna had gone looking for work, no one had wanted to hire them, even though they weren't the ultimate untouchables—out-of-towners. In Ma's case they claimed she was underqualified; in Anna's that she was overqualified. Job Service wouldn't touch them. Employers round-filed their applications. Scavenging took them through the first lean year—that and finding money on the streets, in the runner rims of the washing machines in the Super Suds Launderette, and in the many phone booths around town. They blew what money they held in reserve on bills, until the home cleaning service out in the hoity-toity Willow Hill section of town decided that they'd take a chance on the Sudeks, and offered them office cleaning jobs. (The service also handled in-home care for the elderly, but they were the ones who *definitely* remembered the Miner case.)

During the past six years, Ma had cleaned the FmHA and paper mill offices, while Anna cleaned the Super Suds and two insurance offices. They pulled down enough to keep them selves and their two cats from being kicked out of the county, and the adjusted mortgage on the house helped, too. Surprisingly, though, she and Ma had become friends, getting along better—for a few years, at least—than they had during all the years spent under the old lady's thumb. But it wasn't meant to last, this fragile sense of well-being in the Sudek household.

For Anna kept on getting older, and less marriageable by the year, just as their bills grew steadily thanks to inflation and rising costs, and eventually Ma fell victim to rages of angry words and tiny, self-inflicted wounds after the old lady had called their house two years ago, claiming to have fallen and hurt her hip.

"Claimed" was how Anna chose to think about it; it was funny how the old lady supposedly perked up after Ma resumed relations with her. Of course, Anna didn't know for sure that the old lady had improved; after the fights that precipitated the exodus from the Miner house on Evans Street seven years back, Anna had refused to go see the old lady. Why, for four years she had refused to even speak on the phone with the old woman, when she had called her on little Anna's birthdays.

But Ma had gone back, almost eagerly, thanks to the little gifts of money from the old lady, the latter's little trick to make Ma obligated to do even more for her, to keep giving more and more of herself to the old lady. And Ma spent most of every day with the old woman, doing the very odd jobs that had helped spark the original fight seven years ago, listening to the old lady's tales of what her father had done so long ago.

And the more time Ma spent with the old lady, commiserating, griping about how this or that person had crossed her or Anna, the more Tina Sudek grew dissatisfied with the marginal existence she and Anna had carved out for themselves. Suddenly, Dumpster diving was no longer an honorable, if slightly messy way of steering clear of welfare. And suddenly, every little thing the cats did was wrong, filthy, *evil*—just as the old lady used to say about things that displeased *her*.

But Ma had been duty-bound to go back to the old lady, to help her out, just as Anna had considered herself duty-bound to stay at home with Ma, and give over her money to her. That sense of duty, of obligation, had been drummed into Anna's head by the old lady since she was small—that, plus other things.

"Good girls stay at home. Only *bad* little girls go out and play."

"If I could have, I would have taken care of my Ma all the time, even when she was old."

"Boys are bad. When they put that *thing* in you, it makes an ugly sound, like ham fat jiggling."

"I knew you were no good from the time you were born—lying there, kicking off your blankets, showing off your plum."

"Mark my words, Tina, she's no good—gonna be knocked up by the time she's sixteen, and kicked out of school."

"You'll both *starve* without me. You'll be back in a *week*."

No, they hadn't come back in a week, and they hadn't starved, but the old lady had Ma back, and had gone to work on her, until now all Ma did was sit scrunch-faced, mouth and eyes bitter under her light fringe of bangs, flailing at Anna with words and fists, jabbing elbows and kicking feet.

Anna watched her mother sit and cry, without covering her mouth or eyes with her hands. In a high, quivering squeak, she bawled, "I am so *tired* of this all, you hear me? *Just so tired.* And it's all your fault—everything. This is all because *you* can't stand her."

Unable to watch her mother, Anna glanced down at her watch. It was almost five, and the launderette's automatic doors opened at five-thirty. Leaving the bags where she'd dropped them, Anna quietly got up and went into the kitchen, grabbing an old sweet roll before she hurried to her bedroom, peeked in to see that the cats were all right (Bruiser was cornering Mouth, but they were both big cats, able to stand each other off for hours), then rushed out of the house.

She supposed that she should have gone over to her mother and done something, said something comforting, but that time was long past between them. She was sorry for her mother, even as she wasn't sorry at all.

Anna could never forgive her mother for the way she had turned her back on the warmth and friendship they had finally shared, all because of one of the old lady's all-too-transparent "I need help" ruses. Lucy Miner had been using the same sympathy-seeking tactics on Anna and Tina for years. It just didn't cut it with Anna anymore.

FOUR—Arlene (1)

Arlene Campbell sat on her sofa, old rotary-dial phone perched on her lap, the cats playing with the Velcro flaps on her shoes, for even she wasn't sure how long, before she finally dialed the police. Even then, she hung up before the last number went through. The actual calling to report what she'd seen wasn't the problem; it she wasn't even afraid to give her name. But what did bother Arlene was the thought of the questions:

What were you doing out at that time of the morning?
What were you in the woods, off the path?
What were you looking for?
Why did you wait this long to call, ma'am?
Why didn't you come right to the station?

Arlene put the phone back on its little black painted phone stand and sat down on Don's old wing chair, the one she had never been allowed to sit on when he was alive. *Screw you, Donald*, she thought, picking petulantly at a loose thread in the right antimacassar, while mulling over her dilemma.

Clearly, she had a choice here—either tell what she knew and have her name splashed all over the paper (and even if they kept her name out of the paper, people would know anyhow—you couldn't break wind in Ewerton without everyone and his third cousin knowing you ate beans for supper), and worse yet, have people know for a fact that she was nothing but an old garbage picker, ("See, I tole you Don' didn't leave her squirt—"), or sit back and wait until someone else found the body. If she waited long enough, Chief Stanley or

Sheriff Sawyer would be able to smell it for themselves, and save her the trouble of coming forward.

But then again, if there was a murderer about, he or she might have seen her, and be waiting to shut her up before she told. In that case, it would be best if the police were at least aware that she was in danger.

Brushing her cat Silky off her lap, Arlene got up and went to the phone, fishing in her smock pocket for a handkerchief as she did so.

FIVE—After Work

Anna let herself into the house early that afternoon without bothering to knock. Even though Ma got done with work an hour or so before Anna, the young woman knew better than to expect Ma to open the door for her, or for there to be any meal on the table. *Not after one of her "I'm so tired!" episodes.* If things went as they usually did, it wouldn't be until late Tuesday or early Wednesday that Ma would so much as talk to Anna, or quit banging into Anna whenever she passed her in the hallway.

From past experience, Anna knew that things might be smoothed over for the moment if she simply acted as if nothing had happened that morning, so as she closed the door behind her, Anna said, "You wouldn't believe what those pigs did this time. Broke both gumball machines and then threw the gumballs in one of the driers and turned *that* on...the crap was baked on the drum. I had to call Gordy to come down and look at it, and naturally he acted as if it was *my* damned fault."

Silence from Ma. Anna pulled off her knit cap and fluffed her hair out with her fingers as she continued, "And I don't know, if it was the same people or what, but someone dumped a couple of cans of soda all over the carpeting, so I had to mop that up before I could use the vacuum on it. Geez, you'd think they'd drink the whole can after paying fifty cents for it...." Anna let her voice trail off as she wiggled out of her coat, her mouth going dry in the too-quiet house. Apparently, smoothing things over wasn't going to be easy this time.

Biting her lip as she hung her coat up, Anna sniffed deeply and thought, *The least you could have done was change the cat pan. How would you like it if you were locked in an outhouse for five hours?* Not to mention that Anna would have to sleep in a smelly room that night, if she was destined to get any sleep at all. Usually Ma made sure she sat up all night with the TV turned up full blast.

Ma could sleep, open-mouthed and snoring blattily, anywhere and at any time, regardless of any noise around her, waking up only when Anna ventured out to turn down the volume.

Anna went into the bedroom, dodging Mouth as the fat tiger spay ran out into the hallway. Hoping that Ma wouldn't do anything to the cat while she was busy in the bedroom, Anna held her breath and attacked the full litter pan. As she scraped up the used litter and rolls of poop with a piece of cardboard, dumping the offal onto a sheet of newspaper, Bruiser came sliding up behind her, butting and rubbing his massive head against her back and behind, making soft, high-pitched *churrup* noises.

"You're Mama's good Bruiser, huh, boy?" she asked the huge black tom, who *churruped* in reply. Fastidiously, the cat began to scrape the carpet nap over the mound of litter and cat dirt on the big sheet of newspaper spread out before Anna's knees. Twisting the mess into the middle she said, "There, all gone. See? Mama made all gone with it."

Bruiser sat there solemnly regarding his mistress (he was Anna's cat—Ma wouldn't even look at him, or allow him out of Anna's bedroom very often), his wide-spaced green eyes loving and luminous. Ever since he'd relented last January—after two years of roaming around outside the house—and allowed Anna to take him inside, Bruiser had been *her* boy. Ma claimed that the only reason the eighteen-pound male had allowed Anna to take him in was because his hind feet were slightly frostbitten, that the winter of '86 was just too much for him, pride or not.

"The cold killed old man Holiday, didn't it? So, it was enough to make him come to you. The cold, not *love*," as Ma liked to insist, to try and spoil the total, utter affection between Anna and the huge black cat with the thick neck and ropes of muscles across his shoulders. True, Anna still loved her other cat, but somehow, with Bruiser, it was different. And it didn't bother Anna to admit that she loved the cat more than her own family. Bruiser never yelled at her or made her feel as if she was somehow less than human.

"Oh, no, no water. Oh, Brupie, Mama's sorry," Anna crooned, after glancing at the empty blue water dish on the floor. Bruiser rubbed his big head against her palm, snorting softly, as if to say, "I forgive you."

Anna gently nudged the cat back into the room as she backed out, thinking that she had to face Ma sooner or later, so it might as well be now. But Ma wasn't in the bathroom, even though the door was shut *(If I pulled that kind of a stunt, she'd be all over me—)*, and she wasn't in the kitchen, either. The basement light wasn't on, but that didn't mean anything—Ma had superb night vision, and some-times went into the basement without turning on the lights, just to show Anna how wasteful she was when she turned her light on to clean the cat pan down there.

After giving Bruiser his water, Anna swallowed her pride and knocked on her mother's bedroom door. No answer. She cracked open the door and peered in. The bed was unmade, and Ma's clothes were strewn around the room, some in piles on the floor, others draped over chairs. Nothing terribly unusual there. But no Ma, ei-ther.

"Office at the FmHA must have been dirty," she muttered as she went back into the kitchen, finally noticing that her mother's coat wasn't hung in its usual place—on a hanger outside the big double closet in the dining room. If Anna were to leave *her* coat out like that, it would mean another round of swearing and shouting.

Telling herself that nobody had promised her life would be fair, Anna peered in the refrigerator, trying to make out the back in the darkness (the light had gone out months ago—some sort of short in the wiring), gave up, and turned on the kitchen light.

"There you are, my pretties." Anna grabbed the package of freezer-burn-discolored hot dogs she'd found at the IGA last week and went to set them on the counter, before getting a pot from under the stove...until what she saw on the cabinet door made her stand there, arms limp at her sides, the hot dogs fallen to the floor.

It was as if the very wood of the cupboards was bleeding. Vis-cid fluid bubbled up from between the coarse pale grain in huge, misshapen, oozing letters:

I'M FUCKING GONE!!!

Drops of smeary crimson had settled to the counter below, like splatters of arterial flow. Anna looked at them for a few seconds, unable to digest the reality of the dripping words, until she saw the nearly empty squeeze bottle of catsup resting on its side on the floor, where Ma must have dropped it—where Anna hoped that, indeed, her *mother* had dropped it.

SIX—Black Monday

"—fell 508 points, or 22 percent, to close at 1,738.74, the big-gest one-day drop since—"

"Arnie, can't you find anything else on the frigging dial? I'm sick and tired of all this Dow-Jones crapola. Won't mean a hill of beans to anyone around *here*." Palmer Winston, Anna's former English teacher from EHS, banged his squaw-decorated white and red can of Leinenkugel's on the worn Formica table until Arnie the bartender switched channels on small portable wall-mounted TV.

"—the offshore platforms were suspected to be bases for Iranian gunboats—"

"Oh, screw it, Arnie, put on that Empty-Tee-Vee shit. They don't carry any bad news." Old man Winston stubbed out his Lucky Strike in his round black ashtray, then leaned over in his maple captain's chair until he could see Anna, where she was sitting in one of the Rusty Hinge's dim back booths.

"Anna Sudek? Is that my best pupil hiding back there?"

Anna slurped her rum and Coke, then rocked the slightly greasy glass back and forth in her hand, until the ice cubes battered each other under the sloshing brown liquid. *God, I must be blessed,* she thought, before giving the retired teacher a little wave and nod. She was glad that the small, wood-paneled bar wasn't busy tonight, although, for all she knew, perhaps five customers *was* busy for this place on a Monday night. With ten bars to choose from in Ewerton and the surrounding smaller towns, people weren't exactly limited when it came to watering holes.

But the Rusty Hinge was long regarded in Ewerton and the surrounding towns of Lumbe and Hunterstown as an old fart's bar, the kind of place where the "decor" consisted of scenic jigsaw puzzles assembled and glued onto sheets of warped cardboard and thumbtacked onto the smoke-grimed walls; glossy stand-up display cards hung with naked-women car air fresheners, brightly enameled nail clippers, and greasy bags of fried pork rinds. The blackened smoke-eater hung above the bar was permanently on the fritz, and the surface of the tiny pizza oven behind the bar always bore burned-on free-form squiggles of cheese. It was the sort of seedy yet comfortable watering hole where old buddies and tolerated enemies could sit and gas the afternoon and evening away, with no disapproving glares from Ewerton's pseudo-Yuppie upper middle class to distract from their pleasure.

And Anna was especially grateful that no other patron here today was younger than forty-five. Among her former classmates, she was a freak. Among the beer-guzzling, snack-munching oldsters, she was just pitiable, a spinster to be coddled and treated with benign condescension.

Anna had long ago learned that pity was more tolerable than horrified disdain.

When Mr. Winston realized that Anna wasn't about to leave the confines of the orange-seated booth to sit with him, he nodded in reply and fished another Lucky Strike out of his battered pack, all the while keeping one almond-shaped blue eye on her. Anna leaned over her drink, letting her hair fall partly over her face, thinking, *The old fuck must know about it, whole frigging town must be discussing it over dessert. Wouldn't be surprised if they* don't *know where the hell she is now, either.*

After Anna had read the dripping red message on the cabinet (Ma's words had slopped across the whole north set of doors where the dishes were kept), she had gone back to her mother's room and had discovered that one of the suitcases she'd received for a college graduation present was missing (as if to bring the point home to Anna, Ma had taken the smallest case in the set) , along with a couple of Ma's blouses and pairs of pants, some underwear, a pair of shoes, and Ma's bank book. That was it.

Anna had felt a momentary twinge of mingled guilt and relief that afternoon. Ma was gone, but at least they had had separate bank accounts, thanks to the advice of a woman Anna had met in college, whose husband died a few years ago. The woman had been broke for a month, until her joint accounts with her husband cleared through probate. Now, because of that woman's advice, Anna had enough money to live on for a few weeks, not counting what she would earn cleaning. And while Anna never was sure exactly when Ma had left, a phone call she received a half hour after she came home gave her an inkling—Ma had never shown up at the FmHA building near the four-way stop that morning. Considering that Anna had left home around five, and Ma was expected at work around six-thirty, Ma must either have not bothered with work, or left before then. Either way, gone was gone. Anna placed a call to the woman who ran the cleaning service, telling her that Ma wouldn't be coming in for a while, and that she should find someone else to handle Ma's jobs.

Hanging up the phone, Anna knew that she should have taken on Ma's jobs and just kept on sending in Ma's time card, but she didn't care anymore. She didn't mind garbage picking—at least, not the way Ma did once the old lady started filling her head with doubt and shame.

Hope you're happy, old bat. Ma didn't want to live with you any more, so now you fixed it so she wasn't satisfied living with me, either. There was no doubt in Anna's mind as to what old lady had done. Once Anna and Ma moved out, the old lady was truly alone. From what Ma had told Anna after she'd started going to visit the old lady, no one wanted to mow the lawn or shovel snow for her anymore after a couple of years, and after being insulted once too often, even the Meals on Wheels crew refused to drive out and serve her.

Not that the old lady had ever been Miss Popularity *or* Miss Congeniality. Anna remembered the time when several of their neighbors came up to Mom as she hung out clothes in the backyard of the old lady's house, and politely yet apprehensively explained that Ma shouldn't think it was anything personal, but none of them would be talking or paying any attention to the old lady anymore—and the same went for Ma and little Anna.

Apparently, the neighbors had elected Mrs. Armstrong from across the alley to be the main spokeswoman. She was the one who told Ma, "Please don't think we mean *you* any ill will, Tina, but that mother of yours...well, we've put up with about as much as we're going to take. The backbiting, the things she yells at us out the window when you and little Anna are gone, the other things we think she's doing—"

"What do you mean, think she's doing?" At five years old, Anna knew when her mother was ready to blow; that vertical forehead furrow was already in place, even though Ma was only twenty-one years old.

Mrs. Armstrong began wiping her chapped hands on her apron, smoothing it against her thighs with dry, scratchy sounds. "Now, Tina, we don't know for *certain* that your mother is to blame, but... well, it's just an awfully strange coincidence that every time one of us has a tiff of some sort with her, we find—"

Mrs. Armstrong hung her head, cheeks red, so Mrs. Cooper finished for her, arms crossed over her flat freckled chest. "We think your mother is doing...*dirt* on our back lawn. And then scratching grass and dirt over it, like a dog or—"

And that was when Ma threw them out of the yard. But people still don't hold it against Ma. Didn't she have that nice hearty, break-your-eardrums laugh whenever she met her neighbors in some public place? And didn't Ma always smile at everyone she knew?

And didn't Ma take it out on me when we were alone? Anna found herself thinking, as she swirled the last, near-melted nubs of ice around in her half-empty glass.

"—been a shitty year all around, I say," Mr. Winston was pontificating over at the round Colonial table near the door. He and his long-time, also sixty-some-year-old buddy Palmer Nemmitz (whose wife Bitsy made ugly fabric-vegetable refrigerator magnets to sell at the Methodist Market each spring, and she was so popular—and related to so many people—that they sold out) were chewing the fat with fiftyish Lenny Wilkes and that oily middle-aged geek Wayne Mesabi (father of that stick-in-the-cement dip Heidi, who had graduated from EHS two years after Anna), the distributor who furnished the Hinge with Old Dutch chips and snacks. Mesabi was scarfing down a bag of them right now, using a big onion and garlic chip to punctuate his reply.

"I agree with Win—heck, everybody worth a hill of beans passed on this year, and it ain't even November yet. Think about it. No more Rita Hayworth, no Lee Marvin, no Sammy Kaye—"

"Did he take 'Swing and Sway' with him, like Lombardo took New Year's—"

"Shuddup, Nemmitz, you old cynic—"

"—and John Houston, and Liberace—"

"Always said the man was a—"

"Nemmitz, put a lid on it!"

"And don't forget about Lorne Greene and Dan Rowan. Why me and Millie used to watch that *Laugh-In* every week."

"You also watch *Hee-Haw*, Lenny."

"Butt out, Winston. You're as bad as that buddy of yours, and Bob Preston, and Jackie Gleason, and Danny Kaye, and—"

"Pola Negri died, too," Winston interjected, sipping on his Leinenkugel's. Wayne Mesabi stopped pointing his chip at everyone and asked, "Who?"

"Somebody he screwed a long time ago," Nemmitz cut in, then added before Winston could rebuff him, "And Randolph Scott died, and that soup can fella, Warhol, and Buddy Rich—"

"Millie and I, we used to listen to his records," Lenny said, sneaking one of Wayne's chips, even though he really didn't need it.

"Well, the one that broke me up the worst was Fred—"

"Didn't you get enough of that old fuck Ferger when he was around? Didn't think anyone could miss Dead Fred—"

"Wayne, would you let me finish? Astaire. I'm talking about Fred Astaire," Nemmitz said, grabbing Mesabi's chip out of his fingers and tossing it to the imitation wood Formica below.

"So you didn't care when Dead Fred died?"

"That is not the *point*, you lamebrain—"

"Hey, that reminds me. Arnie, switch that TV back to channel thirteen. Almost time for the news. I'm gonna be on—"

"Lenny *lives* for death," old man Winston said to no one in particular, as he glanced over at Anna. Behind him, the other men had rearranged their chairs to face the small set mounted above the cluttered kitschy bar.

Wondering who had died, giving Coroner Lenny Wilkes another shot at TV stardom this year—his round, flat-topped face was a staple for any Ewerton or Dean County deaths deemed newsworthy enough for Eau Claire's nightly news—Anna slid forward along the booth's cigarette-burned orange seat, until she could just see the sharply angled screen.

Seeing her perched precariously on the edge of her seat, Mr. Winston pulled a chair over from an adjoining empty table and motioned to her. Reluctantly, drink in hand, Anna came over to join the four men, but pulled her chair as far away as politely possible.

Above the collector bottle and shlock-filled glass bar shelves, the off-screen announcer on WEAU was announcing the lead stories for the night. After mentioning the Wall Street crash ("Shit, there's no escaping it, is there Anna?" her ex-teacher asked with a smoke-hazed wink), and a couple of Eau Claire events, the announcer said, "And up in Dean County, a body is discovered in a wooded part of Ewerton."

Around her, the other men cheered. Draining her glass, Anna thought, *Must have been someone even more unpopular than my clan.* For a delirious, delicious moment, she wondered if the old lady had finally ventured out of her house, perhaps in search of Ma, but then discounted it. Anna wasn't the lucky type.

Suddenly, she stiffened. Mr. Winston was tracing the design on the back of her satiny stadium jacket. "If you're a regular, how come I haven't seen you in here more often?"

"Huh? Oh, my *jacket*." Anna had found her silvery nylon jacket with the black and gray banded cuffs at the launderette one morning, tossed in one of the brown garbage cans. It was a mess—the flannel lining torn; the sleeves sticky with some sort of pink stuff, the deep gray enamel worn off the buttons. The lining was soon pieced together like a soft Springbok puzzle, the pink glop washed off after three tries, and she repainted the snap buttons silver with enamel.

She had wanted a stadium jacket for years, so she hadn't minded that there was a black screen-printed logo on the back advertising the Rusty Hinge. Everyone in town over fifteen wore stadium jackets advertising *something,* including bars. Wearing that jacket was one of the few things Anna did that people found acceptable, even though she seldom drank, herself. And tonight, when she finally felt that she *needed* a drink, in a place away from the house that still shook with the echoes of Ma's rage, the silvery jacket was her ticket into a place where she might not otherwise be truly welcome. And yet, it was reflective enough for her to be visible during her long walk home.

"Uh...someone gave this to me. For a gift," she added defensively, even though Mr. Winston was well aware of her financial state. The old man's hooded blue eyes shifted to her own hazel ones. A look passed between them—if that's what you want to say, it's fine with me, but I *know* you, kiddo—and then he directed his attention to the screen.

The commercial was going off, and the perky female anchor said, "A grim discovery was made near the Dean County Fairgrounds, in the county seat of Ewerton. An anonymous phone call was made early this morning to the Ewerton Police, stating that there was a body in a patch of woods a few blocks from the fairgrounds. There police found the body of Inez Hibbing, age unknown, the former wife of Norm Hibbing, a Ewerton businessman."

"Businessman, my ass. That novelty shop is a friggin' joke," Winston snorted over his beer, while Lenny reached over and slapped his arm, whispering, "I'm on next, you old fart, so shaddup."

"While foul play was initially suspected, preliminary results of an autopsy conducted at Ewerton Memorial Hospital Nursing Home soon ruled out murder, according to Dean County Cor—"

"Here goes, here goes," Lenny was chanting, as Mr. Winston nudged Anna and rolled his almond-shaped eyes.

"There's Lenny!" Mesabi shouted, while Arnie turned up the volume on the wall-mounted set.

Lenny's broad, bovine face, brown eyes darting around like flies caught in a windowless room, was sweating slightly as he said on camera, "Well, there had been some bleeding from head wounds, which made us think it was a homicide, but after the wounds was cleaned off, we found that they were—"

"We, huh? Since when did you become a pathologist—"

"Shaddup, Nemmitz!"

"—scratches, probably from a bobcat or fox, both of which we got up this way—"

"My God, Lenny, what a marvelous pitch for the hunting season. Chamber of Commerce should put you on salary," Winston reflected dryly, as Lenny's over-amplified voice droned on, "—but Doc Calder, he found evidence of a heart attack, even though Miz Hibbing wasn't too old—"

"That's *your* opinion, Len," Arnie said, as he leaned against the counter drying an old-fashioned glass. "That hussy's been coming in here since, oh, 1965 or 1966, and she didn't need no ID card *then*."

"—so we're considerin' the case closed, although we still don't know how she came to be in the woods, or who it was who called the police—"

"That was Dean County Coroner Leonard Wilkes. And in weather—"

Arnie switched the TV to MTV—David Lee Roth hovering in midair with a microphone stand in his hand. Over at the table, Mesabi said, "You was sweating, Lenny. You looked better when Dead Fred Ferger kicked off. *That* time you had on a better shirt, too. Don't you know, you ain't 'sposed to wear green on TV? Makes you look like a fish."

"Or a corpse. Len, was old Inez really bloodied up good?" Nemmitz sounded as if he hoped the corpse was mangled. Flushed with stardom, Lenny regally took a sip of Bud before saying, "Not all that bad. But she was scratched up in the agonal stage—that's when she was alive, but dyin'—and you know how head wounds are."

"Seen enough of them in 'Nam," Wayne said sagely, and the others all nodded, even though none of them had ever seen actual combat.

"Well, even though it wasn't *bad,* I still didn't ever see nothing like it. She was just sittin' there, head all raked up, and palms, too. Like she was pushin' off something fanged but gave up mighty quick. On 'count of her heart gave out, I 'spose."

"Could she have been startled by an animal, and that brought on the heart attack?" Winston slurped down the rest of his squaw piss, then dropped his cigarette butt into the can. A line of smoke rose out of the can, as if the squaw pictured there had taken up the peace pipe, then was quenched.

"'Spose so. Doc Calder said she was on a toot. Enough alcohol in her blood to douse a bakery full of fruitcake. Old man threw her out, y'know."

"We knew, we knew. Only question was why Norm was dumb enough to marry her in the first place," Wayne reflected around a mouthful of chips.

"Nother question's who called in about the body. Bib Stanley's goin' nuts tryin' to figger that one out. At first, he thought whoever called it in done it," Lenny said.

"What was it, some guy? Inez was with half the town, at the least. Only ones I know she hadn't fucked for sure are you, Wayne, me, and old Arnie back there,"

"And what about me?" Winston pretended to be indignant, yet winked at Anna, who stared down at her tiny melted ice cubes.

"Oh, *you.* I think there's some kindergarten kid over in Lumbe that you haven't diddled—isn't that right, kiddo? You had him in school."

Anna looked up at Mr. Nemmitz. His green eyes were friendly, so she answered, "Mr. Winston knew better than to tangle with *me.* I would've sicced Grandma on him." Calling the old lady *Grandma* gave Anna a funny taste in her mouth, as if she had just chomped down on a piece of bread and butter covered with cigarette ashes.

"That grandmother of yours—I haven't seen her around lately. Is she well?" Suddenly, the mood at the men's table shifted. When old man Nemmitz turned solicitous, Anna knew she had to get her guard up.

"Oh, she's okay. Hasn't been out of the *house* in years, but otherwise, she's doing fine. Ma's been taking care of her, so—"

"You heard from your mother yet? My Bitsy, she says she talked to her before she caught the bus for Eau Claire this morning. Out by the courthouse," Nemmitz added, as if Anna didn't know where the weekly bus downstate parked each week. Anna swallowed down the watery rum and Coke at the bottom of her glass before answering.

"Yeah, she got down there okay. She called before I left the house. She's okay."

The other men were silent for a few seconds; even Mesabi quit his open-mouthed chewing. Anna sensed that they were waiting for her to say something, give a reason why Ma left town. No doubt they knew she hadn't gone in to the FmHA, too. Lenny's daughter-in-law, Heather Wilkes, used to work there, before she got knocked up again. And Heather "worshiped the great phone god," (as Lenny himself had said many a time) as did her former co-workers.... Finally:

"I really hate to run, but I have to get up early tomorrow. It was nice talking to you."

"Any time, kiddo. Just pull up a chair next time you're in. I promise, I won't put out my smokes in your drink." Mr. Winston winked at her, and Anna felt like she'd just drunk down a glass of warm grease. Even though she was one of the few female EHS students who'd never done whatever it was the other girls used to do with him to get better grades in English, Anna felt a flush of guilt and shame just being around him. Bad enough she felt dirty over what her great-grandfather had done fifty-odd (or was it fifty-even?) years ago.

As she began to push open the door, Lenny yelled behind her, "Anna, you want I should give you a lift home? It's on my way."

Anna stood there, shoulder braced against the door, mulling it over. She needed to walk, to clear her head, but still, if there was something out there that caused that old bleach-blonde barfly Inez to croak from fear—"Okay, as long as it's not out of your way." Lenny was safe—a big teddy bear of a guy with penny loafers and shirts that never stayed tucked in his pants. Anna doubted that he and Millie ever got it on much; Lenny seemed almost neuter, like a deballed bull. And he even blushed when Mr. Winston got raunchy. In Ewerton, that alone was proof that a guy was safe.

* * * * * *

"Here's my house," Anna said, as Lenny's ten-year-old Dodge passed her next door neighbor's house. It was the first thing she'd said since getting into the car with Lenny back at the Hinge. From the way he'd been trying to make small talk all the way from Sixth Avenue East to her house over half a mile away. Anna guessed that he'd found out that Ma hadn't shown up for work, but little else that wasn't already known. And that was the way Anna intended to keep it.

Lenny played the real gentleman, stopping the car and getting out to open her door. Anna was glad that the neighbors were out, no doubt whooping it up in some bar at the city. Yahoos like the Downings and the Effertzes tended to hang out where it was okay to bay like rabid dogs and throw ice at the bartender, the better to come home honking and burning rubber come midnight.

And Lenny didn't pull away until after she had the key in the lock and pushed the door open. And even then, as she closed the door, she could hear his car pull very slowly away, accelerating until it reached the corner. Lenny was a buffoon, and a mediocre coroner, but he was okay.

For a long time after she locked the door, Anna stood there in the living room, staring at the house she'd inherited. Part of her mind was calmly ticking off her added responsibilities—*no problem with the FmHA check, they've accepted them with my signature when she's been too angry with me to sign them, and they'll take cash for the rest of the bills, and I suppose I can take on more jobs through the service—), even as the little girl in her raged, Why in hell did you pick up and leave? Do you really think it'll be any better somewhere else? You'll always be you, with the same emotional baggage as before...and you'll see—the old lady will find out where you are, and call you with some imagined complaint.*

"Oh, *fuck,*" Anna said as she stared at the roomful of castoffs, found wall schlock, and cat-chewed houseplants that didn't reflect either her own or her mother's tastes—a sort of hell's waiting room she'd been forced to spend her time in for lack of any other place to go. "Now *I* have to take care of the old lady."

She wondered if the old lady had tried to call her when she was out at the bar. The old lady only used her phone to make outgoing calls. If Anna or Ma wanted to call *her,* they had to use a complicated code of one ring, disconnect, then two rings, then one after another disconnect, and then wait for the old lady to call *them.* All because the old lady claimed that people were calling her and not saying anything when she answered the phone. And considering the delegation of less-than-neighborly neighbors who had spoken to Ma over twenty years ago, there was a good possibility that the old lady's claims were true—even if she wouldn't let the phone company install a tracer on the line.

Guilt nibbled on the sense of grief Anna was just beginning to feel over Ma's leaving her. Letting a stream of air out past her upcurled bottom lip, until her bangs flew away from her eyes in a puff of light brown, she dialed the old lady's number and began the signaling sequence. Afterward, she sat on the edge of the old trunk next to the phone stand and adjusted the shade of the black metal and gold glass lamp that sat on the black trunk, along with a nearly denuded avocado plant and one of the cat baskets.

It was no use waiting, hand on the receiver, since the old lady always took her sweet time calling back. Claimed she couldn't get up too fast out of her rocker, that she became dizzy, or worse, or so Ma said. Anna had tried to argue that the old lady was *only* in her sixties (sixty-three in late December, as a matter of fact), and nowadays, that wasn't old in the least.

("For Chrissakes, Ma, Fred Astaire was still hoofing in his late sixties, and he looked pretty damn good before he died in his eighties—"

("The old lady don't like him."

("So?"

("So she don't care how fit Fred Astaire was when he died. He had things a lot easier than she did—"

("Oh come *off* it. You know she was well-taken care of af-ter...after you know. Her aunts took good care of her—"

("How the hell do *you* know?"

("All right, did they make her work? Sell papers, matches? It was the Depression, and she had a house to live in and food to eat. And clothes on her back, I've *seen* those dresses of hers—"

("The ones you ruined on her?"

("'Ruined,' my *ass*. It was her fault she made me try them on when she knew I was fatter than she was as a kid—"

("That's right, you *were* a goddamn fat moose of a—") The ringing phone snapped Anna out of her bad memories; reaching over, she picked up the beige receiver and said, "Hello?"

"You *rang?*" Ma had been right about one thing. For a woman of only sixty-two, the old lady did *sound* like an octogenarian, or older. What Anna especially hated was that quavery, phlegm-sliding-down-stucco quality in the old woman's voice, and that false, coquettish lilt on the word *rang*. Leaning against the lamp shade, until the room's shadows were all off-kilter, Anna said, "Ma's gone. I heard she's down in Eau Claire. She took the bus. Has she tried to call you?"

"So Mother took *off*. Are you all *right* there? You can sleep in *my* house," she said in that quivering singsong that Anna had hated for years, ever since the old lady's voice went bad back in the late seventies.

"No...no. I have the cats to look after. Unless you want me to bring—"

"Oh, *no*. Ma *told* me about that big kitty of yours—"

"We have two big cats." Anna felt herself getting ready to snap. She wished Mouth would wake up and start caterwauling—anything to drown out the old lady's gravel-in-grease gurgle.

"I know *that*," the old lady said with an explosive hiss. I'm talk-ing about that *big* kitty—the mean one."

"Brupie? He's a sweetie. Big softie of a—"

"That's not what *Ma* says," the old woman warbled, like a knowing child kicking up sand as she pumped herself higher, higher on a playground swing. For a second, Anna pitied the two maiden aunts who had come up from downstate to look after her grand-mother in 1931, after great-grandpa had gone berserk.

"Your Ma says that Bruiser is a vicious animal."

"Because he nipped at her when she touched his frostbit toes. You'd nip too if you were in his paws."

Wheezing laughter drifted out of the receiver's tiny holes. Stunned, Anna thought, *Hey, old bat, your daughter's just off, and you're laughing?* as the old lady went on, "How would I fit them *on?*" followed by more of that hissing mirth.

Rum and cola bile hung at the back of Anna's throat as she snapped. "How would you fit into *what?*" Her grandmother could be worse than a six-year-old who had just discovered knock-knock jokes.

"His *paws!* I have bigger *feet,* you know," she added, as if Anna were too dense to understand her.

Anna's head hurt. For a second, she felt pure empathy for her mother; sometimes Ma stayed with the old lady for hours on end. It was almost enough to let Anna forgive Ma for all the names she'd called her over the years.

Almost.

"—see the news on Channel Eighteen?"

"What?"

"The news about that Inez bitch—the one who fired—"

"Oh, *that.* Yeah. I saw it."

"On Channel Eighteen?"

"No. Thirteen. In the bar—the Rusty Hinge," she added defiantly.

"Oh. Looking for a fella in there? Your Ma, she used to—"

"No, I went because of my jack—Listen, it's getting late. I need to get up early, okay? I'll talk to you later."

"No, you'll *see* me later."

Ye gods, she's right. Tuesday is *the day Mom picks up her bills and stuff. Oh, shit. And I didn't want to see her again until she was on a stand in the Reish-Byrne Funeral Home. Damn.*

"Yeah, well, okay. I'll be around sometime tomorrow. 'Bye."

"Bye-bye," the old lady hissed triumphantly as Anna let the receiver drop to the cradle with a brittle clack.

Leaning against the lamp until the shade began to buckle, Anna looked around her, and thought, *Those jerks in New York don't even know the meaning of Black Monday,* and began to cry open-faced, her hands resting palm up on her thighs—in almost exactly the same position Inez Hibbing had been found that morning.

SEVEN—Inez

Across town, the body of the former Inez Hibbing, until recently wife of Norm Hibbing (who really should have known better than to marry the town mattress), of the Wisconsin Street novelty and used clothing store, was zipped naked into a black body bag lying on the floor of the Reish-Byrne Funeral Home. Such casual placement of her body was not accidental—not after Craig Reish had caught her back in 1978, in the process of trying to get his retarded Uncle Cooper tanked up, prior to attempting to roll the hapless man for the loose change he happened to be carrying in his fatigue jacket pocket.

Craig Reish had never forgiven the bleached-blonde, roach-faced woman of indeterminate race (some in town said Indian, others were sure she was Mexican, while still others, namely Bitsy Nemmitz and Pearl Vincent, swore that the woman was what they called a light "Nag-ro"), nor was he planning to do much of a reconstruction job on her come morning. He wasn't going to let his wife Susie affix false white-blonde hair (from the assortment of many-hued hanks she kept in an old tackle box) to cover the wide-shaved swath that resembled a reverse Mohawk on the dead woman's scalp, nor was he planning to use makeup, wax, or Hydrol tissue builder to fill in the long ragged claw marks that grooved her faintly black-stubbled dark scalp.

And Susie wasn't going to put any fresh nail polish on those cat claws of Inez's, either—not a single drop from the dozens of half-empty bottles she kept close to his embalming supplies.

Considering what Inez had done to Uncle Cooper (whenever someone treated the heavy-set gentleman badly, he became "Uncle Cooper"; otherwise, he was better known around town as "The Happy Wanderer," or, in the Reish household, as "Your nutty uncle"), the dead woman was lucky to be getting embalmed at all, let alone buried at county expense, or so Craig Reish had decided upon viewing the now naked remains of Mrs. Hibbing when Lenny brought them over that afternoon.

He'd grunted over the carelessly black-sutured chest as Lenny explained about her heart attack, thinking, *Heart attack, fart attack. I only hope you suffered, cunt,* before assuring Lenny that he'd do everything possible for the deceased, before her ex-husband came back from his out-of-town trip the next afternoon.

Watery brown eyes anxious, Lenny had said, "You'll make her look nice, won'tcha, Craig? Her landlady sent over these clothes. Norm, he's a jerk, but really a nice guy. You'll do her up right, won't you?"

Craig was upstairs at that very moment, tossing under the covers in gleeful delight over the prospect of seeing Norm Hibbing's farsighted blue eyes goggle out when Craig lifted the lid and exposed the neo-Punk corpse within, as he officiously explained that there was nothing else he could do on such short notice.

And since Craig was so bent on revenge, and since old Doc Calder wasn't the most observant family practitioner-cum-makeshift pathologist in Dean County (let alone Wisconsin), neither man—to both of whom the dead were nothing new, or exotic, or above all, frightening—had taken all that good of a look at the sets of long scratches on Inez Hibbing's shorn scalp. For while the scratches were mostly close set, and in obvious paw arrangement, there were a few scratches here and there that were wider set, with ample space between the separate ragged wounds.

Spaces roughly the width between *human* fingers, and fingernails.

EIGHT—Dream Time

"Don't wanna have my picture taken...I wanna open my *presents!*" little Anna cried. Mommy tried to hush her, but Gramma was listening, as she pretended to sleep under the big blue quilt, and before Mommy could grab Anna away from by the bed, Gramma's hand snaked out from under the covers, nails curved in a horny yellowish line, and before Anna knew what had happened, Gramma's claw-hand had raked her left cheek. Gramma hissed, "Woke me up, you little mutt."

And little Anna felt blood welling in the four jagged furrows on her cheek, and on her earlobe, where Gramma's horny thumb had caught the tender nub of dangling flesh. Anna screamed, "No, Gramma, no!" but Gramma reached up and did it again, and every time the nails raked Anna's cheek they felt like *real* claws, and Mommy didn't do *anything,* but stare while Gramma hissed from under the covers, "Woke me up, woke me *up.*"

Mommy put makeup over little Anna's cheek once the blood was all gone, but the makeup felt all funny—not like the powder in the round compact at all. It was waxy, and smelled like something stale and dead, like when Great-Aunt Joan was in that box and old Mr. Byrne lifted her up to see the husk of a woman, and little Anna had to smile while she opened the gifts under the tree, for if she didn't smile Gramma was gonna be mad, and do the flapping thing that even scared *Mommy* so bad she'd never admit it had ever happened, after it did, but little Anna wanted to cry, not smile, so suddenly Gramma *came* at her, all brown and wrinkled and fuzzy and flapping.

The flapping noise in Anna's bedroom was *real.* The snicking echoes filled her head when she woke up from her nightmare of

Christmas of 1962—the time when the old lady had clawed up Anna's cheeks.

Real *flapping, in this room,* she thought, pulling her sheet closer to her chin. She felt the weight of the cats on her legs, but she was afraid to open her eyes—'fraid of what she might half see against the dark ceiling and walls. She knew there were bats in the sealed-off attic and between the walls of the house; often the cats would sit for hours, listening to the walls. Somehow, one of those filthy things had knocked aside the ceiling tiles and squeezed through.

There was no more flapping, not even the echo of a sound. Her cheek still carried the ache of the scratches and the makeup burning the sore furrows *(weird, that I dreamed of mortician's wax. Ma put Max Factor on my cheeks. You can see how dark they were in the pictures),* and her eyes were actually tearing. Easing a hand out from under the covers, Anna rubbed her still-closed eyes, as she became aware that Bruiser was resting with his body crosswise to her, his bottom up against her right leg, his head facing the window.

The window—that was it. Opening her moist eyes, Anna saw a faint patch of lightness against the dark wall. Bruiser had pulled his old trick again, pawing at her drawn shade until he created enough tension to raise it himself. Often, he was able to raise it only a foot or so, but occasionally, he could make it go all the way up to the top.

She hadn't taught him to do that; somehow, probably through feline observation and with the help of better than average cat smarts, Bruiser had figured out how to raise the light-filtering shade on his own.

His trick had actually scared Ma; inexplicably, she found it utterly terrifying to think that a mere animal had the brains to perform a "human" task. It was around that time, in fact, that Ma claimed she hated the muscular black animal.

"Whatcha see, huh, Brupie? Bunnies out there? Another cat?" Bruiser turned his massive head her way for a second, then resumed looking out the window. He'd butted the filmy curtain aside, and was staring intently at something in the backyard, following its movements with his broad, small-eared head. Tiny burbling sounds escaped his throat as he tensed up, butt wiggling against Anna's leg.

Curious, she leaned forward at the waist and put her hand on Bruiser's smooth back, asking softly, "What is it? The neighbors? What do you see?" as if she fully expected the cat to supply her with a rational answer.

Her own night vision wasn't the best; unlike her mother, Anna needed at least a few street lamps, or even full moonlight, to see reasonably well in the dark, and thus she kept a small but fairly powerful flashlight under her pillow, just in case the cats started acting up. Usually, all she had to do was train the light on them and they'd quiet down. Staring into her dark, tree- and shrub-filled backyard was almost totally useless without the flashlight, since all she could initially make out was the faint sheen of moonlight on frosty ground, and bulking shapes of foliage—until she aimed the flashlight into the yard, and saw what had captured Bruiser's attention.

Something dark and small—quite small, in fact—was moving fluidly across the yard on a northwest diagonal. Against the faint paleness of the frosty grass and leaves, all Anna could make out was a vague sense of thin legs crisscrossing, below a body that refused to come into focus. But her flashlight's beam captured one detail—an all-too-brief glimmer of color against the surrounding maw of blackness that comprised the creature's head.

A reflected glow of green-brown, roundish and fast-moving, as if the head had turned in her direction, then turned away again—a blink-and-you-miss-it movement that had lasted just long enough for her to register one disquieting, irrational fact.

She had seen the glow of *three* eyes on that formless head. And for no good reason, she remembered what Lenny Wilkes others had said in the Rusty Hinge about that Inez shrew being clawed by an animal, perhaps being frightened into a heart attack by some strange beast.

If three eyes aren't strange, I don't know what is. And the way Inez was always snockered, she could have imagined it was the devil himself come to bring her home to Papa.

Anna knew she was safe as long as she stayed in bed, with the comforting warmth and weight of the cats on her legs, but she still felt vulnerable, violated—there was a *whatever* roaming her yard, and there was always the possibility that it would come right up to the window and peer in at her.

As if intuiting her fears, Bruiser began to growl, a low rumble deep in his chest that woke Mouth up. Soon the window was crowded with cats, blotting out the view through the bottom fifth of the window—but not enough that Anna couldn't see the dark shape pause, turn her way again, and quite obviously hiss, the dim moonlight glinting off the incisors within the ill-defined mouth.

And in that instant, Anna saw where the third "eye" was. It wasn't in line with the real eyes, but situated lower down, close to the mouth. It was a tag, a damned *rabies* tag, twin to the ones Anna had for both of her cats—a green cut-out bell shape with a hole poked in the top. But the tags were over an inch in diameter, and quite wide at the bottom, while this spot of green luminescence was small—only slightly bigger than a cat's real eye.

Reflexively, Anna got up on her knees and reached up to pull down her shade, telling herself, *It's an address tag, like they sell at the vet's office. Some of those are tiny little circles of metal or plastic. No, don't think plastic, it doesn't reflect like that.*

The shade safely in place, Anna flopped back down on the bed and pulled her covers over her, not even daring to poke her head out again when Bruiser began to paw at the shade frantically.

In the *morning,* she thought, *I'll go back there and see what kind of tracks the thing left,* even as she prayed that it would turn warm overnight and thaw the delicate frost on the soil.

NINE—*Arlene (2)*

Much like her fellow Dumpster diver Anna Sudek, Arlene Campbell was asleep, dreaming, as her cats crowded around her bedroom window, peering out through the drawn chintz curtains at the strange wandering beast scampering on the lawn below. Hers too was a worried sleep, with awful dreams; a dripping Inez Hibbing, dirty-nailed fingers clutching long tufts of her shorn-at-the-scalp brittle hair, was waiting on Arlene in the store her ex-husband owned, even though Arlene told the woman she'd much rather have Norm handle the ringing up of her purchases.

But Inez was nonplused. Using her bloody, hair-wound fingers, she punched up the numbers on the till, as the dying fluorescent light above made the bare swath of scalp between the bloody, tangled lengths of blonde hair over her ears and neck gleam in the dingy, musty store.

And even when that Sudek girl, Anna, came in from the back room where she'd been stocking new merchandise, Inez wouldn't let her ring up Arlene's order, even though she begged the walking corpse to let Anna handle it.

"Don't you know? I'm going to fire her," Inez's corpse said, without moving its clawed lips. "I don't want no murderer's relative working in *my* store," and then the display window crashed in a shimmer of ice chips and clear confetti, bringing with it a small, dark-furred thing with widespread claws and three glowing, baleful eyes.

And just as Arlene passed from the nightmare into wakefulness, she noticed that the outstretched paws of the sleek dark thing were covered with what looked like pressed face powder.

Snorting, pawing at her face with trembling hands, Arlene sat up in bed, mumbling, "No...oh, please, *no*," for as the hyper-colored dream images left her mind, one last detail filtered into her consciousness—the face of the blackish beast.

It was fur-covered, and chinless in the way of small beasts, but it was not the face of an animal—oh, no, not at *all*. Like a small child wearing a cat mask, the eyes of knowledge, of calculated *intent*, shone through the painted gauze over the eyeholes.

And as she covered her mouth with shaking hands, Arlene Campbell remembered exactly which face she'd just seen all fur-skinned and fangs out in the nightmare novelty shop—a face well-known to little Arlene Weiss and her playmates, from over fifty years ago.

Worse than the dream, and worse than the remembering, was the knowledge that the owner of that pinched, crafty child's face was still alive.

It was then Arlene noticed that all her cats were crowded in the window, watching the yard. Being much older than Anna Sudek, it wasn't so easy for her to bend at the waist to get a good look out the window as she sat in the bed; she had to get up and shuffle around the footboard to look out the window. Past Silky's huge ears, and Puff and Fluff's round Persian heads, she saw a dark shape gliding across the lawn, leaving definite dark impressions in the crunchy white grass.

If her Don had still been alive, he would have charged out the door, shotgun in hand, ready to blow off the beast's nebulous head, and never mind the law against shooting inside city limits. He was Don Campbell, scourge of the city works crew, master of the snowplow and the street sweeper, king of the pickup trucks, wasn't he?

And while Arlene had never shared her husband's temper, she did have a healthy sense of curiosity, that same sense of needing to know that had led her to find the body that morning, and later to phone in that hankie-muffled report of the incident, because she simply had to know what had happened (not that she bought that heart attack story—Clive Calder couldn't tell an anus from an aorta).

In the darkness, she felt for her clothes and put them on, easing her shoes over her bare feet before she hurried downstairs and outside, flashlight in hand. Sure enough, something dark and darting was in the yard. Arlene saw it, and it saw her—with all three of its eyes.

"Shoo!" she warbled, clapping her free hand against her thigh. The beast took off on an angle to the north, skidding across the frost-slippery grass. Not bothering to see where it went, Arlene shone her flashlight at the creature's tracks across her lawn. They were cat prints, or maybe skunk. Only, not exactly right, either, for the gait was all wrong, as if it had been trying to walk *en pointe* on its paws, in a vaguely human, pattern not *quite* like that of a cat or a skunk.

And farther away from her, on her neighbor's lawn, actually, the print became different—almost dog-size. When she saw the odd prints *(That can't be. Things get smaller when they're farther away—don't they?)*, Arlene thumbed off her light and hurried back into her house, knees protesting all the way, and slammed the door behind her with a shotgun-loud report of aged wood hitting aged wood. But if Arlene *had* decided to follow the strange tracks leading away from her house, she would have been very puzzled to see that they changed once more—for one step, to the scrabbly claw of a bird, and then there was nothing at all to mar the white-rimed grass below.

CHAPTER TWO

TUESDAY, OCTOBER 20, 1987

ONE—Bib (1)

As Anna heard the car pull up and come to a stop behind her, and saw the shadow of the gumball machine on top of the vehicle, she thought, *Why me, huh? Terry Von Kemp two days in a row is too much to*—until she heard a different, more nasal voice ask:

"You're Tina Miner's girl, aren't you?"

Anna's hand stopped in mid-grasp around a half frozen grapefruit in the IGA dumpster. Bib Stanley was speaking. He was Ewerton's chief of police, up until now only a disembodied voice to Anna, whose prerecorded warnings about skateboarding on the sidewalks and driving through the city parks played daily on WERT, AM and FM. Anna hadn't even realized that he pulled patrol duty like the other officers.

Not thinking it proper to turn around to face the chief with garbage in hand, Anna reluctantly let go of the grapefruit. She couldn't do anything about the other five already in her bag. If Chief Stanley didn't like it, he was welcome to make a reservation for her in the vertical-bar suite of the Ewerton Hilton.

"Uh...yeah. Yes. I'm her daughter, Anna Sudek."

"You married?" Chief Stanley had the interior lights turned off. Little of the light from the wall-mounted flood above the Dumpsters reached his face or body, save for a wedge of beard-stubbled chin.

"No. My mother was, though." Chief of police or not, Anna didn't feel the man was entitled to insinuate that her mother was as morally loose as the old lady considered her to be.

"Oh, yeah. I forgot about it. Been so long since I've seen Tina. She and I went to school together, y'know."

"She never mentioned you to me," Anna began, before she realized what her words sounded like. But if Stanley was offended, he said nothing about it. Instead, he said, "What I was meanin' to ask was, are you makin' out okay with your mom gone."

You weasely fuck, you, Anna thought as she leaned over to pick up her mesh bag of fruit and used cake pans. *Why didn't you come right out and tell me you knew all about me and Ma?*

"I'm doing fine. As you probably already know," Anna said evenly, making a move to walk away. Stanley didn't say anything until she was abreast of the front passenger window. Then Bib rolled down the automatic window on that side and leaned over, turning on the interior lights. In the faintly yellowish light, every hair of his five o'clock shadow stood out in three-dimensional relief, and the dry wrinkled pouches under his light brown eyes were elephantine. Anna didn't think he looked the way he should have, based on his voice alone.

"Got a minute, Anna? I...I didn't mean to come on like a bad cop before—I was just curious how you're making out. I mean, with your mom gone, that leaves you with your grandmother, and—"

"Yes, a lot of people are worried about me," Anna said, her voice belying her sarcastic intent. "And yes, I know I have to take care *of* the old lady. I'm seeing her later this morning. In case you're curious, she's taking Ma's departure with her usual aplomb."

"Y'know something, Anna? With smarts like yours, you're really wasted out here. Went to college, didn't you?

"Okay, I know you did, considering that you made it out of Ewerton once, *you* shouldn't have come back here—you or your mom either. Y'know that your grandmother isn't as helpless as she makes out. Not to speak ill of your kin, but she's been that way— y'know, sorta *helpless—for* as long as I remember, and I'm forty-six. She wasn't too old then, either."

"My grandmother *is* old, Chief Stanley. Age doesn't have any-thing to do with it when it comes to her. I think she relishes being *old*."

"Well, that's her affair. She seems to like it here. Things always had a way of rollin' off her back—not like with you and me. I re-member, when I was in school with Tina, how the kids—"

Jiggling her bag, Anna began to walk away again, saying, "It's been really nice talking to you, but I have an early morning job, and I have things to do before then."

Bib Stanley slapped the top of his dashboard, exclaiming, "That was it! I almost forgot. Would you be interested in a job that pays better than what you're making, and for about the same amount of time?"

Really been checking up on me, haven't you? Next you'll be telling me when I have to take a shit, Anna mused, before she said, "I don't think so. I'm happy where I—"

Bib was scribbling something in his notepad as he said, "You give this to Marv down at the CEP office—you can type and file a little, can't you?—and tell him I sent you." He extended the ripped-out page through the window. Anna made him wait a beat before reaching out to grasp it. In small, crabbed handwriting, Bib's message said, "A. Sudek—the clerk-matron position at the police office—Brian Stanley, C of P Ewerton."

Anna put the slip of paper into her top jacket pocket, then zipped it shut before asking, "Why the sudden interest in my welfare, Chief? Atoning for old sins?"

Bib leaned back in his seat, arms crossed behind his back. "Feisty little chit, aren't you?" he asked without rancor.

Not quite sure what a "little chit" was, Anna replied, "Not without reason. If I wasn't, I'd have been eaten alive out here, and you know it,"

"Yeah, I know it." Bib yawned and scratched his head under his cap; the bristling sound was loud in the darkness. "Just like I also know that you and your mom have no chance here. It took Tina a while to wise up and get out again, and I don't think she's as savvy as you are, is she?"

"You're the expert on my family,"

Bib slapped his thigh, exclaiming, "Ye gods, you're a pip. You could have tamed some guy but good, y'know that?"

"Not when they think killing might be catching," she replied evenly, speaking the very words her own father had used against Ma—or so Ma and the old lady often told Anna, while she was growing up.

"Well, not some guy from out here, but some guy, anyhow. Heck, my Rhonda, she put the starch in my shorts mighty quick. And I was a wild shit. Worse than these goomers in the rust buckets with the dirty bumper stickers on the back."

"As I said before, Ma didn't mention anything about you to me."

The more reserved she acted, the more Bib seemed to enjoy himself. "If you don't beat all. Seriously, kiddo, you I should think about takin' a page from your mom's book and leave if you don't want that clerk job. With your education, you're only hurting yourself by staying, and you know it. Ewerton's not a town for someone like you. Heck, you don't talk like the rest of us do, let alone act like us. For most people, Ewerton's good, but not for you. Too much baggage, y'know what I mean? And it ain't fair, since it didn't have nothing to do with anything you or your mom done."

His omission of the old lady's name wasn't lost on Anna. Unbidden, the memory of the neighbors telling Ma about the old lady doing dirt on their lawns returned. It was just plain craziness. Anna had read about the exact same behavior in *Sybil* during her psychology class in college. Her professor, a laconic fellow who always wore jeans and baggy turtleneck sweaters to class, had claimed that the real Sybil had lived somewhere near Wisconsin, or in it, and said that there were clues to her hometown in the book—but Anna had never been able to find them—as if she'd actually wanted to know where another family in pain once dwelled.

Maybe it's a Wisconsin thing—nutty middle-aged ladies like Sybil's mom and my grandmother dropping a load in their neighbors' shrubs. Body language to the tenth power or something.

"There isn't actually nothing holding you here."

"Listen, do you think our leaving would have made it not happen? People can find out what they want about you, or your kin. I know—my father did it with Ma. Hiding never works—not if it means hiding from yourself, or your blood. Running away would only mean that what my great-grandfather did does matter."

Unable to go on, yet unable to leave, Anna stood there next to the car, struggling to catch her breath, feeling the familiar, unpleasant tightness there, and blinking back wetness in her eyes.

Bib paused to blow his nose, then, as he pushed his hankie back into his pants pocket, said, "Yeah, well…you just take that slip of paper to Marv, and tell him I recommended you for the job, And don't worry none about paying for any training. CEP takes care of that. Really, it'd pay a lot more than what you're doing now, and the hours are better.

"Y'know, I'm not tryin' to give you a hard time here. You understand that, Anna? It's just that I'm aware of certain things that've been going on, and sometimes a person can do something about 'em, and sometimes not. This is one thing I can do, okay? It don't make up for what's been, but maybe...well, you just take that slip in to Marv. Now you *better get* home, before whatever got that Hibbing witch gets you."

Recovered now, Anna said with a tight smile, "Animals...know better than to mess with me. I bite."

"That you do, girlie, that you do." Bib smiled as he turned on the ignition and began to back away from the rear of the grocery store, Anna took off, mesh bag banging against her thigh, without so much as a good-bye or thank you. She still wasn't sure if she should go see Marv Krumb down at the Concentrated Employment Program office, but as long as she had that note written in the chief's hand....

It wasn't until she was almost home, completely out of breath, as usual, that Anna realized she hadn't once heard or seen old Mrs. Campbell that morning, and figured, *Old bat's probably afraid she'll be the next one to get a frigging heart attack in the woods.*

TWO—The Old Lady (1)

"—and when I heard the news on WERT, I said to myself, 'That was the bitch who fired my Anna'."

Anna toyed with the piece of tasteless, boxed pumpkin pie the old lady had cut for her, mashing the crust crumbs into a flat little cake off to the left side of the china plate. Ma had told her how bad the old lady had become in the years since she and Anna had left, but even with the proof of the old lady's deteriorating voice over the phone, Ma's powers of description had been sorely limited.

It didn't help that Anna knew exactly when the old lady had really been born. When it came to the old lady, sixty-two going on sixty-three come late December was an abstract term, as meaningless a measure of age as saying the universe was older than time, or that hell is forever.

Anna's grandmother was an old, old lady, of seemingly advanced physical age. Oiled parchment and wrinkled tissue old, with dots, splotches, stiff short whiskers and age warts liberally covering her sagging skin. Her cheeks hung like empty purses beneath her high Czech cheekbones. Lank, almost indifferent strands of gray-white hair sparsely covered her domed, slightly shining whitish scalp. Her nose had ballooned with the years, to match basset-lobed ears, and she had a turkey wattle under her weak chin. Her lips were obscene, thickly protruding and shiny purple-wet, like the skin of a blood-engorged vagina. And her slightly nearsighted eyes resembled those of a doll that had been left outside too long in the sun and mud and snow, an abandoned plaything whose time spent in the open had leached the color from its irises, until only the pupils remained, a dark, hypnotic pair of disembodied dots in a sallow sea of red-veined off-white.

But the old lady's hands had to be the worst part, Anna decided as she reluctantly swallowed the cold pie. They were puff-knuckled, twisted, with nails the color of margarine gone bad in the wrapper, lined with something faintly transparent yet dark, like ancient scalp oils or raked-up dead skin—yet *oily*, with dark dappled blotches across the metatarsals, like the underbellies of some spotted hunting dogs.

And if the way the old lady looked wasn't awful enough, she smelled, a rancid, slightly fulsome odor not unlike wet mold or slimy, ripe, worm-pocked meat. The old lady had emitted that stench long before her formerly thin lips sprung, or her skin went slippery-crepey. Anna remembered how Ma refused to wash any of the old lady's things along with the old women's garments. If Ma threw in as little as one pair of the old woman's socks or panties, the whole wash smelled gamy, like an ill-dressed deer carcass hanging in the sun.

The fights they'd had over the wash had helped bring things to a head the summer before she and Ma left the house, even though Ma had offered to do a special load of the old lady's things. But the possibility of not being part of the "family" had freaked the old lady out, made her rage, teeth bared, and throw things, like a caged monkey in the zoo, shouting, "I already lost my other family; now I'm losing it again!" And not long after that, Anna had vowed that she would never look the old lady in the eye again until the latter's eyes were closed for good. Yet here she was, heart aching because being here, in the house where she'd grown up, which contained such mixed memories, reminded her of just how little she had at the house she and Ma had shared on Wilkerson Avenue. And she'd flinched inside when the old lady had opened the door, staring dumbly at Anna before sputtering without preamble, "*My* little Anna's hair was *blonde—you've got dark* hair," before letting her into the house, blithely ignoring Anna's protest, "But I'm almost thirty now. As I've grown older, my hair darkened." And her reunion with the old lady had deteriorated from there, until Anna found herself sitting at the old-fashioned five-legged white enamel kitchen table, eating a miserable wedge of pie she didn't want, listening to the old lady rehash yet another of Anna's past job failures. *Thanks a lot, Ma.*

Anna had worked for Norm Hibbing all of three days before his skunk of a wife Inez had fired her, for "gypping me." What had actually happened was that Anna had been framed. Inez hadn't been able to stand it when Norm spent coffee breaktime talking to Anna about books and writers. They discovered they shared the same alma mater and had both studied English literature under the same professor. On Anna's last day, of employment, Inez had made a phone call to a friend of hers—a blue-eyed Indian woman named Sharon.

As soon as Norm left the store later on, Sharon showed up, a ten-dollar bill in hand, asking for change, singles; Inez was too "busy" unloading a shipment of dirty pens (click the top and the man's shorts fall off), so she let Anna handle the transaction. And then, as soon as Norm came back from the post office, Sharon returned to the store, saying that a mistake had been made—she'd only handed over a *five-dollar* bill, not a ten, and that Anna had given out too much change.

Inez—ugly, ignorant little Inez, with her miniskirts, pinched iodine features, and filthy, filthy fingernails—had squeaked, "I don't want no college-educated *dummy*" manning *her* till, and same alma mater or not, Norm was forced to give Anna the boot.

Anna had been so ashamed of the incident that she never mentioned it to anyone except Ma, nor did she list the novelty shop on her later résumés, even though it was most likely a violation of some law or another. She already had so much going against her....

"Yes, that was the bitch. Nobody in town seems to be broken up about it," Anna remarked, forcing down another bite of the pie, nearly gagging on the mealy crust.

"They *shouldn't* be," the old lady pontificated, cutting herself a second slab of pie. For a woman only five feet tall, and not exceptionally fat, the old lady packed in a prodigious amount of food.

"Because when I heard it on the *radio,* I *told* myself, 'Mark my *words,* that bitch is getting *hers* for all the *bad* she did.' Like *my* Gramma always said, 'The evil get *theirs.' She* had trouble with the scum-bums, too."

"Yahoos," Anna remarked absentmindedly, as she forked off another piece of gelatinous orange but didn't eat it right away.

"I beg your *pardon?*" The old lady was in her coquettish mode again—Ms. Imperious. It was her only standby when she hadn't the foggiest what someone was talking about.

"Yahoos...from *Gulliver's Travels.* Book Four—the part about the country of educated horses."

"I only remember the little people who tied him up."

"Those were the Lilliputians. Gulliver met up with them on his first voyage. We only studied the fourth voyage in World Lit. Anyhow, Gulliver is washed up in this country where the intelligent beings are horses."

"I saw a horse once, on the *TV,* that could *count* with its hooves."

Anna nodded, trying to ward off a complete recitation of the show her grandmother had seen. She had already heard what was on

People's Court the afternoon before, down to every word Judge Wapner uttered.

"Well, the horses were like people, while the people—or what Gulliver eventually discovered were the people—were called Ya-hoos, They were very hairy and dirty."

"Like those *scum-bums* who drive up and down the *street at night,* honking to beat the *band?*"

Anna was pleasantly taken aback to hear the old lady echo her own thoughts. "Scum-bums" was an apt expression,especially for people like Zack Downing and his brother-in-law Elmo Effertz (the Effertzes—a farm family from out past County Trunk QV to the south—had a penchant for weird names. Zack's zit-faced wife's name was Irma), who spent half the night gunning their engines, shouting obscenities, and slamming their car doors while she tried to sleep,

A couple of years back, Zack and Irma moved into the very small frame house next to the Sudek house. The couple used to wait until well after sunset to begin work on the tiny addition they were building onto their house, Not that they weren't home from their re-spective jobs at the Red Owl and Ewerton bakery (he cut meat, she arranged bakery on plastic trays) hefore sunset—they only worked part-time, and got home by three at the latest. They simply seemed to *like* making noise at ungodly hours. And to pile on the insult, they'd taken out their old bathtub and just left it sitting there, next to the rough-looking little barn-shaped prefab shed Zack had slapped up a few weeks before.

And when one of the Sudeks' other neighbors had complained about the tub to their city councilman, Irma of the creamed-corn complexion and whiny voice had called everyone on the block, ac-cusing them of making the "mean call about our tub," Irma's vo-cabulary level matched that of a small, whining child. When her cat was lost (again), she called it "my kitty cat," and when her hus-band's hunting hound was barking, it was "Zack's doggie talking loud again."

More than once Anna wondered who'd bribed the examiner when Mrs. Downing took her driver's test (like Norma Grasnowski bribed the fellow when her retarded son Gary took his test—and passed). She doubted that the examiner was as hard up as potbellied Zack was when it came to getting a freebie in exchange for a passing test.

To Anna, *creatures* like Zack and Irma and her missing link brother Elmo of the perpetual stocking cap and half-unbuttoned plaid shirts were hardly worth the air they inhaled or the food they ingested. It was as if a command from God had gone wrong, and instead of being the goats or swine or *worms* they deserved to be, they had scaled the evolutionary ladder a little too soon. Rather like Jonathan Swift's Yahoos, who looked and even on occasion acted like people, yet were still animals who ate raw ass flesh and smelled each other's asses, unashamedly.

She was never sure if her own family situation made her feel so unaccountably *above* those with less gray matter upstairs, and much less couth in general. If the way she had been treated produced her feelings of superiority, so be it, she figured. Perhaps it was the way the ones who tormented her got theirs back. At any rate, regardless of why she dubbed them Yahoos, they *did* act as if they belonged to a sub-species of the human race.

I mean, how can cruds who put bumper stickers on theircars saying, "No muffs too tough—we dive at five," or "Wanna get laid? Crawl up a chicken's ass and wait" and leave skinned-out deer carcasses in the driveways after bow-hunting season, expect to be treated like decent human beings? You act like an animal, prepare to be regarded like one....

"...and my *Gramma* always *said,* 'Just because it *walks* upright and wears *pants* doesn't mean it has to be *called* a man—'"

Anna put down her fork and stared at the smelly old lady. Doubt filtered into her mind. Had the old lady really been so terrible during all those years, or had some of the badness been in Anna's mind? The old lady was actually making sense for a change, while Anna's memories suddenly seemed surreal, childish in their simplistic black-and-whiteness.

The dichotomy of her feelings was growing too uncomfortable; she had to either change the subject or leave the house. Pushing her plate forward with a forced burp, she said, "No more. It's wonderful, but I'm so full."

Leaning against the back of the white wood kitchen chair, which had been part of the old lady's mother's kitchen set, before Anna's great-grandmother died not twenty feet from this very room, if the old lady's account of the incident could be believed (and if what Bib Stanley inferred that morning was correct, a lot of people didn't believe what the old lady had to say about the night her father went...*strange)*—Anna glanced around at the kitchen, and the rooms visible beyond. Even though Ma had been coming over to clean up for the past few years, the place was still a rat trap, the walls oddly mildewed, with moldy black circles indicating the studs underneath the painted plaster walls, and a funny, sharply stale yet damp odor permeating the sticky varnished woodwork.

Old newspapers, magazines, and *Dean County Shoppers* were stacked in piles everywhere. Anna doubted that the bundles of paper the old lady kept were worth anything; the old lady had Ma religiously deposit her social security checks in the Ewerton Savings and Loan (the old lady had worked only a few years, back in the early fifties when they were strapped for workers at the paper mill), along with her trust fund checks from the combined money her maiden aunts had left her years ago.

Odd, when Anna got to thinking about it, that the two old women (Anna vaguely remembered Aunt Joan, who was all talc and spider-down hair when Anna was tiny) didn't trust their grown niece with a lump-sum inheritance, as if she was still the six-year-old half-orphan entrusted to their reluctant care. The trust fund did work out for the best, though, since it was in interest-bearing bonds. And considering that the old lady had had no husband to count on for a bigger cut of social security, the trust fund kept both the old lady and the family house in one piece.

Not that the house seemed to be of a whole; ever since Anna could remember, parts of it had been inaccessible, off-limits. The old sewing room off the kitchen, for obvious reasons. The basement, at least for little Anna. Ditto for the attic, which was said to have bats fluttering loose in it. A couple of the bedrooms were shut off, empty and airless, because they weren't needed.

And now, without Anna and Ma constantly around to keep things reasonably clean, the place was going to seed within. Flat bats of dust settled under the bigger pieces of furniture; hazy films of it covered the flat surfaces (Anna remembered how the old lady used to tell her, "*I* don't have to dust...that's *your* job"—and Anna was all of four years old, barely big enough to grasp the wooden handle of the feather duster), and the jumble of bric-a-brac assembled haphazardly on the end tables and hanging shelves. One shelf was a geometric black affair backed with several oversized gold-painted wooden leaves. The leaves had gone springlike, all green and soft looking.

The musty tang of mold spores made the inside of Anna's nose sting. Ma had said that when she first came back, the old lady's coffee grounds were piled up in a gray bearded heap on the counter, and that her linens were indescribable. There were torn shreds of towels and washcloths, mended and remended, sitting out, while dusty, fluffy stacks of new, unused towels, part of Ma's bridal gifts (the same towels which the old lady had removed from their packing boxes before they moved out, and replaced with old stained floor rags and dishrags), rested on the high shelves near the bathtub.

And the old lady's toilet still wasn't working. If you wanted to flush, you had to dump in a bucket of water. Anna wondered if the plumbing remained unrepaired by design or accident. It was common knowledge that no repairman would set foot on the Miner house porch unless Ma was there to keep the old lady away from the fellow while he worked.

(Once, a couple of years before Anna and Ma left, during one of Anna's winter breaks from college, they had had the back screen door replaced, and the old lady leeched onto poor Steve Umbert and refused to back off. She made him hot chocolate after he expressly told her he didn't want any, then fumed when he took one sip of it and left the remainder untouched. And worst of all, she'd dragged Anna downstairs, hiss-whispering, "Go on, *flirt* with him!" and Anna shook off the old woman's grasping claw, with a horrified whisper, "How *could* you? The man is *married. I* know his *wife.* You are absolutely disgusting—just because *you* fooled around doesn't mean—"

(If Steve hadn't been there, Anna might not have screamed so much when the old lady hit her, but Anna had to let someone know what was going on—and when Steve came running, wanting to know what was happening, the old lady made it seem as if Anna was doing something to *her,* pulling away, whining, "Don't hit an old lady...I'm just an old woman! But Steve's eyes were knowing as he quickly wrote out a bill and said, "I'll have my brother come over later to finish up," only his brother Chad never did come, of course, and Ma ended up doing the job herself...and for some odd reason known only to themselves, neither Anna nor the old lady explained why Steve left in mid-job....)

Yet those incidents seemed so *alien,* so removed from reality. that Anna found their very veracity questionable, even though there were plenty of people in town who could have either refreshed or supplemented her memory of them, if only they'd realized that she was now doubting. And paddling happily in dangerous depths.

"Yahoos...I do believe that I *like* that word," the old lady was saying. She added, with a phlegmy gurgle, "It's...how do you *say. Asp.*"

"Apt," Anna gently corrected, pulling the plate of pie back for one last polite bite.

"Yes, apt. Like my *Gramma* used to say, 'If it *walks upright* and wears—'"

"Oh, guess what," Anna quickly interjected, before the old lady did a complete rerun of their conversation, "I met Bib Stanley this morning, and he said there was a job opening at the station. Clerking, and being a matron."

Panic shone in those colorless eyes. "*You* can't be a matron, you're not—"

"Anyway, I have to stop at the CEP office and ask about it," Anna butted in, not wanting to hear another of her grandmother's word games. "And I don't know if Marv is going to be there later on this afternoon—I think he takes off earlier than the rest of the workers—so I'd really better get going. The pie was great. I'll be back later on this week, okay? And. call if you need anything before then."

"When you get *home,* be sure and give me the *signal.* I worry about you, *walking* and all." Anna had wondered when the old lady would be getting around to that same schtick she pulled on Ma. The minute Ma got home from the old lady's, she had to go through the same old triple-blind phone routine, just to check in.

"Control," Ma would say. "She wants that same old control. Worried, my *ass.* If she can't get it one way, she gets it another. *Control,*" as her face got red in angry, strawberry-shaped blotches.

Anna nodded, and said, "I'll be sure to do that, although I've been walking like this for years, and early in the morning, too."

"You shouldn't have to *do* that," the old lady demurred, but Anna caught her drift—you shouldn't do that, period. As if she didn't want her granddaughter out doing things she couldn't control or supervise.

"It keeps food in the fridge." Anna shrugged as she looped her purse strap over her right arm.

"Once you get that *job,* you won't *have* to go out early, will you?" That same six-year-old's wheedle that used to drive Ma crazy, and no doubt drove Aunt Joan and Aunt Bella insane—in the latter's case, for *real*—when the old lady was a little girl. What was it that the old lady's father was supposed to have said before they carted him off?

"Take care of my Lucy," or "Watch over my Lucy." Something no doubt suitably romanticized by the old lady over the years, to show how much her father adored and loved her, and to underscore how *mean* and *nasty* her late mother's sisters were to poor little Lucy Miner. In reality, her father had probably been yelling, "I'm innocent," or something better suited to the occasion at hand—said hand that happened to be carrying a dripping, reddened ax....

"*If* I get the job. I'm not counting on it. You find that out in this town. It's all who you know or who you're fucking."

"*Oh, Anna.*"

"I'm almost thirty years old. I've earned the right to say *fuck* once in a while. Really, though, I have to go. See you later, okay?" Anna said as she let herself out the door and quickly shut it behind her, just as her mother used to do. The old lady claimed that getting up and down too much wasn't good for her, yet, despite her claims of dizziness, she wouldn't let either Anna or her mother have a key to the front door, which made Anna come to the conclusion that the old lady's claims of dizziness were just that. *Claims.*

But she didn't consider any other alternatives for the old lady's persistent habit of making her wait for up to four or five minutes while she slowly made her way to the door—alternatives that had nothing—and at the same time, everything—to do with the state of being dizzy.

And as she walked up Evans Street, toward the CEP office at Fourth Avenue East, Anna didn't think to turn around, to see if old lady was watching her through one of the white frame house's many windows. Ma had said the old lady was in the habit of doing so, another example of *control*. But if Anna *had* looked backwards, just a peek, she might have stopped cold—although her grandmother was watching her, she wasn't watching through any window she could have reached in the short time it took Anna to walk from the porch to the sidewalk.

CHAPTER THREE

THURSDAY, OCTOBER 22, 1987

ONE—The Station (1)

"—and you put your coat and purse here, in this locker." Ginny Yarrow, former EHS classmate of Anna Sudek, and current dispatcher for the Ewerton Police Department, opened the door of a small gray enamel locker.

The inside of the door was fuzzy in spots, as if someone had placed a mirror or Stick-Up there long ago, and there were small crumb like bits of debris caught in the inside corners. Anna felt a sweeping rush of *déjà-vu*; her junior-year locker at EHS had been gray, too, and almost as cruddy inside on the opening day of school. And Ginny Yarrow (then Ginny North, but already wearing Band-Aids to cover Lonny Yarrow's hickeys during Phys Ed) had had the locker next to Anna's then, too.

And other things were the same, as well. When Anna walked into the station that morning (thinking ruefully that she'd be late going to the aluminum can recycling truck, and would have to wait while everyone else getting off work got weighed through), Ginny had looked up from her switchboard and said, "Hi, Anna. Bib wants I should show you around. He said your last name's still Sudek. Aren't you married yet?"

The same old shit: "Didn't you get a date for Sadie Hawkins?" "Aren't you going to the prom?" "We will be seeing you at homecoming, *won't* we?"

Anna's guts did a forward roll, but she shifted her purse from her hand to her shoulder and chirped brightly, "Nope!" The way Ginny said, "Oh" was sweet, very sweet.

At least I'm not raising a kid by myself, like you had to after Lonny split, Anna thought as Ginny reluctantly began to show her around.

Actually, there wasn't much for Ginny to do. Anna had already been to a fingerprinting lesson down in Wausau (Bib had driven her down, along with the new personnel for the Lumbe and Hunterstown police and sheriff's departments—two women who chattered on and on about Pat Sajak and Vanna, high priestess of vowels), and Bib had deputized her after they returned to Ewerton in the late afternoon, before she'd even had a chance to get the last of the fmgerprint ink out from under her nails. Bib had noticed it, joking, "Is that the Inez Hibbing look?" as if the dead woman was already the stuff of late night talk show monologues. Anna hadn't appreciated his approach, but smiled and forced out a chuckle anyhow. She didn't need another gap in her employment record.

It wasn't until Ginny had finished showing Anna where everything was, and where to put her coffee mug (once she brought one from home), that it dawned on Anna why she'd been asked to try for this job. *Bib wants to rub it in to all the people I used to go to school with—put the descendant of a criminal in with the crime-stoppers. Whatsamatter, Bib, did one of them piss you off?*

On the morning to afternoon shift, she counted five people who'd graduated from EHS, including two of the officers. And that was only this shift; Bib had told her that if her services as a matron were ever needed (in case Ginny Yarrow or the meter maid were ill or out of town), she was on call for all shifts.

The two officers were from her graduating class, she was sure, but oddly, their names escaped her, even though they had no trouble recognizing her. Anna supposed it was because she hadn't really changed all that much. She eschewed the short, permed "Ewerton" hairdo popular among married or older women and still wore her hair long, with girlish bangs. Repeated pregnancies hadn't had a chance to widen her hips or spread out her bottom; in fact, she weighed only ten pounds more than she had when she had graduated, and she'd gained that evenly over her body, so her basic silhouette remained undistorted.

And if she hadn't found the red White Stag velour top and black cotton pull-on pants she was wearing (both rescued from the trash bins at the Super Suds), Anna might have looked even more the way she used to—she hadn't bought any new work-suitable clothes since her first year of college, back in 1976. Not getting to wear a uniform had been a disappointment to Anna; she didn't have many more "modern" separates suitable for working in the station.

Also, she'd hoped to have a uniform to show to the old lady. When she'd called the old woman after getting home from her fingerprinting lesson, that was the first thing she asked: "When do you get your *uniform?*" For some reason, the old lady felt that if a uniform didn't come with the job, it wasn't worth doing. Anna suspected that the old woman was thinking of the high school Anna, of the pictures Ma used to take of her in her glee club, choir, and flag twirler outfits (unpopular or not, Anna tried out for things; EHS was a joining sort of place, where cliques were actually encouraged by the then-vice principal, Wally Inglass), pictures that still hung in montages on the dust-webbed living room wall in the old lady's house.

Anna had mollified the old woman by explaining that not having a uniform meant not having to pay for cleaning it. Even then, the old lady persisted, "But they *owe* it to you!"

As it was, Anna felt that she was already getting something long owed to her—slight, albeit grudging respect on the part of her fonner classmates. True, she'd never thought of majoring in business or secretarial courses, but she was a good typist, one of the fastest in her typing class her sophomore year. Even that letch of a teacher Mr. Owens, who used to chase girls like Ginny North and Maureen-who-married-Larry Komminski around the tables before the last bell for class rang, had to admit that Anna was a decent typist. He'd tried to get her into the whole secretarial shebang, but Anna wasn't into listening to the future-*haus frau* clucks in that clique talk about Fonzie and *The Love Boat* between lessons.

Ginny handed Anna a stack of arrest reports, mostly disorderly conduct cases with one plaid-shirted, baseball-capped Yahoo calling another such stylishly clad Yahoo (or Yahooette) a shithead or worse in front of one or another of the bars at nine-thirty that morning, and by lunch she had them neatly typed, without having to uncap her Liquid Paper once.

The only bad thing about finishing her work fast was having to sit with Ginny during break. *Happy Days* and *Love Boat* were long off prime-time, but Ginny was now an ardent Wheel-Watcher. Anna managed to salvage *that* line of conversation by asking about Ginny's little boy ("Little? Greg is taller than I am!"), a topic which managed to segue into a discussion of that Monday's Inez Hibbins case.

"I told Greg, 'Don't you go playing out that way, even if your friends are all going. It ain't worth it.' I mean, who knows what did that to her? Could be a big cat, or worse. I know Lenny, he made out like it was nothing, but it doesn't make sense, two heart attacks found out that way in a year. And old Fred Ferger kicked off out there, it was because he was an old goat and wasn't used to walking that much. But Inez wasn't all *that* old, and from what Bib said about the time when she broke the sink off the wall in the old county jail in the sixties—

"She *what?*" Anna had heard her share of strange stories, but that one had escaped her. Putting down her cup of instant (which she hated, but there were no tea bags around), she crossed her arms and leaned closer to her old classmate.

"It was when we were kids. My mom told me about it. Picked up for threatening the Horaks—you know, old man Nemmitz's cousins. Toobie works at the mill, and Troy at Ewerton Savings and Loan. Well, anyhow, they put Inez in the pokey and she got all fired up and either jumped on the sink—"

"Jumped *on* the—"

"Yes. On the sink, or beat it down with her fists. Anyway, Bib, he was only a patrolman then—walked by the cell and saw her sitting cross-legged on the floor, with the sink *next* to her. I 'spose it was really funny, but Bib was so pissed he went in there and grabbed her up by the arm and yelled—" here Ginny rasped through her nose—"'Put that damn thing back where you found it!' Next time you want to get even with Bib for something, you just mention Inez and the sink."

As she was laughing, flicking the tears from the comers of her eyes, a thought suddenly came to Anna. *Ginny's right*—Inez was *a strong little cuss. I saw her lift a whole case of shot glasses onto one arm, and carry a big roll of remainder carpeting under the other. And she was in her forties or older then. Wiry little slut—never a huff or puff out of her. And it did make sense with old Fred Ferger's heart giving out this summer—he was fat, old, out of shape. A good stiff trot to the john might have done* him *in. But Inez having a heart attack really didn't figure. Not unless she was scared, real scared. And someone who could do damage like that to the county* jail, *virtually in front of a whole police squad, couldn't have been afraid of all that much. I'm scared shitless to scribble "fuck you" on the walls of a public toilet. Why, I remember the time when Inez found a mouse in the storeroom...she crushed it to death with her foot. I was almost crapping in my pants when I just saw it scurry by. Even Norm was quaking in his sneakers. No, it makes no sense at all.*

"Anna, are you okay?" Ginny was staring at her with a look as close to concern as Anna had ever seen on the face of one of her contemporaries. It gave Anna a strange feeling she didn't quite know how to cope with.

"Yeah. I was just thinking about what you said. I worked for Inez for a short time."

"Oh? You couldn't stand her either? Norm couldn't keep anyone there."

"No, I couldn't. Anyhow, she always seemed to be in such good health—"

"Except for her Wassermanns—"

"Well, yeah, but that's a given. But she was so strong—not the type you'd think would just drop off like that, even an animal got to her."

Ginny scratched her scalp, making her head of short permed brown hair ride around like a loose wig. "I see what you mean. Of course Lenny and old Doc Calder, they don't see it like that. She was a big pain in the ass, and they were just glad to see her go. I guess all of us around here were glad on Monday. Y'know, the way they made it sound on the TV, it was like Bib wanted to prosecute whoever called in about the body, but Joe and Quinn and the others on the day shift, would have liked to have kissed her."

"It was a woman?"

Ginny put her fingers over her full lips and giggled."Whoops. Well, you're working here now, so I guess it's okay, That was Bib's big secret. Some broad called in the sighting, hey, c'mon." Ginny got up and motioned to Anna to follow. They made their way down the narrow, green-walled hall connecting the vending-machine-filled lunch area to the office, where whoever was dispatching received incoming calls.

"I wasn't on duty, but we tape incoming calls for verification. And Bib sometimes checks 'em to make sure nobody smarts off to the public. Hi, Kurt, can I show Anna something? Kurt, this is Anna, Anna, Kurt. C'mon, move it, Kurt. We can't fit in the same chair."

Kurt, a tall, balding young officer who Anna vaguely recalled as being from the class ahead of hers at EHS, stood up, stretched, and said, "Fine. I'm going for coffee. You man the store," and loped off down the vacant hallway. Ginny rolled her big brown doe eyes and shrugged. She picked a cassette out of the drawer and put it into a small portable machine next to the switchboard.

"I don't know if they do it this way in the bigger cities," she explained, as she wound the tape to a certain section, "but Bib's found that it works pretty good. I think old Stu Sawyer over in the sheriff's department runs it differently, but he and Bib are on the outs, so I don't know. Ah, here it is, I think."

Ginny pressed the Play button, and a hissing garble of words cameout. Muttering, "Bib should run a head cleaning tape through this thing," she thumbed the volume control wheel on the underside of the machine and said, "Listen good, the woman's voice is muffled or something."

Bending down close to the speaker opening, Anna heard:

"Hello, Ewerton Police Department. May I—" The voice was young, masculine, somewhat like Kurt's.

"I want to report a body." Muted, and very, very soft, almost a whisper filtered through something.

"A body? May I please have your name and—",

"In the woods by the fairgrounds. To the left of the road, in the trees. It is a woman, and she's bleeding." Considering what the woman was relating, her voice was remarkably calm and measured.

"When did you see this body?"

"Never you mind. Now, go find it before some kids stumble on it. Good—"

"Wait!

"...bye."

The "never you mind" was a tip-off for Anna; she'd heard her grandmother use the same phrase. An older woman, then, and very tough, judging by her choice of words.

This time, Anna didn't let her thoughts show on her face; she shook her head and said, "Sheesh, not much to go on there."

"Yeah. Bib's really ticked that the dispatcher couldn't get more out of her, but like you heard, she wasn't very talkative. At first, Bib and the others thought the woman was just injured, but...well, at least she was fresh. Not like old Dead Fred in July. Old goat was *ripe*. On Inez, the blood had hardly had time to clot up. If you can believe Doc Calder, she wasn't dead more than half an hour, or so. Lenny was telling Bib Tuesday in his office."

"Telling Bib what?" Kurt was back, coffee and a doughnut in hand; he edged Ginny out of his chair with his hip. Ginny gave him a bump and grind with her fleshy bottom before leaning against one of the file cabinets and saying, "That you're a dink. Hey, do you know if they buried that Inez bitch yet?"

"Uh-huh," he replied between slurps. "They planted her yesterday. No service. Norm didn't even close the store. I dunno. if they have a headstone bought or what."

"Maybe they can use the sink from her cell," Anna said, and her two new co-workers began to laugh as if she was just another person, and not Anna "Where's Granny?" Sudek. She even felt a twinge of camaraderie, something alien to her.

But tentatively accepted now or not, Anna still wasn't able to give up other, less warm but still tangible ties. For even though she was almost certain that she recognized the voice on the tape, she couldn't turn in the caller.

Even if old lady Campbell *did* get to the bakery Dumpster, before Anna did that Monday. For the old woman "understood" a part of Anna's life that Anna's new co-workers might never be able to comprehend, and that in itself was important.

Besides, she didn't really know whether the old woman was considered a suspect. *Remember, Ginny's only been your "friend" for all of three hours—and she brought it up about you not being married, didn't she?*

But later that day, when Ginny asked Anna if she'd be interested in apartment-sitting when Ginny and her son had to go out of town late next week, Anna said, "Of course—isn't that what friends do?"

TWO—At the Bakery

"Phone for you, Irma," Pete Quill, the head baker at the Ewerton Bakery shouted testily, as Irma Downing was busy composing a letter to her next-eldest brother, Maurice, during her morning coffee break. Irma didn't hurry to get the phone (*I'll bet it's that puke, Maurice*), instead choosing to scan over the words she'd written on the back of some custom cake order forms:

Maurice—

You asshole, you make dad feel unwelcomed. If you had any brains you'd go duck hunting with him—not your fucken friends. Why do you think he bought the boat up so you can *go* with someone else? You better shape up or I will hate you you son of a bitch. Dad has to tell me if Maurice would rather go. with that kid, I could go to Hunterstown or something.

Where are your brains. You talk to him and plan something together. Forget Tony forget your dad. Think about me & Zack for a change.

"Irma, I've already *told you* about having your family call here at work. Now answer this damned phone or I'm hanging it up."

"Coming, coming," Irma pouted, pausing to push a strand of hair back under the saggy hair net she was required to wear, before quitting her chair at the back of the bakery and taking the phone from her increasingly irate boss's floury hand. Leaning against the pink-painted cement bloc wall, Irma snapped, "Yeah?"

"Where the fuck were *you?*" said Elm, her next-youngest brother, calling from *his* job at the Gas 'n' Go Service station.

"Oh, writin' that creep Maurice a letter. Now Pete says you can't be callin' here."

"Yeah, well, I am. And Zack told me to tell you that your cat got out again, so. you better get your butt back come lunchtime and put it back in the house 'fore the county shelter people come 'round and get it."

"He *didn't!*" Irma squealed. From where he stood by the pastry machine, Pete Quill shook his head and mumbled to the woman who fried doughnuts, "Stupid stuck pig."

"Yeah, well, Zack said it slipped out 'tween his legs, and he wasn't gonna chase it all morning, so you better. And he said if the county catches it, you gotta pay."

"Yeah? You just tell him—"

"Irma, get off the line. You've been warned about personal calls. C'mon, your break's over," the head baker warned, while Irma's co-workers tactfully kept their heads turned and their eyes averted. Irma mumbled, "Gotta go," then hung up, but before she got back to work—in the back of the bakery, well out of the line of vision of any customers who might lose their appetites at the sight of her pustule-laden complexion—Irma said matter-of-factly, "I gots to go home for a while, 'kay?"

Normally, Pete Quill would have said no, you just get back to work, but spending an Irma-free lunch was worth it—and he could always add her unauthorized departure to the growing list of complaints, infractions, and just plain gripes about her poor work he kept in her employee file.

I might even get lucky—too many more demerits and she's outta here, the baker thought, as he continued arranging long loops of pale yellow sweet dough on the huge greased baking pans in sloppy spiral convolutions, prior to spooning dollops of apple filling in the center of each. And no one working around him in the sweet-spicy ambrosial combination deli-bakery disagreed when Pete said to himself, "Don't let the screen door bounce you in the butt."

THREE—Irma and Elmo (1)

No sooner had Anna put the phone down after giving the old lady the signal that she was home after work ("Now remember, you *call* me, just so I know you're all *right*—") than it began to ring again.

Tucking the receiver under her chin so she could finish taking off her killer good shoes, Anna said, "Hello?"

"I want my kitty back. I know you got her and I want him back and I think you're real mean for taking him and—"

"What?" Anna dropped her shoes on the floor and grabbed the receiver before it slipped off her narrow shoulder. She thought she recognized crazy Irma Downing's high-pitched babble. The woman was jabbering something about her cat again, the big tiger-striped tom who roamed the neighborhood, sans collar or the accompanying rabies and Ewerton cat license tags (if indeed the cat had any to begin with), shitting on people's lawns and digging up any root vegetables it could find. Irma was always bugging people to be "looking out on" the cat when it got loose on her again, but Anna had seen her neighbor shoving the cat out the door on many a morning when Anna was coming home from a Dumpster run, so she took the short, vapid young woman's usual cat stories with a good-sized sprinkle from the Morton's box.

Anna tried to say, "If you didn't put your cat outside like that, it wouldn't run off," but Irma shrieked, "I know you stolded her! I seen him in there!"

Anna sat down on the trunk and began itching her right foot as she very calmly said, *"Oh?* Were you looking in my windows, then?"

"Yeah!" came the inarticulate blat.

"Really? You were looking in my house?"

"Yeah! And I want her back! I know you got him!"

"How can one cat be a he *and* a she? Does *he* happen to be neutered?" she asked, even though she'd seen the double marble-sized scrotum under the wandering tom's tail.

"No she isn't neutered. I haven't had a chance to get him fixed yet," Irma wailed, her voice climbing higher and higher. Anna had once read an article in the *Milwaukee Journal* about how to spot a liar. A rising tone of voice was one tip-off. That Irma was lying wasn't so unusual, but that she was such a miserable *stupid* liar got on Anna's nerves.

"Well, listen, Mrs. Downing, I do not have your cat in my house. I do not own a male tiger-striped cat, so you could not have seen one in my house."

"I looked in your window and saw her!"

"You did?" Anna never let her voice go above a pleasant, conversational tone, especially when speaking to a volatile ignoramus like Irma Downing, and this conversation was no exception—yet.

"Yes, I *did*," her neighbor replied in a petulant huff." And I *seen* him in there! She was setting on some kinda box, by a doorway."

"A trunk, perchance?"

"Uh, big and black, whatever it was. And he was there. And I want her back!"

Anna glanced over at Mouth, who was now curled up near one of the registers. Mouth was huge, tiger-striped, and most definitely female (at least she was before she was spayed), and she did resemble Irma's straying cat, especially when viewed through a window.

"Now, you did say that you were peeping through my window."

The word *peeping* must have made the single-watt bulb above Irma Downing's overgrown shag-cut head light up. In subdued voice, she said, "I wasn't doin' no peeping in your window. I was *looking*."

"Oh?"

"Yeah," Some more of her old belligerent tone returned, along with a new threat. "If you don't give him back, I'm gonna send Elmo after her and he's gonna get her outta there, 'cause I seed him in there and—"

"Who, Elmo or your cat? And by the way, whether you call it peeping or *looking*, it's still the same thing as far as the—"

Anna was talking to a dead line, Dropping the receiver on the phone, she picked up her shoes and was about to walk into the bedroom when she heard a wild pounding on the front door. Elmo Effertz was such a long-legged drink of water he must have made the trip from his house to Anna's in three strides. Before Elmo had a chance to pound the door in splinters, Anna ran to answer it.

Elmo didn't have his sister's pasty, vacant face, but his hot-wired expression wasn't much of an improvement, under these circumstances.

"Where's my sister's fuckin' cat?" he bellowed, trying to push forward into the house, but Anna let herself out, shutting and locking the door behind her. Arms crossed, face growing flushed and hot, she said, "Listen, Elmo, your sister saw my spay in there, when she was *peeping,* like some kind of pervert through my windows.And I've seen how she and her husband let that cat of hers out when they have no business doing so. Now, either she puts that cat on a leash, or I'm calling the sheriff's office and reporting it as a stray. And once the pound picks it up, she'll have to pay ten dollars to get it back. So—"

"Let me in the fuckin' house an' we'll settle this right now."

"Get off *of my property this minute!* I will *not* have that kind of language spoken to me, do you *understand*?"

Elmo stood there, stubble-covered mouth hanging open, big knuckled fists dangling from his too-short flannel sleeves, Skoal tobacco mesh hat askew on his head of matted, curly hair, chuffing like a tethered bull. At over six feet, he towered over Anna, but she stood her ground, glaring up at him.

"I said I wanted you to leave."

"My sister, she said—"

"Your sister doesn't seem to know the difference between a male and a female cat, let alone where her own animal is. Before you leave, I want you to take a message for her. If she ever so much as sets foot on my property again, or even glances through one of my windows, I am calling my boss—"

"What's Gordy Grey gonna do?" Elmo sneered, referring to the owner of the Super Suds Launderette, a small, slender young man even younger than Anna was,

"Oh, I'm sorry, I didn't tell you or your *sister.* I don't work for Mr. Grey anymore. I work for Bib Stanley—short, thin fellow? Works for the police department."

"Oh fuck!" Elmo sputtered, before he lumbered across the lawn and down the street with his shirttails flopping behind him like wilted batwings. Anna stood there watching him until he went into his sister's house; she could hear him shouting from a distance of over fifty feet, and through a door and screen door. "You got me in a fuckin' *jam,* you dumb cunt."

Back in the house, Anna had the receiver in hand, and was dialing the station, when Bruiser came winding around her legs, mewing up at her, as if to say, Why bother with those idiots? Let them brood about it all night. Pay attention to *me, okay*?

Putting down the receiver, she scooped up the cat, cradling his broad black head under her chin. Bruiser began to purr, wiggling in her arms. At eighteen pounds, he was too big to hold up and onto at the same time. Anna sat down on the, trunk and let his broad-hipped hind end slide down into her lap.

"You're one big kitty, aren't you? Too bad you aren't big enough to sic on Elmo. With those fangs, you'd make short work of him, wouldn't ya?" Bruiser ducked his head and rubbed his forehead on her upper arm, as if to say, Nah, Mama, not me, I'm an old softie.

"Oh, not *again*," Anna sputtered when the phone began ringing. Fully expecting to hear Irma's inarticulate bleat again, Anna snapped, "What is it *now*?"

"What's *wrong*, Anna? Bad day at *work*? The old lady's querulous garble had never sounded so good, or so welcome.

Rubbing Bruiser's head with her free hand, Anna said, "Sorry. I was expecting someone else."

"Someone who was *bugging* you?" came the singsong gurgle.

"Yeah." Anna sighed, as Bruiser looked up at her with adoring, tan-flecked green eyes. That look of unconditional affection never wavered as Anna told the old lady about Irma's quest for her "she-him" cat and Elmo's efforts to reclaim it (including detailed, feature-by-feature recreations of her Cro-Magnon neighbors, after the old lady asked her for them), but when she let out a louder-than-usual, "You don't *say*!" the cat suddenly growled and jumped off Anna's lap.

She listened as the old lady said, *"I* wouldn't do *anything* if I were you. Let them stew in their own *juices."*

"That's just what I was planning to do. Besides, calling the cops does no good with their kind. Swift's Yahoos didn't obey any authority."

"Whose Yahoos?"

Anna wasn't sure if the old lady really didn't remember what she'd said about the Yahoos, or was playing one of her little games, so she said, "You remember, in *Gulliver's Travels.* I've seen this bunch of yahoos in action. The only thing they understand is a shotgun pointed between their little pig eyes."

Which was true. Last fall Zack and Elmo had a fight, and Elmo settled it by running outside after his brother-in-law and, whacking him in the behind with the butt of his hunting rifle. When Zack turned around, Elmo pinned the fatter, shorter man to the cab of his four-wheel drive with the barrel of his gun applied to the spot where Zack's scruffy eyebrows almost met in the middle. while Irma stood near their front door, screaming her pustule-laden head off.

As Anna finished telling the old lady about the incident, her grandmother singsonged impishly, "I know something else they'd understand."

"Oh, really?" Anna was just about to ask what when Mouth finally noticed that Bruiser was wandering around. The tiger female began arching the fur on her spine and hissing, which meant that Bruiser's honor was in question. Before the two cats could begin a fight that would end in the basement, in some place where Anna couldn't reach either cat before some fur-ripping had commenced, Anna said quickly, "Sorry, I have to go—the cats." She heard the old lady say, "That big bad *cat* again!" before she dropped the phone and ran after the already fighting animals, but was already down the stairs and in the basement before she remembered that the old lady had never had a chance to tell her what else might work against yahoos like the clan next door.

If Irma or Elmo came nosing around again, Anna was ready to try almost anything.

FOUR—Lucy (1)

It was quiet in the big old house. Silent and vast, the walls and wooden floors reverberating with echoes every time the old woman moved forward in her rocker, or let out a loud, sighing breath.

Gramma knows what to do, she thought with a ponderous shake of her head. *She always did know then, and she knows now—oh yes she does,* she told herself as she rocked back and forth in an easy rhythm. The bones in one of her feet cracked as she pumped the rocker forward, then let it fall back. With the soft popping, brittle sound, old Lucy's right hand crept up to her neck, to feel the tiny cotton drawstring bag attached to the long cotton cord there. Her fingers kneaded the white bag, just as they'd kneaded the hem of the old night skirt, in this very house, so long, long ago, on that special, horrible, *wonderful* night when everything had changed for her.

And just as it did then, that which rested dormant in the little cotton bag flexed under her loving touch, like a pet cat rubbing against its master's stroking hand.

Lucy's fingers were no longer small and soft; age-hardened and tough, bigger now, too, they covered what curled and uncurled in the tiny drawstring bag—a leftover from little Anna's obedient years on her Baba's knee, which once held jagged bits of brightly colored chewing gum—and let the tiny coil bask in radiant body heat.

Leaning back in the rocker, making it go as far back as possible (as she used to do when she was small, going back, back, *back* on the playground swings), Lucy closed her eyes until red-tinged light poured through her fragile, slightly greasy lids. She thought of what her grandchild had said about those awful creatures. Calling them *people* was an *insult,* an outrage. She knew *her* Gramma would have agreed, too.

Just like those nasty Parks people, she decided. *The one's Gramma got revenge on. Lots of nasty, horrible people out there, always ready to hurt my little Anna. They breed like animals, so there's always more and more of them. But not always—right, Gramma? Sometimes, we do something about it.*

Lucy's rocker pitched forward and back, in a delicious, chain-swing, high-in-the-air motion, as her fingers caressed the worn cloth bag.

Eyes still closed, she remembered how those rotten county men's Ford had gone end over end in the ditch. It was so easy for Gramma to do, too! At first, Lucy hadn't been able to understand the *how* of it all, but then, after the *special* night when the night skirt revealed its secrets to her probing fingers, it all became so clear, so *simple* to comprehend. Now that little Anna was all alone in Ewerton with her Gramma, wasn't it the time for Lucy to be a *good* Gramma to her little granddaughter? Lucy's Gramma never had to revenge *Lucy,* like she'd done with those county men, but things were just *different* for poor little Anna. People could be so *mean.* But they didn't know that Lucy could be *meaner.* Oh, yes, so much more.

The golden thing had worked for Lucy right away, hadn't it? And the first time she'd used it, she had only been *six.*

FIVE—Second Kill

Although it was just as illegal as standing on that Sudek bitch's porch and yelling "Fuck!" Elmo Effertz wasn't about to let a little thing like the *law* get in the way when he wanted some brewski while driving his black Ford custom cap four-wheel-drive pickup down Lakeview Road. Steering with his bony knees, Elmo grabbed a can of Miller's from one of the six rolling around the floor of the cab by Irma's feet and popped the top, making sure he aimed the opening at his sister.

"Elmo, knock it off!" Irma wiped beer spray off her bumpy check, then wiped the beer on her palm onto her jeans. It left a darker stain among the older, stiffer stains on the worn denim.

"Can't you take no joke?"

"No," she pouted. "I don't like it none when you do that. Dad warned you 'bout drinkin' beer while you drivin'. You crack us up an' Zack'll beat the shit outta you."

"He does that an' I'll pop Zack a goodun. Dumb fuck of a—"

"Elmo, you're talkin' 'bout my man!"

Elmo drained his can and threw it out the window. It hit something metallic in the darkness outside with a hollow ping!

"Elmo, you gonna get us both in a jam," Irma warned, as she rolled the remaining cans around under her sneakered feet. When Elmo reached down for one, she stepped on his big-knuckled fingers. In retaliation, Elmo unlocked the automatic lock on his sister's door and reached over to release the handle.

"Elmo, you fucker!" Inna bit his arm just like she used to when they were kids back on the farm, until Elmo released the door.

"Scared you, didn't I?"

"Not as scared as you are. I didn't go sayin' filth around that thief next door. Why didn't you just go in an' get Kitty, huh? You're bigger 'n her."

"Bitch locked the door b'hind her. And you know Dad tole us never to go hittin' no woman."

"She stole my—"

"Fuck your cat. If it was up to me, I'd take the bastard out behind the garage an' shoot his lights out. Unless that's illegal in the city, too," he added, remembering how that little Sudek shrew had bested him.

"You don't even know if she does work for the police. You didn't ask for her badge or nothin'," Irma grumped, crossing her arms. Warming to the subject, she added, "She just said 'Git' an' you *got*, like you was some runt pup. Dad'd be ashamed of you," she wheedled.

"'Dad'd be ashamed.' Who's the one who jumped in whose truck, beggin' to get outta town 'fore the cops show up? Huh? Who left a note for Zack to not tell the cops nothing? Huh? Who's the one who's scared that the bakery'll fire her for makin' trouble? Huh? An' who's the one on probation at work, for gettin' all those warnings from her boss."

"He's a mean puke," Irma said, drawing her knees up under her chin and sliding back as far as she could in her seat. "I hate that place, anyhow. They make me work too fast."

"Trouble with you is, you even fuck slow."

"I do not!" she screeched, pounding on her brother's right arm as he made the turn onto Byrne Avenue, prior to heading north on the old unnamed county road, in the direction of their parents' farm over near the county line.

"Do, too. Zack said so. Said you screw so slow he can watch your pimples come to a head."

"You prick!" Irma screamed, as she went to open her door and jump out of the truck cab, but Elmo turned on her automatic lock just in time.

Irma—never the most rational member of the Effertz family, and most certainly not the best-looking of her parents' seven children—sat there pawing at her bumpy forehead, as if more acne was rising there, and said, "Well, I heard you don't screw too fast, neither. Heard it from plenty of girls."

"That's 'cause I can find more than one who'll go with me. Only one guy nuts enough to stick it in—"

"Shaddup. This is all your fault, 'cause you pussied out back there. I did the looking for Kitty. All you was supposed to do was—"

"And what if it ain't your cat? What then, huh? If Zack don't keep lettin' the damn cat out—"

"Well, he wants to go out! She gets too hot an'—"

"See, Sudek's right about you. You're too *dumb* to know if your cat's a she or a he. Raised on a farm an' you don't know balls when you see 'em." Elmo leaned down to grab another beer. Popping it open, he said, "Maybe I should follow Zack into the can someday. Maybe he's a she, too."

Irma punched his arm again, hard. "You just leave Zack alone. Now shaddup and—Elmo, watch out!"

His sister grabbed the wheel and began to spin it to the right before Elmo could stop her. The truck went kitty-corner across the road, and came to rest half on and half off the dusty soft shoulder.

"What the fuck you do *that* for?"

"The *dog*, you stupid. Didn't you see the dog?" Irma pointed to something white hovering just outside the headlights' twin beams—a big fluffy shape, with eyes that flashed pinkish-tan in the light. There was another quicksilver flash of color, too—just out of easy sight.

"You dumb slit butt," Elmo fumed, pulling the car back onto the road. "Almost wrecked my truck over a dog."

"But you were heading right for it," Irma whined, trying to make herself tiny in the truck cab. As she spoke, the dog circled the front of the truck, keeping just at the rim of the headlights' beam, both in and out of sight.

Elmo was unimpressed by her concern. "Shit, no fuckin' dog's worth a *truck.* I paid good money for this sucker, an' no dumbbell, pus-faced bitch—"

"Elmo!"

"—is gonna wreck it on me! Not over some fuckin' dog, she ain't!" Elmo threw his half-full can, of beer at the dog. As if anticipating the missile, the animal stayed in place until just a second before the can impacted on the road, sending up a spray of liquid that glittered in the high beams. A few drops of beer landed on the dog's thick fur, and with a delicate disdain it shook itself, then licked off the remaining droplets.

Elmo watched the dog's performance with growing rage. No sphincter-assed mutt was going to make a fool out of Elmo, Jr.—no, sir! Elmo put his foot on the gas pedal and gunned the truck. Irma's head whipped forward and snapped with an audible pop.

"Elmo, no!"

But Elmo was past listening; he wasn't going to let some mutt get the better of him! "No way," he muttered as he sped after the dog, which managed to start running a second before he went after it, and was keeping just far enough in front of the car to prevent Elmo from running over it outright. Shifting the truck into a higher gear, Elmo said, "You are bird meat, you fuckin' hound. You are a doormat on the side of the road."

Irma was shouting something in that high-pitched babble of hers, but Elmo's blood was roaring in his big ears, drowning out everything but the sound of her voice, so he didn't even realize that the dog was no longer running ahead of the truck until Irma grabbed his arm and screamed so close to his ear that his collar was damp from her spittle, "It's alongside us!"

Elmo eased up on the gas, until the truck was bumping half on and half off the right-hand soft shoulder, and the sound of gravel pinging against the sides of the truck stopped, but Irma was still screaming, her pale eyes scrunched almost shut, "He's trying to get in here!"

"How could—" Elmo began to say, before he saw the lights of an oncoming car playing over his sister's bas-relief skin, and then he saw the dog jump up, almost hovering there, to stare at him through the passenger-side window, and noticed the winking, shimmering greenish glow in the middle of the dog's neck, even though no collar was visible against the animal's long, white fur.

And in the endless second before he realized that in his horrified astonishment he'd put his foot on the gas instead of the brakes, Elmo swore that the damn-fool dog was grinning at him.

SIX—Bruiser (1)

As she lay sleeping, her cats curled up against the bends and hollows of her quilt-covered body, Anna didn't hear the wailing blat of the police sirens as the squad cars sped down Byrne Avenue, far to the north of her house on Lister Street. And while the whoop-whoop-whoop of the ambulances speeding from the hospital to the west of her did bring her half out of her sleep, she mumbled something incoherent about "Don't wanna see it, Baba...scary!" into her pillow, then drifted back into her nightmare of the old lady and the shining, moving thing in the tiny drawstring bag that rested between her Baba's flat breasts, under her dress and slip.

And the truck bearing the Jaws of Life (a gift to the city from The Hospital Ladies Auxiliary), removable gumball light on its cab, made no easily heard noise as it raced down Lakeview Road to the north.

But the sound of a car door slamming, hard, and that same car laying down two wide swaths of melted rubber on the street, did wake Anna up. After figuring out the direction the sound was coming from, she pushed her pillow up against her ears and mumbled, "Goddamn Downings—don't they know this is a residential street?" before she began to breathe deeply again and returned to her nightmare.

Unfelt and unheard by his mistress, Bruiser moved from where he'd been resting, parallel to Anna's right thigh, to the window. He diligently pawed at the pulled-down shade, until enough tension was created to raise the plastic a few inches the above sill. Pushing aside Anna's pink curtains, Bruiser positioned his fat paws on the bottom of the sill and rested his enormous head on them, green eyes aimed at the window and what lay beyond, in new-moon blackness.

Bruiser had been a wanderer for three years before Anna and her mother took him in, and he'd been a house cat for a year before that, until his old People threw him out, for the unspeakable crime of no longer being small, cute, and cuddly. Bruiser had known love, then nothing, then love again. With the return of love and warmth, he learned something else: loyalty.

Bruiser loved his Person, the one the other woman called Anna. He loved her smell, especially the scent of her that clung to her discarded clothing. Often, he'd rub his head against her pillow, filling his nose with Person smell, sating himself until her return. Come nighttime, he'd pad around her as she slept, nuzzling her here and there, dotting her skin with his scent in return,the only tangible sign of his affection he could offer. There was no other way to show his gratitude to his Person, no way to show the other cat in the house that she was *his Person*. But more important than that, he knew she was the one who protected him, who kept him safe when the words in this little house grew loud, sharp, and ugly sounding, and by this alone Bruiser more than once intuited that his stay here was in danger of ending. But the younger Person had stuck up for him, that much Bruiser knew, even if the finer nuances of Person language were beyond him. And when the other Person left, Bruiser's Anna-Person had come home, on that day when Bruiser and Mouth cowered in the bedroom, shaking inside after the last, worst fight.

And as his Person protected him, Bruiser was determined, in his own cat way, to protect her, even if she didn't know she needed protecting. Even if she thought the voice of badness was a good one.

But Bruiser had heard the bad modulations in that voice, just as a dog hears sounds no human can utter or discern. He had left his Person, not knowing how else to show her that there was badness on the other end of the speaking-thing, a hissing, spitting bad that made the short fur on Bruiser's broad, muscle-rippled back rise with the memory of it.

No, Bruiser's Person could not hear with his sensitive, all-hearing ears, but Bruiser was going to make sure she would not actually need to. Just as he was determined to watch out for the bad for her, his eyes seeing crosshatch hazy false-lightness where no human eye could see it.

Snuggling his wide hind end against Anna's leg, Bruiser let out a soft sigh, a delicate exhalation which belied his massive girth and bed-denting weight, as he watched the yard for all the rest of the night, on the lookout for the darkness darker than the night beyond, as he kept silent vigil by his sleeping, unsuspecting Person.

CHAPTER FOUR

FRIDAY, OCTOBER 23, 1987

ONE—The Wreck (1)

Anna had barely shut the door on her little locker prior to work when Ginny Yarrow came up behind her, saying, "Some excitement last night, huh?"

"Excitement?" Anna echoed, before squeezing past Ginny's wide hips as she made her way to her desk in the room beyond. Ginny trotted after Anna, her hard-soled shoes making a loud bright noise on the linoleum-tile floor.

"Out on the old county road, close to the Nemmitz place. Both ambulances were called out, not that it did any good, but to try, I guess. And it gave them a chance to try out the Jaws of Life. The women at the—"

Ginny's large doe eyes were glittering with excitement when Anna turned around to face her. Switching on her electric type-writer, Anna asked, "Ginny, I don't have a scanner at home, and I don't usually listen to WERT. What happened?"

"A crash, out on the old county road past Byrne Avenue," Ginny explained, as if Anna were a dense, sleepy child who didn't understand that she had to wake up and go off to school on a Monday morning.

"Oh," Anna replied, shutting off her typewriter. The motor died with an annoyed rumble. She _had_ seen a couple of vehicles—a car and a truck van of some sort—both mangled beyond recognition of make or year, in Yogi Hoveland's used car lot, across the street from his Chevrolet dealership. Yogi (so nicknamed in high school long ago for his beer belly and ever-present necktie) owned a tow truck, and since most county wrecks wound up on his used car lot, Anna hadn't paid much attention to the smashed car and truck when she had passed them while Dumpster diving early that morning.

"I guess I was tired last night—the sirens didn't wake me," she said, even though she half-remembered hearing something, even as she claimed not to have.

"Didn't they? Lucky. I didn't get to sleep until two in the morning. Greg got all scared, and I had to try and comfort him. And don't expect the chief to be in until late—he was out notifying the families and all that crap. Rhonda called and said he was sleeping in," Ginny said with a fillings-exposing yawn, before adding with a conspiratorial wink, "So that leaves us inmates in charge."

"Were there fatalities?"

"Look at the reports. Bib left them here for you to type up before he went home last night," Ginny said before going to her desk in the outer office.

Anna switched on her machine again. Over the rumbling hum of the typewriter, she muttered, "That's me, alway asleep when something interesting is going on," and then stopped in midsentence, as she read the names of the victims on the ftrst page of Bib's neatly written report.

Elmo Effertz, Jr., and Irma Effertz Downing. Both dead. Passengers in a Ford truck which had been on the wrong side of the road going north before crashing into a southbound station wagon. The driver of the wagon, a man from Huntertown whose name Anna didn't recognize, was in the hospital, condition not listed.

Anna leaned back in her nubby-upholstered office chair, scrubbing her slightly chapped lips with a clammy palm; whispering, "Oh, my God," she began rocking back and forth in the chair, until its persistent squeaking brought Ginny trotting down the narrow hall between the offices.

"Anna, are you all—Anna, you're white," Ginny exclaimed, going over to the coffee pot over on one of the file cabinets and drawing a cup. She put the paper cup into Anna's hand, sat down on the edge of the desk, and asked, "Friends of yours?" as she glanced down at the report.

Wrapping her hands around the warm, waxy cup, Anna said, "No, not really. They're—they were my neighbors. Next door. I'd only spoken to them yesterday afternoon—"

Patting Anna lightly on the shoulder, Ginny said, "Don't feel bad. From what I've heard about those two, it's no loss. They were both cruds. Rhonda said that when Bib went to talk to their folks, they were less broke up than when their barn full of cows burned two years back. They've got a bunch of other kids. Me, I always thought that kind of people had a brood so it wouldn't matter so much if they lost a couple. Farmers are like that. Always having kids squashed by combines or something, or getting arms torn off. Why, the other day I saw something in the *Milwaukee Journal*—or was it the *Sentinel*? Anyhow, about this kid, who lost his—"

Half-listening to Ginny's account of a gruesome farm accident downstate, Anna reluctantly sipped her coffee, and thought, *Geez, first that sleaze Inez kicks off, and now those two. Ginny's right— they were trash—but still, it's so damn sudden. And I heard car doors slamming over there last night. I thought they were home.*

"...so we'll end up footing the kid's hospital bills, 'cause his folks didn't have accident insurance, naturally. Couldn't, not with the other bills and all. I don't know if you saw it, but a long time back, on that *Ripley's Believe It or Not!* they showed a little Russian girl who lost both feet—they showed pictures of them resting under her legs on a gurney—and they managed to put both of them back on just fine. One ankle looked kinda funny, but it was so cute, the kid was walking on a table in front of all these doctors, afterward, and I just got to thinking that maybe the docs here in America just don't try hard enough. As if we don't already have enough people on welfare out here."

"You mean Welfare Wonderland?" Anna said with a wan smile it to show Ginny she was all right again, so her co-worker would leave her alone.

"Uh-huh. Well, I gotta get back out front. You'll be okay? Ginny paused in the doorway, until Anna said, "Fine. I was just kinda stunned. And you're right, they were cruds. Why yesterday I was go—"

"Sorry, gotta go, the phone," Ginny said, as she hurried to her desk, Behind her, Anna said softly, "It's just as well you didn't know. After what happened, my wanting them arrested would sound ghoulish."

TWO—Bib (2)

Tossing and writhing under absurdly pink flowered sheets in the bed he and his wife Rhonda shared, Brian "Bib" Stanley' drifted deeper into his dream, as the rising sun, filtered by diaphanous pink Priscillas, dappled his lean, fiercely stubbled chin and cheeks with a bright pinkish glow, giving his flesh a scalded look.

The image of the wreck, starkly illuminated by the portable floods, kept returning, each time more clearly, the details more de-fined, each rivulet of blood sparkling with tiny points of reflected light.

And there was so much blood—spidery legs of it wrapped around the crumpled door, moving slowly down the warped metal like paths of condensation winding their way down a steamed kitchen window in the winter. And the little pools of it under the chassis of the black Ford truck. Bib's subconscious was haunted by the way it picked up miniaturized reflections of the accident scene, tiny portraits of closed-fan pleated metal and surrounding portable floodlights in a ring around the vehicles, And when he or the other officers moved, minute, versions of their legs and torsos could be seen moving along with them, trapped on the flat, moist gravel below.

Bib had just stared and stared at his own Lilliputian self until that boor Stu Sawyer lumbered over and barked, "Move over, Bib, you're in the frickin' way." Sheriff Sawyer of the baggy pants seat and the bristling bald cut, peered on tiptoe at the mash of metal and diamond-chip glass that had been the front of the truck, trying to see what was causing all that blood—as if he didn't know.

Dizzily, the dream-Bib's actions mirrored those of the real-time Bib; he trotted over to the left shoulder of the road and puked up his supper of meat loaf and baked beans. It steamed whitish in the cold, and the dream-Bib turned away quickly, thinking, when he saw the scratch-marks in the frosty field of stubble-high weeds beyond the soft shoulder.

There were long, deep furrows in the ground, with the soil raked up in several parallel sets of lines. *Just like a dog after it drops a good load,* the dream-Bib thought, in echo of the real Bib. *I wonder if one of the cars swerved to miss a dog or something. Most folks out here go out of their way to hit them. Either way, those are big scratches—damn big dog. Ground's harder than a diamond-tip boner,* he thought, trying to scrape up the surface of the dirt with his hard-toed shoe. And just as it had in reality, at first the ground refused to budge, but then, as the Jaws of Life uselessly pried open the truck with a metallic *scree,* the ground under Bib's feet suddenly gave, the soil gone soft, skin-tender, and as the blood oozed up to lap at dream-Bib's feet, he let out a thin whine, but Stu Sawyer only barked, "Ain't you Keystone Kops got nothing better to do than scream?"

And just before Bib came to startled, heart-lopping wakefulness, the stubbled soil became dark brownish, like the exposed scalp of that Hibbings woman, and the surrounding grass grew long and bleach-blond brittle.

Lying there there hyperventilating, Bib wondered why he'd dreamed of Inez Hibbing's wounded head, until something shook free of his subconscious and drifted into his conscious: not the victims, but who they knew—something about the home address of the brother and sister who'd been crushed. And squeezed in that truck cab. A name casually mentioned in the autopsy room this past Monday afternoon clicked in Bib's mind.

Lenny Wilkes had mentioned that he was glad Inez Hibbing got hers, especially "after how she fired that poor Sudek kid, the one everybody dumps on." Bib knew where Anna and her mother lived—the same street where the Downing woman and her brother had resided. Sitting up in bed so fast his eyes throbbed in their sockets, Bib reached for the thin yellow-covered book under the bedside phone, and turned to "S."

THREE—The Station (2)

"—expect to see *you* here today," Ginny Yarrow was saying out at the front desk. Anna looked up from the page she was typing in time to see Bib Stanley's lean face and crookedly tied tie looming over her desk.

Shutting off the machine, she said, "Hi. Ginny said you'd be in later on today."

Without preamble, Bib said, "Could you step into my office? Please?" then took off for it without waiting to see if Anna was following him. Hoping that Ginny hadn't overheard him, Anna quietly got out of her noisy chair and stepped into Bib's office, shutting the door softly behind her. Half afraid that Bib was about to fire her, that someone had complained about Alvin Miner's great-grandchild working for the police, of all people, Anna sat down on the hard wooden chair across from Bib's padded one, and gave him a weak smile, waiting.

"Did Ginny get a chance to break the news to you? Some folks you know passed on last night."

"She told me," Anna said with what she hoped was suitable regret, secretly relieved that Bib hadn't fired her—yet.

"Real bad scene out there. If the woman didn't have longish hair, it would have been real hard to tell her from her brother. They was all mangled up. Must have been instant, if you get my drift. The truck's out by Yogi—"

"I saw it," Anna said a little too quickly, then added, "but it was very dark and I didn't recognize the truck as Elmo's. When I walked to work, I went a different way."

"Yeah, they were a real mess," Bib reflected, oblivious to what Anna had been saying. Putting his feet up on the desk, he leaned back and stared at the ceiling, saying, "I even made a fool of myself out there, barfing like a rookie in front of that fat fuck, Stu Sawyer. Mr. 'Elected by the People,' as he likes to tell me whenever he can. Like that makes a whole lot of difference. In his clan, every damn male gets elected sheriff, 'cept for that pansy-ass son of his who went to liberal art-farts college downstate. And when Stu's too old to aim that friggin' bullhorn of his into somebody's business, they'll have to drag old swishy Brucie up here to take over. You'll see. Give 'em ten, fifteen years, and we'll get a new Sawyer sheriff. Been Sawyers in that post since the glaciers."

Anna shifted uncomfortably in her chair. Bib's speech reminded her of one she'd heard many years ago, when she was in Junior high, and Wally Inglass had plopped his pudgy little body next to hers in open study hall in the auditorium, and proceeded to give her a *sotto voce* explanation of why she wouldn't be appearing in the school play—a piffling little murder mystery called *Somebody Screamed!*—*despite* her glowing audition:

"Lots of people in this town still remember what your great-grandfather did. The publicity for this town was pretty bad, and at least one manufacturer who was thinking of locating in the old lumberyard pulled out when the news went statewide. And that happened during the Depression, when this town needed all the help it could get. And a good many people had parents or grandparents who could have used those factory jobs, too.

"Why, you just say the name Miner out here, and noses start to curl." Inglass had gone on with that oily little smile of his, which showed his short, squared-off gold-rimmed rotten teeth through his slick full lips. His narrow blue eyes were glittering behind his wire-rim glasses as he went on, his voice growing steadily louder and louder, until the whole auditorium of study hall students could hear, "So how do you think people will react if they see *your* name under the name of a play about *a murderer?* People know that you're Al-vin Miner's kin, and I for one don't want to spend my time speaking on the phone to outraged citizens. You wouldn't want for no one to come to the play after your classmates worked so hard on it, would you? It would break the school's spirit, and we don't want *that,* do we," he'd asked, leaning closer to her than was really proper, and Anna had just stared at him, wishing the hardwood floor under them would split open, to suck the pudgy, balding little bastard down into hell, where he belonged.

Damn Wally Inglass and his precious school spirit. Wally Inglass, who followed her like a stubborn stray dog into high school, to become the little Napoleon of Ewerton High, defender of pep rallies, the vice-principal who blithely ignored students who were skipping class to smoke out in the outdoor "island set aside for smokers," yet pounded the halls, shirtsleeves billowing around his pumping arms, to sniff out students who dared to skip the first pep rally of each fall semester, badgering them as he marched them back to the packed auditorium with the hissed threat, "You don't want to spoil this school's spirit, *do* you?"

And each year, Anna and the others who didn't give a tinker's fuck about the EHS Rams and Ewes, or the semi-mythical "school spirit" Mr. Inglass so ardently defended, would plod along after him, prior to being delivered into the first ring of the inferno sarcastically dubbed a pep rally.

Just thinking of that smarmy toad Wally Inglass gave Anna severe heartburn. Stifling back a belch, Anna listened to Bib ramble on about the Sawyer clan, until he suddenly shifted gears by saying, "I suppose those neighbors of yours gave you a pain in the ass like Stu gives me."

That's it—he thinks I had something to do with them dying. Cripes, I thought Bib was above all that "murderer's kin" shit.

"You could say that," Anna said carefully, since anyone in the neighborhood could have heard her argument with Elmo the afternoon before. For all she knew, someone could have phoned in a complaint about it. Deciding to make a clean breast of it, Anna briefly outlined her dual fight with Irma and Elmo; Bib even chuckled about the changeable gender of the lost cat. Dutifully finishing with her account of the argument to the old lady, Anna said, "—and then I went to bed. I think I heard a car door slamming later on, but that could have been Zack."

"It was. That dumb cluck Stu called him, had him to come out to view the remains on the spot." Anna winced. As much as she hated her tubby, slackfaced neighbor, that was something she wouldn't wish on anyone, save for Wally Inglass, perhaps.

"That's too bad. I'll bet they didn't look so good," Anna demurred, looking down at her weather-roughened hands. *Have to stop rooting for garbage in the winter. My hands will be cracked all over and no one will understand why.*

"Nope, they didn't. They were in pieces. Goddamned Stu, he didn't even think to have them laid together like they *was* in one piece. Thinks he's so damned smart—like being elected adds to his

IQ or something. He forgets I knew him from school. Biggest shit-for-brains in his class.

"But cruds or not, he should have had them assembled, for cryin' out loud. He was as bad as that dinkus Craig Reish, over at the funeral home. Norm Hibbing's old man, he called in a compaint to Lenny Wilkes, on account of Craig not doing anything with that Inez's body. Can you imagine, he *left* her looking like that?"

Anna knew a loaded question when she heard one, but her job might depend on her making a stab at an an answer.

"Like what?" she asked innocently, hoping that kind-hearted big mouth Lenny hadn't blabbed to anyone about taking her home on Monday night.

Bib made a moue. In a flat voice he replied, "Pretty awful. Skunk stripe down the middle of her head, dark against white. All the scratches showing. And zipped in a body bag with only the head peeping out. Damn Craig—thinks he's some kinda god because he was homecoming king and quarterback of the ball team. Damn team lost homecoming that year, that's how smart Craig was even then."

Anna had to smile at Bib's assessment of Craig Reish. Craig had been in Anna's class, and he *was* a putz. Always air-washing his spongy pale hands. And she remembered Wally Inglass screaming at him the Monday after the game, the glass wall of his office all but shaking as he chewed Craig out (if Craig had been shorter than Inglass, the vice-principal never would have bitched him out like that, but once some of the guys grew over five-seven, they were fair game for Wally, businessmen's sons or not).

"Of course, then Len called me and wanted to know why I didn't do anything about the body, like it's my goddamn concern. Like I really cared what happened to that woman in the first place."

"Was she the one who broke the sink?" Anna blurted out before she realized it. True to Ginny's word, Bib's face grew red, and he sputtered, "Damned slut. Wiry little shit. Still don't know if she jumped or what on it. Say," he asked, his tone of voice subtly shifting, "You had a run-in with her, too, didn't you?

"Who hasn't?" Anna parried lightly. "She fired me. Framed me is more like it. I...I didn't put the job down on my list of previous employers," she added with downcast eyes, remembering that the omission could get her fired.

Bib sat up in his chair and said, "Forget it. She's dead, and her husband probably wouldn't remember it in his state of mind. I'm not going to let you go over that. You got paid cash, no? Good. Then there's no real record of you working there anyhow. Just forget it. That wasn't what I wanted to know, anyhow. Now, this is kinda difficult, and I want you to know that you aren't a suspect, or anything like that, 'cause the Hibbing woman was animal-scratched and all, but, well, I was wondering, did you possibly see anything on Monday, maybe, up in the woods?"

"No. I don't go up that way—not looking like this," Anna said, crossing her arms over her bust. Bib laughed, leaning, forward. "I don't blame you—pretty rough crowd parties up that, way. Probably what Inez was doing up there herself—getting tanked up again. After Norm threw her out, she'd been haunting the liquor department at the IGA. Anyhow, I was just wondering if you'd maybe seen something, 'cause it was a woman who called in the sighting of the body. Voice was—"

"Disguised?"

"Yeah. And I know that you usually go uptown early in the morning, but come to think of it, I've never seen you that far uptown."

Then why did you ask me about it? Anna wondered.

Bib continued, "I just wanted to make sure, that's all. On account of whoever saw Inez out there might have seen what kind of animal got to her. Never know if it was rabid or what, or vicious. Kids still like to party up there."

"Would a curfew help?"

"Nah. Kids' folks have to be home to enforce it, and they're out getting tanked up themselves. No, the fewer warnings we give for kids to stay away, the better. Best thing, would probably be to tell 'em to go there. Then *nobody'd* want to."

"Yeah, like Wally Inglass and the pep rallies," Anna said, relaxing slightly. Whatever it was that Bib wanted to know from her, apparently he'd learned it, and Anna seemed to be out from under the gun—for the time being.

"Oh *that* fat little weasel. He's even worse as an educator than that old diddler Palmer Winston was—only they didn't make *him* principal. Don't tell me—you got rounded up by Wally's Pep Patrol."

Nodding, Anna said, "Four years running. Me and Dusty Parks and Bobbie Grey, and their girls. Usually we never spoke to each other, but come pep rally time, it was off behind the gym or in that little wooded spot near the parking lot—anywhere but in that gym. Not that the rally itself was so awful, but the slavish way Wally made everyone go was sickening. I mean, we knew the team was a joke—the cheerleaders were all sleeping around with the jocks, even though they were supposed to be virginal and rah-rah. And every year the homecoming elections were fixed by the faculty advisers.

"And what got *me* was how he'd see Dusty or Bobbie skipping classes all quarter long, and never say so much as, 'shouldn't you be in class?' to them, yet he'd go into a screaming meemie fit when they didn't show up at a silly *pep rally.* As if attendance at them was going to count toward graduation or something. The man is just absurd," she finished, thinking, *And I had his number long before I made it to high school.*

"Me, I always thought Wally should have stayed down at the elementary, with the small fry. At least he was bigger than them," Bib remarked, before his phone rang. Mumbling, "'Scuse me, he picked up the receiver and said in that incongruously nasal voice, "Chief Stanley speaking. Oh, hello, Wally," before putting his palm over the receiver and whispering, "Speak of the frigging devil—"

Anna stifled a giggle as Bib said, "Uh-huh. I know what today is. Well, I don't know, Wally. My men are awfully busy, and anyhow, do you really think that's necessary? Sounds kinda—I don't know what, Wally, but"—he winked at Anna—"shouldn't you spend your time looking for the kids who cut classes, instead?"

Anna couldn't believe it; Wally Inglass had finally flipped, wanting the police to enforce his pep rally attendance rule. Something like that could only happen in Ewerton High School, she decided, as Bib went on, "No, Wally, I do *not* think it is a good idea. Wally, I had a rough night, and I'm not quite up to—what do you mean, you want a face-to-face on this? Wally? Wally?"

Bib began to set the receiver down and say, "I think old chrome-dome finally popped his cork," when the door began to rattle furiously.

"Come in," Bib said, and Wally Inglass bustled into the small office, the creases on his short-sleeved shirt bayonet sharp, eyes darting behind his glasses. Not noticing Anna at first, he strode up to Bib's desk and leaned over it, short hairy arms planted on either corner of the imitation oak, saying, "You have no idea how difficult it is to instill school spirit into those youngsters. The Rams need every student on those bleachers, cheering them on."

"Wally, did Ginny say you could come back here? I already know you bullied her into letting you use the desk phone," Bib began, before Wally started to pound the desk, sputtering, "You have no idea! This is a serious matter here, and I cannot round up all the students in time for the whole rally anymore. It may not sound important to you, but I have to think of the team's standing in the conference, and believe you me, Brian, this is *very important.*"

"Oh, yeah. Anna and I were just discussing it before you called."

Wally Inglass whirled around so fast Anna felt Arrid-scented air displace around him. His eyes narrowed and his head reddened under the few combed-over strands of crinkled hair, but his mouth smiled as he said, "Oh, have you had some trouble with Miss Sudek, *too*? When she was in school, she and I had a few—"

"No, so far she's been doing an excellent job as a clerk here. 'Course, I still don't know if she can brew up a decent pot of coffee, but it's hard to screw up a Mr. Coffee, isn't it?" Bib interlaced his fingers, cracking them to fill in Wally's stunned silence. Inglass's face hardened before he turned his back on her and said in that soft, oily voice of his, "Brian, I hope you haven't forgotten about her—"

"Grandfather?" Bib leaned back, hands still folded, and in a tone of voice that indicated that he had, instead, forgotten about Anna's presence, said, "Oh, come off that shit. You're worse than a kid on a playground, Wally. It's amazing you actually made it past puberty. No wonder Anna's had such a hard time of it, with ding-dongs like you pestering her and her mom." Anna tried to breathe quietly, to make herself completely unobtrusive, almost as invisible as Bib's words made her feel right now.

"God sakes, Wally, if the parents out here realized that their kids were right when they say you're a nut case, they'd pull them out of school and teach 'em at home in a minute—and you'd miss out on all that state credit for near-capacity attendance."

Standing up, thumbs hooked in his belt, Bib continued, "I'm really surprised that I haven't had to answer a call telling me to come to the high school and arrest some kid who blew your brains out with his dad's deer rifle. I know it's gonna happen someday. Because you are *asking* for it. I mean, who the hell do you think you are, blustering into my office and ordering me to send my men to police a stupid pep rally? Come on," Bib said, in a voice that reminded Anna of the way Ma's voice used to get all harsh and desperate, at once.

"For cryin' out loud, Wally. Not ten hours ago I saw two bodies pulled out of a truck in messy little *pieces*. And I saw that Hibbing sleaze on a slab with her innards exposed not four days ago. *That* is what is important, Wally—dying and making a damn messy job of it. Because it's what's going to happen to all of us. That is what is important in life. Not some asshole pep rally that means nothing, you hear me, Wally? They don't stop you from dying, and they don't teach you how to live before you have to die." Bib's face was white under his five o'clock shadow, and his eyes were bloodshot, scary red around the irises.

But Wally Inglass was unimpressed. He crossed his arms (for the first time, Anna noticed that they were short in the humerus and that Inglass's elbows didn't reach his brown-belted waist), and said to Bib, "You are wrong. School spirit is vital to the health of a school."

"Weren't you listening, Wally? Get your nose out of those textbooks and get real. Your school is a *joke*," Bib said, unconsciously lifting Anna's earlier words. "I have some of your illustrious EHS graduates in my department. Some of them could hardly fucking *read*. I ended up sending them to adult education classes on my own dime, just because I felt they had the makings of good officers. But they went to pep rallies, didn't they? Couldn't read half the words on their applications, but they went to fucking pep rallies!

"And now you come here, bullying my dispatcher, harassing my clerk—"

"You're crazy to hire her, " Wally said smoothly, half glancing at Anna. "People, will call in complaints—you'll see."

"Yeah, and I'll bet they'll all sound like you, your wife, or those daughters of yours," Bib said evenly, as he stepped out from behind his desk to face Inglass toe-to-toe. Bib wasn't much taller than Inglass, but he was thinner and fitter. And his arms were much longer, the hands rough and carelessly manicured, unlike Wally Inglass's fussy soft hands with the lightly buffed nails.

Quietly, Bib said, "If you and your rah-rah-rah mentality aren't out of my station in five minutes, you're under arrest for unlawful entry."

"I don't think there is such a charge," Wally countered, chin held high, but he wilted when Bib replied, "When I get through with you there will be. Now *scat.*"

Wally left the office, but before he slammed the door behind him, he shot back, "Just you wait, Stanley, you'll get calls. *Boy,* will you get calls about *her*!"

Anna sat there, shaking, feeling thirteen years old again, shamed in front of the whole study hall, when Bib sat down on the edge of his desk, saying, "Don't let that little fart bother you. If he tries anything, we'll both go before the school board when it meets next month, and tell him what we just heard. Only reason the man's still in power at the school is because his wife is related to Superintendent Young *and* Mayor Perry. You know how this town is run. It's all who you're related to."

"Don't I know *that*," Anna replied with a wry smile.

FOUR—The Pep Rally

Wally Inglass knew they were out there, somewhere, hiding from him—that Precious Isaacs, and her boyfriend Martin "Mayo" Parks, the little punk with the white-blond hair. He walked down the blue carpeted hall of building five (English and Math), glancing into each of the open doorways on either side of the rectangular building, on the warpath.

Bad enough that stubbly ignoramus Bib Stanley wouldn't go along with his request that some of his officers round up the miscreants who refused to show proper school spirit, but to have that Sudek girl listening in—that was war, pure and simple.

The few long crinkled hairs combed over Wally's ever-growing bald patch ("Walter has a high forehead," his wife was fond of explaining) flopped back to their natural side, exposing his ever-deepening pink scalp to the pitiless glare of the banks of fluorescent lights above.

"Whole school's going to pot," he told himself, as he poked his head into Mrs. Evans's classroom, peeking past the burlap-covered wall divider that hid her classroom from the open hallway beyond, just like all the other wall dividers in all the other rooms in the building (save for music, art, and shop classrooms), which were supposed to conceal the class within and mask out hallway noise. Unfortunately for Wally Inglass, they also masked sounds within the classroom from the hall outside.

The two students he was looking for weren't there, Breathing hard, Inglass strode down the hallway, pausing at the next classroom—Mr. Ulquist's math center. No wimpy little white-headed boy, no tall girl with dark blonde ringlets and too-big hips. Inglass marched up the set of four steps that joined buildings five and six (sciences), pausing to glance in the inner court that lay between the circling buildings. Just three stone benches, and brittle dead grass ringing the spindly red maple the Ag class had planted two years ago. No Precious or Mayo Parks.

"Damn!" Inglass panted, even though he almost without fail would gleefully suspend any student who said such a word in his hearing (unless the student was a male shorter than Inglass himself). "Where are the little bastards?"

Every year, the students grew bolder, yet more insidious in their disrespect for him and what he stood for. They wouldn't sing the school song during commencement exercises.They'd snap gum during fire drills. They failed to station themselves on Ewert Avenue en masse during the homecoming Parade, prompting him to threaten the whole student body each fall. With revocation of the privilege of being excused from the last four mods of classes on homecoming afternoon.

Even then. some of the little smart-asses would yell (always from the safety and anonymity of the last three rows of the auditorium), "What's the diff? Even detention mods are are better than the parade!"

Pounding the tiled halls of building six, loose strands of hair flopping wildly, Wally Inglass was certain he could pinpoint just when things had gone bad at the high school. That was the year Anna Sudek had shown up, spawn of the murderer, Alvin Miner, the man who had caused Wally Inglass's father to lose his shirt when that canning factory had refused to come into Ewerton in 1932. Wally's father had stood to make a pretty penny on the deal, and then Alv Miner had go hack up his mother-in-law, and do whatever it was he did with most of her.

Oh, things were starting to go bad in junior high, when Anna was enrolled, but Wally was sure that he'd be able to break her down once she got to high school—or the teachers would do it for him. But Palmer Winston never did manage to get involved with her, even though she was just the type of girl the old English teacher liked (short and chesty), and Mr. Owens in Business kept clear of her, and even Wally's prize teacher, good old Una Winston, couldn't work her old verbal magic on Anna—the girl managed to avoid all of Una's classes, instead getting Mrs. Evans. And then Una had let herself get all flummoxed over that Lawton girl, and eventually got herself suspended from her job.

That had been a bad time for Wally Inglass, losing Una Winston. She and her husband were the last of Wally's favorites, the kind of teachers who weren't afraid to go after what they wanted from these little brats, the kind who didn't hesitate to let students know when they weren't welcome, and make sure everyone else knew who was to be accepted and who was to be castigated.

Wally Inglass was a firm believer in cliques and castes. How else would these young people learn how the world *really* was, how a person had to lick ass to get ahead, and bed down the right people if the need presented itself? Just as he'd done with his wife, Louise. Old Superintendent "Yucko" Young's baby girl—all three hundred flubbery pounds of her. Grimly, as he poked his head in the chemistry lab, Wally remembered that joke making the rounds of the students about women like his Louise: "How do you fuck a fat woman? Roll her in flour and bang the wet spot."

Oh, he'd been banging the wet spot for years—every wet spot necessary to get ahead, and therefore, it didn't bother him when any student was smart and opportunistic enough to follow his example. So he had turned his head when the Winstons and Mr. Owens and all the other teachers who grabbed a little in exchange for better grades, or lead roles in the school musicals, or whatever, even after the school board started breathing down his neck after the Una Winston fracas in 1978, two years after Anna Sudek had gone— actually *graduated*, not been given a useless Certificate of Attendance, as he'd hoped.

Wally Inglass was prompt to show those elected idiots that he was on top of things at EHS—he made sure there was perfect attendance at the pep rallies, didn't he? And pep rallies were the visible backbone of school spirit, which was what the educational system was all about, wasn't it? As long as he got all those little scumbags and bitches into the gym for the rallies, he was being a good principal. He was Making a Difference, as he liked to point out to the school board each time it met and started to question his methods.

Why didn't he police the students who were skipping class? They'd ask. Simple, he'd say. Who was going to police them when they skipped out of work after graduation? Another doubt quashed, another gold star on Wally Inglass's brownie-point scoreboard. But by requiring 100 percent attendance at pep rallies, he was imposing order and discipline on his charges.

And besides, Wally enjoyed seeing those little pom-pom girls and cheerleaders expose the thin bands of black or gold cloth covering their crotches when they did those kicks and splits. Surely, for marrying Louise, he deserved some reward in this lifetime. And how better to enjoy himself than to know that the eyes of all the students were aimed in the same direction as his, without the worry that some scummy future dropout might be watching him through the narrow gap in the fire doors opposite the bleachers where the students were all seated, instinctively knowing that their principal was taking sly peeks at the pep squad's wet spots?

That old dud of a principal, Mr. Villiard, who retired back in 1979, was so ineffectual, so willing to simply hide in his office, only venturing into the students' hearing when he made his often aborted announcements over the PA system ("This is click—cipal Villiard, with *today's*—click—list of students who are to—click—to detention—"), that it was easy for Wally Inglass to become actng principal long before the real job was his. And that in turn meant that all the losers were fair game for Wally, to do with what he wished, however he wished.

Was a student too tall for him to stare down? Suspend the bastard. What to do when he ached to cop a feel? Haul some little piece of goods in for a "warning talk." Did he still feel the sting of not having quite enough after Dad's lumber yard deal fell through? Then go after the relative of the man who wrecked things for Dad.

It had felt so good to bring up the Alvin Miner case when Anna Sudek was in junior high; such a glow of triumph to hear the kids taunting "Where's Granny?" later on in the day. And if any kid didn't know the details, wasn't joining in on the fun, Wally Inglass always had the time to explain the facts of the case to him or her. *That* felt good, too, rehashing all the grim, unexplained details for an eager audience.

Far away, in building one (the gymnasium, shower rooms, and weight room), the first blats of the school band were faintly audible, followed by a roar from the students. *Damn.* The rally would be beginning soon, and he'd miss first pom-pom routine—all those black and gold exposed cracks between high-kicking legs. And that was when he saw it, scribbled on the creamy yellow wall right before building seven (shop and drafting).

A new bit of graffiti, freshly written in black felt-point marker, the ink still moist:

"Wally Inglass sucks dirty donkey dongs."

It had been a favorite phrase of furtive wall-scribblers since, oh, 1973 or '74 (around the time Anna Sudek showed up at EHS), surpassing even "Yucko Young" or "Viney Villiard" in popularity.

But this particular bit of student expression hadn't been here when Wally had searched building six fifteen minutes before. Standing on tiptoes to reach the scribble, Wally found that his soft fingertips were smeared blackish-purple after he touched the inscription. Far down the hallway, he heard a soft chortle, followed by a higher-pitched giggle.

Precious and Mayo, those two lowlifes who sat around the outside courtyard, holding hands and sneaking nibbles of each other's earlobes when they thought no one was looking. Wally remembered surprising Precious's parents in the act of conceiving her, back in 1971. Her dad, Dickie Isaacs, was already in high school, but he had to come down to the junior high for language enrichment, which was the school board's fancy way of saying his inability to read had been caught by some "dogooder" teacher at EHS. Her eighth-grader mom, Pam French, was one of those ripe bits of goods you just knew was doing it with some guy on Saturday night after the Youth Center closed.

Pam was even better than Wally's expectations. She and Dickie were doing it in one of the practice rooms down in the basement music room during lunchtime recess, when it was Wally's turn to make the rounds of the building. And she'd been a cool cookie, too, even as Dickie gulped and blushed and turned to zip up. Saying, "Either get it up or get out," Pam had stared Wally down, not making a move to pull down her skirt until he left the room, a huge smile distorting his full lips.

But Precious was another matter. She was too tall, like her dad, for one thing. And too big bottomed—too much like his Louise—for Wally to keep the thought of his wife out of his mind when he looked at her.

That in itself was no good, no good at all. And Precious hung around with the youngest Parks boy, that Mayo. Not that young Martin was too tall, or anything like that, but his brother Dusty was over six feet, and before he received his Certificate of Attendance, he had publicly vowed to mow down Wally's fat little bottom with his secondhand rust bucket should the vice-principal ever venture out near Dusty's part of town late at night, or touch his younger brother.

As Wally slowly walked down the shop building hallway, pausing at each glass-windowed door to look around at the sawdust-floored rooms within, he said in a loud, no-nonsense voice, "Martin, you're free to go—it's your girlfriend I want to see.

"If you hear me, Martin? Mayo? You don't have to go to the rally. You're excused. But I have a bone to pick with Precious Isaacs."

Farther down the hall, in the drafting room near the fire exit of building six, Wally heard a faint but intense exchange:

"Mayo, you crud. If you go he'll—"

"I'll go scare up Dusty. Him and Bob Grey will—"

"But I'll be here *alone* with the little prick!"

"Dusty and Bob'll—"

"*Fuck* Dusty and Bobbie Grey. They won't stop him from—"

"From doing what, Miss Isaacs? Martin, I said you're free to go," Wally started to say as he stood in the doorway ofthe drafting room, staring at the two juniors. Mayo and Precious were both clad in the ubiquitous T-shirts, torn jeans, and flannel overshirts their kind had been affecting for the past ten years or more, were standing by the desk closest to the windows and the open cupboard where the drafting boards were kept in slotted niches.

Precious said, "Go on, Mayo. The little donkey sucker says you can go," all the while keeping her eyes locked on Wally's, and began to run her right forefinger along the neck of her T-shirt, pulling the taut fabric lower and lower on collarbones, until the barest hint of cleavage was visible—and until Wally didn't notice that Mayo had edged over by the drafting board cupboard, keeping his hands behind his back. With her free hand, Precious crooked her forefinger, and began to motion for Inglass to come forward, saying, "Bet you get tired of those donkey dongs, don't you? Mom told me how you saw me being made and all—she gets a big kick out of it. *Now, Mayo!*"

Wally Inglass had been so entranced with the sight of the Isaacs girl's breasts—so like her mother Pam's, on that wonderful lunch hour sixteen years before—that he hadn't paid any attention to Mayo Parks as the blond youth pulled a T-square out of the cupboard and positioned himself behind Inglass.

Mayo Parks wasn't on the EHS baseball team, but he should have been. With the broad, flat side of the black-toped T-square, he hit a home run on the back of the principal's head, then grabbed Precious's hand and ran out of the drafting room to the fire door in the back of the building.

Wally slumped forward across the desk, rubbing his sore scalp with one hand while he slowly raised himself up with the other. And through the big window, he saw the couple running off through the wooded area in back of the school, hand in hand, Precious's long, dark blonde hair flying like a swarm bees behind her.

"You can run, you little shrew," Inglass muttered, as the pep band tooted and blatted its way through the school song in the gymnasium. "You can run all you want—you and that punky boy friend of yours—but remember, I know where you live.

"I know *exactly* where you live. And I know how your folks don't come home very early on Saturday night."

And in nearly empty building six, the walls of the drafting room echoed in piercing, lunatic harmony with the pep band members, who were playing their hearts out in the faraway gymnasium, as the pom-pom girls and cheerleaders kicked their black-and-yellow stockinged legs high, higher, exposing narrow swaths of spandex uniform panties, as Wally Inglass laughed until his head ached and his eyes flowed with tears of gleeful anticipation of the next night.

"Remember, Precious, *I know where you live.*"

FIVE—The Old Lady (2)

"Bib says to Wally, 'Now *scat*,' as if Wally was a dog or a cat on his *lawn*." Anna was laughing so hard she could hardly get her words out. The old lady seemed to understand Anna's gist just fine, despite the younger woman's laugh-distorted words.

Folding her knobby hands in the fuzzy lap of her blue wool robe, the old lady nodded her head, saying in a wildly modulated garble, "Served him *right*. Do *you* know what *I think* Wally *Inglass* is?"

Anna knew what was coming, but said anyway, "No. What do you think old Wally is?"

"I can't *say* in polite *company*!" It had been the old lady's standard line since at least 1975 or so. Since no amount of bored questioning would make the old lady reveal whatever it was she thought the current person in question really was, Anna instead remarked, "But the thing that got me was the look on Wally's face when Bib told him I was working for the department. I wish you could have been there to see him."

"And I'll bet Wally would have wished I *wasn't* there," the old lady babbled cryptically, before saying, "Even if you did wish I could *see* it, I can't *because* I don't know what it looks like.

Anna paused in her dusting of the knickknack shelf next to the refrigerator and said, "Run that by me again."

The old lady pursed her lip and said with exaggerated emphasis, "Your *wish* about *Wally*."

"Oh, oh, oh. I forgot, you haven't seen him in years, have you?"

"Did *I* ever *see* him in the *first* place?"

Anna wanted to snap, "How the *hell* should *I* know?" but instead she made herself dust off another china squirrel before saying evenly, "I just figured that since Wally is in his late forties or early fifties or so, you probably saw him somewhere around town. His father was about your fath—um, his father was in his nineties when he died a few years back. I figured you'd seen someone in his family."

"I've seen *lots* of people in town," the old woman sputtered, her pendulous lips moist and shiny in the late afternoon sunlight.

"Wally you'd be hard pressed to forget. He's a short plump little banty rooster, with short arms and—"

Tsk-tsking as she moved, the old lady shuffled in her moplike pink slippers, heading for the bookcase in the dining room. "Gone from here only a few years and she *forgets*," the straggle-haired woman exclaimed as she pulled out a thin, imitation-leather-covered volume and came back into the kitchen with it. Anna saw that it was the EHS Ram Charger yearbook from 1976, her senior year. Putting aside her dust cloth, she sat down at the white wood table opposite the old lady and began paging through the book with distaste.

Anna had felt so negative about her alma mater and her ex-classmates that she'd left all her annuals behind when she and Ma had left the old lady's house; in fact, she hadn't paged through them since 1977—long before she'd moved out. As Anna had often told Ma, "The only way you'd get me to go to a reunion of those creeps is to hand me an Uzi and a belt of clips, or whatever an Uzi uses."

And now, flipping through the glossy black-and-white pages, Anna's fingers longed to caress a trigger. Not allowing her eyes to focus on the face of anyone pictured, she quickly found the section devoted to the EHS faculty. To Anna, the rows of small, mostly can-did pictures resembled mug shots.

"I knew *him*—" the old lady's horny fingernail was tapping old man Winston's picture. With a start, Anna realized that her grand-mother was most likely the same age as the beer-swilling ex-educator. Even as dissipated and scruffy as Winston had let himself become, he still looked a good ten years younger than the old lady. And she didn't keep the ink in the black at the Rusty Hinge. To be honest, Anna didn't think that her grandmother ever did drink, or do much of anything besides get herself knocked up by "Father Un-known," as Ma's birth certificate had stated.

"You went to school with him, didn't you?"

"I would have *been* in his class if I'd *gone* to school after eighth *grade,*" the old lady cheerfully warbled, and Anna suddenly re-membered the story the old woman used to almost proudly tell little Anna:

"After Daddy went away, my aunties came to take care of me, but once Aunt Bella got older, *I* had to help take care of her and her cat, Mister. And I'd be so *worried* about her and that cat during school that I'd get distracted. You see, back then, elementary school was up to eighth grade, and that building was only two stories, so *that* wasn't hard to figure out, but once I started *ninth* grade, in the high school"—her grandmother was talking about the old brick building on Riverview Road, overlooking the Dean River, which had still been in use when Anna was small—"it was so *confusing. Every* time I wanted to go up the stairs, there were always students going *down.* I felt like *a fish!* And when I wanted to go down, they were going *up!* And the funny thing *was,* there was another staircase across the building that nobody ever thought of using! *So...*I finally figured that it wasn't *worth* it, getting trampled every day, and Aunt Joan, she *agreed,* and to let them have their stairs to *themselves!*"

Even at an early age, Anna had realized what her grandmother was incapable of understanding—the two staircases were designed to keep the students moving up out of the way of the students moving down. Anna hadn't needed Ma to explain it to her, either, despite being only five years old or so. Later on, Anna supposed that that was when she'd gone from being "Gramma's girl" (as Ma often and bitterly would throw up to Anna when she was enraged at her for some reason or another) to first secretly, then openly doubting and challenging the simple old woman's stories and opinions.

That the old lady *was* quite simple in the head wasn't a surprise to Anna; after all, she *had* seen some rather hideous things when she was six, and losing both her parents—one to violent death; the other to the insane asylum downstate—plus her grandmother, within the space of twenty-four hours, must have been a mind-rattling experience. And for all Anna knew, little Lucy Miner might have been a bit dimwitted to begin with: after all, she was a late baby, born when her mother's eggs were getting old.

But the old lady's *pride* was a source of constant, and growing, vexation to Anna as she herself grew more intelligent and mature. It was as if *nothing* she had done in her life either embarrassed the old lady, or gave her reason to be anything less than boastfully proud.

She even managed to brag about her unwed mother status: "They tested the blood of a *dozen* young men in town—that *horny-toad* Palmer Winston included—and they *never* found the one who did it," she related with the air of someone who had pulled off an incredible, mind-defying stunt. And the old lady never passed up the opportunity to bring up how her Aunt Bella had gone crazy shortly after Ma was born, as if that, too, was some sort of *coup* whose special significance was known only to Lucy Miner herself.

Maybe she was happy about the old woman going nuts because she inherited her frigging cat, Anna now reflected as the old lady slowly pored through the yearbook, head lowered close to the page, her finger laboriously tracing each teacher's name as she read it off. Anna had briefly majored in education in college; she'd taken enough courses to realize that the old lady read at perhaps a second- or third-grade level. At any rate, that's when Ma claimed that the old lady stopped helping her with her homework.

The names and pictures of the EHS administrative staff were grouped at the end of the faculty section, When the old lady reached

Wally Inglass's image, she bent her gnome-like head closer to the page to better read his name, pursed her lips, and said, "He *looks* like a *bad* person. Little *bird* eyes, and Negro lips."

"Don't *say* things like that. It's an insult to black people," Anna scolded gently, crossing her arms and leaning back in the hard white wood chair.

"I didn't say he *was* a—"

"Never mind," Anna sighed, thinking, *No, you never* say *anything. That's the problem. You just blather on and on.*

The old lady tapped the shiny page with her knobby forefinger until Wally Inglass's brow was dented with nail-shaped crescents. She said, "I don't think I remember *him*. I'd know that hairdo."

"He wasn't always bald—he had hair when he taught elementary, I remember. But you weren't missing much, anyhow."

Abruptly, the old lady sat upright, shutting the book on her still-positioned index finger (as if her skin was absorbing Wally's image off the slick paper), and said, "Not to change the subject, but when Bib was telling you about those *yahoos in the* truck, did he show you any *pictures?* I imagine they took some, *didn't* they?"

Uncrossing her arms and placing her folded hands on the table, Anna said, "I suppose they did, but Bib didn't show any to me, no. I mean, why *would* he? It was obvious that it upset him."

"Like it upset *you?*" The expression on the old lady's puffy, saggy face was hard to read, but her voice had an edge of disappointment in it.

"I wouldn't actually say *upset*—more like shocked. You know, first I had that fight with them, and then...*blam. Wipeout.* I did hear that the guy who rammed into them is going to be okay. Before I left work, Ginny called the hospital for Bib, and she said they told her the guy was out of intensive care already, and they figured he'd walk and everything, But he didn't remember the accident, which was what Bib was wonder—"

"But that's *good*," the old lady countered quickly, her colorless eyes darkening to a semblance of their former gray-blue.

Anna gently pulled the yearbook off the old woman's finger. As she walked into the dining room to put it away, she said, "No, it isn't. With the people in the other vehicle gone, they won't know what really happened, or whether the fault was really with Effertz or not. You see, his family called Bib and wanted to know whether Elmo had pulled into the wrong lane on purpose, or by accident. They really got belligerent when Bib told them there was no way to know for sure, anymore—not unless the other driver suddenly remembered what happened, which doesn't seem likely," Anna finished as she sat down again.

"I don't see what the *point* is—it won't bring them *back*," the old lady argued in that quivering-fat voice of hers.

"No, it won't, but there's responsibility to figure in there. Dead's dead, but some people need to have a reason to cling to. Even if they are idiots," she added, thinking, *And it takes on to understand one, doesn't it, old lady?*

With a *harrumph*, the old lady crossed her arms over her breasts. As she did so, Anna noticed that there was a strange bulge in the place where the two wings of the old woman's collar bones met. Glancing at the rounded neckline of the old woman's flannel nightgown, Anna saw something that had either escaped her during earlier visits, or hadn't been there—a cordlike string pulled taut in the middle. Apparently, the old lady was wearing a heavy pendant of some sort under her clothes, in the same manner favored by the late Andy Warhol. But recalling that Warhol did that to hide expensive, flashy jewelry, and knowing that her grandmother owned nothing more expensive than fair-quality costume jewelry, Anna thought, *What is this, some sort of Czech thing you people do when you grow older? Or is this your way of attracting attention, making me ask you what the big secret is? Either way, I'm not biting this time.*

But the thing under her grandmother's nightgown *did* niggle at Anna's imagination, long after she'd told the old woman that she had to get going if she wanted to get home before dark—things always were crazy on homecoming night, especially if the Rams happened to win—and was actually on her way to Lister Street.

She wondered just how long the old lady had been hiding that bulky *thing* under her clothes...was it after she'd given up wearing street clothes, and took to schlepping around the house in her fuzzy woolly slippers and billowing cotton or flannel nightgowns, topped by layers of sweaters and her robe? Had there always been something hanging around her neck, concealed in the valley between her smallish breasts? A vague wisp of memory wavered just out of Anna's mental grasp—the best she could do was brush it with fingers of recollection:

She remembered herself at five years old, maybe less, sitting on "Baba's" lap (Anna's almost forgotten nickname for her grandmother, in honor of a small lamb toy the old woman had gifted her with one Easter), while the old woman dangled an object that stubbornly refused to come into focus in front of Anna's eyes—a thing that a quarter century of time had diffused into a nebulous *some-thing* of a (maybe) golden or yellowish hue.

With a touch of *green* on it, of that much Anna was now quite certain, although why she should be was unclear to her as she fitted her key in the lock and let herself into the house, without so much as a backwards glance at the cars and battered pickups lining the street near the empty Effertz house and the Downing house next door to it.

And as the cats wound around her legs and raked their paws on her thigh while she stood at the kitchen counter eating a sandwich, Anna knew that whatever the dangling, glittering thing was, something about it had made her cry and try to squirm out of the old lady's lap; but Mommy was out shopping, and Anna was all alone in the house with her Baba, only now she had wanted to run away and hide from her grandmother, who was trying to put the thing on her skin, trying to make her hold it.

As she tore off bits of her lunch meat and threw them to the waiting cats, Anna was certain that the object had been doing something, but just what was beyond her ability to recall or so locked in her subconscious, perhaps for her own good, it refused to come to the surface.

It wasn't until she was putting away her package of pickle and pimiento loaf that Anna remembered that she'd forgotten to give the old lady the signal. As she stood there dialing the phone, she thought, *I'm beginning to see why Ma griped about this "call me so I know you're home safe" rigmarole so much. I mean, who the hell would want* me? *The old lady shouldn't worry about me not making it home. Considering that I could be related to just about any family out here, no guy is gonna want to take a chance on raping me—I might be kin to his father or mother.*

And while she listened to the phone ring three times over at the old lady's, Anna heard something on the porch. She stepped over to the window and pushed aside the drapes. It was Kitty-Kitty, Irma Downing's tiger tom, climbing the scrolled metal porch supports. The cat had most likely been out prowling. Anna tapped the window with her finger until the cat ran off for home, quickly finished giving the rest of the signal, then dialed the Downing number.

She told herself, *You're being nasty, Anna,* as she heard a strange woman say, "Hello?" Before she made a complete fool of herself by snapping, "Tell Zack his wife's cat is back," she slammed down the receiver without speaking.

You can't let yourself sink to their level, Anna told herself as she stood next to the phone, hugging herself with suddenly cold arms and hands, *or to the old lady's level, either.*

SIX—Lucy (2)

Lucy paced the living room, her mop slippers leaving wide, shapeless tracks in the film of dust on the bare hardwood floor, eyes darting back to the phone. Briefly, she lifted the receiver, then quickly put it down lest she accidentally break the connection her granddaughter might be trying to make.

"Ring already," she hissed with bubbling urgency, gooey voice slurring as her gnarled fingers reached into her nightgown gown and lifted out the tiny cloth sack.

The bag crinkled slightly. Inside the thin white cheesecloth sack was another bag—an old-style lunch bag, without the thick, zipper-type closure on the top.

And inside the inner, clear plastic bag, Lucy could feel the *thing* flexing, coiling and uncoiling with slow, sensuous undulations.

"Where *are* you?" Lucy asked the silent phone as she made fresh tracks on the floor, her slippers now ringed with a pale fringe of collected dust. And as if it, too, were anticipating the night ahead, the coiled thing in her doubled bag (doubled out of necessity, to keep the golden thing from taking over whenever *it* wanted to) jerked impatiently, straining to be free of the inert, nonorganic prison of the plastic sandwich bag.

Lucy had been quick to learn the lesson of the night skirt—oh, yes, indeed. Her Gramma's skirt was wool, which was once part of a living, breathing animal, and close contact with something that had once been alive was opportunity enough for the tiny thing hiding in Gramma's rolled hem.

Gradually, it had worked its wonders on the skirt itself, becoming one with the swirling black fabric, making a home there, until a touch to the skirt was a touch to the small, moving thing secreted within the hem.

Lucy hadn't thought to ask Gramma if *that* part of it all was an accident or something she had planned when she had hidden the thing in her hem. Things were just too hectic that night to think of everything. Especially when Lucy was only almost seven, and there were so many things to be done.

Like a granted prayer, the phone began to ring. One ring, then silence, then three, then—

But then Lucy wasn't bothering to listen anymore. She was too busy unknotting the little yellow drawstring, and then undoing the green plastic and wire twist that kept the crinkly plastic bag closed, hoping that she wasn't already too late to do she had to do for little Anna.

SEVEN—The Wreck (2)

It may have heen traitorous to his own alma mater, but Deputy Sheriff Terry Von Kemp was always relieved when the Ewerton Rams lost a homecoming. For one thing, it shafted that dink-donk Wally Inglass, who had handed down many a suspension to the then five-eleven and growing Terry, for infractions as mild as chewing gum outside the gymnasium, or cutting in in the lunch line because he had only one mod to eat his lunch in on Wednesdays. And for another thing, it made his evening-to-early-morning shift in the squad car a heck of a lot more interesting.

Usually, all Terry had to look forward to on this shift was checking the Super Suds Launderette for any dumb clucks trying to sleep one off after a night spent at Pearl 'n' Earl's or the Wooden Keg (the Rusty Hinge's crowd was composed of duffers who called it a night long before the mandatory two o'clock closing time), and cruising the alleys, eyes peeled for anyone rooting in the Dumpsters that he could give a hard time to (except for old Don Campbell's widow—she was off limits, partly out of fear that the ghost of Brush-head Campbell might ride Terry's ass for all eternity, and mainly because Mrs. Campbell wasn't above telling *anyone* off).

But if the Rams (or the Ewerton Sheep Fuckers, as the other teams in the conference dubbed them) lost homecoming things really cooked overnight. Bottles were cracked over heads in anger, tires on the cars belonging to anyone who happened to go to the winning school, and was stupid enough to try and stay in Ewerton after sundown, were either slashed or punctured, or deprived of hub-caps, and fights broke out next to soaped-on pro-Rams slogans on store windows, as members of the opposing team tried to scratch "flattering" remarks about the Sheep Fuckers into the dried soap, and the members of the Rams tried to flatten *them.*

Oh, it was a blast, all right. On nights like that, the hours went fast for Terry, as his arrest log swelled, and he had an opportunity to get out of the smelly squad car, too, which had never been quite the same after some knucklehead had stuffed a dead skunk in the glove compartment. Stu Sawyer had blamed the guys in his department for the stunt, mainly because if he had tried to blame Bib Stanley's men, the city council would have ridden Stu's butt all the way to kingdom come, or so Terry thought. After all, Stu was always calling Bib's men the Keystone Kops, so it wasn't as if Bib didn't have reason to pull the skunk trick, as well as access to the squad car.

So far, as Terry began the ten-to-eleven hour of his shift, he'd made three disorderly conduct arrests, chased a pack of six or more kids away from a car whose chrome they were trying to remove, and honked his horn at a group of cheerleaders in the purple and gold uniforms of the victorious team, who were in the process of scraping "Rams Suck!" in the soap lettering on Clausen's Hallmark and Gift Shoppe. And he'd made them scrape it off, too, ogling them as they reached up on saddle shoes tiptoe to reach all the letters, and their little skirts rode up over their butts.

Terry especially liked that. He hoped the next time he drove down Ewert Avenue, the girls would be trying the same stunt at another window, but no such luck. Feeling slightly disappointed, but optimistic, Terry swung the squad car around to Yogi's Chevrolet, to take a gander at the two wrecks parked in the used car lot across the street from the dealership proper. One thing that was missing from tonight's post-game activities was Elmo Effertz cruising in that black Ford, honking his musical horn and screaming obscenities out the window at anyone who happened to be driving the other way. Every year that the Rams had lost since Terry had joined the Sheriff's Department, he had logged in some sort of complaint against Elmo, and often as not, his brother-in-law Zack, too. One year, when Zack had first married that zit-brain Irma, Terry managed to arrest all three of them outside the Wooden Keg for fighting in the street. As Terry now recalled it, Elmo was trying to tip the ice machine outside the beer garden fence on top of Zack, and Irma was riding on her brother's back, trying to knock *him* over. That incident hadn't happened after homecoming, but it was just about as good.

And now Elmo and Irma (*sounds like some sorta polka band, Elmo and Irma and the Polka-Aires!*) were lying in assorted bits on the two slabs in the hospital morgue, until the funeral home director over in Lumbe could come pick them up. Zack Downing had gotten wind of what Craig Reish had done to Inez Hibbing and had told Lenny Wilkes (who promptly told Stu Sawyer, since those two all but lived in each other's blow holes, or so Terry thought). "I ain't takin' no chances—not with their old man an' old lady wantin' to view 'em."

It was hard to see the two wrecked vehicles; the used car lot was positioned exactly midway between the two streetlights on the block, and with no moon above, and only an ineffectual dotting of stars peeking through a filmy scud of clouds, Terry was hard-pressed to make out much of anything besides the occasional wink of passing headlights on twisted chrome, or the cheap glitter of crushed glass chips that were pooled in the deeper dents on the accordioned hoods.

Aimlessly, knowing full well that he had many hours left in which to stare at the aftermath of the wreck, Terry left the block to casually check out the rest of town, but he kept returning to the two ruined chunks of metal and rubber, moving slowly past them, his lights on high beam so as to pick up whatever details he'd missed on his previous run-bys.

He wasn't certain whether he saw the animal on his third or fourth run past the parking lot, but he was reasonably sure that the thing running across the street was a cat, or maybe a small dog—a sleek one with tiny, upright ears. All Terry was sure of was the fast liquid wink of a green rabies tag, attached to a collar as dark as the animal itself, positioned close to beast's pumping shoulder.

"Should buy the thing a flea collar—one of them white ones," Terry said and crossed himself when he almost ran into the animal. Terry Von Kemp may have been kind of rowdy in high school, but he had never intentionally car-hit an animal.

Terry had once run over a baby duck that didn't get out of the way out by the four-way stop. He'd scooped up the mess of down and pomegranate-seed innards and placed it in a Styrofoam burger box in the nearest Dumpster, then parked the squad car behind the "Ewerton Welcomes *You!*" sign out on County Trunk QV and bawled his eyes out for five minutes.

So that was why Terry slowed the car down the next time he cruised past the car lot—he was worried about the animal he'd almost hit. And that was why he saw something he hadn't seen before, on his other trips past the two demolished vehicles—a limp white plume, hanging down from the half-popped-open rear door of the car.

Sure that he hadn't noticed the fluffy white thing hanging there before, Terry slowed the car and backed up until his window was even with the car's ruined door. Squinting in the darkness, oddly reticent to turn on his flashlight lest any passerby find his preoccupation with the totaled car and truck ghoulish, Terry took in the crush of clothing, small suitcases, knapsacks, and the like that had been forced from the back seat of the car into the area that had been the dashboard, the pried-open passenger-side door which the Jaws of Life had mangled in its efforts to get the driver out—the force of the crash had broken his legs, flipping them over his shoulders; the tiny nub of an antenna, the stress-blistered paint job...and the long, flaccid fur-covered thing which was (Terry was willing to swear on a stack of *Playboy*s) just a couple of inches closer to the ground than it was before. As if whatever the white plume was attached to was slowly sliding down, out of the ruined car....

Something just didn't feel right, so Terry stepped on the gas and turned the corner, but found himself drawn back to the wreck, and the mysterious white streak against the crumpled dark maw of the car and the gritty asphalt below. It definitely *was* longer, and there was more to the animal than what Terry now realized was a long-haired tail. Rolling slow past the scene, Terry saw the twin curve of furry canine haunches jammed into the flattened backseat of the auto. In the faint breeze the tail began to twitch, as if the poor dog was still alive, as the curved lower back and folded hips of the animal slowly began to squeeze out of the car, fractions of an inch at at a time.

Terry didn't remember anyone mentioning that the driver of the car had had a dog, nor did his relatives ask about any animal when they called Stu's office that afternoon. *But the guy could have picked it up on the road. Farmers are always dumping animals just for the hell of it. Or maybe it was one of those out-of-state geeks passing through. See a lot of dumped dogs at the shelter.*

Slowly, gravity was pulling the dog out of the twisted wreckage. Now the bent hind legs and some of the lower abdomen were visible, as the sluggish wind made the tail seem to wag in the barely illuminated darkness. But something about the somber tableau of dead dog and mangled metal was wrong, even though Terry couldn't immediately put his finger on it.

It was on his next run by the car that he figured it out. When they'd pulled the guy from the car he'd been ribboned with blood, his clothes and body striped with it like a sunburned zebra (Terry hadn't actually been there on the scene, but he did take a look at the color pictures Lenny Wilkes shot of of the scene, plus the black and whites Stu took, just after they came back from the department darkroom). And the people in the truck had been so covered in shiny crimson that they registered in some of the shots as shimmery, reflective shapes, returning the glare of the camera's flash attachment, almost hovering above the dark gravel below.

That dog's as white as an albino's ass, Terry thought with awed fear. *Not even so much as shit stains on its behind.* And Terry had seen enough road-killed things, and the occasional human hit-and-run, to know that dead things shat on themselves. There was no such thing as a totally clean death, yet this dog's fur was snowy, full-moon-on-a-clear-night white.

And as if challenging Terry's powers of observation, and his knowledge of just what death was and wasn't, the dog continued to slowly ooze from the car. Now the well-defined rib cage was showing, followed by the beginning of the shoulders.

Unable to watch the dog's descent from the car, Terry happened to glance up at the line of elms beyond the parking lot, and eyes wide, gasped in the close, piss-sharp-smelling confines of the squad car.

Most of the leaves were already torn from those elm trees, but not so many that Terry couldn't see that not a single fall-yellowed leaf or denuded branch was moving. *There was no wind.*

Yet a quick glance at the dog *(oh sweet Jesus on a boxcar, it's almost out)* showed him a still-wagging, bushy tail.

Terry stepped on the gas so fast he almost flooded the engine, but he made it past the parking lot anyway, eyes glued to the dim yellow line on the road ahead of him, thus just missing the sight of the large dog wiggling free of the wreck and running in a southeast direction, and how the streetlight picked up the emerald glint of something odd-shaped and green embedded in the fur of its thick, collarless neck.

EIGHT—Irma and Elmo (2)

Had they still been alive, and able to relate what they'd seen in those last nanoseconds before Elmo's truck had been slammed by the oncoming car, Irma Effertz Downing and Elmo Effertz, Jr., might have told Terry Von Kemp to turn the car around and follow the running dog with the odd glowing green thing positioned near its neck to see where it went, and what it did when it got there.

They might have told him what the dog had done to them, how it had baited Elmo into that murderous position on the wrong side of the old gravel road. And Elmo could have told Terry how the dog had glared at him in those last seconds, as if it actually recognized his face from somewhere, and Irma's, too. If they had been able to tell Terry that, he just might have remembered the Gas 'n' Go "Safe Employee of the Month" notice in last week's *Ewerton Herald,* which showed Elmo presenting a certificate to Clark Umbert, or the big, full-page ad, the one with all the pictures of its workers, that the Ewerton Bakery had run the week before that.

It was crazy to think that a dog could have looked through a paper, let alone recognized someone's face from a grainy picture. But after witnessing the slow emergence of the dog from the ruined car, Terry might have been open to any sort of clue as to what had happened on that lonely gravel road.

CHAPTER FIVE

Saturday, October 24, 1987

ONE—The Years of Cock and Dragon

Thanks to lucky scheduling on her predecessor's part, Anna had weekends free (aside from being on-call matron), and today she needed every free minute she could scrape together in a stretch. First, she needed to make the rounds of the Dumpsters. Friday nights usually marked a flurry of shelf emptying, prior to a thorough cleaning of the stores over the weekend. In the IGA Dumpster alone, Anna found seven badly dented cans of soup, a nearly full box of macaroni whose plastic "window" had split, a couple of frozen deli pizzas with only a slight tracing of mold on the cheese (which she could remove before she baked them), and coup of coups, a five-pound bag of cat chow with a tear in the side.

Knowing she couldn't make it home without having one arm permanently pulled longer than the other, Anna decided to drop the food off at the old lady's house, behind the solid lower walls of the porch. Ma had done the same thing during her turns out in the morning *(Saturdays used to be our day to dive together,* Anna recalled ruefully), then either call the old lady to let her know the stuff was out there, or go back to the house before heading to work uptown.

Ma never knocked on the old lady's door, asking to be let in, because the old woman was never up at that hour, and even if Ma had knocked, it would have been a good fifteen-to-twenty-minute wait for the old lady to rouse herself, get up, throw on her robe, and shuffle to the door. Since Anna had to go shopping for both herself and the old lady later on that morning, she intended to dump her stash of food and run back uptown, but when she saw both the bedroom and living room lights on, she couldn't resist knocking.

The inside door opened after the remarkably short time of four minutes (Anna checked her watch in the faint spill of light from the overhead lamp on the corner). Through the storm door the old lady queried in that bubbling gurgle, "Who is it?"

"Me. I've got some stuff here. Can I leave it until I come back later?"

When Anna walked into the living room, the old lady's familiar fuliginous reek hit her nose, overlaid with something she couldn't quite identify—a metallic, slightly musty stench, like old rusty farm machinery. Anna wasn't sure what it was, but it was teasingly familiar, nonetheless—it had a sweetish, almost coppery tang.

Passing through the dining room on her way to the kitchen, Anna noticed that the crooked piles of old newspapers, checkout rags, and Sunday supplement magazines were all askew, and a few had pale, irregular vertical stains running down their folded spines, and dried, slightly caked pools from moisture on the hardwood floor next to them.

"Grandmother, did you get yourself a pet?" she asked, thinking of the messes Mouth made when her bladder got the best of her.

"A *pet? Me?* You know me and *animals.* We don't always get along.

Anna wished that the old lady wasn't shuffling behind her; she longed to see the expression on her face as she'd spoken. Resting her full bags on the kitchen floor, Anna turned around in time to see the old lady settle herself into one of her antique hardwood rockers, which the old lady had apparently pushed from the living room into the kitchen and positioned close to the kitchen table. Anna noticed that the old lady had had to place several crocheted throw pillows onto the seat of the maple to bring it closer to the level of the table-top.

Noticing Anna's quizzical stare, the old lady smiled and said, "I still like to *rock.*"

Not knowing if the old lady meant that as a play on the meaning of the word "rock," or if her remark was yet another regression into her little-Lucyhood, Anna merely nodded and mumbled, "Uh-huh...."

The old lady clumsily settled herself in behind a spill of writing paper scattered on the cluttered kitchen table, next to a yellowed sheet of paper torn from a checkout rag. She took up her pen, leaned down close to the table, her watery eyes mere inches from the paper, and started to scribble something on one of the sheets.

"What's that?" Anna began rummaging under the kitchen sink, looking for a paper bag to put the torn bag of cat food into.

"Our *fates*," the old woman sputtered teasingly, *knowingly,* then, after several enormous, incredibly loud jaw-unhinged yawns (which reminded Anna of a sick seal), she went back to her writing.

As Anna shoved the cat chow into an old Red Owl bag, she glanced down at the sheet of checkout rag newsprint. Over a circular chart of twelve pie-shaped wedges, each decorated with a line drawing of an animal positioned over a series of years, was written in half-inch block letters:

ORIENTAL ZODIAC REVEALS 1976 FATE

And on the sheets of paper her grandmother had already filled, Anna saw charts of more years, most in the nineteenth century, in series of twelve. Nineteen seventy-six was the year that Anna had graduated from EHS; it was a terribly long time to hold onto a rag magazine.

Placing the now double-bagged cat food on one of the empty chairs, Anna sat down opposite the old lady, asking, "Looks like you've been working on that a long time. Couldn't you sleep?"

The old lady yawned again, then consulted the chart, jotted something under a long column of numbers (the slight movement of her arm sent a wave of rancid effluvium Anna's way), before replying, "No. Darn *neighbors* kept me up all night, *hooting* and beeping their *horns,* and burning rubber on the *street,* so I gave up around *midnight* and got up. I was looking through my *paper,* and I found *this*." With a deeply ridged nail, she tapped the yellowed sheet of newsprint, then went on, "And I got to *wondering* what year my *Gramma* was born, and Mother and *Daddy.* So I got to work and—"

"Lemmesee." Anna turned around one of the sheets until it faced her, and read "Lucy—1924, Year of the Rat; Tina—Year of the Horse; Anna—early 1958, Year of the Cock.

"What's this about *early* 1958?" The old lady turned the sheet of newsprint so that it faced her granddaughter, who leaned forward to look at the circular chart. Above it was a warning:

> Remember, if your birthday falls between January 1 and February 5, place yourself under the influence of the preceding sign.

If Anna hadn't been born on January 19, she would have fallen under the influence of the rest-of-the-year sign of the dog.

As Anna glanced at the chart, the old lady explained between yawns, "It's a *good* thing you were born when you were—otherwise, you and I wouldn't have gotten *along.* See what it says under the *dog*?" The old woman's sulfur-tinged nail tapped the last lines of the paragraph under the heading DOG:

> The dog is well-matched with all signs of the Orien-
> tal zodiac save for the years of the cock and the rat.

"*See? I said* it was a good *thing*—"

"Uh-huh," Anna said, thinking, *A whole lot of good it did us— especially that time when you took out after me with that knife. threatening to tear my throat out. Oh. yeah. The cock and rat get along famously. Tell me another one, old lady.*

"And here, look at what it says about your mother," the old lady prattled on, referring to Anna's mother, Tina. Anna couldn't help but wince slightly; she hated it when her grandmother (or any older person, for that matter) insisted on calling her own child "Mother" in front of Tina's daughter. It was as bad as that dippy old couple the Wooddards (the ones who practically *lived* on their Roberts Street front porch), calling each other "Mother" and "Father."

The article claimed that the Yang horses were strong, swift, and had great stamina *(she had to, to do all your running for you),* and were well-liked and popular. Remembering Ma's loud, so-frantic-it-hurt laughter, Anna said, "Let's see what it says about you. Hmmm, you're Yin—intuitive. You need to rest a lot so you don't tire yourself out."

"Amen to *that*," the old lady said with an intensity Anna thought was uncalled for—after all, the old lady never went any farther outside than her front porch floor, and her slippered feet hadn't touched concrete for at least five or more years, thanks to her hip injury. Perhaps being lazy was tiring in itself. Anna never *could* figure the old lady out, and now wasn't a good time to start.

"And you should avoid people born in the year of the dog—"

"*That's* why my mother and I never *did* get along—she was a dog. *They're* naggers."

Anna quickly read something about dogs being Yin—watchful, alert, unselfish, tending to give more than is reeeived, and "nagging others in order to get them to move into necessary action."

"See how I figured it out?" The old lady shoved a piece of paper covered with row after row of figures on it to Anna. Since the pie chart on the page only went up to 1900, the old lady had had to calculate backwards from the year of the rat in that year to 1886, as well as figure out the rest of the twelve-year cycle going back to the 1850s.

Looking over her grandmother's neatly written figures, Anna thought, *You couldn't even get the change right in the envelope when you gave Ma the money to pay your bills, and yet you can do something like this? Something of no consequence whatsoever? C'mon, old bat, give me a break already.*

"*Daddy* was born in the year of the *snake*. The paper *says* he should've been *fortunate*, but that wasn't the *case*."

Anna noticed how the old lady breezed past the rest of the description of those born in the year of the snake—Yang, powerful, masculine, treacherous, prone to profit from the losses of others, either slippery or adaptable—and decided, *Your Daddy was adaptable all right—he adapted himself to using an ax very well. Too bad he didn't notice that he'd gotten his feet bloody when he walked out of the house, and adapt himself to not walking on the bare pavement. Bloodstains are harder to see on grass.*

"It says here he should have married a *monkey*, but I don't suppose it would've *sounded* very nice."

"What?" Anna knew what was coming, but the old lady got testy if her jokes were spoiled.

"Asking some young *lady* if she was a *monkey*!"

Anna chuckled, just long enough, then asked, "How many people were you figuring this out for? These lists go back quite a ways."

"Only for the *immediate* family. I couldn't care *less* about my aunts." The old lady pronounced the word in the manner of southern people Anna had heard on the TV, with an "aw" sound in the beginning (another of the old lady's pretentious affectations that Anna hated). "But I had to go way, *way* back to figure out Gramma's year. And wouldn't you *know*, it's the best one of all."

The year of the dragon. According to the rag paper, dragons were Yangs of "rising power," who could profit by adapting to change, and had the ability to transform their personalities to suit the situation. But there were warnings, too—dragon's chameleon-like personality could tend to get worse, not better, and dragons hated to be pushed around, often resorting to violence in a pinch. According to the article, printed in late 1975, 1976 was to be a time of "offensive successes" for those born in a dragon year, a prediction that seemed self-contradictory to Anna. At any rate, it was of no help to her late great-great-grandmother—the old woman had kicked off in 1931, and was in her seventies *then*. The best she could have hoped for was to last into maybe the early 1960s or so.

"But see, at the *end*? You and *Gramma* would have gotten along."

"Oh, yeah," Anna said, reading aloud the line. "'They find fulfillment with those born in the year of the cock'." Anna could just imagine it—a 102-year-old woman finding great fulfillment with a newborn baby. Sighing out loud to avoid laughing, Anna said, "I can see you worked really hard on all this, but—well, what's the point? I mean, you can't always plan on what year your parents are born in, or the person you fall in love with"—Anna noticed that the old lady hadn't figured out any year-sign for the "Father Unknown" listed on Ma's birth certificate, and wondered, *Didn't you ask him how old was, or didn't you care?*—"so what good is it? It's like zodiac signs—once you figure in the rising signs, and cusps and all twelve houses of this and that, it ends up that everyone has a touch of all twelve signs in them. I mean, *it's fun* to figure it all out, and I even read my horoscope if I find a paper that's current, but—I dunno. People are too variable to pin down with a set of year or month signs."

"But the *Orientals,* they put great *store* in this, and look, they're *ahead* of us in trade. Mark my words, you'll find out *they* were behind Black *Monday.*"

Sensing that the old lady was about to go off on one of her idiotic tangents, which in turn meant hours spent in useless argument, Anna got up, saying, "Sorry to leave you, but I have some more—" the old lady hated the words "Dumpster diving," so she instead said, "*looking* to do this morning. I'll bring the shopping cart along when I go shopping, and take this stuff home then. Oh, did you make out your list for the store?"

"*List?*"

Anna felt her temper rising; the old lady had absolutely no sense of priorities. Ma claimed that they went through this rigmarole every weekend. Ma asked the old lady on Friday night to make out her list of on-sale items from the *Ewerton Shopper,* which came out every Tuesday afternoon, and come Saturday morning, the old lady would say *"List?"* every damned *time.*

"Is there anything you need? Anything on sale in the *Shopper*?" Anna coaxed, her temper seething.

"I don't *think* so."

Just like Ma had told Anna. First the old lady claimed not to need anything, then after Ma did the shopping, she would whine, "Well, I saw *this* advertised...."

"Okay, then, because after I do my shopping, I'm *not* going back," Anna warned, knowing she'd go back to the store anyway after the old lady remembered what she wanted.

Anna couldn't recall the old lady ever being other than helpless. When Anna was small the old lady had *only* been in her forties, and early forties at that, but she'd nonetheless come across as very old, like a regular grandma who hadn't had a child while relatively young, and whose child hadn't had a child while in her mid-teens. Even in the time when the old lady actually worked, she'd been helpless. She couldn't walk the less-than-half-mile distance to work, but had to hitch a ride—hell, *pay* for a ride each day, since she wasn't friendly with any of her co-workers—and she never could do housework.

Ma claimed that she was wringing out sopping clothes by hand when she was only four years old, and had done the old lady's income tax since she was twelve. Tending to Aunt Joan supposedly took up most of the old lady's free time, but a county nurse stopped by quite often, so Aunt Joan (skin husk-dry, body withered, with hair like frosty spider-webbing and a mouth that drooled decay-scented saliva) wasn't *that* much of a problem.

Ma later claimed that Anna's grandmother had seemed old when Ma was small, when in reality the old lady had been in her twenties. "She *liked* it," Ma would say. "She *enjoyed* being old and sickly—like some grandmother in a fuckin' chair. Always dressed old—in the winter, she wore some damn shirt *her* grandmother had worn. All she did was shorten the thing a little. And it *stank* like a wet dog."

"—have some coffee on for you when you come *back*," the old lady was saying, getting up to get the coffee pot. Anna sighed; the old lady *still* couldn't remember that she preferred tea. But to sit up half the night charting out stupid *zodiac* signs for a bunch of dead people, *that* she could do. While the old lady ran the faucet above the glass coffee pot, Anna noticed that her forearm was scraped raw along the outer side, as if she'd raked it along something jagged. But the wound didn't look deep or infected, so Anna merely thought, *Don't think I'm going to ask widdle Wucy about her owie. It ain't gonna work this time. Go get sympathy somewhere else.*

As Anna picked up her now-empty bags and headed for the door, the old lady was prattling on about how well Anna and Gramma would have gotten along, and before Anna had a chance to escape the cluttered, smoky-musty-smelling house for a few hours, the old lady crooned, "When you get home, give me the signal."

Pausing in the half-opened door, Anna said, "But I'll be coming right back in less than a couple of hours."

"But I *worry*," came the plaintive reply. Anna shouted back, 'Oh, all *right*," before slamming the door behind her and stepping back onto the frost-swirled sidewalk.

And as she walked back into town, cutting down alleys and jaywalking across the streets, Anna thought, *Next, she'll have me phone her every time I have a bowel movement. It's as if she wants to live my life as well as hers, knowing every thing I do.*

And although she still didn't know it yet, Anna was right—but also totally wrong.

TWO—Lucy (3)

Swiftly, her hands claw-hooked in rage, Lucy crumpled the sheets of paper on the kitchen table, sparing only the brittle zodiac chart. Wrinkled paper drifted to the floor like sheets of snow, to blanket the red-and-gray-check linoleum below.

The girl refused to understand—refused to come *around*—and if she didn't want to consider certain things just a *shade* beyond the norm, how could little Anna ever accept the *facts,* in all their wonderfulness and strangeness? As Lucy herself had accepted them—without hesitation or reservation?

She is too old now, a voice much like Gramma's whispered in Lucy's mind. *I should have tried harder when little Anna was small. I went too fast, and frightened her. Gramma had her night skirt, to make it easier. I understood in stages—not all at once, like what I tried to do to little Anna. She just wasn't ready—and Tina didn't help matters. Keeping me away from her, keeping the child in her room, holed up with all those fairy tale books and things. Tina was jealous, that's all, because she was so much like Mother—oh, not the same year sign, or other zodiac sign, but they're the same. Neither of them could understand that grammas and granddaughters belong together. It's so natural—a perfect circle, Gramma—Granddaughter—Gramma, with no room for mothers.*

If things had only *worked* last night, if little Anna had given the signal earlier, Lucy might have been able to do what she had set out to do before leaving the house, before she spent a futile evening looking, searching, almost getting caught. And then she'd had a *change,* again, only she'd had no time to *think,* and so the *thing* had done the thinking for her, and changed into the white dog—the same dog that had scared those two *yahoos,* and it wasn't the right time or place for such a change. She'd been seen, and almost caught—and all for nothing. She had spent a futile night roaming, working off a rage that still wasn't played out when she fluttered in through the chimney, her arms, legs, and sides scraped raw and bloody. And then little Anna asked if Lucy had any *pets*. Was Lucy lucky that she was walking in back of the girl when little Anna said that!

Lucy shuffled over the crumpled sheets of paper, slipping slightly over the scattered, blue-shadowed sheets. And as she shuffled into her room, Lucy told herself, *Once I finally get it right little Anna will understand, and* then *she'll be ready to join us, like she should have when she was small—when it should have been an* adventure. *We could have done so much together, had such fun. But Mother almost ruined it for me, and Tina did the same with little Anna. But I made them both pay. didn't I? It was messy with Mother, and Aunt Joan and Aunt Bella had to come, which* almost *made it no good anymore, but I fooled* them, *didn't I, Gramma?*

Getting rid of Tina was even easier. It took longer, but now there's no one between me and little Anna, she's got *to like Gramma. That year sign chart* proves *it, even if little Anna won't pay attention to it now. After tonight, she will.*

Smiling until her thick purplish lips pulled away from her rotted-from-behind teeth like two bloated leeches, Lucy whispered, "You'll see, little Anna. You and Gramma will *really like each* other—the chart *said* so."

THREE—*Shopping and After*

"—so I says, 'What you think *you're* lookin' at, girlie?' but the waitress she don't say anything more, just sorta makes this little hitching noise, down in her throat like this—" Wayne paused in the middle of his story to demonstrate to one of the IGA stockboys what sort of gagging noise the waitress at the Four-Way Café made, while Anna pretended to be extremely interested in the row of children's breakfast cereals before her. She'd been standing with her back to the Old Dutch salesman and part-time Ewerton ambulance driver when he'd first started talking to the stockboy, and after he'd said no more than a dozen words, Anna realized that she didn't dare move.

"—and then Scooter he says, 'She must not have seen the ambulance when we came in,' on account of me having parked it out back, well, *anyhow,* I still don't see what all the fuss is about, until I notice how some of the customers at the counter are turning sorta greenish, and then I looked down and noticed all the blood on my clothes—"

"Mean you were dripping?" the stockboy asked; his awed voice made Anna wince.

"Nah, just smeared up pretty good. Scooter, he had all these little cuts in his shirt and jeans, on account of him having to crawl into the station wagon through the back window—cripes, you should've seen the driver. His feet were draped over both shoulders—legs were like over cooked noodles," Mesabi added with an audible licking of the lips, as the stockboy whistled and asked, "What about the ones in the truck?"

"Could've sucked 'em out with a straw. Once the doors came off, some of 'em just plopped out. Like something in 'Nam. Bits here, bits there—"

Gorge rising in her throat, Anna tried to inch her way down the aisle unobtrusively, wanting to just get away from Mesabi and his bloody anecdote, but a pair of old ladies—each pushing a cart—came around the corner of the aisle, effectively blocking her exit.

"—clothes was all that held some of the pieces together. Trying to carry the bodies was like hefting a quartered frying hen in a tissue bag. I got smeared pretty good on my legs when one of their jackets gave way. Funny thing was, I didn't even notice it until I was in the café. Didn't even smell it, not until I was in there. Then it was like iron, like melted-down iron filling my nose—"

"They make you guys get outta there?" the boy asked, as Anna found herself squeezed tight between the marshmallow-laden cereals and the slowly-cruising old women's carts.

"Nah, you ever know a time when Flossie would turn away customers less they was barefoot or shirtless? Don't say nothing on the door 'bout wearing bloody shirts—"

"I suppose...but what about the other customers?"

"Some left, more came in. Once we were at the counter it was all right. Our backs wasn't messed up too bad. I wish that Scooter would've washed his hands before he ordered that sandwich, but it didn't seem to bother him none. Made me a little queasy when he went to lick the mayo off his fingers and it'd gone sorta pinkish—"

"*Sheesh.*" The stockboy's awed tone was simply too much for Anna; without apology she pushed her way out of the aisle and hurried over to the canned foods section, trying not to remember what she'd just heard, trying to tell herself, Yahoos *don't* know *better, they don't*...even as a small voice within her reminded her that she was—at least in part—to blame for the macabre recitation she'd just overheard.

And the worst part was, Wayne hadn't even bothered to call the victims by name, as if they were nothing more than meat. Inhuman, nameless, freshly slaughtered *meat.*

Sick at heart, Anna told herself, *Don't show them what this is doing to you. They won't understand—they can't understand. Just don't think about them...don't care, don't bleed. Just...go on. Keep going, without* thinking—

Anna was putting a price-reduced, dented can of Camp's Beef Noodle soup into her cart when she heard a nasal voice say behind her, "C'mon, Anna, don't we pay you better than that?"

Bib Stanley. Anna finished setting the can in her cart as she said, "How else am I going to save what I make?"

"I was just teasing you," Bib said quickly as he walked beside her, a plastic jug of milk under one uniform-jacketed arm, and a box of Hostess Ho-Ho's in his other hand.

"Sorry," Anna said as the cart rumbled past the frozen foods section along the west wall of the store. "I've never been able to take a joke. We didn't do a lot of it when I was a kid. Except for mean stuff."

"Like what?" Bib's tone was casual, but Anna knew that he'd known Ma, and figured he was fishing for something.

Anna steered the cart away from a knot of women blocking the snacks and soda aisle (she wanted to pick up some paper goods, which were located at the opposite end), and took the long way around, past the deli counter, saying, "Oh, gross things. One time my grandmother found a little screw, from something or other, on the street, and she handed it to me and told me to give it to Ma, when Ma opened the door. I was supposed to say, 'This is what you need—and it's a good one,' but I screwed it up when I went to say it, and Grandmother ended up getting ticked off at me. I didn't figure it out until I got to junior high, and by then I realized it wasn't funny to begin with. But my grandmother thought it was."

"I went to school with Tina. She would have thought it was funny. Your Ma, she's a load of laughs, was then, too. Always had a joke or something silly to say. I 'spose it was on account of her dad and all."

"Whoever he was," Anna added without obvious rancor, to which Bib quickly said, "Oh, no, I don't mean it like that. It's just, you know how cruel kids can be."

"And the teachers, too."

"But she'd beat 'em to the punch with jokes about herself, so it wasn't fun to bait her. Your Ma, she doing all right?"

"Uh—okay, I guess. She still can't afford to call much. But I haven't heard anything bad, so that's something." Anna rounded the aisle and picked up her paper towels after making sure that she had the right coupon in her wallet.

Anna didn't notice that she'd acted strangely until Bib said, "Do you always do that?"

"Do what?" Cold dread trickled through her veins; she'd done something so wrong that she'd offended her boss.

"This." Bib went to move past Anna, and pulled his elbow in close to his ribs in an exaggerated manner, bowing his entire body away from hers. "You did that when you were about to graze my arm as you rounded the aisle. Same thing you do at work whenever anyone passes by you in the hallway. I was just wondering if—"

Deeply embarrassed, Anna mumbled, "I have to finish my shopping. My grandmother's waiting for me," and tried to get away from Bib, but he grabbed onto the handle of her cart and said softly but forcefully, "Whoa. I'm not getting on your case, or anything like that. I just wondered if there was some reason you go to such pains to avoid touching people. Heck, sometimes it's unavoidable. Nobody minds, but they do get to feeling offended if someone looks like they might die if they touch someone."

Pulling her lower lip into her mouth for a second, and kneading the flesh with her front teeth, Anna stared up at Bib's mild eyes, feeling her own water, until she could say tersely, without crying or raising her voice above a whisper, "I do this because if I didn't, I'd get my face slapped, or worse, when I was a kid. Because if I brushed against Ma or the old lady, I was accused of pushing them on purpose, out of spite. But they could bang into me all they wanted, and it was all right. Do you realize that when I was small, and Ma and the old lady would give me cards for my birthday, or Christmas, or whatever, the old lady always asked me whose I liked best? And no matter which way I answered, someone was mad at me. It was always 'Who does Anna like best?' As if the old lady was a little girl on the school ground, vying for the attention of the teacher.

"And when the old lady realized that I had discovered that she wasn't the wise, all-knowing Granny she tried to be, but an ignorant, weird old bat, she hated me, just as Ma hated me for not being like her. Ever hear of a no-win situation, Bib? There are rules, but they change with the playing of the game, and no matter which ones are in effect that day, they're always against you.

Anna jerked the cart out of Bib's hands, turned it around, and headed away from him, not wanting to roll it past the women blocking the other end of the aisle.

Rumbling past the meat and cheese counter, Anna didn't realize Bib was following her until she heard him say, "I didn't know. You could have said something, or gotten out while you were still in college. Tina could have handled the old lady alone."

"I doubt it. She hadn't the money to put down a deposit on another house. I did."

"But for cryin' out loud, Anna, you didn't owe them, not after what they did to you. And this town—not to put you down, but you don't belong here. You're too smart—you have a degree, for Chrissakes. How many people here have one of those and still do the kinds of jobs you—"

"I was so overwhelmed by the offers of work I couldn't decide—"

"Well, I'm sorry, all right?" Bib said, stopping in his tracks behind Anna, who paused, thought it over, and turned to face him, oblivious of the two white-coated workers who were unloading foam trays of veal cutlets and pork chops from rolling carts as she replied, "No, it isn't all right. I can't believe that nobody realized that things weren't right with my family. All people could ever think about was something that happened before I was even born, or my mother, either, for that matter. Nobody noticed how I was being treated, right then. And when the old lady was doing all those sick things when I was little, going on lawns and all, nobody really did anything about it, just smothered us with silence. I'll bet nobody ever reported her to the police, did they?"

"I wasn't in office then, but I don't recall—"

"Don't bother looking. You won't find any report about it. The neighbors just ostracized us as punishment. It didn't faze the old lady—she's been in her own world for ages."

"Now, Anna, you know what she went through," Bib began, keeping his voice as soft as Anna's, but she overrode him with, "Oh, she wasn't the first kid to see something horrible, and she won't be the last. What about those boat people, huh? The ones the Lutheran church sponsored? Some of them spoke to my political science class in college. They saw things a lot worse than what my great-grandfather did to his mother-in-law and wife, and on a daily basis. And they're okay—heck, their kids win frigging national spelling bees. And there have been others...in this country. They've seen much worse than she did—if she even saw anything that night. For all we know she probably was asleep when her father went berserk. You know what he said about her when they carted him off—'Look out for my Lucy'—why, she probably wasn't even there when it happened."

"Now, that's not what I heard as a kid. Lenny Wilkes's grandfather August used to claim that she—"

Anna sighed and said, "Even if she was there, I doubt it bothered her in that way. Not if you'd heard how she talked about her daddy. She idolized him, even after what she did or didn't see him do. Any normal kid would have hated him for chopping up her beloved Gramma, even if the old bat *was* already dead when he did it. And I can't see her forgiving him the way she did, not after whatever it was he did with the rest of the old woman.

"No, Bib, the old lady is weird, but not because of what she saw back in 1931. She never acted like she was suffering from suppressed trauma. I think she was always that nuts, but she got away with it because of what happened to her family. People excused things they shouldn't have—for her, they made allowances, but for me and Ma they just made fun. Or tried to, if what you said about Ma is true. I used to hear the rowdies yelling 'Where's Granny?' when she'd walk me someplace when I was small—it never seemed to bother her. She'd just sort of smile, like their words rolled off her back. It bothered me, and no matter what you believed before, it bothered Ma, but the old lady has been living in never-never land all her life. Just her and her Gramma. She tried that routine with me, but I wasn't buying."

"Anna." Bib waited until she had cooled down a bit before walking up to Anna and asking as she began to move forward again, away from the hidden but curious stares of the butcher's assistants, "Listen, you can apply for a county nurse for your grandmother. I can arrange it for you if they balk about it. Now what you should do is go. Get yourself a car, renew your license—I know you had a license once, I checked—pack up your stuff, let the FHA reclaim the house, and leave this dump. Seriously, what's holding you here?"

Anna walked in silence for a few feet before saying, "There are too many people I'd be making happy if I left."

"Fu—screw 'em," Bib said. "They don't owe you nothing, do they? Sure, some of 'em would be glad to see you go—nut cases like old Wally, or a few of your grandma's neighbors. But it's the same for all of us—heck, Stu Sawyer'd love it if I skedaddled. The man resents me for being able to keep my job subject to the approval of the city council, while he's gotta go through the whole rigmarole of getting himself elected every couple of years, depending on the whole county to still be liking him come election time. He can't even go after any pot growers close to election time, for fear their families'll all join forces, down to the last second cousin seven times removed, and vote him out of office. And that's not to mention anything *serious.*

"Why do you think they didn't do anything much when Alvin Miner did what he did? Just shuffled him on downstate to the loony ward, without so much as a trial? Stu's grandpa wasn't about to dirty up his record with a messy trial and a lot of publicity. It was sure a lucky break for him, finding Alvin with the ax in his hand, and his feet painted with—"

"I know the story," Anna snapped, before saying, "I really do have to get going. My grandmother is probably looking out the window right now, wondering where I am."

"Does she rule your life that completely?" Milk sloshed in the jug as Bib shifted it in his arms.

"You have to have a life before someone can rule it," Anna replied, then maneuvered her cart into one of the checkout lanes, turning her back on her new boss. Bib didn't say anything in reply, but Anna could imagine what advice he'd offer her—*Go out and make a life, then.*

And in reply to his imaginary retort, Anna thought, *How? It's like trying to paint a picture without ever having seen colors. You can't do it if your eyes have been scratched out of their sockets before they had a chance to open.*

* * * * * * *

"Why, Anna Sudek, I haven't seen *you* in a month of Sundays," Mrs. Campbell said to Anna in the IGA parking lot. before Anna had a chance to notice that the whip-thin old woman was walking behind her. Resisting the urge to say, "Don't you remember beating me to the bakery Dumpster on Monday?" Anna fell into step with her and replied, "I've been busy—a new job, plus taking care of my grandmother. It's been a hectic week." *And if you think I'm filling you in about Ma you're dead wrong, you old prune.*

"Handling your grandmother must be a job and a half," Mrs. Campbell mused, as the brisk wind whipped the loose ends of her head scarf, making them flutter with a dry, snicking flag-like sound. It wasn't what Anna had been expecting, this apparent commiseration.

"You see, I knew Lucy when she was in school. If you don't mind my saying so, she was a caution even then," the older woman said in a voice that suggested she was going to say what she felt whether Anna minded or not. And after her exchange with Bib a few minutes earlier, Anna was quite past minding much of anything.

"Were you in my grandmother's class in school?" Anna's pace was slowed both by the cart she was pulling behind her and her shortness of breath, but the older woman didn't seem to mind walking slowly. At least she was dressed for the blustery weather, in no-nonsense men's dark jeans, sturdy socks under her running shoes, and her ever-present worn pea coat. Most women Mrs. Campbell's age wouldn't be caught dead wearing so many clothes in such chilly weather; they suffered in flimsy unlined nylon jackets or thin fluffy sweaters, over cold polyester pants and tops, and only thin nylon, between their feet and their low-cut dressy shoes—and never mind their red ears under wispy, poufy hairdos.

Glancing at Mrs. Campbell, Anna felt some admiration for her and also thought, *That's you, Anna, in thirty or so more years. A dried out pea pod of a woman wrapped in layers of men's clothing, without a bump or curve in sight. You won't have to worry about any of the goomers trying to bang you if you venture too far out in the boonies in the dark. If they jumped her, they'd get bruises from her hip bones and rib cage.*

"My grandmother always has been—how do you say, um, different."

"*Nuts* is the word you're looking for, dear," Mrs. Campbell said not unkindly as she reached over to give Anna's arm a friendly squeeze. They paused at the intersection before crossing to Dean Avenue, then proceeded toward Evans Street.

"I've known Lucy Miner since she was a small, small girl—before her grandmother died. She was the same—shall we say *sweet*—little thing before her Gramma died as she was after."

Noticing the IGA bag in Mrs. Campbell's arms, Anna realized that the old woman must have overheard her conversation with Bib. Anna felt warmed by Mrs. Campbell's words. Without actually coming out and saying so, the woman had let Anna know that she cared, and at least on some level understood what Anna had had to put up with. Or so Anna chose to believe, wanted to believe, now that Ma was gone, as she had no one else to turn to, aside from the old lady, which in itself was as bad as having no one.

Now, I don't have absolutely no one, but how many people count cats? Nobody would understand about how Bruiser "talks" to me and comforts me when I'm down, any more than Ma wanted to believe how he can raise the window shade by himself. It scared her—maybe because she realized his size and shape were the only things differentiating him from humans?

"—live here?" Mrs. Campbell was looking expectantly at Anna, her eyes watering in the wind, her slightly bulbous, large-pored nose red around the nostrils, and Anna had to say, "I was woolgathering. What did you say?"

"I said, does your grandmother still live here? In this house? She pointed a wool-mittened hand at the bricked façade of the old prairie-style house. As Anna glanced toward it she saw one of the curtains fall quickly back into place behind the living room window.

"Yes—she's never left it, in fact. Except for when she's absolutely had to. She even gave birth to my mother in there."

Mrs. Campbell muttered something the wind tore from her mouth; all Anna caught was a fragment—"...ceived in there, too, I'd wager"—but Anna had heard enough to not want to hear the rest of the other woman's thought. Then, hefting her bag, Mrs. Campbell said, "You'll have to stop by my house sometime, Anna. I live on Polk Street, in a little 1930s bungalow. It's gray with white trim, and there are always animals in the windows. Why, it's not far from where you live, actually. Say, terrible news, wasn't it, about those youngsters."

"Pardon?"

"That brother and sister—the ones who died in the truck. And them being neighbors of yours. My Don knew the boy. Elmo. Hated the little bastard. Every day in the summer when that boy was helping the city crew paint the curbs yellow, Don would come home and say, 'I hate that little hick bastard.' Just like that. No inflection or anything, like saying rain was wet. 'Course Don, he hated everyone 'cross the board. Why, it got to the point where I couldn't have a body over without him saying this or that against the person right to their face, or worse. After a while, I didn't have *that* problem to worry about anymore. Only thing was, people took to blaming *me* for not making Don shut up." Mrs. Campbell let her voice fade, but the look in her eyes said to Anna, *Don't feel alone, kiddo, I know where you're coming from—I've walked that path myself.* Then, as if she was mentally sweeping aside old dirt, the woman went on, "I suppose you had trouble with Elmo, too."

Assuming that Mrs. Campbell now wanted to hear some fresh dirt about the crash, maybe even what the victims now looked like, in exchange for that small revelation about her life with Don Campbell, and thus feeling as if she'd been taken for a sucker again, Anna blurted quickly, "I'm sorry, I really have to get inside."

"Yes, I saw Lucy watching us," Mrs. Campbell said wryly before shifting her bag in her arms and adding, "Well remember, drop by any time. And Anna—"

Anna stopped on the porch, in the middle of pulling the cart up, and waited with slowly eroding politeness.

144 * *THE AMULET*, BY A. R. MORLAN

"—watch out for Lucy, won't you?" And then Mrs. Campbell was gone, trotting down the street on thin ankles, her wrinkled face pointing into the wind like a flinty arrowhead, resolute and unmoving.

Behnd Anna, the old lady cracked the front door open and burbled,"What did *she* want? You didn't tell her anything, did you?

"Tell her what?" Anna asked as she pulled the cart with difficulty into the house, around the unmoving old woman. The old lady hovered near the door, lower lip more pendulous than usual, her no-color eyes vacant, purposefully blank, saying, "Oh, nothing. She's just a nosy old biddy. She don't have to know nothing."

"*If* there's nothing to tell her, she won't know it, will she? Anna could feel a headache building behind her eyes, both from the cold buffeting her face and from anger. First Bib, then that strange, but sort of nice Arlene Campbell, and now the old lady.

("Nuts is the word you're looking for, dear.")

All Anna wanted to do was go home, get into her nightclothes, and crawl into bed—just press her face into Bruiser's heavily muscled flank and make all the craziness go away. But she couldn't do that—at least, not yet. Her nose told her that the old lady had fixed something to eat—something slightly greasy-meaty smelling, with a tangy-piquant vegetable on the side. And she knew from the times Ma had tried to leave without eating the proffered meal that the old lady would pout if Anna tried to refuse whatever had been cooked.

Deciding that eating might help her headache, Anna followed her grandmother into the kitchen, wincing as the old woman sing-songed, "You'll never *guess* what's waiting for you in the *kitchen.*"

* * * * * * *

"Lunch was good," Anna lied, getting into her second sweater, pulling on her coat. At the table, seated behind her plate of fatty pork hocks and sauerkraut, the old lady smiled vacuously and said, "You *know* that coat is too *big* for you."

"That's because the two sweaters are so bulky." Anna was about to explain that when it was this windy, she preferred to wear layers of clothing, because a single heavy coat wasn't enough when the old lady said, "Not bulky sweaters—bulky *strangers.*"

Anna looked incredulously at the old woman, whose greasy face was pulled up in a parody of a smiling mask, while the old lady laboriously explained, *"Bulky...*like *Balki,* on that show *Perfect Strangers*—the character, he's a *shepherd* named—"

"*I know* which show," Anna said with a gentleness she didn't feel, as she wondered, *Why me? Out of all the people on earth, why was I blessed with her?*

"It's a *joke,*" the old lady explained, as if Anna were the dense one in the room, then added, with a solemn nod of her grizzled head, "It's only make-believe, you know. None of those shows are *real.* I *know* what's *real,* you know."

As Anna put her coat on over her sweaters and buttoned it up, she bit her lip to keep from snapping a retort and said. "I'm going home. I have things to do."

"You'll give me the *signal,* won't you? I get so *worried.*"

"Yeah. But don't go getting in a panic if I don't call right away, okay? I never know who I might meet in the street. People expect me to stop and talk. It's the polite thing to do—"

"You just tell *them,* you have an *important* call to *make,* Someone is *waiting,*" the old lady said, rocking forward and back in her seat, making the wood protest feebly.

"I can't always do that...but I'll call as soon as I get home. Is that all right with you?" Anna put her purse strap over one arm and pushed the cart in front of her to the front door . Behind her, the old lady persisted, "Just *tell* them, 'I have an important *call* to make.'"

Anna slammed the door on the old lady in midspeech. Walking down Evans Street, she wondered, *What would she do if I didn't call? Keep trying my line? Call out the National Friggin' Guard? Harangue me about it the next day? Cripes, it isn't even worth it to disobey her. At least with the signal, I don't have to listen to her Gravel Gertie voice.*

FOUR—*Arlene (3)*

About three-quarters of an hour after she'd spoken to Anna in front of Lucy's house, Arlene Campbell saw the younger woman trudging past her own house, full cart rolling behind her, knit-hatted head bent down against the wind that blew trash into her face.

Arlene was tempted to open the door and invite the young woman in, but decided not to; the poor girl looked exhausted. *I'd be after a row with Don—and Lucy is much, much worse than Don ever could be. He was simply a mean Esso-Bee. Her grandmother is something far more insidious than plain old mean. Those neighbors of hers thought shitting on their lawns was the worst of it—they didn't know Lucy Miner like I did, nor would they have wanted to know her, or know what tricks she had up her little sleeve. The way she'd make all those awful noises when the teacher's back was turned—sounds so disgusting the teacher would never believe a girl made them. How she'd leave the swing seat all wet and slimy after she'd sat on it, so no one would want it after she got off. Or the way she could make the earthworms come slithering up out of the ground, just by lying down and drumming her fists and heels....*

Mrs. Campbell walked away from her kitchen window, gracefully dodging the cats and dogs that wound around her thin ankles. Sitting down on her chair, after pulling over Don's ottoman to rest her feet on (something she'd have never dared to do in his presence), she sat staring up at her walls, at the pictures framed and hanging there.

Pictures of Don she was still too cowed inside to take down, snapshots of her cats and dogs, grouped by year of acquisition, and older, more faded studio photographs of her school years.

Ewerton Elementary School used to hold a graduation ceremony at the end of the eighth grade year. And while Lucy Miner had been older than Arlene Weiss, Lucy hadn't graduated from elementary school until the same year Arlene had, too many missed days of school.

Arlene's eyes weren't perfect, but she could see the photograph of her elementary graduation clearly enough to make out Lucy Miner, sitting in the middle of the front row, holding the little placard that listed the name of the teacher and the year of the class, in the spot the eighth grade teachers reserved for the class dummy, to make sure he or she wouldn't the able to do something to ruin the class picture.

But Lucy Miner had this superior look on her face, as if being smack-dab in the middle of the front *row*, in the dummy position, was a mark of high honor. Lucy had worn the same "I-know-something-you-don't-know" look ever since her mother had been killed, and her dead grandmother had been dismembered, and mostly disposed of, save for one half of a limb.

Even when Arlene and the others had taunted Lucy, asking that old, silly question, "Where's Granny?" something about Lucy's reaction bothered Arlene to this day. She and her friends had expected hurt, anger, rage, and more, but Lucy would only give them that smug sphinx smile, and keep swinging higher and higher, jerking the stout rope holding the swing to the overhead bar until the hemp sang. She looked like a bird, waiting for the right second to alight into the clouds, her braids flapping behind her like thin, almost prehistoric wings, her then-thin lips pursed into a beak-sharp pucker.

It was as if she didn't care—as if she knew it all, Arlene recalled, and also remembered something else—something little Lucy Miner had showed her once, after Arlene had come to school wearing a new locket, a gift from Mamma and Papa. Lucy obviously envied the little oval of opal and filigree gold, and managed to pull Arlene away, to a corner of the playground during recess, ostensibly to show her something.

And "something" was the only good word for it. Whatever that horrid thing was—if it was, indeed, just a thing, Arlene told herself with a shiver, even though she had two cats on her lap, and one standing on the back of the chair kneading her shoulder, and shouldn't have been cold at all.

To this day, Arlene couldn't really remember what it looked like, but she swore it moved, in that little tobacco tin Lucy kept it in. She only wished it hadn't been overcast that day—she couldn't really see the whole thing.

But of one thing Arlene Weiss Campbell was sure, as her babies purred and kneaded and snuggled in against her—the coiled, shining thing in the Plow Boy tobacco can didn't remain coiled in there for long. It was just a pity she'd screamed and run when that greenish head poked out of the can, casting about for her, like a dog scenting a hidden fox, for then Lucy never brought the thing out in Arlene's presence again.

After that day, Arlene Weiss never joined in when the other children made fun of Lucy, for whatever the coiled thing in the can was, it wasn't just something to wear, something more special than Arlene's new opal locket. It looked like it should have have been wearing Lucy, if it wasn't doing so already.

FIVE—Bib (3)

Driving his special Ewerton Chief of Police car (deemed "special" because it lacked the usual rectangular bar of blue and red lights across the top) down Riverview Road, Bib Stanley wished that he hadn't taken such a threatening stance (or what most likely seemed like a menacing stance) with the Sudek girl in the IGA a few minutes before.

He really hadn't intended to come on like gangbusters, he assured himself as he made the slightly angular turn that marked the spot where Riverview Road turned into Abigail Avenue. All he'd wanted to do was find out if she was all right. He knew she was old enough to take care of herself, but yet, she seemed much younger than twenty-nine or so, more vulnerable in certain almost indefinable ways. *That, and try to warn her,* his mind added as he drove down the little dirt road shootingoff the avenue, into tiny Ewert Park.

Ewerton only had a population of 3,300 or so, give or take a hundred, yet the city boasted three officially designated parks, plus numerous small scatterings of benches and big metal trash bins in and around the numerous wooded patches on the west side of the Dean River. Elm Park and Maple Park were on that side, too, along with the tacky Wood lawn Development, the hospital, and the swanky Willow Hill section, where Bib couldn't afford to live even if they made him mayor, police chief, and Dean County sheriff combined, and threw in garbage hauler for good measure.

The parks on the west side were likewise tacky and swanky, too. Maple Park was filled with wobbly kiddie rides on big springs, lots of swings, slides, monkey bars, and two of those lazy Susan type rides with the bright enameled handholds around the circumference, and the rusty garbage bin-dotted grass was worn to bristly nubs by the hundreds of running feet. Elm Park was Yuppie-heaven—volleyball courts, basketball hoops, horseshoe squares, covered gazebos among the birches on the rise, fancy-schmancy benches, *painted* metal garbage bins, and a restroom with air blowers near the sink. Bib liked to think of the two parks as Daddy Bear and Mamma Bear. with Baby Bear tiny Ewert Park being the proverbial just right.

Every Saturday, while his wife Rhonda was off worshiping at the Holy Church of Bingo on the Indian Reservation, Bib liked to buy himself a little treat, a box of Hostess or Little Debbie snacks, plus a jug of milk, and drive down to Elm Park to eat and think in peace, away from the station.

Won't be coming down here much more this year, he thought, looking at the surrounding trees and the steel-gray river beyond. The birches, maples, and elms were all but denuded of leaves, their dark branches angular and forlorn against the leaden, cloud-scudded sky. A mix of soggy and crisp leaves covered his favorite bench, the one closest to the sand-filled horseshoe square. Brushing them off with his leather-gloved hand, Bib realized that it wouldn't be too long before the snows came—not just the false whiteness of early morning frost, but the real thing, covering and chilling the land, and taking away Bib's Saturday time to himself.

Bib both loved and hated autumn—hated the way the land grew browned-out and sad, and bones of the trees and weeds were exposed, yet he also loved the stark beauty of their intricate shapes and subtle play of brown on brown against muddy green-brown. Bib likewise liked the way autumn brought tourists into the area, how it filled the cash registers and motel beds in town—yet, too, autumn sometimes brought bad things to Ewerton.

Like the Alvin Ewert case, Bib thought, unwrapping a Ho-Ho and popping one of the log-shaped cakes into his mouth. A fine spray of crumbs settled on his leather uniform jacket like soot, but the few remaining birds twittering in the trees didn't mind his messy clothes.

And the birds didn't care when he slopped some of his milk on his jacket, the white liquid leaving a faint glistening snail trail when it dried on the dark leather. Unwrapping another cake, Bib burped lightly as he remembered the Miner case, the one which both did and didn't still keep the town buzzing after the passage of fifty-six years. No one who was anyone in town would think of mentioning the case. It was those considered "beneath" Ewerton's up-and-coming crowd (which, because of the relative lack of real wealth and class in town, included such people as the city refuse haulers and the lowly clerks in the treasurer and city clerk's office): the crowd who hung around Lenny Wilkes's video arcade-cum-bowling alley-cum-pizzeria, the haggard women who frequented the Super Suds, the ding-dongs whose names made up most of the weekly list of arrests for drunk and disorderly, disoderly conduct, DWl, and the like, *they* kept the Miner case truly alive. *Them and the children,* Bib told himself, but kids didn't really count. You almost had to expect them to act stupid, and more than a little mean. It wasn't nice, and it wasn't fair, but that was the way it was, just as fairy tales were nasty and life was likewise brutish.

Just as the Miner case itself was brutal. In fact, until the case had exploded down in Plainsfield, Alvin Miner was jokingly known in northern Wisconsin as the semiofficial state murderer and all-around wacko. Some people in Ewerton were so smug and tasteless as to publicly cheer on what Ed Gein had done—if only because it shut off the burner under Ewerton's pot.

Bib Stanley's people weren't among those who were awfully relieved in 1957, after that dressed out old dear was found in ol' Ed's garage, but Bib and his family were in the position of knowing just a little more about the Alvin Miner case than most Ewerton residents, save for the Wilkes clan. Even the Sawyers didn't know quite as much, and then-Sheriff Sawyer was one of the first people into the house early that morning.

Bib's Grandpop Andersen, his mother's dad, was the one who had found Alvin Miner wandering around Crescent Lake that blustery October morning—one week before Halloween. And Grandpop liked to tell it this way:

Thought at first Alvin had done hisself up as an Injin, for an All-Hallow's Eve joke—Alvin was always one for the pranks and such. But then I reccamembered that Halloween was a week away, and Alvin may've been a scamp, but he wasn't no fool, neither. Yet Alvin was a hootin' and a hollerin' like an Injin, which made me wonder if he hadn't looked at the calendar wrong.

But he still had what I thought was 'sposed to be a tomahawk in his hand, all painted up Injin red, I but then I walked alittle ways closer and seen that it was sparklin' in the light too much to be paint, and lemme tell you kids, Alvin was covered with it! With what, Brian? Blood! All drippin' from his peejammers legs, and pooled between his toes. He was barefoot, which was crazy. It was in the teens that morning, So cold your breath just kinda stayed behind in a little cloud long after you was shut up and gone.

So I waves to Alvin and hollers, "Alvin, you'll catch your death o' cold out here without no shoes on! C'mon in the house with me!" even though I knew my missus wouldn't appreciate red footprints all over the floor. And to tell the truth, I really wasn't gonna invite him in anyway, but I hadda get him closer to me, so's I could see if it really *was* blood or jusl something red and slippery he'd dipped hisself in.

Well, he didn't have to come no closer than two feet for me to know he'd been doin' more than liberating chicken heads from their bodies out in the backyard. Now Alvin, he was a little man, with a sunk-in chest and not much meat on the bones, but he was a wiry little Bohunk—that's a *Bohemian,* from Europe, out near the Krauts. I think he changed his name or something. When he was a kid it was something different, with a "nink" on the end, I think; oh *dammit,* kids, where *was* I?

Alvin bein' wiry. He worked in the paper mill, liftin' big rolls of paper and such, so his arms were corded like knotted hemp. And when I seen them arms of his all lumped under the skin with tensed muscles, and seen that ax in his hand with the silver all red-sheened, I just said, "Why Alv, Halloween's but a week off yet," and at first, Alv don't say nothin', just smiled at me, this goofy grin with his eyes like flint, and I said real calming like, "Alv, won't your missus be wonderin' where you are on a cold mornin' like this?" And through the steam from my lips I saw Alv all cloudy, but still just as red and drippin', and up closer I seen that someone had tried to push him away or somethin', only their hand was so slick with blood it just left a palm and finger smear on his P.J. top and kept on slidin' off the cloth.

And lookin' off to where he had come from, I seen these red blotches on the street, and I thought to myself, "Alvin's finally had it with that woman of his." Mrs. Miner was a withered string bean of a— well, your mamma don't want for me to talk like that. Woman was a worker, but jerky-tough, and about as cuddly. Funny, I don't recollect her name now. Any-who, I figgered that the handprint belonged to the hand of his missus, and the first thing that came to mind was, Lucy. He's done killed his little girl, too.

Not that she was a particularly nice little girl, but killin'a little 'un never set right with me, be the child a whining pesky brat or no.

So, I says, "Oh, Alvin, I hope you ain't done nothin' to that little girlie of yours," and Alvin *really* smiles at that point, I mean his eyes and all, and he says in the calmest voice you can imagine, "Don't worry about *Lucy.* No, don't worry about her at all— she's just *fine,*" he says, only when he said *fine,* it didn't seem like he meaned it in the way I was used to understandin' it. Like he meant it but didn't, all at once.

Lemme tell you boy, *that* was when I was gettin' scared but good of Alvin. I didn't even make a move to stop him when he started wandering north of us, off across the grass toward Byrne Avenue and the fu-neral home beyond, and then was when it hit me— my missus had been at Alvin's house the night be-fore, helping his missus with the body of his mother:

the old shrew had kicked off—burst appendix, or some such thing, and not a minute too soon, lemme tell you.

Right then and there, I realized that Alvin had done gone and drummed up some more business for the Misters Byrne and Reish, and they was both sick in bed on top of it.

It wasn't until Alvin was crossing Seventh Avenue, walkin' free and easy as you please, that I come to my senses and ran back home to phone up the police. Even then, they didn't want to believe me, since Alvin was known to be a joker, but when the Byrnes placed a call right after me, then they believed.

And sure I was there at his house when the police cars showed up. I figgered I had to follow up on what I'd sorta started, just in case it *was* some sorta prank on Alv's part. But when I seen all the footprints clustered near the front door, which was hangin' open, and saw how the prints kept on going across the bare wood floor—no, I don't know why they didn't have no rugs. Maybe Mrs. Miner didn't like cleanin' 'em.

Where was I? Oh, the prints. Me and a few of the city police, plus Sheriff Sawyer, we walked in there, callin' out, "Mrs.Miner? Lucy? Anyone in there?" but we didn't get no farther than the little room off the living room—the one they'd done over for Mrs. Miner's mother—than we seen her. Not her mother, but *her.*

She was lyin' on her back, palms up and bright red, her face all awash in it, too, except for the places where the bones was showin'. And where her eye was hangin' on her left—no, it was the right cheek. Her eye was kinda deflated, like a ball that's lost a lot of air.

All right, all right, Mother, I'll skip that part to make you happy. Now, since there wasn't too much we could do for Mrs. Miner, we kinda skirted around her, bein' careful not to step in the blood and add our footprints to the general confusion of tracks there. Alvin's were easy, being big and, bare, but there was a lot of other prints, some tiny and bare, some bigger and slippered, and some—well, August Wilkes and Sheriff Sawyer said them prints were not really prints, but traces where robes and such had dripped in blood and trailed out behind folks, but I dunno. They was too regular for that, and too strange-shaped, but I didn't get that good a look at them, on account of some of us wasn't too careful and stepped on them and messed them up with tracked-in leaves and mud.

Well, it's funny, now, but I took it all right with Mrs. Miner, and even the tracks didn't bother me much, but when I seed that hand and a little bit of the arm just lying there on the floor with nothing else of the old woman's body to match it up with, that was when I got myself out of there, 'cause the room wasn't big enough and the bed wasn't high enough to hide her, but she wasn't there anyhow.

Tossing his Ho-Ho wrappers in the metal trash bin next to his bench, Bib slowly unwrapped another confection as he mulled over what his grandfather had told him on many an occasion during Bib's youth. The story never progressed beyond the point where the elderly man saw the lone limb on the floor of the converted sewing room in the Miner house. And it wasn't until Grandpop Andersen died, seven and a half years ago, that Bib finally heard the rest of the story, or what rest of it was known to the few remaining relatives of those who had gone in the house that October morning.

Lenny Wilkes had come up next to Bib after the graveside services, sweating slightly in his too-tight sports coat, his crew cut beaded with it, as he said, "Sorry about your granddad, Brian. He was a good man."

"He was the last of them, you know," Bib had mumbled absent-mindedly, fumbling with the Kleenex in his pocket, and wondering where in the hell Rhonda had gone off to.

"Last of who?" Lemiy was huffing to keep pace with Bib, the new pennies in his loafers glinting in the noon sun.

"Last of the men who were in the Miner house, the day they went *in*," Bib said after spotting Rhonda standing with some of her bingo friends, over by the Crescent mausoleum.

"That's right. My grandfather went ten years ago. I can still remember his stories about it—used to scare the bejesus out of me when I was in Dr. Dentons."

The inage of Lenny Wilkes stuffed into a pair of footed, drop-drawer jammies was too much for Bib; he erupted in a shout of laughter which Lenny mistook for stifled tears.

"Aw, Bib...."

Wiping his nose, Bib had remarked, "My Grandpop, he was always telling us about it. Usually at family gatherings, after we ate. Mom was always furious—and always, the story stopped almost the same way—'but she wasn't there anyhow.' And then he ran for home."

"You mean he didn't see Lucy Miner?"

"Well, yeah, afterward, at the funeral."

Lenny had come to a chuffing stop near the front gates.Leaning against one of the iron doors, he said, "No, no, no. I mean that day. In the house."

"I just said he left."

"Oh.Yeah. So he didn't see her?"

"No. He skedaddled home after he seen—saw the arm. If he knew more, Mom and Grandmom wouldn't let him tell it."

"If that was the case, I don't blame them none." Lenny fished a grayish hanky out of his pocket and mopped his face before going on, his reedy voice suddenly eerie, out there in the brassy sun and stillness of the graveyard:

"My grandpa, he told me time and again that he'd never seen nothing like it. They come into the house and found Bekka Miner all claw-handed on the floor, like she'd been fighting when she got whacked and went down still tryin', and then beyond her, they found some of her mother. 'Where's her mother?' one of them asks the others, and next thing you know they was scootin' around the floor on their hands and knees, peeping under the bed, and pushing aside the clothes on hooks, looking *everywhere* in the room, then the bottom part of the house.

"But the rest of her wasn't *nowhere.* And there wasn't blood anywhere but in the living room and that room where the old lady was living. Finally, my grandpa, he tells the others.

"Maybe Alvin took the rest of her out of the house and put her in the sewer or something. It wasn't no secret that Alvin Miner's mother-in-law was causin' a little bit o' friction in the Miner household, even if Alvin was a tolerant fellow, so his putting her somewhere disgusting didn't seem too unlikely. Well, as Grandpa told it to my dad and later to me, he and the others was about to leave the house—they posted one of the men to stand guard, of course—when they remembered that they hadn't seen Lucy Miner. I mean, they'd been calling for her, but when they seen the old lady's arm, they kinda forgot about Lucy, on account of she wasn't much to remember anyhow, kind of a colorless little girl, and a brat, or so Grandma said.

"So Grandpa starts calling for her, and the others join in, and one of them notices that some of the footprints was hers only they didn't seem to go nowhere, just in a tight little pattern around the rest of the prints near the old woman's bedroom doorway. Like her daddy had lifted her up and taken her out somewheres.

"Someone said, 'Alvin must've killed her, too,' and somebody else supposedly said, 'No loss,' but Grandpa wasn't sure if he just imagined it or if someone was that rude out in public, even if it was the truth.

"So they split up and some ran off for the basement, and some ran off for the upstairs, and one man went outside to have a look-see. Grandpa, he went upstairs with one of the policemen—Vern Campbell, I think he said. Don't really matter who it was, I guess. Grandpa and Vern went slow up these stairs, and Grandpa, he noticed that the bare wood treads was all splintered, and said that he hoped that little girl didn't get splinters in her feet, and the other guy says, 'Naw, no blood. see?' on account of there wasn't none on the treads. There was plenty elsewheres.

"When they reached the top, they saw the two opened bedroom doors, and peeked in each one. Lucy's bed was pulled back real neat, or so Grandpa said, like she'd taken her time getting out of the bed and had time to arrange the blankets and sheets nice. Her folks' bed was a mess, the covers all trailing on the floor, and tangled, like they'd fought out of 'em. Then and there, Grandpa decided that it was Lucy who'd gotten up first and maybe gone downstairs before her momma and papa did. Couldn't prove it, but he thought it.

"Lucy wasn't nowhere, in any of the other rooms, neither. I wanted to get the hell out of there, but Grandpa said, 'What about the attic?' The other guy didn't want to go up there, on account of it being an open attic with no rooms and floor, but Grandpa said, 'We gotta *look*,' so Vern says, '*Fine, you* do it,' and takes off, almost sliding down the banister he was so anxious to get gone.

"Now, then, Grandpa starts to thinking about bats and all up there, on account of the house is making these funny little noises all around him, like old houses used to do in the cold and he don't want to go up there, 'cause he thinks he hears mice, but all of a sudden, he don't have to.

"'Hello,' comes this chirpy little voice behind him, and Grandpa claimed he nearly wet his drawers when he turned and saw

Lucy Miner standing there in her nightgown with all the strips and splotches of blood on it, and her feet all bare and rusty-stained.

"She was standin' next to one of the rooms Grandpa and Vern had just been looking through, and there wasn't enough furniture for a cat to hide behind, let alone a kid over three feet high. In a white nightgown. Grandpa, he said he hunkered down and asked, 'Tell me, what *happened?*' although he wasn't expecting much out of her, but Lucy piped up and said, 'Gramma died but now she's better, and I think Daddy killed Mother.' Just in a rush like that, with no tears or *nothing.*

"Lemme tell you, Bib, that's the scariest part for me. Think, if she had all the blood on her, she *had* to have been when some of the blows was bein' landed, and her footprints was all among the others, but all she has to say about it, 'I think Daddy killed Mother.' Like she don't care neither way if the woman was or wasn't really dead. Mentioned how her Gramma was in heaven, or whatever the Miners had taught her about death being a better place. *That* she was more worried about. Now don't that beat all?"

Bib remembered telling Lenny something about kids acting strangely under certain circumstances, but Lenny, mopping his stubble of hair with his limp hankie, said, "Wait, there's more. You ain't heard the *weird* part. Later on, Grandpa figgered that Lucy had been *playing* upstairs, while he and whoever it was was looking up there. The kid had on some stuff she'd taken from her momma's jewelry case—some earrings, and a big bead necklace, and wrapped around one of her arms was this really fancy golden bracelet, something like one of them slave bracelets Theda Bara used to wind around her upper arm—"

"Huh? Theda—?"

"She was one of them sirens in the silent films. Grandpa had a thing for her. Anyhow, that was what made him notice the bracelet, or whatever it was on her arm, over her nightgown. The thing looked expensive, not like something a factory worker's wife would wear, or even own. Grandpa said it was gold, with some kinda bug on one end and a lizard or something on the other."

Bib had felt dizzy from the scent of the river and the flowers in the cemetery, and asked, "If it was a bracelet, how come it had *ends*? I thought they're round."

"That's why Grandpa always said 'bracelet or *whatever.*' It wasn't a circlet, but a long wire of gold, wrapped around her arm. With doohickeys on each free end. A bug and a—"

"Yeah, I heard you before. And a lizard."

"Uh-huh, and there was stones set in it, too, or some shiny enamel work. Grandpa wasn't sure, on account of being color blind. Reds and greens all looked black to him, or at least gray. He was never too good at figuring out any stones but diamonds and sapphires. And opals."

"And what else about the girl?"

"Oh, yeah. Lucy. Well, when she saw Grandpa lookin' at her bracelet, she sorta slid it off her arm and did something with it before he carried her downstairs. Probably on account of she wasn't supposed to be playing with it. She left on the necklace and the earrings, so maybe her grandmother had given them to her or something."

"Hadn't they hauled her father back to the house by then?" Rhonda was coming their way, and Bib wanted to hear the rest of the story before she showed up.

"Yes. He was in cuffs, and somebody threw a jacket around his shoulders. Lucy said 'Hello, Daddy!' when she seen him, wanting to run over to him, but he just stiffens and says, 'Watch out for Lucy... just watch out for Lucy!' and then he wouldn't say no more, so they led him off. And after that the girl's aunts came up from downstate, and there wasn't no trouble until her aunt went crazy, but I think that was on account of Lucy getting in a family way and—*hello, Rhonda.*"

Bib put the empty box of Ho-Ho's in the bin, and followed it with the empty milk jug; afterward, he just sat, staring at the road, watching the few cars slowly roll past, their drivers intent on looking at the diminishing fall colors. They were mostly out-of-town plates from Minnesota and Illinois.

He again wished that he could have gotten Anna to listen to him when he tried to warn her about her grandmother. The old woman was no damned good, right from the start. Stealing her mother's jewelry while the woman was lying cold and bloody not sixty feet away, And the way she was when she got older. Bib hadn't told Anna about the complaints the department *had* received about Lucy Miner crapping on lawns and doing whatnot, when Bib was a rookie patrolman. No one had wanted to follow them up, and so they had buried them rather than face Lucy Miner's wrath.

And besides, no one wanted to further embarrass Tina or her little daughter. Bad enough they *lived* with Lucy "Where's Gramma" Miner?

Odd, Bib thought, as he half watched the cars slither down Abigail Avenue, *how everyone comes to the same conclusion—that Lucy knew where the remainder of her grandmother's body was dis-*

posed. I 'spose it was because she was in the house all along. But still, it is strange, sheesh, burying a hand and a little bit of arm like that. Too bad Lenny's granddad didn't get a good look at that bracelet or whatever. Maybe it belonged to someone who did take the body.—someone who bribed the kid into shutting up about it. Or maybe her daddy gave it to her to keep quiet.

Bib was so deep in thought he didn't notice that one of the cars was moving faster than the rest down the avenue by the park—a custom-painted maroon Pacer station wagon, with new red-on-white Wisconsin scenic plates. And he didn't take a second glance at the driver, even though he knew the man's face quite well.

Once Wally Inglass had made the sharp turn that put him on Lumbermill Drive for a block, before turning again, this time southwest, in the direction of the hospital bridge which fed directly into the four-way stop, Bib couldn't see him anymore without turning his head and staring through the mostly bare trees behind him—which he didn't do.

But if he *had,* he might have seen the maroon Pacer Speed down the westbound arm of the four-way stop, as if trying to outpace the lone, darkly speckled bird that was resolutely flapping a few yards behind it, as Wally's car headed for the dilapidated trailer park a couple of miles beyond the westbound stoplight—

—where Precious Isaacs and her family lived, and where Precious was always home alone on a Saturday.

SIX—Third Kill

Precious Isaacs's parents may have started out their married lives in a less than conservative mode, but now that they were both in their early thirties, the elder Isaacses did share something in common with their more staid fellow citizens in Ewerton—they were avid bingo players, a fact Wally Inglass knew well. His Louise (Mrs. Staid herself, in Wally's less than unbiased opinion) always sat in the seat ahead of the Isaacs clan—even their younger kids played—on the bus that took the players from Ewerton, Hunterstown, and Lumbe to the reservation, listening to them unconcernedly discuss the fact that Precious and Mayo would usually spend the evening alone out in the trailer, and wonder out loud when they'd become grandparents.

Louise was always so shocked and appalled, but Wally found the whole scenario most titillating...and quite convenient for his purposes.

And so, while Bib Stanley finally brushed the crumbs off his jacket and got back into the squad car, debating out loud whether he should call Anna to try and apologize, Wally Inglass slowed down his Pacer slightly, relishing the sweet approach to the Isaacses' run-down forest green trailer, where the Parks boy's rust bucket was parked sideways across the lawn. Wally had all afternoon, and he didn't plan to spend it in direct confrontation with Mayo, before he got rid of the punk and concentrated his attentions on Precious.

Remembering what the girl had written about him on the wall of building six, Wally Inglass smiled a tight, even little smile in the ovetheated confines of his maroon car, and said, "You'll wish you *could* do it with a donkey after I get through with you—if you have the strength left to do so much as swallow spit."

* * * * * * *

"What stinks?" Precious Isaacs shifted slightly, allowing herself to slide slowly off Mayo's splayed legs and her frowsy quilted pink nylon comforter, until her bare feet and uncovered knees hit the matted-down carpeting next to her poster-decorated bed alcove. Mayo raised himself up to a half-sitting position with his elbows, clearly displeased at the interruption of the aftrnoon's foreplay. Brushing aside the slippery spray of hair that had fallen, unnoticed, into his eyes, Mayo watched his girlfriend get to her feet and pad the yard of floor space that separated the bed she and her sister shared from the doorway, her small, slightly sagging breasts jiggling with each step. Her nostrils were quivering, turning slightly pink around the edges, as she said:

"I *smell* something...." Her forehead wrinkled under her pale bangs, making her resemblance to her mother more obvious and slightly ominous. Precious didn't venture out into the narrow swath of brown shag-carpeted hallway that connected all the abysmally tiny rooms in her parents' trailer home; instead, she hung back, her lower right leg raised and protectively wrapped around her left calf, her bottom lip caught under her small white teeth. Watching her, Mayo felt his erection slowly droop; he didn't like the pinched, frantic look on her face. It was too much like the way she'd looked when that dweeb Wally Inglass was hassling her yesterday.

"Mayo, go see what it is. The kitchen, go look in the kit—" and Mayo was halfway down the hall before she finished speaking, stepping into his jeans as he made his way to the grouping of tiny grease-runneled electric range, mildew-scummed stainless steel half sink, and small magnet-encrusted fridge Mrs. Isaacs dubbed "the kitchenette." The tiny corner of the trailer had its own grimy, oily odor, but this smell was different. It was a harsh, greasy, yet very *organic* redolence, one that Mayo had never before encountered. It was vaguely...dangerous, like the noxious warm smell of an electrical fire.

Mayo patted the walls next to the ivory-colored outlets, sniffed the range's twin burners, and opened the oven—nothing. But still, the sickening reek lingered, seemingly sourceless, yet *there.* Just when Mayo thought he heard a tiny sliver of sound, a cut-off squeak, something else captured his attention—Precious, screaming.

"*No!* Mayo, come back! It's *hiiim—Mayo!*"

Mayo Parks needed no further explanation of who "*hiiim*" was—that fat fuck Inglass. Mayo'd warned Precious over and over again about messing with the dude—didn't Mayo's brother Dusty have enough hassles with the shifty creep?—but Precious had kept on *pushing* the geek, goading the fat prick until he was good and mad.

Precious was glued to the narrow bit of beige paneled wall next to her bedroom doorway, holding her jeans and Def Leppard T-shirt across her pale, exposed body. Mayo elbowed her into the hallway itself when he saw Inglass's face pressed up against her bedroom window, but Mayo was too late to stop the inevitable. A second later, the window burst inward in a spray of glass and torn plastic screening. Shards of glass were everywhere—on the frowsy bedspread, the carpeting, Precious's long hair—and Wally Inglass was trying to hoist himself into the room, his hairy forearms exposed, his face shining with sweat and excitement, as he was saying in a voice all the more horrible for its calmness: "I don't have a bone to pick with you, Mayo, so you just go home now."

"Mayo, *run.* Go get *help,*" Precious urged as she pulled on her clothes. The boy started to say, "But the ph—" until she screeched, "It got took *out!* Go, Mayo, *go—*"

"You'd better listen to her, *Mayo,*" Wally taunted, and it was then that the teens saw the knife—a Lilliputian mother-of-pearl-handled penknife, not big enough for even a decent game of mumbley-peg, held in Wally's left fist. The EHS principal was unable to squeeze through the window, so he dropped out of sight. Mayo grabbed Precious by the arm and dragged her, still barefoot, to the front door, but Wally was already there on the front steps, pulpy purplish lips drawn back into a self-satisfied smile.

He nabbed Precious by the arm just as she and Mayo started to pass him. Mayo tried to yank her away, but Wally made a swipe for the boy's exposed chest, drawing a thin, beaded red line across the swath of skin between Mayo's nipples, leering with steaming breath, "I don't want you, unless you'd care to watch."

Mayo started to reach for Precious, but she shook her head and screamed, "The *car*. Go for *help*," before Inglass dragged her toward the scruffy-grassed backyard. Panting, Mayo looked around him, but in the rapidly gathering dusk, he saw no neighbors' cars parked outside the other trailer homes. Snow was beginning to fall, spinning hard pellets coming from every direction at once; as he tried to start his rust bucket, Mayo watched the snow collect on the hood in scrabbly, almost-dry-looking drifts.

The engine wouldn't turn over. And Mayo could hear his girl screaming something, her voice seeming to echo from every*where,* swirling around Mayo, while Inglass was saying something too low and garbled to be understood clearly. Panting, his breath hitching up in scared-child gasps, Mayo abandoned his car *(didn't I* warn *you, Precious, the guy's plugs are missing from the engine?),* and ran onto the road into town, looking for a light in a window, a passing car, any sign of sane life.

Cursing himself for pussying out, yet unable to go back and face Inglass and his knife, Mayo Parks didn't notice the unwholesome-smelling yet oddly sleek rat scurry out of the trailer's open door, down the cracked cement steps and onto the snow-dusted grass...nor did he see what happened in the rear of the Isaacs trailer before the sky behind him came alive with a squawk and flurry of oily, fluttering black wings.

SEVEN—Behind the Trailer

"Gramma!" the horse whinnied, with a nostril distending snort. "You must *go to Gramma!"*

"You'll like Gramma—the paper said *so," the rat chittered from her towering nest of urine-stained, tooth-shredded newspapers. Anna tried to flap away, but her wing tips were blunt, lopped off, useless in the hot, fetid, dragon breath gusting in misty waves from the little sewing room.*

Anna heard the dragon, a chitinous crunch of horny scale, rubbing against horny scale, and she saw the mangled body of the dog lying across the doorway, but the horse and rat didn't seem to notice, or care, as they nickered and squeaked in unison, "Get in there with Gramma—she wants you...she wants you." Then the Snake slithered across the smeared and odd-tracked threshold, glistening red banding its dark-scaled smoothness. The tips of its tongue flut-

tered with a sibilant, utterance, "Waaatch out for Luuucey...
waaatch out, Annnna—"

Until the horse crushed its head with a single, floor-pounding
hoofstrike, and the rat took Anna's right leg in her teeth and
dragged her across the floor, the bristly stiff yet yielding body of the
dog, and over the threshold of the lair of the dragon, past the single,
withered claw as the horse whinnied, "Gramma doesn't need that,
so don't pay it any mind, you hear? You hear?"

Flapping and fluttering, Anna pecked at the rat's mangy, offal-
scented fur, but the lumbering horse was close behind, sharp hooves
treading on dragging feathers and trailing hairless tail, making the
rat move faster, faster. The dragon shifted and heaved a fulsome
sigh within, her heavy breath shaking the knickknack shelf, making
the china whatnots rattle and knock against the shelf, until the
pounding was a live, fierce thing—louder than the horse and rat
combined.

* * * * * * *

Still half in her dream, Anna tried to burrow her head, deeper
into her stacked pillows, until their flannel-covered softness masked
the horrible pounding of the dragon's breath, but it didn't grow
softer. And the cats were both awake, marching around her legs,
their paws hard and painful against her soft thighs and calves.
Bruiser padded up to the top of the bed and tried to dig her out of the
covers, raking up her quilts with a sharp-clawed paw, while snuffling her with his huge, short-muzzled nose.

"All right...all *right*," Anna moaned, sitting up at the waist and
draping her arms around Bruiser's broad shoulders. The cat kept
poking his wet nose into her eyes, her cheeks, while the pounding
kept on, a heavy wooden drone.

"Oh, *damn!*" Someone was knocking on her front door, most
likely had been for quite a while. Anna screamed, "Coming!" as she
swung her legs out of bed, toed on her house slippers, and hurried
across the bedroom, pausing only to grab her robe off the gold hook
on the back of her door.

Whoever was knocking was patient but persistent—not the
break-the-door-if-I-feel-like-it pounding of her late neighbor Elmo,
or the timid tap-on-the-glass tinkle of the old ladies who went
around with issues of *The Watchtower* tucked in their mesh bags,
but a steady knuckles-on-door-frame rapping that could have been
going on for minutes.

Glancing at the lit LCD display of the clock near the doorway—6:37 P.M.—Anna kept repeating, "I'm up, I'm up—who is it?" as she padded across the worn-out shaggy carpeting until she felt the doorknob with one hand, and the switch for the porch light with the other, but didn't move either hand until she heard a muffled voice say, "It's Terry Von Kemp. Bib Stanley said for me to come get you—matron duties."

Simultaneously, Anna opened the door and flicked on the porch light. Through the narrow opening she peered out at Terry's shock of limp, greasy hair hovering a few inches above his fur-collared uniform jacket, and the fuzzy-cheeked face between, and said, "But you're in Sheriff Sawyer's department."

"Stu doesn't got a matron, least not one on duty tonight. Bib loaned you out to him. He said it was okay."

"Oh." Anna glanced past Terry's shoulder. The white sheriff's car was parked parallel to the overgrown patch of weeds and gravel she and Ma called their "driveway."

Not knowing how long Terry had been standing outside, and being too embarrassed to ask, Anna said, "C'mon in, Terry. I'll only be a couple of minutes. Sorry about the wait." She stepped aside to let him in, and hurried over to turn on the lamp on the trunk. Pulling her robe tighter across her blue-trimmed pink fleece pajama top, she said, "Lemme get dressed. It'll only take a minute. Please, sit down, or—"

"Can I have a glass of water?" Terry asked almost shyly, as he stood in the middle of the living room, hat in hand, his eyes careful not to rest anywhere close to where Anna was standing. He seemed more subdued than usual—not at all like he'd been on Monday morning.

On her way back to the bedroom, Anna said, "The kitchen is through the dining room, to your left. There are clean glasses in the draining rack," and it wasn't until she had shucked off her pajama bottoms and top, and was wiggling into her long johns, that she remembered Ma's catsup-scripted message blackening the cabinet doors. As she pulled her boots over her night socks—Bruiser and Mouth were "helping" her by butting their heads against her legs and feet—Anna shouted through the closed door, "Don't mind the mess. It's just me and the cats, and the maid hasn't been in for ages!"

Over the gurgle of water gushing through the tap, Terry shouted back, "This place is a lot cleaner than your Ma—it's really neat for someone who works all day," amending himself quickly and covering his gaffe with a noisy slurp of water.

As Anna pulled on the White Stag top she'd worn Thursday, finger-combed her hair before pulling it all back with a big barrette, and gave both cats a good-bye squeeze, she thought, *What did you used to do, Ma—tell everyone the house was a pig sty just because the kitchen floors weren't always clean enough to eat breakfast off? Or did you do it to make* me *look bad, even though you were the one who used to leave your dirty clothes all over the house?*

"I'm ready," Anna said as she stepped out into the tiny hallway that joined the bedrooms and the bath, and abutted the dining room. She could just see the edge of Terry's left arm as he stood facing the cupboards, reading what Ma had scrawled there. When he heard her voice, he jerked and angled his head around the cupboard, a guilty look on his face.

"Geez, you dress fast. I wish my wife could to that," he said, setting his half-empty glass on the counter before he followed Anna to the front door.

"That's just it, it's a trick. In the winter I sleep in underwear and socks," Anna said without embarrassment, adding as she shouldered her purse and patted her jeans pocket to make sure she had her keys with her, "When I get up early in the morning, I don't feel like doing much of anything, so I take what shortcuts I can." All Terry said in reply as she shut and locked the door behind them was, "Oh...I guess that makes sense."

As she stepped off the porch, Anna noticed that it had snowed a little—the first snow of the season—and wished she'd thrown on a jacket.

During the short, slippery walk to the car, Anna said, "I'd appreciate it if you wouldn't say anything to Stu or Bib about what was written in the kitchen—my mother wasn't herself when she did that."

"You can't wash it off?" Terry sounded more puzzled than accusing as he opened the door for her and then walked around front of the car to get into the driver's seat.

Anna sighed, waiting until Terry was seated beside her in a crinkle of newish leather and squeaking upholstery, before saying, "You wouldn't understand. It's the principle of the thing. Something between my mother and myself."

Like Ma always dropping her dirty clothes on the floor and furniture, making a mess like a two-year-old, and then making me clean it, and then blaming me if I didn't have the time to clean up the rest of the house. Like when Ma would get frustrated with her job at the FmHA, and throw a pot of food on the counter and leave the slop all over the walls and ceiling until I had to scrape it off with a spatula, rather than admit she'd caused the mess in the first place. Or like when I'd be delayed coming home, and Ma wouldn't lift a finger to touch the litter pans, even if they were overflowing. And then she'd claim that I was the one to blame for the house being "an outhouse, a fucking outhouse."

Instead of giving Anna a hard time, all Terry said was, "Yeah, sometimes you gotta live with a person to understand the stuff they do."

When Terry said no more for a few minutes, Anna settled back into the front seat of the squad car (there was an unpleasant, tangy odor, like the faint vestiges of skunk, lingering about the dashboard, but after smelling the old lady's lardish stink for years, Anna wasn't overly offended), and half closed her eyes, just barely watching the streets whiz past.

Terry drove down Lister Street, crossed Ewert Avenue, continued down Anna's street until he hit Railway Drive, went north on that street and made a left on Lumbermill Drive, his headlights making the snowy streets glisten. When he made the angular turn that took the squad car past tiny Ewert Park and across the hospital bridge, Anna straightened in her seat and asked, "Terry, where *are* we going? I thought we going to the station."

"Oh, sorry, I didn't tell you. It's something out of the city. That's why Stu's in charge, but he needed more manpower, so he called out the city police, too."

"What do you mean, *something?* I thought you had some woman under arrest and needed—"

Terry drove past the cluster of bright lights circling the hospital's emergency entrance in the already cocoon-like darkness, saying, "Once we find her, we'll need you. But she's not under arrest yet. At least, she wasn't when Stu sent me to get you."

The lights out this way were set far apart on the county Trunk, faintly illuminating the looming trees and weathered farm-type houses and sag-roofed barns set farther back from the road. Above the squad car, there was still no discernible moon, only a vague haze of light behind the scud of cloud overhead. And the farther they rolled out of Ewerton, the darker and more scattered the houses became—smaller, ruder structures set at odd angles to the road, each almost surmounted from the rear or side by huge silvery fuel tanks, and surrounded by the dark-laced hulks of rust bucket cars and trucks, and brand-new snowmobiles covered with plastic tarps.

Anna had seen this part of Dean County seldom, and always from the safety of a school bus going to a music festival or forensics meet, but never on foot, or in a car by herself. "Yahoo country," was what Anna always called this place, for sometimes, as the EHS bus whizzed past, she'd glimpsed the feral-eyed, wild-haired, flannel-shirted beings who lived in those barely human quarters. The thought of someone, some *woman*, being out alone and hunted in the boonies where the kooks roamed was a terrifying prospect to Anna—regardless of *what* the soon-to-be-arrested woman had done.

Now the houses on the right side of the road were of a more uniform size, and set in close rows near the road—a trailer court. At the far end of the court was a brilliant cluster of lights, gleaming like unblinking, fallen stars—flashing reds, whites, and blues; cones of sparkling headlight yellow; and the steady, greenish-tinged glare of floods. There was movement among the lights—dark figures with shining badges and buckles that alternately merged and detached themselves from the pockets of darkness around the long green trailer set back a ways from the other, slightly newer trailers. Yellow police tape imprinted with blocky black lettering was strung on leaning metal poles pounded crookedly into the scrubby lawn, further separating the garishly illuminated trailer from its neighbors.

Terry stopped the car close to the soft shoulder but made no move to get out, saying, "Don't look like they found her yet; it's a good thing you were asleep when I came to your house."

Anna looked at him quizzically, then said slowly, "I wasn't feeling that well this afternoon. Does it really *matter* that I was in bed before?"

Terry fumbled the key out of the ignition, not looking at her as he replied, "Oh, not really, it was just when Bib got out here and told me you were on-call matron, he said something about hoping that you had yourself a damn good alibi for the past few hours, on account of what happened out here." He headed in a rush before getting out of the car and slamming the door behind him. When Terry opened the door, Anna just nodded her thanks and then followed him across the uneven, snowflake-crunchy mixture of fallen leaves and scrubby grass that led to the spotlighted green trailer.

She wished that she'd thought to ask Terry if she'd be needing something heavier than the velour top she was wearing. She shivered as she walked a couple of paces behind Terry, over and past the snicking yellow tape, into the circle of lights, cars, and movement. It wasn't until she saw the strobe-like flash of a camera blinking one-two-three times, and wagging wiggle of dogs far behind the trailer, that a twangy, folksy voice began to speak-sing in her mind:

*They was using up all kinds of cop equipment
that they had hanging around the police officer station. They was taking plaster tire tracks and footprints and dog smelling prints.*

Suddenly Anna smiled—Arlo Guthrie was singing in her head,
that protest song, "Alice's Restaurant," from when she was a little
girl, about "the biggest crime of the last fifty years" in Stockbridge,
Massachusetts, home of the "three stop signs, two po-lice officers,
and one po-lice car," which managed to blossom into "five po-lice
officers and three po-lice cars" after Officer Obie found that envelope with Arlo's name on it under that half ton of garbage from Alice's converted church home, which Arlo and his friend had removed from Alice's home with the "shovels and rakes and implements of destruction," packed in the red VW microvan, and then
dumped off the side of that cliff onto the *other* pile of garbage already at the bottom of the cliff, before having a Thanksgiving dinner
that "couldn't be beat" at Alice's place.

Anna hadn't thought of the song since she'd heard it the past.
Labor Day, during a special radio countdown of the best sixty songs
of the 1960s on WBIZ, but as she tagged along after the sheriff's
deputy, passing what had to be a dozen city and county officers
she'd never even *seen* before, all busy talking coded gibberish into
their squawking, sputtering car radio mikes, sweeping the frost-crust
with their flashlights, snapping photographs with brilliant-bulbed
cameras, or simply conferring with one another, she stopped hearing
whatever hub-bub was going on around her, her ears instead guided
by Guthrie's funny-sad narration about the *"Twenty-seven eight-by-
ten color glossy photographs with circles and arrows and a paragraph on the back of each one, explaining what each one was to be
used as evidence against us."*

Anna had to suppress her giggles when Terry finally stopped
next to where Stu Sawyer and a state trooper were standing, close by
a ratty outbuilding big enough for a lawn mower, a gas can, and not
much else. Judging by the cloying reek of gasoline, that was about
all the little blister-sided building contained.

"Hey, Stu, you guys find her yet?"

Apparently, Stu Sawyer found being called "Stu" in front of the
new matron offensive, judging by the way his sagging cheeks darkened and his small eyes grew smaller and harder as he grumped in
reply, "No, we have not, *Deputy* Von Kemp; if you got any idea
how to flush her out, you go do it. I wasn't gonna do no touching of
her without a female officer present—or a matron, at worst." The

last was obviously for Anna's benefit, but Stu's usual blatty bark was filtered through Arlo's twangy voice sing-songing, "I don't think I can pick up the garbage with these handcuffs on," so if Stu meant to offend her, it didn't work.

Anna smiled in reply, shivering stoically behind Terry as Stu went on speaking to the trooper, oblivious to both of them: "'Cording to her boyfriend, they were approached about two, two and a half hours ago, and he was on foot at the time."

"Now *who* was on foot—the victim, or the girl's boyfriend?" The trooper, a man of about fifty or more, looked both cold and annoyed, but whether the latter condition was due to the former, or due to Stu's muddled, overly cautious account was difficult for Anna to tell. But Anna could tell one thing old "Satchel-Ass Sawyer" (so dubbed because his pants seats hung down flat and saggy) was trying to cover up something or more specifically, *someone.*

Reluctantly, Stu mumbled, "The *victim,"* then resumed his monotonal ramble. "And after he told her boyfriend to get lost, the kid tried to get in his car, but he found that someone had done something to it so it wouldn't start, so he had to hoof it to the nearest house where there was a phone. And since most folks out this way don't stay home come Saturday night, the kid had a long hike."

Terry was standing there, hands in his jacket pockets, his breath pluming out faintly multicolored and amorphous in the lights, until Stu mentioned the part about the kid having a "long hike." Snorting a couple of times, Terry interjected, "Didn't know that any of the Parks clan knew what to do with their feet, aside from puttin' them on a gas pedal."

"Shaddup," Stu barked, but in Anna's mind his remark became Officer Obie's terse reply to the handcuffed Arlo—"Shut up, kid." This time, Anna giggled out loud. Stu cast a sour glance her way but kept on talking to the trooper.

"So it wasn't until an hour and a half ago that he made it to a phone, and at first he wasn't making much sense, so my man didn't see the need to follow up on the call right off."

"In other words, you delayed responding to the call because you doubted the veracity of the girl's boyfriend—this Parks boy?" the trooper asked, obviously tired of Stu's little "no names, please" game. Terry Von Kemp squirmed in delight when the trooper said "this Parks boy," and Anna giggled again, when Arlo continued, "They took pictures of the approach, the getaway, the northwest corner, the southwest corner, and that's not to mention the aerial photography."

"You got a problem or something, girl?" Stu asked, turning his attention to Anna, but Arlo had already translated his question into Officer Obie's words: "Kid, we found your name on an envelope at the bottom of half a ton of garbage and just wanted to know if you had any information about it."

Giggling helplessly, surrendering to the utter, crazy, cover-up formality of the situation, Anna shook her head no. It was just like Guthrie's song: the mock seriousness that led to nothing, the glittering toys dredged up from the storerooms of the police and sheriff's department, all the elaborate "he said, he did" runaround, all for the purpose of hiding how totally inept Sheriff Sawyer really was. He hadn't responded to a call in time, and now someone was "the victim," and a woman was being sought for a crime (*a woman, Terry said "she" remember that...a woman is hiding out here in Yahooland, in the cold and dark*—), so here Stu was, trying to cover his flat, saggy ass and blowing his relative lack of cool when his new matron had a giggling fit.

"For cryin' out loud, Stu, aren't you going to get that girl a jacket? Can't you see she's freezing?" Anna turned around at the sound of Bib's voice. The police chief was coming from behind the trailer, having apparently caught the last of Stu's words to Anna.

Eager to get behind the winning—or at the least less stupid seeming—team, Terry quickly shucked off his jacket and draped it across Anna's shoulders, while Stu glared and the trooper sighed, kicking at the frosty grass stubble with his boot.

Bib moved closer to where Anna was standing before he said, "I think we've got her cornered. She's down in that patch of trees across from that gully behind the trailer."

("—till we came to a side road, and off the side of a side road was another fifteen-foot cliff, and at the bottom of the cliff was another pile of garbage. We decided one big pile was, better than two little piles and—")

"My officer heard something in the trees, and when he shone his light out that way, we all saw a flash of blue jeans and blonde hair. I know Precious, and it looked like her. But this isn't quite my jurisdiction, so if you'd come down with—"

"By now, the little bitch is probably halfway to Wright County," Stu grumped as he followed Bib behind the trailer. The state trooper and Terry joined him, as did Anna—after Terry doubled back and got her.

She was still half giddy with suppressed mirth, cold, tiredness, and what she now realized was a slow-blooming sense of fright, for aside from the still-hidden female, Anna was the only woman walking around in the light-pooled darkness.

Out in Yahoo country.

And even if all the men around her *were* policemen, they were still men, and ever since she had been small, the litany had been drummed into her head by the old lady, always when Ma was away, and little Anna was all alone with her Baba: (Men are bad. They have black ugly things in front, like old bananas. If they stick it up into you, it breaks off and rots inside you.) "Know what ham fat sounds like when you slice it off the meat? That's what sex sounds like."

(And the worst, although seemingly most innocuous statement, made to the steady back and forth beat of the rocker: "My Aunt Bella—that would be your *great-aunt—she* went crazy when she found out who I had your Ma with, but that was all right. I didn't like her *anyway*.")

Between the old memories of her Baba slowly, insidiously poisoning Anna's mind about the opposite sex, and her more current recollection of "Alice's Restaurant," Anna didn't actually *think* as she stumbled across the uneven lawn in back of the dark green trailer. Each thing she saw was automatically matched by an oddly appropriate—or ironically inappropriate—fragment of conversation or song lyric, completely freeing her brain from the need to formulate any fresh observations, rather like a very dark, very bloody little snuff film running on a continuous eight-track film loop in her skull, the actions of the celluloid beings repeating and repeating endlessly.

Off to her left was a circle of lights set up around a speckle-sheeted figure, anonymous save for the single black-shoed left foot sticking out the bottom, and the fisted right hand curiously high-set in relation to the rest of the shrouded body—

—*"shovels and rakes and implements of destruction—"*

("*rots* inside you—")

—and the pair of officers standing next to the body were smoking and flicking ashes past the cameras hung around their necks, and one said to the other, "Think they'll want to stick these in the annual?" before both of them snorted back stifled, oddly frantic laughter—

"—*color glossy pictures with circles and arrows and a paragraph on the back of each one—*"

("And if any boy comes up to you in school, and wants to hold your hand or anything like that, you tell him, "My Gramma says you're *bad*—")

THE AMULET, BY A. R. MORLAN * 171

—which they hushed to muted coughs as Bib and Stu passed within hearing range. And in the darkness beyond, the trees sharp-edged and deep *black-black-black* against the sooty, grayish sky, there were officers moving around, flashlights aimed at the snow-dusted ground, keeping in a line parallel to the barely leaved trees, and one of them was saying, "You have nowhere to go, Precious, and it's getting colder. Wouldn't you like to get into a nice warm car? C'mon, Precious, you can't stay out here all night. You don't want we should send the dogs after you," to which another officer remarked, "Why not? They didn't pick up her scent before—"

"—and footprints and dog smelling prints—"

("Men have an *awful* smell. You don't want to go with one of *them*. See where it got your *Ma*?")

"—mollycoddling the little bitch already," Stu grumbled, grabbing for the white bullhorn hanging from his belt that Anna had somehow missed seeing before. Next to Anna, Bib whispered, "Like a kid with a new toy," before Stu bellowed loud enough to be heard clear into the Upper Peninsula and parts of eastern Minnesota, "Precious Isaacs, you get out of those woods now!!! I'm not fooling around anymore, miss! You are under arrest! Now get out!!!"

The officers played their lights over the tangle of trees and wicked scrubby bushes, a thick blackish cluster of branches and thorns; curled, withered leaves; and even metallic strands of barbed wire that would have intimidated a grown man suited in armor—yet a woman was hiding in there.

Coming back to her own mind for a moment, Anna realized why the officers hadn't ventured into that thicket—if they weren't careful, they'd be razored to ribbons. And a dog would be little more than Alpo chunks. And that name kept drumming against her subconscious—*Precious Isaacs*—until realization sapped like a chilly wind through her body, past Terry's slightly sweaty-smelling jacket, through her velour top, right into the core of her being.

Precious Isaacs—that little blonde girl with the big mouth and the even bigger eyes. She was a grand-niece of the old lady's former neighbor, Mrs. Cooper. The little girl used to hang around Evans Street every summer—a thin little thing in Dean County Clothing Center castoffs, and no shoes, ever. But perceptive—

Anna recalled the summer when she and Ma were painting the old lady's house, trying to do a two-story-plus-attic brick house by themselves. Since Anna suffered from mild vertigo (even standing on a kitchen chair was a sickening experience), Ma was up on the ladder painting the second story, while Anna handled the first, so she alone heard the little girl ask, "Are you guys going to move?"

"Why no, Precious. What makes you think that?"

The little girl had twisted a long strand of blonde hair around one grimy finger before replying, "Because that's what people do when they're going to move out here. They paint and fix up a place." And Precious had been only four or five when she had said that. Even the child's mother (a broad-featured, babied-out, drab young woman who was close to Anna's age but looked ten years older) admitted that Precious was smarter than both her parents combined, when she told Anna about the time Precious and her siblings (three girls and a boy of indeterminate age—they were all undersized) unlocked a padlock on a backyard gate by figuring out the combination from viewing it backwards and from above.

But after Anna and Ma moved away from Evans Street, she hadn't seen Precious Isaacs, and gradually, the memory of the little girl and her weasel-faced siblings filtered from her consciousness. And now, with a start, Anna realized that the girl had to be in her mid-teens now—high school age. And if she was going with a Parks boy, that had to mean one thing: both Precious and her boyfriend would be likely candidates for Wally Inglass's annual pep rally hunt, and the corpse she'd seen had oddly short arms.

As unobtrusively as possible, Anna drifted away from Stu and his echoing bullhorn, away from the officers pussyfooting in front of the tangle of frost-sharpened growth beyond the gully, and made her way back to the floodlit body. Coughing lightly to announce her presence, she said when one of the officers turned around, "I'm with the department. Bib said I could take a peek."

Grinning, the pale officer who had turned to look at her nudged his companion, winked, and said, "This your baptism of fire? Go ahead—but don't touch the corpus delectable, okay? Lenny Wilkes still has to get his butt out here."

Anna felt their eyes on her back as she stepped into the ring of lights and knelt down next to the lone hand pokng out from under the sheet. With sick fascination, she recognized Wally Inglass's wristwatch, the metal band embedded with stray arm hairs.

"Now, don't sick-up on the sheet, 'kay? We can't go blaming it on old Wally," the other officer—a shorter, darker skinned man— said behind her, as Anna took the edges of the sheet in her fingers. The cloth was rough, the weave coarse and nubby, slightly cold-damp where it had rested on the snow.

The lights cast multiple, crisscrossing pale blue shadows on the sheet, and the many places where it peaked up, then settled down. And through the cloth, Anna could see bloody outlines—part of a belt buckle, two buttons, and the underlying shirt seam; a fleshy, uprising curve nestled in the hollow between the legs....

("Black, like a ripe banana. And when they put it in you....")

"See, she didn't sick on the sheet. Hey, just don't do a Lenny Wilkes and puke on your shoes. He's already famous for that," the shorter officer called behind her as Anna stumbled away, into the unlit darkness beyond the body. To her right, she could hear Stu bellowing through the bullhorn, "Give yourself up now. We have the area surrounded. You have nowhere to go."

"Kid, I'm gonna put you in the cell—"

Between Stu's oddly metallic, amplified words, all Anna heard was the delicate, fragile scrunch and crackle of her booted feet slip-sliding along the hoary grass. Pressing her hand over her mouth, she told herself, *You will not throw up* in *front of all these men. You will not do a Lenny Wilkes. You will hide yourself and then let it all rip,* while something heavy banged against her left side with each stride she took—a flashlight.

Holding her breath, feeling the ache in her diaphragm and upper palate as the vomit strained to get out, Anna pulled out the flashlight and aimed it at the ground. With her dark jeans and Terry's uniform jacket covering her pulled-back hair, Anna might pass for an officer to the most casual observer—and she hoped the moving flashlight beam would enhance the illusion. After all, officers were known to occasionally get sick during post-mortem duty.

Luckily for Anna, Stu's incessant bullhorned commands masked the sound of her retching. She had to contort her body so as not to splatter Terry's jacket, which made her diaphragm feel as if it were adhering to her lungs with each breath. By the time she was through, and merely spitting up bubbles, she was quite aways away from the trailer, deep into the blackness of dying countryside. In the distance she saw scrubby copses, their bases pooled in shadows, and a line of abandoned telephone poles along a distant dirt road, the uprights tilted in crazy directions. Looking backwards, she could see the thicket where Precious was hiding. True to Stu's blared-out word, there were officers circling the trees, their flashlights bright flecks in the blackness.

Figuring that she had no good business being this far away from the the murder site *(Oh, Wally, you pompous little putz. She should've bitten it clean off)*, Anna started to make her way back to the scattering of bright lights and incessant noise, taking the time to poke her arms through the sleeves of Terry's jacket, so she could close the snap front against the growing cold. In the distance, she heard Lenny Wilkes's exclamation, "never seen *nothing* like it!" and wondered if he'd be the one to lose his supper on the snow-thick frost.

Quickening her pace—her ears were going numb under her pulled-back hair—Anna professionally cast Terry's flash back and forth in an arcing motion, looking down as she did so, even though she expected to see no tracks but her own. But apparently she had set off on a slightly different angle onon the return trip, for Anna didn't even see her own footprints—those of a rabbit and some small rodent, most likely a rat. And a skittering of tiny bird tracks, in neat, winding rows.

And then she saw the bigger tracks—ring-necked pheasant size—that started out of nowhere, as if the bird had just landed but not shaped anything like those of the big game birds recently let loose in the county for breeding purposes. Hunkering down for a better look, Anna aimed the yellowish beam at the faint tracks, examining the odd gait with more than curiosity. *Birds don't walk like that,* she thought, as she backtracked a few feet, to follow the huge talon prints into the darkness, until they stopped being bird prints altogether and changed.

Into footprints—bare ones. Child-tiny, they continued on a ways, winding around to the west, until they, too, stopped in the middle of nothing. No tree to jump into, no tire tracks of a waiting car that could have picked up the child. And the new-fallen snow was undisturbed, unmarred by anything else for yards around, save for a few blurry dog tracks near the edge, as if someone had tightly reined in a running dog, then pulled it away.

"Anna Sudek. Wherever you are, get back here. We need you right now," the bullhorn blared. Glancing at the place where Stu had had been standing, Anna saw a cluster of flashlight beams, and in the middle, a smaller, bent shape, hugging itself. It was Precious—bigger, older, still recognizable.

Taking a last glance at the bizarre footprints, Anna ran back to the group of officers. Lenny Wilkes was whining by the prone body, Bib was relaying information over his radio, Terry Von Kemp was shivering in his light quilted vest, and Stu Sawyer was holding court in the middle of a circle of officers, standing next to Precious Isaacs like a fisherman holding up his torn-lipped catch of the day. Anna resisted the urge to knee Satchel-Ass in the groin as he said, "Here's your charge. From here on in you watch her, until we can scrounge up a real matron."

Stu's prize fish was shivering; her thin Def Leppard T-shirt was soaked with sweat and iridescent with unmelted snowflakes along her shoulders. Burrs, thorns, and bits of broken branches were tangled in her long sweep of matted hair, and her cold-reddened bare arms and face were crosshatched with abrasions and scratches. Worse yet, her feet were bare, the nails standing out brilliant red against the mottled pink-white white of her dirt-stained flesh.

One of the state troopers asked something about appropriate juvenile facilities, but Stu bullied him off with a gruff, "We got that taken care of," before he told Anna, "You and her get into that squad car. In the back. Wait, lemme get these on you first."

Before Anna knew what was happening, Stu had snapped a set of cuffs around her left wrist and Precious's right, then steered them toward his car and opened the back door. Shoving Anna in first, then boosting Precious in after her, he said, "I read the suspect her rights. She didn't want no lawyer, so if she says anything, you tell me."

"This girl is a *minor*," Anna snapped, not caring what he thought about it, and hoping that one of the state troopers might hear her. "She doesn't understand about waiving her rights."

Stu leaned into the car, across the shivering, hiccupping Precious, and growled at Anna, his fat face crammed almost directly into hers, "Listen, Miss File Clerk, I'm the sheriff around here, and this is my county. If you don't like it, you can go take a running leap into that gully there. You come from a family of experts when it comes to causing trouble, so I don't want to hear nothing out of you but 'Yes, sir,' okay? Now, Bib thinks you're a swell worker, and we all know the man's an asshole, which tells me what kind of worker you *really* are, so until I can round up Ginny Yarrow, who is *supposed* to be on duty tonight, I am stuck with you as matron. And if you hear some stuff that I should know about, you are duty-bound to tell me about it. You understand, Miss Sudek? If *she* says it, *I* hear about it."

With that, Stu backed out of the car. Anna bit her lip to keep from laughing when the sheriff grazed the top of his bear-like back against the door frame.

After Stu slammed the door shut, Anna was alone in the car with Precious. Even the interior light had winked out. Some illumination from the floods and flashlights spilled into the car, enough for Anna to see that Precious's eyes were glazed, her pupils large and glassy-black, as though she'd seen something so immense, so unimaginably vast, that the sight of it had permanently distended the windows of her eyes.

"Precious, do you remember me? Anna Sudek? I was painting my grandmother's house that summer? You wanted to know if we were moving?" Nothing. Anna could have been shouting from the surface of the moon for all Precious noticed her. Anna tried rubbing the girl's right hand with both of hers. No reaction. As she tried lightly running her fingernails along Precious's forearm, trying to rouse the girl from her catatonia, Anna watched Stu lumbering around, thinking, *You flat-bottomed creep. Too bad it isn't you under that sheet*, Precious began sniffing violently, her nostrils quivering like those of a rabbit.

"Precious, you okay?

"...stinks?...smell something...."—*sniff*—"Mayo, see what it is. Kitchen. Look in the kit—no, Mayo, come back! It's him. Mayo—" The girl's voice was a warbling squeal. Unable to hold Precious because of the cuffs, Anna shifted around so that she could rub Precious's back with her right hand. "It's all *right*," she said. "Wally's gone. He won't ever hurt you again. Wally's been...taken *care* of. He won't bother anyone again."

Precious began to breathe more evenly, her breath faintly bubble-gum scented, with an underlying sharp odor Anna guessed was semen. Not that she'd had any firsthand experience (to Anna, fellatio made about as much sense as sucking a milk shake through a used catheter), but Wally Inglass hadn't bitten himself down there. And in all likelihood, her boyfriend Mayo *(Mayo Parks? I knew Dusty had a little brother)* had been long gone before Wally got down to serious business.

The girl's eyes finally began to focus. When she noticed Anna, she grabbed onto Terry's jacket with her free hand as she rambled, "Stu said I did it, but I didn't. You gotta believe me. I know it looks like I did, but I *didn't*. I didn't even bite him, like Stu said. Inglass, he was *watching* us, from in the backyard, while me and Mayo was making out, 'cause Mom, and Dad and the little kids, they're gone. Left me alone for the weekend 'cause they trust me and Mayo, they like him. We weren't doing nothing *bad*, just making out. Then I thought I smelled something, like from the kitchen. Mayo went to check, and when he left, Inglass was at my *window*, looking in and grinning and...and I screamed. Mayo came, but Inglass pushed in the screen and the glass and everything. Glass was all over me and Mayo and Inglass said for Mayo to leave. He had a knife and he'd stick Mayo if he didn't get going, 'cause he didn't have a bone to pick with Mayo, and I told Mayo, 'Run, go get help,' 'cause our phone got taken out last month, and we ran for his car, but it didn't start, and Wally *grabbed* me. I was so scared and—and"—Precious swallowed back tears—"in the backyard, Inglass unzipped his pants and said, 'I didn't appreciate what you wrote about me in building six. Now, what do you suppose you're going to *do* about it?' I said I didn't know, and for him to just go away, and he just *laughed* and pulled out his di—his—"

"Never mind, I know what," Anna said quickly, patting the girl on the back, while an odd thought hit her: *I'll bet it smelled like bacon—rancid bacon.*

"So he said, 'First you can suck this, you little donkey,' and I said 'No way,' but he reached over and grabbed my hair to pull me level with it and then...then *it* swooped down and went for his eyes, and he let me go, and then I—"

"His *penis* swooped down on you?" Anna didn't understand.

"No, *no*...the bird, the big black *bird.* I don't know where it came from, but it flew down and got his eyes, then it went for him all over, pecking everywhere, and Inglass even got out his knife—it was a little penknife, just a dinky thing—and he tried for the bird, but it wouldn't let go of him, and I was screaming, 'Good for you, Wally, I'm *glaaad,*' but nobody was around to hear us, and it was just Inglass doing a dance around the backyard with his pants slipping down his legs and his dick flopping outside his briefs and he got all tangled in his pants and fell down in the snow and the bird kept at him, until he dropped the knife, and then the blood went out in this big arc from his neck, y'know, and then the bird...then it went for his—"

Precious looked at Anna from behind that tattered curtain of hair, her eyes wary yet undeniably vindicated as she whispered—"...*dick,* and it went at it until it was like a worm that a fish chewed and left on the hook. I never saw a bird *do that.* And then it got real big—like a pheasant, only bigger and black, except for this place on its one wing where it was sorta greenish against the black and red. It flew around Inglass, looking at him, and then it...then it *pooped* on him, like he was a statue or something. It was so quiet out I heard it splat on his pants. And then it flew off *that* way..."—Precious raised her free hand in the direction where Anna had seen the tracks in the snow—"...and when it landed, it...it...oh. *shit,* you won't *believe* me, *nobody* will." The girl's voice lowered to an anguished sob, and she leaned back of the seat, her eyes scrunched closed.

Anna glanced out the window. Stu was starting to head toward the car, walking slowly and still showing off, playing king of the sandpile. She had a minute, maybe two at best.

"Precious, *what* happened? Tell me, please, I *will* understand," she pleaded, as Stu lumbered closer and closer to the car.

"Promise you won't tell?"

"*Yes, yes—*" Stu was perhaps forty feet from the car.

"This bird...it *changed*. So fast I couldn't, like, make it out, 'cause the sun was going down and it was getting dark real fast, and it was still snowing a little. But there was that bird on the ground, walking around, and then there *wasn't*. It like—*like melted*, only not down but *out*. Know what I mean? It melted *out into a little girl.* The black went gray, then whitish, and there was this little girl walking in the field, in some sorta nightie, and in the last rays of light I saw this thing glittering on her arm, like a bracelet or something, and it was green, a green stone, and it was hard to see, but I looked real hard and it looked like a little bug or something, on a golden twist, up here"—Precious clutched her upper arm. Stu was twenty feet away, and hurrying—"...and I started to head toward her, calling for her to come back, to *thank* her, y'know! and she heard me and got scared and started to run off. And then she *melted again,* only this time *up,* and then she was back in the air, flapping away...it was a bird again. And *nobody* will ever believe *that*," Precious whispered as Stu opened the driver's door. Cold air and Stu's woodsy aftershave wafted into the car before he slammed the door. Terry Von Kemp entered through the front passenger door, looking back longingly through the mesh divider at his jacket.

"She say anything?" Stu asked, not bothering to look at the women in the backseat. Anna shifted until there was a hand-space between her and Precious. Glaring at the back of Stu's boar-bristle head, she said, "No."

"Better not have," Stu grumped, starting the car as an ambulance pulled up, siren off, lights off, rolling quiet and secretive in the night, all the better to not attract attention.

Leaning back in the seat, the handcuff cold around her wrist, Anna tuned out the crackle of the car radio, Stu and Terry's cryptic coded replies, and Precious Isaacs's snuffling breathing, as the memories crashed down on her.

"—like a bracelet or something. It was green, a green stone... and it looked like a little bug or something, on a golden twist."

Yes, Precious, Anna thought, *you're right—it* is *a little bug. A beetle, to be exact. A beetle like Ann Blyth used in that old* Twilight Zone *episode about the movie queen who lived forever by sucking out people's juices with a scarab beetle. And the other end of the twist was a snake, but the "bracelet" wasn't just a bracelet—it could be twisted into a coiled ring, or pulled out wide enough to be a necklace, especially if you're small in the neck, like a little girl. When you're small enough to think scarab sounds a lot like* scareab, *which is what it did to me. Oh, Lord, did it scare me. Ye gods, I thought I'd forgotten it—I wish I had—but it was real. Every bit of it* wlth *the old lady was real. Those scratches on her arm—where did she get them? How? Ohmigod. And those crazy stories she told about her Gramma, and that "night skirt"—they had to have been true, too. Ohmigod, I didn't want to believe...I couldn't believe it... can't believe that and remain sane...*but it's true. *The thing in the old lady's little bag is alive. And it is magic, just like she said.*

And all those stories the old lady used to tell, of her Gramma "gctting even" with people—true, all of them. And she loved her Gramma for doing those things.

Anna watched the lights whip past the windows, closer now. with the red four-way stop hung high over the approachiag intersection, and thought, *You knew all along, didn't you, Anna? When they all died, deep inside you had to have known, had to have suspected. Bib suspects, too—oh, not what you do, hut he sees the pattern, suspects that I'm behind it, not the old lady. No, not Lucy. Little Lucy and her missing Gramma—the one she's so sure I would've liked....*

Anna felt cold horror roil in her guts as she wondered, What are *you up to, old lady? Why? Why now? Is all this for you, for me...or for her? Is it for your Gramma, wherever she is? Because you know, don't you? You knew where Granny was all along, and only you knew why you wouldn't let anyone take her away. You let your father go to the nuthouse, just so you could have your fun. "Watch out for Lucy." Oh, you were so right, Great-grandpa, you were so right.*

"Watch out for Lucy," Anna whispered so softly no one could hear her—so very softly she could repeat it again.

"Watch out for Lucy."

INTERLUDE

OCTOBER 24, 1931

Lucy dropped to the floor of her Gramma's room like a snowflake hitting a griddle—first all tiny and flapping and white, and then big again, her nightgown hem wide and drifting around her thin calves.

And the pretty-yet-ugly golden thing that had been a greenish glint on Lucy's wing *(My wing! Wait'll that Veenie Nemmitz sees this!)* uncoiled from around her right hand before it tightly wound itself into a spring-tight ring, the bug head snugged close to the snake head, and went to sleep in her palm. Lucy prodded it with a small blunt fingertip, and the golden ring jerked slightly, like Daddy did sometimes when Lucy tried to make him wake up on a Saturday morning, and he pushed her away with his shoulder without moving anything else, or opening his eyes.

"You can't sleep *now*," Lucy protested softly, poking the thing in her palm into wakefulness. "You gotta work for Gramma. Come *on*," she pouted, rubbing the shiny greenish stone back of the bug. It looked like one of those bugs with the big, hard shiny backs that lived under the old clay flower pots Mother kept out on the narrow walkway behind the house, only the legs were funny. And the snake was like the little garter snakes Vernon Nemmitz (that ugly Vernilla's twin brother) liked to pick up by the tail and throw at the girls at recess, only *this* snake didn't have a skinny little tail. Its tail was the bug, which Lucy thought was pretty funny, but right *now,* she was mad at the coiled thing.

Giving it a squeeze, she whispered, "You go on *Gramma* now. You don't need her skirt anymore. Here, I'll set you on her."

Lucy tiptoed forward, her bare toes casting for splinters in the plank flooring as she neared the bed. The light was better now, and Gramma was easier to see—a big rise on the bed, with two floating white patches where her face and hands should be. Lifting the cloth in the middle of the old woman's body, Lucy dumped the thing out

THE AMULET, BY A. R. MORLAN * 181

onto Gramma's folded hands, and held it in place with her own tiny palm.

"There," she whispered, oblivious to the soft sounds of floor-boards upstairs, as someone walked slowly down the hallway between the bedrooms. "Now, you make Gramma all better, so she can watch me when I take you upstairs." Lucy was planning what she was going to do up there. Mother was first—that much was for sure.

Just *what* Lucy was going to do to her was something she was going to keep secret until Gramma actually saw it. Her Gramma loved surprises, and Lucy loved it when her Gramma was happy, so she wanted what was going to happen later to be just right.

Under her down-pressing hand, Lucy felt the thing working against the cold, stiff flesh of Gramma's big hand. The golden thing uncoiled to loop itself around Gramma's hand and wrist, like one of those vamp bracelets that fat old rich lady, Mrs. Holiday, wore. The kind of bracelet Mother said was "crass."

Sensing that the thing knew what to do once it had been coaxed onto Gramma, Lucy stepped back, watching, hopping from one foot to the other on the bare floor like this was Christmas Eve and she was seeing Santa Claus's boot heels emerging out of the fireplace flue, only Christmas wasn't for another two months.

At first, nothing happened. Granhna was still quiet, still *still* and the only sound in the sachet-and-wool-scented room was the sound of Lucy's hitching breath, and the first hint of a welling sob.

And then, so slowly that at first Lucy thought she was imagining it, *wishing* it, Gramma's hands began to move, flexing stiffly under the white handkerchief, the fingers slowly arching with soft cracks of rigid bone to form a little raised steeple.

"—open the doors, and out come the people!" Lucy chanted the finger-game rhyme under her breath as the hankie on Gramma's face fluttered, then sucked in and out around the peak of her nose, and Lucy stopped hopping in place, and pressed her legs together tight, like she did when she had to tinkle, and recess time was only a few minutes away. Heart racing in her tiny chest, Lucy's ears were pounding, almost drowning out the sound of the linen handkerchief slowly sliding off old, dry skin with a faint, whispery, snake-shedding-its-scales sound.

"Oh...*Gramma*," Lucy whispered in awe and delight. This was *better* than Christmas, and *much* better than Halloween, which was only a week away.

And as Lucy's Gramma shifted her white head on the cross-stitch, lamb-embroidered pillowcase with a barely audible, rusted-hinge motion, Lucy reached out one of her hands to pat Gramma's wrinkled, still death-withered cheek. The little girl saw and heard only her beloved Gramma. She didn't notice at first that someone was coming down the stairs, panting and moving quickly, frantically, through the living room, long quilted robe and flannel nightgown swishing, and satin mule-slippered feet *scuff-scuffing* across the slightly dusty plank flooring.

PART TWO

THE BEETLE AND THE SNAKE

The master horse ordered a sorrel nag, one of his servants, to untie the largest of these animals and take him into a yard. The beast and I were brought together,and our countenances diligently compared, both by master and servant, who thereupon repeated several times the word *Yahoo.* My horror and astonishment are not to be described, when I observed, in this abominable animal, a perfect human figure.

—JONATHAN SWIFT
Gulliver's Travels

On what wings dare he aspire?
What the hand, dare seize the fire?

What the hammer? what the chain?
In what furnace was thy brain?
What the anvil? what dread grasp
Dare its deadly ferrous clasp?

When the stars threw down their spears,
And watered heaven with their tears,
Did he smile his work to see?
Did he who made the
Lamb make thee?

—WILLIAM BLAKE
'The Tyger"

Little lamb, who made thee?
Dost thou know who made thee?

—WILLIAM BLAKE
"The Lamb"

CHAPTER SIX

SUNDAY, OCTOBER 25, 1987

ONE—Anna (2)

Anna Sudek hadn't arrived home until well after four o'clock that Sunday morning, and as a consequence, she didn't wake up until she felt the weak, only slightly warm beams of the sun branding her cheek as she curled on her right side, facing the west wall of her room. Mouth, still full from the hurry-up meal of Meow Mix she'd sprinkled in a big foil sheet cake pan a few minutes after Terry Von Kemp had dropped her off at her door, was curled in the valley of her bent knees, while Bruiser was staring out the window at the backyard.

Anna pushed up the sleeve of her White Stag top—she hadn't bothered to remove more than her shoes before crawling in bed—and glanced at her Lorus watch, a birthday gift to herself the previous January: 12:27.

"Eight hours?" she mumbled into her pillow as she let her head flop down weakly. Judging from the hung over way she felt, she would have guessed she'd only had a minute's rest. With her right knee she nudged Bruiser, saying, "C'mere by Mama," and patted the empty space next to her pillow. The neutered tom padded over to her, his huge feet making the bed alternately sink and rise, then flopped down on his left side so that he was facing her.

Massaging his wide cheeks and broad skull with her left hand, Anna whispered, "What are we going to *do*, Bruisie? Hmmm? I can't tell Stu or Bib what I saw, what I heard. They'd have me locked in a cell next to Precious in fifteen minutes, and have me shipped down to the loony bin with the old lady's dad within the hour. *If* the old goat is still down there. Probably six feet under, he is."

Bruiser regarded her with his wide-set, deeply green eyes; they were somber eyes, yet loving, too. He reached out a paw to touch her cheek, stroking her skin with the rough-skinned pad. Anna took his furry paw in her own fingers, and gave it a squeeze before pressing the fleshy pad against her check. Tiny nail tips dug into her flesh as she went on, "I still swear I you can understand what I say to you—can't you?"

Bruiser blinked in reply, making Anna laugh bitterly as she continued, "Figures—'spose you'd have to be an animal to sort all *this* out. Not that any of it makes much sense to begin with...."

Closing her still-burning eyes, Anna remembered what had happened after Stu had driven the squad car to the station. Anna had had to fingerprint the girl ("might as well use some of that CEP-money training you got, Sudek"), but she'd balked at strip-searching her. And since the men couldn't do it, they'd just put the girl in one of the cells—after all, they'd found Wally Inglass's almost absurdly tiny pocketknife, and since it roughly matched the size of his many wounds, it was being held in evidence as the murder weapon. Anna had said nothing when she'd seen the Baggie-enclosed knife; she *couldn't* say anything without getting herself either fired or arrested, most likely both.

While another of Stu's deputies drove around Ewerton and beyond, looking for Ginny Yarrow's car in the parking lot of every watering hole between Lumbe and Hunterstown, Anna had to sit outside the girl's cell, watching her to make sure she didn't try to strangle herself with her T-shirt, or attempt some other unlikely form of suicide.

For a brief moment, Arlo Guthrie's mocking voice was in Anna's head again, explaining how Officer Obie took away the singer's belt so Arlo couldn't hang himself for littering, and "took out the toilet seat so I couldn't hit myself over the head and drown," and even removed the roll of paper, so Arlo couldn't unfurl the strips out the window and shimmy down the tissue-sheets: "Obie said he was just making sure." And if it hadn't been for what Precious had said, and for what Anna had seen out there in the yard, Arlo's recitation of his troubles in the Stockbridge, Massachusetts, jail would have sent her into another round of helpless giggling.

But by that time, even Arlo's littering troubles seemed bleak and dire, impossible to ignore or get out of, even if *his* judge had the Seeing Eye dog, and would *never* be able to look at those "twenty-seven eight-by-ten color glossy pictures with the circles and arrows and a paragraph on the back of each one.

While Precious had curled herself into an armadillo ball on the bare mattress in her cell, Anna rested her head against the squared-off cell bars, the cold metal almost hot against her forehead, thinking.

The old lady had followed Wally out to the Isaacs trailer, either trailing him from his house, or spotting him as he was driving. She had slithered or trotted or flown. It didn't really matter *which* animal guise the old woman had taken—she had done it. And now Wally was pecked to death. Only, the beak wounds looked so much like knife wounds—especially to "forensics geniuses" such as Lenny Wilkes, Doc Calder, and all the rest of the bottom-of-their-class physicians employed at Ewerton Memorial—no one was bothering to question their origin.

Anna seriously doubted that they'd be sending old Wally down to Madison for an expert autopsy—from what she'd overheard Stu saying to his men, and to that state trooper Anna had good reason to believe that this was already regarded as an open-and-shut case. Wally Inglass had had problems with both Precious and her boyfriend, and he'd merely come out to the Isaacs trailer to have a talk with the girl's parents.

That was what Stu told the state troopers. He'd made a few calls to some of the young couple's teachers, and they'd agreed that Precious and Mayo were just looking for trouble, and they'd finally found it. Mayo Parks's story was partially discounted; he was considered "unreliable," thanks to his own run-ins for disorderly conduct and DWI. Also, Mayo failed the Breathalyzer test Stu insisted he take after Precious was booked, and he was brought into the station for questioning.

While Anna hadn't actually seen the boy—the cells were a distance from the main lobby—she half recognized Mayo's voice as he shouted at Stu, "But I wasn't drinkin' in a *car*. No law on the books 'bout drinkin' in a house, in a *bed*. Precious and I wasn't the ones who broke into her bedroom. The glass was busted *in*—"

"Which you and her done to cover up!" Stu had thundered, and Anna knew then and there that the case had been tried and won already, without the need of a judge, jury, or fat-cat lawyers in their sheer socks and three-piece suits. And the ironic thing was, no one would really *care* about what happened to the girl; Wally Inglass had always been getting this or that award for "Educational Excellence," or whatever claptrap the Jaycees or Kiwanis or Lions saw fit to engrave on those little wood and brass plaques they handed out every year at their respective banquets, even though he was crazy.

Wally had helped to give a leg up to the sons and daughters of area businessmen who, in any rational and fair educational system, would have been kicked out as unteachable back in the third grade, so a lot of people *owed* him for that...even in death. And when one of the cruds from the blistering-paint-and-missing-shingles trailer park out past the four-way stop was present at the scene of his death, and her equally trashy boyfriend had witnessed part of the incident, whose version of the truth would be believed by all those grateful businessmen, and their marginal-but-well-established Jaycee and Jayceette offspring?

Listening to Mayo Parks shout, "I ain't sayin' *nothin'* till I get me a lawyer!" Anna felt a strange stab of pity for the boy and his girlfriend. They weren't what she ever would have considered "her" type of people, yet what she had seen and heard only an hour before made her realize that she had a lot more in common with "their" type of people than she could *ever* have in common with Stu Sawyer's brand of truth and justice.

Why did you ever think you were above these people? Anna had asked herself, as Stu Sawyer barked, "Well, then, you have the right to remain *silent*—but you still ain't goin' nowhere!" *Everyone has thought of you as a no-good, a crumb, ever since you were born, and all because of what your great-grandfather did. And because of the old lady—don't forget that. My god, Anna, at least this girl's grandparents didn't go crapping on people's lawns, like a dog.*

Things got crazy out in the lobby when Dusty Parks and his father showed up to take Mayo home. While the men out-shouted and outswore Stu Sawyer, there were sounds of a scuffle, and the sound of something heavy and at least partly glass crashing to the floor. When Ginny Yarrow came in to relieve her, Anna saw that Mr. Coffee had been permanently relieved of his duties. Ultimately, Stu hurried past Anna, half dragging Dusty Parks through the cell block, and shoved him into the cell at the end of the hallway, saying, "Cool off, string-head...don't go weavin' those locks of yours into a rope, hear? Anna was tempted to add, "Don't forget to take away the toilet paper and the seat," but thought better of it as Stu thundered past, hardly giving her a second glance as he went back to the lobby.

Watching his squared-off, flat rear end shifting under his saggy trousers, Anna was reminded of the way an ape walked, or a grizzly bear, and told herself, *Must have been born in the year of the boar. Nothing else on that chart of the old lady's would fit something like him. What was it the old lady said she was—the rat? Wonder if she ever "did" that animal. I know she was the bird Precious saw...but how do I tell the girl that, let alone the rest of them? It's like Professor Nuzzi used to tell us in Composition 201—"I don't want to know what you know, I want to know why you know it."* Her short, ener-

getic, histrionic college English professor had been deeply opposed to intuition, or gut feelings, saying with a wave of his pale, thickly black-haired hand, "Emotions aren't enough—I want logic in your writing!"

Anna hadn't seen her professor since she'd graduated from the small liberal arts college over in Wright county over seven years before, let alone thought of him, but for some reason his bespectacled face remained projected on her memory-screen for the rest of the night and into the early morning, even as she tried to puzzle out just what her grandmother had been *doing* this past week.

The old woman had killed Inez Hibbing, and caused the crash that had left Anna almost neighborless since Thursday. How or even *why*, Anna didn't really know, but she suspected it had something to do with an animal—one with an odd green patch somewhere on its body.

For now Anna remembered that time, on an afternoon roughly a quarter century before, when Ma had been out shopping or whatever, and little Anna's Baba *(God, when did I stop calling her that?)* was taking care of her. And she was sitting on Baba's lap, in the big old rocker that had belonged to Baba's grandmother, and Baba was telling Anna her "Gramma" used to rock little Lucy in *just* the same way, when she suddenly said to little Anna, "Do you want to see your great-great-gramma, Anna?"

Confused, little Anna had said, "But we visited her last week. In the cemetery, when we took the flowers out."

"Oh, Anna, that's only her *hand* in the coffin. Didn't your momma tell you that? Oh, now, don't cry, it's not that bad," Baba had soothed, as little Anna had begun to sob at the thought of having been to visit a disembodied *hand* resting in a big old box in the ground—a hand that might come clawing out of the earth like the one in that old black-and-white movie Ma had let her watch on the Saturday horror movie on channel five the week before, to come hitching and scrabbling down the long road and finally hide under little Anna's bed, waiting to clamber up her sheets and try to strangle her, like it strangled the fat man with the bugged-out eyes and oddly accented whining voice in that movie.

"It's just her *hand* out there...but I can make you see her," Baba had cryptically promised, as she fumbled with the neckline of her cotton print dress, adding, "Before that happens, you have to show me you're big enough...and *brave* enough." And little Anna saw Baba bringing out the little white drawstring bag from inside her dress, the cotton bag from Anna's bubble gum—the one she'd been looking for herself, wanting to give it to her Tammy doll for a clothes bag.

"*My* bag—" little Anna started to say, reaching for the cloth pouch, but Baba grabbed Anna's fingers and gave them an unpleasantly hard squeeze.

"No, no, my baby lamb, you don't open this—only *Grammas* can do that. It might *bite* you," Baba had teased, but the...oily sound of her voice didn't make little Anna laugh.

And then Baba opened the knotted drawstring, as she explained something little Anna didn't understand—something about cotton being good because it was "real, and was once alive, yet plastic was good, too, because it *hadn't* lived, and all the while Baba's semi-opaque nails were glinting in the weak sunlight as she untied the bag and slowly opened it up, to reveal a coiled, golden object wrapped in a piece of slightly greasy-looking, dog-eared plastic.

And Little Anna watched in awe and terror as her Baba unwound the plastic from around the thing and began to play with it, like a child fooling with a Slinky, shifting the sinuous, golden, wormlike body from one set of fingers to the other, making the ugly double heads flop and jerk. The tiny, glittering dark eyes of the glassy, green-winged bug and the pointy-snouted, mean-looking snake were looking at little Anna, and then Baba stretched the coil out to its full, slightly slimy, length, just long enough to wrap around Baba's wrist, and just barely long enough to go around little Anna's neck.

And while Precious alternately shivered and jerked in her in her cell, Anna watched but didn't watch the girl, as she remembered how little Anna felt like she was burning up, only from inside—everything within her puddling like candle drippings, melting and squishing together—until the too-hot-inside feeling went away and then she remembered how things looked all funny, yet *wrong,* after the strangely warm metal-that-wasn't-hard touched her skin.

For suddenly, nothing was itself. Everything looked alien, like little Anna's eyes weren't hers anymore, and just those few seconds had been enough, almost *too* much.

Now I remember. The old lady had scratches on her arms and neck after I worked the thing off somehow—as if a cat or some taloned bird had scratched at her, trying to pull away from her. But she only put on her old lilac woolen sweater with the horny yellowed ivory buttons, and told Ma that she'd become chilled, and she didn't stop wearing the sweater until the scratches were healed over. And she never showed me the golden thing again. But there was that time, that Christmas, when the bat flew out of and then into her room, the time when she scratched me, and later on, Ma wouldn't admit that it had happened—she claimed that I'd dreamed it all up. What was it, Ma? Did she put the golden thing on you, when you were my age? Or did you see her changing-melting, as Precious described it? Whatever it was that happened that afternoon when the old lady placed the thing on my neck, it must have meant that I wasn't brave enough to see her Gramma...if that's whatever it was she had in mind in the first place.

And now, as Anna curled up under her covers, and Bruiser pushed his vaguely urine-smelling paw against her face, she again tried to think of the old lady, and the golden ring that moved...until something connected.

The *bug*—the green, glasslike beetle on the one end of the ring—was a scarab beetle, like the Egyptians used to adorn their jewelry, and their talismans. She had taken a course in mythology, which had included an overview of magical practices in various ancient cultures, as a prelude to the myths themselves.

They hadn't spent much time on Egyptian magic or mythology, only a couple of class sessions, but Mr. Nuzzi had made the students buy a couple of paperbound books about that culture—Mr. Nuzzi *always* ordered enough books to fill a small bookcase for each upper-level class he taught, most of which he never referred to during the course of the semester, let alone made assignments from. Usually he chose such esoteric, difficult texts that they were impossible to unload after the class was over (and his constant shifting around of texts each time he conducted a certain class didn't help), let alone try to sell them for cheap at a garage sale, as Anna had tried to do shortly after she and Ma moved to Lister Street.

Anna got out of bed, remembering that she'd piled all her textbooks in a cardboard carton and stored it in the basement to keep the cats from getting into the box and peeing on the books.

Bright sunlight turned all her pulled-down shades into brilliant gold-white rectangles, but Anna didn't pause to raise any of them as she hurried through the silent house and made her way down the narrow, vinyl-covered steps to the basement, Bruiser following close behind her. He made it downstairs first, and "helped" her sort through the many boxes of old clothes, too-good-for-the-dump items she and Ma had picked up from after garage sale refuse on their scavenging runs, and plastic Christmas garlands and ornaments.

Finally, in a detergent carton shoved next to the bigger box that contained Anna's college notebooks and term papers, an entire education compressed within four corrugated brown walls and covered with a fitted lid, she found the books. Pulling the box down off the cat-splintered, built-in wooden shelf, Anna let out a gurgling squeal when a silverfish slithered off the top flap and onto her hand.

"Oh, great—now I'll never sell the bastards," she muttered, shaking her hand before she took the books out and set them down next to her on the cement floor. Bruiser sat a short distance from Anna, regarding her solemnly.

"Am I doing this right?" she asked him, and he padded forward to rub his huge head against her crouching thigh, purring and letting out little crying noises.

Anna lifted out a purple-and-black-covered trade-size paperback and whispered, "Bingo."

Egyptian Magic, by E. A. Wallis Budge, "WITH 20 ILLUS-TRATIONS," the cover promised. The Dover book had never been opened; the creamy white pages smelled ink-fresh as she paged through the volume.

"Okay," she said aloud. "We're going to find out why I know what I know...whether I understand it or not."

Two hours later, the dining room table was covered with the remains of Anna's brunch—freezer-burned lunch meat and bread—and page after page of spiral-bound notebook paper, covered with Anna's sprawling, chicken-tracks handwriting. She scribbled down notes whenever she noticed something that seemed important. That was how she'd done it in high school and college. She'd read the information and jot it down before actually digesting it, then study the notes later—and she'd been seventh and fourth in her respective graduating classes, and *magna cum laude* in college. As far as booklearning went, Anna did fine; it was only in personal relations that she'd failed, and as far as college went, that had been enough to keep her out of the education department ("Anna, you're smart, and highly motivated, but I just think you'd have trouble relating to the students in a classroom," her adviser had told her before he had coerced her into dropping her education classes and concentrating on her ultimately useless liberal arts course of study).

Today, Anna was determined to teach herself something beyond the idle study of an ancient race and its arcane beliefs, even if the lesson was an obscure one, and even if the knowledge gained couldn't actually help her.

Slowly, Anna scanned the pages, jotting down phrases and longer passages, not really thinking of how they all fit together, just knowing that they did, somehow:

...Egyptians...famous for their skill in the working of metals...attempts to transmute them...employed quicksilver...

...belief that magical powers existed in fluxes and alloys...

...magical powers..."Khemia," "the preparation of the black ore" (or "powder") which was regarded as the active principle in the transmutation of metals.

...perpetuate the reputation of the Egyptians as successful students both of "white magic" and of the "black art."

Historian Mas'udi mentions an instance of powers of working magic...a native of village of Zurarah...employed his time in working magic... transformed himself into a camel...made the phantom of an ass to pass through his body;...having slain a man, he cut off the head and removed it from the trunk, and then, by passing his sword over the two parts, they united and the man came alive again... recalls the joining of the head of the dead goose...and the coming back of the bird to life....

amulet...Arabic root meaning "to bear, carry," hence *amulet* is "something carried or worn"...name is applied broadly to any kind of talisman or ornament to which supernatural powers are ascribed... not clear whether the amulet was intended...to protect the living or the dead body....was originally worn to guard its owner from savage animals and from serpents.

Amulets...(I) those which are inscribed with magical formulae, and (2) those which are not.

...at...early date words of magical power and prayers were cut upon the amulets, which thus became possessed of a twofold power...the power which was thought to be inherent in the substance of which the amulet was made, and that which lay in the words inscribed upon it.

...deceased to be provided with these *hekau, or* "words of power."

...earliest Egyptian amulets...pieces of greens schist of various shapes, animal and otherwise....

...and when he had gained mastery over his heart, the heart, the double, and the soul had the power to go where they wished and do what they pleased.

...a hard, green stone scarab....

...amulet would then perform for him the "opening of the mouth," for the words of the chapter would be indeed "words of power."

...the amulet of the heart...directed to be made in the form of the scarab at a very early date.

...since the heart is taken from the body...and the body has need of another to act as the source of life and movement in its new life, another must be put in its place....the scarab or beetle itself possesses remarkable powers, and if a figure of the scarab be made, and the proper words of power be written upon it, not only the protection of the dead physical heart, but also new life and existence, will be given to him to whose body it is attached.

...beetle chosen...to copy for amulets belongs to the family of dung-feeding lamellicorns...generally of a black hue...some adorned with the richest metallic colours.

...scarab denoted "only begotten"...was a creature self-produced, being unconceived by a female.

...having made a ball of dung, the beetle rolls it from east to west....

Here Anna double-underlined her words:

> ...unseen power of God, made manifest under the form of the god Khepera, caused the sun to roll across the sky, and the act of rolling gave to the scarab its name kheper, i.e., "he who rolls." The god Khepera also represented inert but living matter... and at a very early period he was considered to be a god of the resurrection...the insect became at once the symbol of the god and the type of the resurrection.

The amulet of the scarab has been found...in untold thousands...varieties are exceedingly numerous... green basalt, green granite, limestone, green marble...

blue-and-green-glazed porcelain, etc.; and the words of power are usually cut in outline on the base.

...green stone scarabs are often set in gold....

15. THE AMULET OF THE SERPENT'S HEAD...placed on the dead body to keep it from being bitten by snakes in the underworld or tomb.

After Anna finished writing, she closed the book, its spine now creased with half a dozen fine white stress lines, and placed it face-down on the table as she picked up and sorted through her notes. As she read, answers formed in her mind—answers that ultimately added up to a question:

The guy who wrote this book may have thought he was dealing with legends, with things dreamed up in some drug-inspired haze by temple priests and magicians back in Egypt, but somebody, somehow, actually made an amulet that worked. Maybe he was trying to protect himself from animals and serpents—must have been really scared of the serpents, to add one on the end like that—and figured that the only way to beat something is to join it, get on its level. He created some special alloy, maybe threw quicksilver in the pot, and inscribed some extra-strength words of power on the back of the thing, then took off from there.

Scholars scoff at things like words of power and amulets, now, but were they around in those days to either prove or disprove what the ancients wrote about? Just because they didn't believe in our gods, did that make their gods any less worthy of belief...or producing miracles? Maybe the ancient Egyptians wouldn't believe in the Ascension, either.

...And I've seen that thing. I'll bet others in town have, too, even if they didn't realize what they were seeing, or couldn't bring themselves to believe it. Like Ma. I think she knew—she had to have seen that bat flapping out of the old lady's bedroom that Christmas, but she was afraid, or refused to let herself believe. Maybe she was afraid she'd become like the old lady if she believed.

But the old lady, little Lucy back then, had no trouble. Hell, she had a hard time dealing with everyday life couldn't even figure out she was going down the up staircase, so why shouldn't she latch onto something that made up for her inadequacies, made her better than those who were really smarter than she was? She was always telling me or Ma, "I know something you don't know," whenever she heard some tidbit of news before we did, like that temporary knowledge made her superior.

And I can't deny that she began to hate me once I advanced be-yond her mental level—she claimed she couldn't help with fractions because they hadn't been invented when she was a little girl. I hated her for trying to make me buy that line of happy horseshit. And she turned on me, claimed I was born a whore, when I began to defy her, just because she had always stayed home with her aunts, even stayed with them after that man supposedly raped her when she was eighteen. It was like, "If I can't control you, you aren't worth con-trolling."

But there's something you have that you can control, isn't there? That amulet you have, which your Gramma probably glom-med onto somewhere, God knows how, maybe before she set sail for America from that place that became Czechoslovakia years later—although how an Egyptian scarab amulet got there I have no idea. You can control that, can't you old lady? My god, you can be any-thing with that amulet...even yourself as you were. And you can do anything, to anyone you wish. It's a good thing you're a little slow upstairs, old lady. If you were halfway smart, you'd be selling this thing to the highest bidder.

Anna leaned back in her chair, absentmindedly stroking Bruiser's shoulder as he draped himself across her lap. She hadn't examined the coiled ring when she was a child, but she guessed that it was roughly seven or so inches long when extended, which meant there was room for more than a few words of power on the back. What had the book said? There was power both in the words *and* in the substance of the thing itself.

And no matter what *hekau* were inscribed on the thing, the metal itself was the substance of nightmares, for it *lived.*

TWO—The Old Lady (3)

"No, I *didn't* hear it on the radio about Wally Inglass...I was there," Anna said simply, shifting the receiver from her right hand to her left in order to turn down the volume of *60 Minutes*, as she thought, *You're not the only one in this family who's into little sur-prises.*

"You were *there?*" came the old lady's tremulous hiss, and Anna kept her voice calm as she replied, "I had to accompany the suspect back to the jail. Stu Sawyer didn't want her coming back later on and claiming they'd molested her out there. The girl is only—"

"A *juvenile*," the old lady said with her usual over-emphasis of the first syllable, her trademark way of showing people how *well* she spoke, how *smart* Lucy Miner was.

"I heard it on the *radio*. On WERT *and* the religious station."

"Oh, you listen to that one, too?" Anna asked nonchalantly, thinking, *What you have hanging around that turkey-wattle neck of yours would make any religious leader quake in his turned-around collar or yarmulke.*

"Only for the *news*. I don't *believe* all that *hoo-haa* they spout. Not after what *I* saw on the *TV* about that Jim and—"

"Uh-huh, I've heard about the PTL crowd." *On the TV*, she thought with barely contained spite. The old lady prattled on, "I heard that the *suspect's* family can't be *located,* and the person is being held in loo of bond."

"That's *lieu*—it means—"

"*I know* what it *means,* I just *say* it the way it *sounds.*"

Spoken like a true idiot...a very powerful idiot, Anna thought, before cutting in, "I'd really like to watch *60 Minutes*, Gramma—"

"I never would *watch* that show...it's always the same *story on there....*" The old lady began to pontificate, but Anna cut in with deliberate—and difficult—gentleness, "I'll tell you all about the case when I come by with the groceries, okay? I didn't get any sleep after I came home and I'm really tired. Talk to you later, okay?" Anna said, and then hung up before the old lady could finish sputtering her good-byes.

Anna leaned against the couch back and forced herself to breathe in and out deeply and evenly, telling herself, *I just can't go over there and rip the thing off her neck. Who knows if it responds to her, or what? It could be in synch with her—go into action when she's in trouble. After she's been wearing the thing for over fifty years, who the hell knows what it could do? I have to wait, study this a little more before I dare act.*

It's just lucky she doesn't realize that other people would find it a lot more useful than just a means of getting rid of a few people who barely deserved to be alive in the first place—who you didn't think deserved to live. Remember that, Anna, before you get as bad as she is. That's how all this trouble started. Ma and I had to tell the old lady all our troubles, even though I didn't realize she had a means to end my miseries hanging around her scrawny, bony neck.

Although I did hear those stories about her Gramma since I was knee-high to a flea; she never tired of telling how her Gramma "got even" with those men who took her house. I thought it was just good old wishful thinking, but now....

Now I'm glad they only confined what they did to a few well-planned "accidents," Anna told herself, smug in her complete misunderstanding of the situation. For while she now remembered most of what the old lady had been spouting about "gettng even," she regrettably forgot the old woman's other favorite story—the curious, never-actually-completed one about her much-hated Aunt Bella. The maiden aunt, who went crazy when Lucy laughingly revealed the identity of her baby girl's father...and the abominable answer to *that* question wasn't to be found in any book on amulets or Egyptian magic—

—because Lucy, uninstructed in the ways of her wonderful coiled treasure, had performed some unholy, desperate improvisations, the knowledge of which had already led her Aunt Bella to almost instant insanity, moments after Lucy uttered the words relating what she had done, and with whom—especially the "with whom" part.

CHAPTER SEVEN

MONDAY, OCTOBER 26, 1987

ONE—The Station (3)

Fingers dancing over the keyboard of the Ewerton Police Department's IBM typewriter, eyes flitting from the handwritten report at her left side, to the bobbing silver element, to the the paper rolling up behind it, Anna Sudek forced herself to concentrate on the words she was typing so she could extract as many clues as possible from Bib's scribbled words:

> —victim was found in the backyard, lying on his back, with his right arm extended, and his right hand lying palm up. The legs were toes up, with the feet at right angles. The victim's fly was unzipped and the male organ was removed from the undershorts. The organ had suffered trauma, type undetermined, as had the exposed surfaces of the arms, face and neck. Agonal bleeding was observed.

Anna stifled a snigger. "Trauma, type undetermined" was so like Bib, so understated. Over the persistent hum of the IBM, Anna thought, *Precious said it better...claimed it looked like a bird-gnawed worm.*

And if her old, old memory of the afternoon when she'd briefly worn that ring-amulet was correct, old Wally Inglass's male organ probably did look like a worm to the old lady.

Too bad you didn't rip it off—but then again, you don't really like men, do you?

Anna paused to decipher a particularly scribbled word, then kept typing:

—as was pre-death trauma to the eyes. The body was surface cold, but rigor had not yet set in when this officer arrived on the scene at approximately 5:45 P.M.

Leaning back in her squeaky office chair, Anna tried to set up a timetable in her mind, utilizing what she'd just read and what Precious had told her Saturday afternoon.

It had been late afternoon when Precious had seen Wally looking in her bedroom window. Just how late, Anna wasn't sure, but it was already late enough for the first flakes of snow to begin coating the grass. Saturday *had* been cold. Before Anna had gone to bed at three-thirty, the temperature had been only twenty-eight or so, and the sky was beginning to clear.

But Wally had to have been waiting out there long before that. Hadn't Terry and Stu said something about the officers not finding any tracks leading to or from Wally's car after they got that report on the car radio about one of the other deputies finding it parked half a mile away? Anna wished she had been able to understand what had been said over the radio, but it had sounded like pure static. She was sure Terry had mentioned something about it being funny that Wally had been sitting in the Isaacs yard without any coat on, because Stu told him to shut his mouth. She definitely remembered that.

But regardless of when Wally had parked himself out in that. Backyard—*sans* coat or jacket—somehow, the old lady must have known where Wally would be *before* he drove out to the Isaacs trailer—or else she followed him out there from his house. Which in turn meant that the old lady had left home between the time Anna left the Miner house early in the afternoon and whatever time Wally Inglass had left *his* house.

Finding his place was no problem...she likes to sit around and read her damn phone books, just rocking and poring over the numbers and names. Ma said the old bat always did that, and I've seen how she likes to go grubbing through those piles of papers of hers. The puzzle of the urine-sprayed papers was now solved with the imagined image of the old lady melting into a spraying dog, but Anna didn't dwell on that, at least not *now*—*and it's no mystery how she figured out what the bastard looked like. But everything hinges on when Wally left his house.*

As she went back to typing the report, Anna soon had her answer, a few lines farther down the page:

Identification of the victim was initially made by the officers at the scene, and by witness Martin Parks, but formal identification was made later that night by the victim's wife, Louise Inglass.

In her mind's eye, Anna saw fat, round-faced, polyester-slacked Louise Inglass standing out in a parking lot with about a dozen or more similarly attired women in their late forties to early sixties, gray- or dyed-haired women like Rhonda Stanley, Bitsy Nemmitz, and Val Sawyer—the Devoted Sisters of the Holy Church of Bingo, so dubbed by the official town wit and uptown bench-warmer Palmer Winston—waiting for the bus to the Indian reservation. The big blue bus that left Ewerton around noon every Saturday.

Which means Wally probably headed for the Isaacs place around then. Just about the same time I was giving the old lady that signal to let her know I'd arrived home.

Without thinking about it, Anna thumbed off the machine and sat staring at what she had typed. If she hadn't given the old lady the signal, Wally Inglass might very well be alive today, probably basking in the afterglow of the best forced blow job of his life...and Precious Isaacs would be a free—if nonetheless traumatized—person.

For the old lady needed to know—if only for her own peace of mind—that Anna was safe at home before she left her house in a guise no one in Ewerton but Anna would recognize.

Or Ma, for that matter. She never admitted it to me, but I think she realized...she had *to, after seeing that bat flapping out of the old lady's bedroom that Christmas. No real bat has a greenish patch on its wing. I'm* sure *I saw a flash of something greenish before the thing flapped back into the room, before I ran screaming into the kitchen to get away from it.*

But why the old lady had been venturing out in the first place, and even then only in the past few days, was beyond Anna. She had known that Anna hated Inez Hibbing, Elmo and Irma, and Wally Inglass long before last week. Anna remembered telling the old woman about Wally herself, and Ma often told Anna how she'd told the old lady this or that about the neighbors, or old bleach-blonde Inez—anything to get her to stop telling her what Judge Wapner said on that frigging *People's Court.*

Anna realized why Ma had stuck to talking about other people around the old lady. Talking about *their* relationship was too painful, potentially too explosive a subject. Anna remembered the trouble the old lady would get into, how she'd sneak upstairs and paw through Anna and Ma's belongings, doing childish, petty things like drawing big, blue ballpoint pen eyes over the images of her own flash-closed eyes on Anna's high school graduation pictures, or re-folding all of Ma's socks because she didn't think that Ma knew how to fold them right, as she'd half-shouted, half-bawled when confronted with evidence of her meddling.

And the tampering with their belongings was the most minor thing: Anna unconsciously cringed when she remembered the time she had been in one of the stores whose P.A. radio was tuned in to WERT. The old lady's quavery, distinctive voice came on line for the afternoon talk show *Speak Your Piece*, and she grew so abusive in her assessment of how the "*shitty* council" ran things that the an-nouncer had to cut off the connection. After Anna ran home that af-ternoon, she was so enraged she ended up throwing a glass of water in the old woman's face, just to stop that inane laughter as the old woman gleefully explained that nobody could touch her. And, of course, when Ma came home later on, Anna was the one who got smacked, for "hurting" a harmless old lady.

Biting her lip against the inner pain, Anna turned on the IBM again and resumed typing up the report, all the while thinking, *Whatever it was that set her off, the old lady isn't about to stop this until the whole town is wiped clean of the "crumb-bums," as she likes to call them. But if everyone I've ever publicly crossed, or who even knows me, ends up dying in these "accidents" and murders, someone is bound to start connecting me to them...and I've always been home alone when this stuff has happened. It was lucky that Wally Inglass got his so far from the house, but Terry Von Kemp did mention how fast I managed to get dressed. If he ever mentions that to Stu, I'll really be knee-deep in it...except for Precious being found on the scene, plus that little knife lying on the grass.*

But somebody's bound to bring it up in court that she didn't have any blood on her T-shirt or jeans. Even I noticed that. And the way Wally bled, she should have gotten some blood on her, if she'd been anywhere near him—which she wasn't, of course. My God, Anna, you're just lucky the law enforcement personnel out here aren't that well-trained. What is going to happen if her folks get her a good lawyer—if they ever locate her folks?

When Anna came to work that morning, Kurt the dispatcher told her that no one was sure where Precious's folks were—the neighbors stated that the pair were still rather free spirits, and thought nothing of taking off, occasionally with the rest of the kids in tow, and the girl's grandparents told the sheriff's department "we're washing our hands of that brat," so Precious was still sitting in a cell, in a form of legal limbo. No charges had been formally filed yet—Kurt said he thought those would be made later in the day, at the Dean County Courthouse, "if Judge Hauser gets back from vacation," so there was no bail to be paid, either. And there was no one willing to assume responsibility for the girl, even if she was released.

Over the weekend, Stu had finally gotten around to deputizing his wife. She had balked at the prospect of being a matron, but Kurt claimed that Stu had told her, "she ain't about to kill you through the bars or nothing," so Val Sawyer was sitting with the girl now, taking over from Ginny Yarrow, who had babysat the prisoner over the weekend. Ginny came in to work late, her eyes raccoon-ringed as she sat at the front desk downing cup after cup of black instant coffee.

As Anna finished typing up the report, and was about to take it over to Bib's office, Ginny turned around in her chair and called down the hallway, "I heard you were there Saturday night. Wanna fill me in? Bib wasn't talking."

After placing the papers on Bib's desk—he, too, was late that morning—Anna walked up to the front of the police station half of the law enforcement building and leaned against the wall that separated the police offices, after getting herself a can of Classic Coke from the vending machine out in the camera-monitored lobby beyond the office door.

Between sips from the chilled can, Anna told Ginny what she'd seen—leaving out the throwing-up incident that led to her discovery of the strange tracks, and Precious's confession afterward—as her co-worker nodded emphatically, and clucked in approval when Anna mentioned the stuck-down reddish spot by Wally's groin.

"He had it coming," Ginny whispered, with a cold smile that stopped short of her melting brown eyes. "I dunno know if you remember, but when I was going with...my *ex,* in our junior year, old Wally Inglass would ride our butts if we so much as touched *fingertips* in the hallway, but when Paula Tish and Yancy Young"—Paula was the daughter of "Tooth-Puller Tish," and Yancy's dad owned a feed and supply store; they eventually were the 1976 Homecoming King and Queen—"were making out in the commons between the buildings—y'know how he used to stick his hand in her blouse down to *there—Wally* just used to stand at the glass door leading out there and bob up and down on his toes, watching them like they weren't doing a damn thing wrong. Like he was *enjoying* it. Like, no wonder that kid is curled up in a ball in her cell. Can you imagine having to..."—Ginny glanced at the lobby to make sure no one was coming—"...*to blow* that geek? I'm surprised she didn't bite and swallow."

Anna made a face, asking, "Would *you*?"

Ginny crossed her arms and leaned back in her chair, saying, "The look on his face would've been *worth* it."

Slowly sipping the rest of her soda, Anna thought, *I'll bet you would. I underestimated you in school, Ginny. They had you back in the "B" stream and I had you pegged for just another party hanger-on, like that crowd you hung around with. But did you hang out with them because you liked them, or because those of us in the "A" stream wouldn't accept you? You were so quiet, I just assumed you were dumb. Wonder who else I've misjudged lately?*

"Goddamn Sam, gone half a day and this place goes to pot," Bib said through the glass as he stood outside the door, waiting for Ginny to notice him and open the automatic lock. Ginny hurried to press the release button on the door, and Bib walked in, wiping toast crumbs off his shirt front as he went down the short hall to his office, saying over his shoulder, "I'll be wanting that report on my desk."

"Done," Anna called after him, crushing the empty can under her foot prior to placing the squashed round of aluminum in her pants pocket.

Bib paused by his door. "In triplicate?"

Anna ran her fingers through her bangs and muttered, "Oh, *shit.*"

"What?"

"I said I'll do the rest right away," Anna said, giving Ginny a wink. *Act normal, act normal,* she told herself, walking to her desk and placing a fresh sheet of paper into the machine, while her mind was flapping high above her work, on green-dotted black wings.

TWO—Bib (4)

As he listened to the IBM clack-clacking in a jerky, repetitive rhythm, Bib Stanley slowly read the typed report of the Inglass case. running a square-nailed finger under each line of slightly indennted black type. This case wasn't really his baby; the trailer court was actually in the county, not city limits, but Bib needed this report for his own edification.

Right from the start, Stu Sawyer had bolluxed things up—he hadn't cordoned off the area in time, and those damn dogs were a crazy idea, what with all the wild game that was common out that way. *What the hell did you expect them to track? Frigging birds or something?* Bib asked himself as he fished around in his side desk drawer for that box of rolled fruit treats Rhonda had bought for him.

Pulling the sticky flap of mashed cherries off the slightly opaque sheet of plastic, then wadding the rolled fruit into a small ball which he then stuck between his cheek and gum like a plug of chaw, Bib pondered the report before him.

Something just wasn't right here. All the pieces of the crime were there in black and white, but try as he might, Bib couldn't make them fit. Swallowing down cherry-flavored saliva, Bib reread what he'd written about the condition of the prisoner upon her emergence from that thicket:

> —suspect was wearing a blue T-shirt, jeans, and no shoes. The suspect's arms and face were scratched, and she appeared to be in shock—shivering, blue and—

Bib again scanned the line about Precious's clothes. He remembered how wet her shirt was in spots, revealing the outline of her bare nipples under the fabric, and how snow had actually dusted her shoulders, but her clothes weren't blood-soaked—not like they should have been. He'd seen Wally's neck after they had hauled the short bastard to the hospital and tried to get him cleaned up a little before Louise came in, leaning on Rhonda's arm, and blubbering so hard that little bubbles of nose-drippings had collected around her nostrils.

Wally's carotid artery had been severed, cut clean through with those odd paired stab wounds, as if the girl had jabbed the tiny penknife in and out each time she struck in a certain spot, like equal signs. And Bib knew that neck wounds bled like a sonofabitch—he'd seen his Uncle Raymond butcher enough cows and pigs to remember *that.*

In fact, Bib now remembered that the girl's hands were scratched and *slightly* bloody, but they weren't stained with blood—at least not the way that knife handle had been when Stu Sawyer had nudged it into that plastic bag with his shoe-tip.

But Wally's *hands were bloody—I saw the deep red creases in the palms. The little fucker was* covered *with it—parts of his shirt were burgundy. And that kid's T-shirt was almost clean—too bad Stu didn't think to dust her hands with benzidine, just in case she tried to scrub the blood onto the ground. But* he's *so dumb you couldn't even make head cheese out of his brains if you butchered* him. *And* I *sure as hell wasn't about to intrude on Stu's precious investigation to let him know he was fucking up. Let the voters tell him that he blew it come next election time. If they even give a shit about this case, or remember it by the time the election rolls around. Hell, they know Lenny Wilkes is a Grade-A Prime Asshole, and they don't think nothing of—*

"Here's the rest of the reports," Anna Sudek said, poking her head around the half-open doorway.

"Put 'em on the 'In' pile," Bib said as he swallowed down the gummy ball of cherry fruit mash, but before Anna left the office, he added, "Anna, shut the door and come over here. I want want to ask you something."

The girl—Bib knew she was pushing thirty, but she *seemed* girlish—quietly closed the door and sat down on the hard chair before his desk, a carefully composed look of expectant wonder on her wide-cheeked face. Bib paused before talking. Anna had those unreadable kind of eyes he always found disquieting—not dark in color, but *dark* nonetheless.She had a way of not letting them roam much, but keeping them trained on a person the way a cat does, almost unblinking and very steady. *Purposefully* steady, so as not to jerk or shift whenever she heard something that surprised her. It was rare for her to glance away from someone, unless it was *at* something specific.

Bib remembered that her grandmother, old Lucy Miner, was the same way. Once, Bib had been in the checkout line of the Red Owl back when they were doing some sort of instant cash game. Anna and Tina had just moved out of the Miner family house, so the old woman had to do her own shopping because winter delivery hadn't started yet, and on that day, old Lucy—not that she was *old* old, but she *seemed* it—had a full cart of groceries, plus a fold-up shopping cart in the store cart, and she'd let a pair of teenagers who only had a few packs of pop and gum go ahead of her in the line.

The instant cash game consisted of little rectangles of paper with rub-off silver spots covering either a "Sorry" line or a dollar amount. The two girls paused to rub off their silver spots while the checker was counting out their change, and one of them won ten dollars. Everybody in the checkout line either groaned good-naturedly, or congratulated the girls—except Lucy Miner.

The old woman, her thinning hair drawn up into a silly-looking, tightly wound topknot, her powdered face a mass of deeply shadowed valleys and ridges, let out a hiss—a low, whispering exhalation that made Bib's balls feel like melting ice cubes, and caused several people to crane their necks to see where the odd noise had come from.

Unconsciously, Bib had found himself reaching for his holster, even though this was the Red Owl, and the girls had only won ten bucks, not stolen the old woman's life savings in a pigeon drop. But when he looked at the checker, he realized that his fears were justified—the girl's smile was frozen as she woodenly said, "Here's your prize...sign here, please," while Lucy Miner began to shake in her shapeless cotton dress, the oddly cut old garment (Bib remembered his *mother* wearing a dress like that—a Hooverette, she called it) actually rippling from the old woman's agitation.

That was when the girls noticed what was happening and hurried out of the store, but Lucy Miner yanked her fold-up shopping cart out of the larger, boxy store cart and told the checker in that bubbling tar voice of hers, "*Stuff* it," and marched out of the store, leaving a rancid, meaty odor in her wake. By the time the checker had had one of the stock boys pull the abandoned cart out of the way, and had rung up Bib's Ho-Hos and milk, it was too late for him to catch up with old lady Miner, but he found the girls standing next to their bikes out by the Coke and Pepsi machines, sniffing back tears.

"That old *bitch*," one of them sobbed, "she took OUR money. She said it was *hers,* like some spoiled little *brat*."

Bib tried to get the girls to come to the station and press charges, but for some reason they clammed up and refused instead jumping on their bikes and pedaling away. And after that, Bib used to see the IGA delivery truck stopping by the Miner house to deliver groceries, until the day when they, too, got fed up with the hissing, stinking old woman, and her daughter Tina had to start doing her shopping again.

"Chief Stanley, did you want to speak to me?"

Anna was perched on the edge of the chair, short-nailed hands loosely folded in her lap. Anna Sudek never flicked her fingers or cracked her knuckles or anything like that—she always had her fingers still, and her hands palm-in. Bib remembered how her mother Tina was always flicking at the dead skin on the sides of her nails, or rubbing her fingertips against her palms, always moving her hands. *Funny how that never hit me before. Tina was nervous, even when I used to think she was the easiest-going person around. Shows how good my powers of observation are.*

"Yeah, I did want to ask you something. You were sittin' in the car with the Isaacs girl, weren't you, before Stu and Terry got in?"

Those steady eyes didn't jerk or flicker; Anna evenly blinked once or twice as she said, "Stu told me to. I didn't have a choice about it, since he cuffed us together. But Precious was no trouble. She just sat there, shivering. If we hadn't been cuffed, I would've draped Terry's coat around her shoulders, but...." She let her voice trail off with a "you know how it is" sigh.

Bib also realized that she'd just fended off his next question before he had had a chance to ask it. If the girl *had* anything to Anna (as Stu suspected; Bib had heard him talking about it to his deputy on Saturday night), she certainly wasn't going to repeat it. Not that Bib really blamed her; he was well aware of her feelings for Wally Inglass, and realized they were justified—but not to the point of obstructing justice.

"So Precious just sat there. She say anything?" he asked quickly, but not quickly enough. Anna looked at him with the blankness of a cud-chewing cow, and said in an even voice that didn't rise up sharply or quiver, "No."

Damn, he thought. *Either she's telling the truth, or she's a damn good liar...probably been expecting this conversation for a couple of days.* Realizing that that line of questioning was useless—for now Bib began to crumple and then smooth out the piece of plastic from the rolled fruit snack, saying, "I was just looking at this report. I noticed something weird, thought you noticed it, too. The girl's shirt—"

Ahh...gotcha. Your eyes jerked.

"—was really clean, considering what she done—*did* to Wally. Did you notice it, too?"

Anna swallowed briefly, but she kept her hands still in her lap—quiet and unmoving. "She was shivering so much I really didn't notice her shirt, but now that you mention it, she didn't have much blood on her. Of course, it did depend on where she was standing," Anna finished quickly, obviously having thought of something Bib hadn't.

"Come again?"

"The angle of trajectory," Anna said with self-effacing simplicity. Bib realized that *she* realized that he should have thought of this himself, long ago.

"If she was standing out of the path of the blood flow, especially near his neck, the spray might not have hit her. But the blood tests on her shirt would show that, wouldn't they? I mean," she went on when Bib sat silent, "her arms and face were bleeding, so it had to be on her shirt. When they tested it, they probably noticed which was her type and which was his."

With a sick feeling, Bib wondered if Stu *had* had the girl's shirt tested, and instantly doubted it. If only the trailer park had been in Bib's sole jurisdiction.

Anna lapsed into silence, her perfectly composed hands resting in her lap, her eyes politely withdrawn. Whatever she was thinking, it was probably better thought out and more logical than whatever Stu *or* Bib had come up with in regard to this case. Bib was briefly stung by her insights into the murder, and her knowledge of police procedure—until he realized that she knew a little *too* much.

What was it she had said about the blood spraying from Wally's neck? Quickly scanning the report, Bib realized that nothing there was written about Wally's severed artery, just a vague remark about the trauma to the body, and how it involved the face, arms, and neck—*but nothing specific was mentioned about the carotid artery.* It couldn't be—Bib didn't even know the *word* for that artery until after he'd written up the report, prior to speaking to Doc Calder once Wally was stretched out on the slab. True, it could have been a logical guess on her part, but Bib's policeman's gut feelings told him otherwise. Anna had sounded too sure, too authoritative, when she spoke about the blood gushing out, as if she'd either heard about it...or seen it herself.

Precious did talk to you, didn't she...but what did she say? For some reason, you won't or can't tell me...and that girl doesn't seem like the type of person you'd champion—not a crud like that. I know you fairly well, Anna Sudek. You were never *one to get chummy with someone you thought was beneath you. Not like Tina. You don't even talk* like *a native of this town, not with all your "doesn't"s instead of "don't"s, and your precise way of pronouncing everything. Even when you're ass in the air, leaning over a Dumpster, you've got them airs about you...so why are you protecting that little bum? Or are you protecting yourself? Terry Von Kemp told me how you were dressed and ready to go not two minutes after he walked through the door. He thought it was funny, but now that I think about it—*

Anna began fidgeting on the chair, until she said with obvious embarrassment, "May I *please* be excused, Chief Stanley? I drank a can of Coke before you arrived and—" She gave him a face-crinkling smile that effectively hid her eyes as she got up and hurried out the door with a little wave before she shut the door behind her.

The cherry fruit snack Bib had swallowed began to backup in his throat, a cloying, bitter cherry syrup that hung around his soft palate before he force-swallowed it down. The girl was definitely acting hinky—that much Bib was sure of—but it still didn't *tell* him anything, at least nothing he could relate to Stu Sawyer. Bib did dial Stu's number, and left a message asking how the blood test on the girl's T-shirt had gone. Even if Stu had't done one, he would now, unless he'd been stupid enough to let his wife Val wash the shirt— but he didn't ask for Stu to call him back.

First of all, he hated talking to the bear-big sheriff, and second, part of him hated the thought of getting someone like Anna Sudek in hot water over a snaky creep like Wally Inglass. The Isaacs girl would have wound up in the Ewerton Hilton sooner or later, either with or without that scuz-bum Mayo Parks for company; it was just happenstance that the girl was in for Wally's murder. As it was, the fact that Wally's weenie was outside the bun was more than likely going to go in the girl's favor, if and when she decided to talk about what had happened. Mayo Parks had hinted that Wally had more than a missed pep rally on his mind when he came to the trailer court; Bib could see the girl getting justifiable homicide, or pleading self-defense, if she was waived into adult court.

And then there was the matter of how Wally had been acting on Friday morning. Bib was honor bound to relate what happened when the time came, and not only because Anna Sudek had been sitting there listening to the whole thing. *Hell, Wally should have been fitted for a straitjacket years ago. The guy was nothing but a Froot Loop without the milk. But he was an* important *Froot Loop— remember that, Bib. And his wife's family is big shit around this town. Now don't forget that, either.*

Bib tossed the crumpled sheet of plastic into his waste-basket. It made a soft, rustling-crinkling noise as it unfolded agaist the papers already resting in the round metal container. For some reason, the sound reminded him of old Lucy Miner's cotton Hooverette, rustling like a pile of fall leaves around her smoky-smelling wrinkled body in the Red Owl, and Bib rested his beard-stubbled chin on his stee-pled fingers and thought, *What I wouldn't give to look into Anna's head for just a minute. Only a minute....*

THREE—*Terry*

If the powers above had granted Bib Stanley's wish about read-ing Anna Sudek's thoughts for that single minute, the police chief would have been disappointed, for as he sat listening to the faint snakeskin snicker of the piece of plastic shifting in his wastebasket, Anna was leaning against the snack vendor that stood next to the Coke machine (she didn't want to trap herself in the department lunchroom, where Bib might corner her), trying to make up her mind between a bag of Doritos or some Old Dutch fried cheese puffs. She couldn't stand the Old Dutch distributor, Wayne Mesabi, but the nacho-flavored chips didn't *weigh* as much, and if she hadn't been so preoccupied with thoughts of writhing rings and green-stone scarabs that morning, she would have remembered to bring along a lunch, and wouldn't be standing here in the first place.

"Take the cheese puffs. I seen Wayne bring 'em in fresh this morning. Them chips've been there a while—see the dates?" Anna didn't turn around at the sound of Terry Von Kemp's voice, but she was surprised at his tone. No more "Where's Granny" leer; he was still as nice as he'd been Saturday evening, which Anna found puzzling. She'd known him for years; Terry had always been a snot, at least in her presence. And she doubted that her lowly clerk's job had suddenly made her his equal in the law enforcement field.

Shoving her quarters into the slot, Anna pushed the plastic bar in front of the cheese puffs and then took the bag out from the bin at the bottom of the machine. Terry likewise bought a bag of the fried puffs, then purchased a can of Mello Yello. Anna chose another Classic Coke. Terry commented, "You don't like that new Coke, either?"

Anna smiled and replied, "No more than I like Pepsi...and this new stuff's even sweeter than that." Terry nodded, his greasy bangs sliding across his slightly domed forehead. He was being *awfully* agreeable, almost to the point of anxiousness. Anna guessed that he still felt funny about seeing her in her PJ's and all, or perhaps was wondering about what Ma had written on the cabinet doors.

That has to be it. Terry's married, I'm sure he's seen women in nightwear before. And it wasn't like I had on baby dolls or Dr. Dentons with the flap hanging open. But you don't always see stuff written on people's kitchen cabinets—especially in moldy black catsup.

Terry was hanging around the machines, munching his cheese puffs and slurping down his Mello Yello, not making a move to leave, so Anna motioned to the long, low armless bench that rested along the wall adjoining the police department offices, and said, "I'm on my lunch break—might as well eat sitting down."

Terry sat down a short distance away from her, pushing free-form orange puffs into his mouth faster than he could swallow the ones he'd already begun to chew. Whatever it was he wanted to talk to her about, he wasn't about to bring the subject up himself.

Opening up her red plastic bag, Anna casually remarked, "Did Stu ever round up Precious Isaacs's parents?"

Terry spoke around a mash of bright orange half-chewed cornmeal. "Yeah. Couple of hours ago. Didn't go to Bingo that afternoon. They were up in Rhinelander, of all places, with the other kids, in some cabin. Visiting some relatives. They'll be down tonight, maybe. Stu was looking into getting them flown down. But the kid, she ain't been arraigned yet."

"What's Stu waiting for?" Anna took a sip of Coke and watched Terry chew fast, then swallow before replying, "Who knows, when it comes to Stu? He claims it's 'cause Judge Hauser is outta town, but I think he just wants to make the kid sweat it out." Terry leaned forward until his shock of no-color hair was an inch from Anna's fluffy bangs before going on in a cheese-scented whisper, "'Tween you and me, Stu's...Stu. Get my drift?"

Anna nodded and took another sip of soda before carefully adding in a soft voice, "I've always suspected that Sheriff Sawyer makes his own rules. I mean, it *is* his department, but—"

"His department?" Terry slapped his thigh as he laughed. "It's more like his fu-frigging *inheritance*. Been Sawyers in that office since before the glaciers. Don't tell nobody I *said* that," he added quickly, glancing up at the small surveillance camera mounted close to the ceiling. The camera's images were best described as nebulous, aside from being in silent black and white, but Anna understood Von Kemp's concern. Stu seemed like a vindictive cuss, and there were always new applicants for the sheriff's department.

"Cripes, I could tell you stories about Stu. Take that car crash on Thursday, f'rinstance. You know he made Zack Downing look at the bodies right out in the *open*?" Without waiting for a reply, he went on, "And he *still* hasn't released the cars to the families, but if the guy in the car reports any of his stuff stolen out of that car, it'll be *our* asses that'll be in a sling, not Stu's."

"You mean to say Stu still hasn't removed the belongings out of there? He has someone posted by the car, I hope."

Terry rocked back and forth on the wood bench, laughing. "You *kiddin'*? Hell, there's been animals rootin' in there already," he added with a slightly uneasy look, before picking up his yellow can of pop and chugging some down.

Something about his voice and expression made Anna sit there, a big corn curl halfway up to her mouth, until she said, "What kind of animals were rooting in it? Skunks?"

"Nah, the squad car just smells like 'em. You notice that on Satur—"

Anna nodded and went on, "I can't imagine anything being able to *fit* in that wrecked car—it looks like a pretzel without the spaces between the loops. Doesn't it bother Stu that animals might be—"

"Stu don't know," Terry said quickly, as the color slowly faded from his slightly pitted cheeks and forehead. Anna paused a beat, then said softly, "I know it isn't any of my business, but I'm... curious. What kind of a thing did you see around that car? Was it something wild or—"

Terry said something, but his voice was so soft Anna couldn't make it out over the crinkling noises his red cellophane bag made as he grubbed his fingers around in it.

"Pardon?"

"A dog. There was a dog in there, only I don't see *how* it got stuck in there. It was in that little space—you seen how small it is—between the rear door and the frame. At first I thought it was, y'know, *dead*, 'cause of the way it was hanging, and—"

As Anna listened to Terry's tumbled, agitated words, she thought, *That had to have been Friday night...and Terry's right. there wasn't a dog in that car before, and there isn't room for one—not to go in head-first. But suppose something crawled in when it was smaller, and then got stuck?*

And in answer to her unvoiced question, Terry was saying, "It was the second animal I seen around there, actually. 'Fore that there was this cat running around—you know how they can smell blood, and the guy *did* bleed like a stuck pig in that wagon."

And I know how cats can squeeze into the smallest places, just as long as they can get their heads in. Rats can, too. Were you returning to the scene of the crime, old lady, or couldn't you find Wally Inglass that night? You didn't think that he'd be at the football game—you don't even know where the new playing field is, do you? You never went to any games, and you only were out to the school once, for my graduation. and then you were too busy blathering in the back of Mrs. Petersen's car to notice where we were going. I remember how surprised you were when the car stopped way out in the county.

You meant to get Wally on Friday night, didn't you? But I didn't give you a call until it was too late to get to his house in time. He'd already left, hadn't he? And you didn't dare leave before I called, just in case I was still walking around town or something, and might have seen you flapping away from the house, or however you left that night. After you got lost, you panicked and hid in the wreck when Terry passed by. What was it—did being in the wreck make that pet of yours remember the last *time you were around that car... and Elmo's truck? Hmmm? You must have realized Elmo would just as soon run over a cat...but a dog might be a different, eh?*

Precious said you changed in and out of a bird shape—what's the matter, do you forget yourself? Or are you like that magician in ancient times—the one in the book of Egyptian magic? He changed into a multitude *of forms.*

"—a license, so I couldn't haul it in," Terry was saying around a mash of cheese puffs, andAnna said, "Sorry, I was woolgathering."

"The dog. It wasn't a stray. It had tags, or at least the rabies one. I didn't see the silver city tag, but it had the colored one for rabies."

"Oh, yeah, the little green bell," Anna said, thinking. *You're just lucky this year's tags* are *green, old lady. What did you do, find out about them from Ma? You're always asking her so many stupid questions, she wouldn't have even noticed one about the pet tags.*

"Yeah, that one. Only it didn't look like a bell—it was more like an oval."

Noting Terry's slightly dubious tone, Anna said, "I think the shape depends on which company issues the tags. I've seen some different ones on dogs around town—not like the ones they issue at the clinic. Here they rotate between the bell, a blue flower, a red heart, and a yellow doghouse, but I've seen a sort of sloppy rectangle, with sides that slope like this"—she held up her hands with the palms angled in a bottomless vee—"so the dog you saw probably was vaccinated out of town. People do that to avoid paying the city license fee," Anna prattled on, all the while thinking, *Shut up, already! He'll think you're acting hinky, just like Bib was staring at you funny in the office. Quit blathering like the old lady.*

"Yeah, my next-door neighbor does that. Hauls his dog all the way up to Rice Lake to get its shots. Like nobody notices that there's dog shit on his lawn. I keep thinking I should turn him in. My wife Cindy says if she steps in another pile of it again she will. Cindy even put up a little sign on our lawn, 'This is not a dog toilet,' but it ain't done no good. Guy still takes his dog to squat on our lawn. Like I told Cindy. 'Once you make him mad, he'll only get worse.'"

Anna nodded, remembering the fight she had with Elmo before he got into his truck with his ugly sister and drove off into the big wrecking yard in the sky. Anna had been quick to tell the old lady all about it, down to what her rube neighbors looked like, and now she imagined the old lady bat-fluttering out the chimney, hurrying to the address she'd no doubt looked up in her well-thumbed phone book, and getting there in time to see the brother and sister climb into that black Ford truck. Once they were moving, the old lady could move as fast or faster than Elmo was driving, not only following them, but actually overtaking the car. She had been able to take her time, wait around, decide how to kill them, and choose the proper form in which to do it.

For Precious Isaacs had told her boyfriend that she had smelled something, some odor she associated with her mother's kitchen, and for as long as Anna could remember, the old lady had smelled like rancid lard, or rotten animal flesh, only with a more ozone-like undercurrent. A *hot* odor. And even in darkness, it hadn't been hard for Anna to see what bad shape the Isaacs trailer was in, how there were dark lines running along the broad green siding that had to be gaps—gaps where something small could burrow, to perhaps watch Wally Inglass's intended prey, even as Wally himself was waiting outside, thinking whatever it was that frustrated, oversexed little men like himself were wont to think in such a tempting situation.

Anna was smart enough to realize that the old lady's constant talk of how *awful* sex was still was about sex, no matter which side the old lady professed to be on. The old lady had this childish fixation about the subject, that much Anna had been able to see from early on, so it would have been natural for her to want to take a peek at what was going on, see what she'd been missing...after all, didn't little Lucy used to sleep in that tiny bedroom next to the master bedroom? Anna remembered how thin the walls upstairs were, how sounds carried so well. Surely, little Lucy had heard her parents doing it at least once before what happened that October of 1931 happened...and Lucy had never heard about the facts of life from them—certainly, they wouldn't have told a six-year-old about it, not in the 1930s. Hence, Lucy Miner's love-hate fascination for the subject.

How long did you spy on those poor kids, old lady? Until Wally went and spoiled your fun? No wonder you made sure you bit that up good. He stopped the show for you.

"Oh, shit, Stu's gonna be on my tail," Terry said, suddenly getting up and brushing fluorescent orange crumbs off his uniform trousers. As he got ready to leave, Anna figured she owed him something in exchange for the information he'd unwittingly given to her, and said, "About what was on the cupboards in my kitchen...I don't know what you've heard, but my mother and I...well, things were kind of hairy at the end. She was upset about a lot of things."

Before Terry walked down the hallway that led to the sheriff's department, he nodded his head and said, "Your grandma...listen, I understand. Remind me to tell you about the time my kid went trick-or-treatin' there. Gotta run, see ya later," before loping off and out of sight.

Anna took a last sip of her soda, then went to crush the can, stopping as she positioned her heel over the opening. She'd forgotten about Halloween. She had candy she could give out, but she didn't know if the old lady had any. She hadn't wanted to go visit the old lady just yet—at least not until she had a better idea of how to get that amulet away from her without both of them ending up hurt or worse—but now she realized she didn't really have much choice.

FOUR—The Old Lady (4)

"—then Judge Wapner told *him,* 'You're in the *wrong,* and you have to *pay* this woman—'"

Just once, Anna was tempted to actually tune in *People's Court* some afternoon. After listening to the old lady give her word-by-word recitation of what the almighty Judge Wapner supposedly said to the people who came before his bench, Anna had come to the conclusion that either the good judge used exactly the same childish syntax her grandmother did, or the old woman was a liar. Anna preferred the latter option; it relieved her of having to actually watch the show itself.

"If he owed her the money for the job, he should've had to pay it," Anna replied rhetorically, as she reached for the bag of groceries on the table between herself and the old lady, then pulled out a bag of assorted wrapped candies and suckers.

"Here, this is for Saturday evening. I didn't know if you had any candy on hand."

The old lady's grease-sheened face—she'd been slathering on some sort of thin, oily cold cream when Anna had knocked on the door—wrinkled into a fair approximation of one of those loose-skinned Chinese hunting dogs, the ones all the Yuppies were dying to own in the big cities, or so Anna had read in the paper. "The heck with 'em. They don't need any candy."

Anna placed the crackling cellophane bag squarely in front of the old woman and said quietly, "Last year Ma said the kids egged your windows *because* you wouldn't give them any candy. And she'd bought you a bag of suckers, so there was no exeuse." Anna was also tempted to add, "And Terry Von Kemp told me you did something to his kid," but thought better of it.

The old lady pushed at the rippled paper label attached to the top of the bag of candy with a ridged yellow nail, fingering a hole punched in the top of the label before sputtering, "They got *other* houses to go to. Who's gonna give *me* candy, huh?"

Anna sucked in her breath and held it for a couple of seconds. Letting it out, she said as evenly and sensibly as she could, "You won't have to give out much, anyway. Before I left work, Bib got a few calls asking if Halloween was going be postponed or canceled because of all the deaths this past week. Some of the mothers on the PTA thought it was disrespectful to go out after what happened to Principal Inglass."

When Anna mentioned Wally Inglass's name, the old lady's eyes lit up, an infinitesimal widening of the pupils, like a cat's eyes in darkness. Anna actually found herself glancing at the old lady's yellowed teeth, wondering, *Did you brush the blood off...or lick your teeth clean?* And the old lady openly began fidgeting with the bag of candy, pushing it around the slick surface of the worn oil-cloth, saying, "I thought the kids would be *celebrating* after he died. I didn't know that the *high* school kids went trick or *treating*."

"No, no, that's not what I meant. That's not the point. He's a school administrator, and some people still aren't sure how he died. The girl who saw him killed still hasn't talked," Anna added non-chalantly, pretending to be engrossed with one of the bright foil-wrapped pieces of candy in the clear bag. Outof the corner of her eye she noticed the old lady's week-old ham-colored tongue circle her liver-colored lips lizard-quick, before disappearing behind her rot-discolored teeth, as Anna's stomach did a forward roll in free fall, tumbling with no support. Then:

"The *radio* said that the *girl* killed him."

Momentarily taken aback by the mental image of a radio speaking like a human being, the speaker grille moving with a lip-like pucker, Anna finally said, "No, that's not quite how the news put it. They *said* a juvenile suspect is being held on *suspicion* of the murder, pending arraignment and—"

—that poor kid is sitting in jail because of what you *had to go and do. If you wanted to kill Wally, why'd you have to go and do it in front of an audience? Couldn't you wait? Or did you enjoy showing off, like a blasted six-year-old? But what you did wasn't like anything a child would do—at least, not a* normal *child.*

"—and, uh...setting bail, stuff like that," Anna finished lamely as she nervously gave the bag of candy a push across the table. It stopped just short of falling into the old lady's lap. For a second, Anna saw the start of that hissing rage in the old woman's colorless eyes, those peculiar spots of golden-white light that pooled near the outer corners of her eyes. And Anna knew what was bound to follow next—the tea kettle-shrill breathing, the flushing cheeks, and then the balled, fisted hands, pommeling flinching flesh.

Quickly, Anna smiled and reached for the bag, saying with false cheer, "Oilcloth's slicker than I remembered it being," then watched as the old lady's eyes lost that weird light, and her saggy, greasy face composed itself into a calmer expression. Any other time, Anna might have been up to a fight—it certainly wasn't as if she hadn't the *motivation* for wanting to beat the old woman to a pulp—but today, she needed to make her trust her, and (she hoped) confide in her a little bit.

Moving the candy to the center of the table, Anna said, "If any kids do come around, you'll be ready. If you don't want to keep opening the door, just put the stuff in a big bowl on the porch and attach a note to it. Tell the kids to take a piece and then go. Something like that. Ginny, this woman I work with"—Anna was careful not to mention any last names, not anymore—"she told me she does that every year. And most of the kids are pretty good about it, especially if their parents are with them, which accounts for most of the little kids. When it comes to the bigger ones, it's catch as catch can, but at least she's not getting up every five minutes to get the door."

"But what about the *bowl*?"

"She uses an old plastic thing. If they drop it or steal it, well, no loss. Really, you should put out candy. I just don't have the time to wash egg off your windows, not with this job of mi—"

"*I* know how to solve *that*," the old lady said smugly, her odorous skin glistening like adipocere flesh in the dim kitchen light.

"How?" Anna asked, guessing the answer before the old woman opened those pendulous lips.

"You quit *that* job, and get your *old* one back. You had more *time* before."

"And a lot of time on my hands where I wasn't getting paid. No, this job pays better than the others I had. Even if I'd taken on Ma's old jobs, I still wouldn't be making what I am now. And it's not hard work."

The old lady defensively pulled her robe around her neck with quivering fingers, pouting, "Well I don't like the *idea* of you being on *call* all the time."

"Just for the matron's job," Anna said, adding, "and Saturday night was an exception. They needed someone that minute and the other matron was out of town. And it was no problem taking care of the suspect. She hadn't much to say—she was too busy shivering."

"But she said *something*?" the old lady said, too quickly, leaning forward across the table, her knobby, gnarled fingers interlaced into a cage of bones and shiny flesh.

Staring at the old woman, Anna abruptly wondered why Lucy *chose* to stay so old, so horrible looking, when she obviously had the power to appear as anything or to be any age she wished. Anna looked for the cord that held the small white bag under the old woman's dingy white nightgown collar, but couldn't see it, nor could she see the accompanying bump that was usually level with the woman's collarbones.

Anna gave her grandmother a slight smile and replied, "Not much—just that she was so cold. The poor kid wasn't dressed for the outdoors."

"And being *barefoot* didn't *help,* I'll bet."

Anna couldn't remember for sure if she'd said anything about Precious Isaacs not having any shoes or socks on, so she didn't pursue the subject. Instead, she simply answered, "You said it. Uh, not to change the subject, but I was wondering, could I borrow some of your costume jewelry for Saturday night?"

"You're not going *out* with a *man*—"

"You kidding?" Anna asked with what she hoped was light joviality, then went on, "Oh, hardly. I was going to dress up myself for Halloween. It's a new thing people have been doing in town, getting dressed up for when the kids come knocking. And then later on they go to the bars, since the bartenders give free drinks to every adult in costume."

The old lady recrossed her arms and leaned back in her chair, her face smugly incredulous. "*You* don't *drink.*"

"Coke, I do," Anna shot back. At least some of what she'd said was true—the Rusty Hinge and Pearl 'n' Earl's did give out free drinks, and Anna supposed that at least a few adults in Ewerton donned partial costumes while handing out candy, and she certainly did drink Coca-Cola.

"All that *trouble* for a glass of *Coke*?" the old lady asked, shaking her head of thinning limp hair.

Pressing the subject, Anna persisted with frantic joviality, "Oh, it's *fun*...and anyhow, in Ewerton, people are expected to be joiners. Most of the cops who'll be off duty that night will be out"—which was true. Kurt and Ginny had both mentioned what they planned to wear that night—"and if I don't show up, Bib'll end up hearing about it, think I'm a party-pooper"—which Anna doubted, since Bib wasn't into bar-hopping himself, and didn't care who was—"so I might as well go. Besides, the Rusty Hinge is okay. Lenny Wilkes and the two old Palmers hang out there, and *they're* no problem."

"That Palmer *Winston* was a real *rake* when *he* was young," the old lady said with her "isn't sex *awful*" lip-licking leer, but Anna fended off that line of conversation with a hasty, "The way he drinks now, Mr. Winston couldn't lift it with a crane. But c'mon, could I please borrow some of that jewelry? The earrings and the bracelets, you know—the ones with all the faux stones."

"*Foe* stones?"

"*Faux*—French for fake. *Y'know,* the costume jewelry," Anna urged, thinking, *And whatever else you have in that jewelry box, too. I see you did take off the little bag with the amulet in it—was your pet getting too strong for you? Have to hide it away, give it a rest?*

"I don't *know*," the old lady said dubiously, as she began lacing her fingers together. Her age-coarsened palms rasped as the surfaces rubbed, the noise loud in the silent house.

"I'd bring the stuff back on Sunday morning, first thing. That way you'd see me an extra day," Anna coaxed, dangling her time and attention before the old woman like a merry-go-round brass ring. The old lady eyed the shining ring, and finally decided to grab for it.

"You'll bring them back *first* thing in the *morning*?"

"Of course. I take a run uptown anyway to buy the Sunday paper. I could stop off here on the way in, sit and talk a while."

The old lady paused for a second, then got up and shuffled for her bedroom—the same room Lucy's Gramma used to sleep in, and died in, over half a century before. The door was always closed when the old lady was out of the room, but as Anna's grandmother padded noisily across the uncarpeted floor in her *slappy* slippers, Anna rose from the table and quietly followed her, her own rubber boot soles making little noise as she stepped carefully on her toes, making sure she kept a good five paces behind.

She got a brief glance in the old lady's room as she opened her door—pink-papered walls with tears of brown staining the place where walls and ceiling met, a quilted comforter, and the arms of a light wood rocker, partly covered with something black draped over the curving wood, and a puff of scent Anna couldn't identify at first, for it was too mingled and musty to recognize after only one good whiff.

And Anna had to move out of sight as the old woman half turned to shut the door behind her. When she heard the privacy lock click shut, Anna thought, *You still have that on the door even though you're alone in the house? Whatever for?*

Anna wished she could listen at the door, try to hear any strange sounds the moving amulet might make, but she doubted that even such a small sound would carry very far. And besides, she didn't dare linger outside the doorway—not when the old lady would be out any second now. Anna just made it to the kitchen table when the old lady's lock clicked open, and she began her slow shuffle back to the kitchen, her white jewelry box tucked under one arm.

The old lady leaned over to place the box before Anna. The younger woman caught the familiar warm odor of spoiled fly-blown meat overlaid with a more nauseating tinge of something she didn't *want* to identify (because it literally could've been anything, pure or impure), plus another whiff of the bedroom odor, as if the old lady had been rubbing her hands on something scented. This time, Anna identified the odor—peaches, tinged with a sweet vanilla-spice scent. Probably a sachet of some sort—most likely a vain attempt to disguise her vile body odor. She must have had Ma buy it for her, or picked up something while she was still doing her own shopping.

At any rate, where or when the old lady obtained something sweet-scented like that wasn't worth worrying about, Anna decided as she opened the white-leather-covered hinged box. Inside was a scintillating jumble of multicolored faux stones that glinted like rainbow flecks against sun-washed snow, plus luminescent yellow-ivory paste pearls, and strings of tiny beads, with metal bases and clasps of tarnishing gold and silver metal. Anna made herself look slowly through the jewelry, picking and choosing among the gaudy clip-on earrings, wide jeweled bracelets, and childishly ornate neck-laces, and placed her choices on the table, trying to hide the disap-pointment she felt as she reached the bottom of the pink-satin-lined box. No little cloth bag, no writhing hard double-headed spiral within.

This jewelry was cold against her fingers, the stones touched here and there with chipping-away flecks of metallic paint to enhance their shine, bright, but obviously fake, under the weak glow of the dim-bulbed overhead lamp. The base metal and glass surfaces made unpleasant *scritching* sounds as the pieces shifted against each other, and out of nowhere came the memory of the time little Anna had done something or other that had displeased her Baba, but instead of hitting her, or making her stand in the corner (as Ma used to do when she misbehaved), Baba had instead disappeared into her room for a minute, then emerged with the leather-covered jewelry box. Making little Anna sit at this very table, in this very chair, Baba had opened the box of glittering, beautiful-to-a-child baubles, saying solemnly, "You were going to get *all* of this when I died, but now you don't get *any*—*not* this bracelet, or those *earrings*—*none* of it. And it was to be *all* yours, every piece of it—" until tears ran hot and streaming down little Anna's burning eyes.

And now, sitting here pretending to be interested in a cheap box of junk jewelry—there weren't even any truly valuable pieces—no Bakelite bangles or rhodium-finished platinum-look rhinestone pieces, the kind she'd read about in some Sunday supplement magazine—Anna realized that the old woman had chosen her punishment well that long-ago afternoon. A slap or harsh word would have been quickly forgotten by a child, but to this day, the sense of panic, of a treasure almost won and then cruelly lost, had stayed with her, even as she now realized that the jewelry she'd cried over, that she'd begged for, only to be smilingly refused with a solemn, "You've *lost* it, *forever*," was only a pile of garbage, of clanking *junk*. For the *denial* had hurt Anna—the sense of losing something she could never, ever regain, no matter how good she was in the future, or how well she behaved.

And the old lady had played that same trick on her later on, or crafty variations of it. When Anna had wanted a birthday party, and Ma broke down and actually bought the invitations for it—little white cards with a party-hatted pair of children adorning the fronts—Baba had sat her down in her front-room rocker, asking, "Do you like your toys, Anna?"

Of course she did.

"Do you want to see them all broken? Your Tammy doll with its hair all pulled out? Your teddy bear ripped apart?"

"No, no, *no*," little Anna cried.

"Then *you* don't want to invite any of those *children* to the house. They'll pick up your *toys* and rip them *apart,* and make you *watch."*

Little Anna began to cry—what could she do to *stop* it?

"Tear up those *invitations.* I remember how *my* Gramma didn't want any children coming over when *I* had a party. She said they were *mean,* and later on, they *were.* Oh, the *things th*ey did to your poor Baba—the terrible *things."*

And Ma had slapped Anna when she had found the torn invitations hidden in the kitchen garbage bag, not listening when she tried to explain about her soon-to-be-shattered toys, and she never did get to have a birthday party of her own, let alone attend anyone else's—the fact that she was never invited to any notwithstanding.

And it was almost the same thing when she decided to try out for one of the high school music festivals, and actually sing solo. She'd gone so far as to order sheet music, but when she told her grandmother about it, the old lady said with a knowing hiss and sputter, "They'll all *watch* you, and first *one* person will snicker behind their *hand,* and then *another,* and they'll all be laughing so *hard* no one will be able to *hear* you, and you'll get judged *down."* The music teacher was pissed off at Anna for pulling out the way she did, and made her pay for the music anyway, which was really no more than right, but for years, she had nightmares about the room of people laughing as she sang, even *after* she learned from her classmates that the music solos were performed in private rooms at the festivals.

Letting a cheap, greenish-gold metal necklace slither through her fingers, Anna thought, *And even after the old lady wasn't around to tell me how I'd fail at things, I made myself fail anyway. I held myself back in college, until I had to leave the teaching department, just to prove to myself that it was* me *who was the failure, and not the old lady urging me to quit, to fail, to hide away and just be* Baba's *little girl. I was taught to hate and fear men so I'd never want to up and leave Baba, never run off and get knocked up and married and divorced like Ma did. Baba and her Anna, just like Lucy had* her *Gramma all to herself.*

"Isn't that *pretty?"* the old lady gushed, looking at the necklace Anna was loosely holding. Anna glanced down at the tarnishing metal, thinking, *Pretty to what—a nearsighted magpie?* before saying sincerely, "Yeah...it is. Really nice," as she let the necklace fall in a mesh heap on the bottom of the jewelry box.

Scooping up the pieces she had set aside with her right hand, Anna said, "These will be fine, but I really need a ring or two to set it off. I was going to polish my fingernails, and I thought a couple of rings would—"

"I don't *have* any," the old lady snapped, reaching over to shut the jewelry box with a muted chuff of leather hitting leather.

Anna slipped a couple of the bracelets around her wrist, cringing inside when the cold base metal touched her skin, as she persisted, "I thought I remembered this one ring you had—a cheap gold thing with a bug on one end." She relished the look of suppressed indignation on the old lady's grease-valleyed features as she went on, "I *know* I saw it when I was small. It was in a coil, kinda like a Slinky, but golden, and there was a little snake head where the tail end of it should've been, and a green stone beetle on the other end. It sort of pulled open, and you could wrap it around your wrist...or around my neck," she finished nonchalantly, all the while staring the old lady in the eye and thinking, *And don't you sit there and say I imagined it, either, you old witch.*

"*You're* thinking of the workings of a ballpoint *pen* your *mother* had. You took it *apart* one afternoon and—"

Anna made a show of furrowing her brow and shaking her head slowly as she replied, "No, no, I remember *that*. I'm thinking of a piece of jewelry that was *real* gold. I know it was very malleable, and shone like—"

That cold gold-white light shone in the comers of the old lady's colorless eyes as she said tersely, with hissing undertones, "It was the *pen* spring. You were a *bad* girl and you broke your *mother's* pen, and she—"

Anna glanced at her watch and said, "Oh, geez, look at the time. Isn't *People's Court* going to be on soon? I'll bet the cats are thinking I went and left them forever," she prattled on, tossing the rest of the jewelry in her grocery bag and hurrying for the front door, while the old lady scrambled to her feet, her thin suede slipper-soles not gaining purchase on the linoleum floor as she wheezed, "Your ma whipped your bottom for it! Know *why* she whipped you?" the old woman called after Anna, who was opening the front door.

Over her shoulder, Anna said as sweetly and solemnly as she could, "No, Grandmother—why *did* Ma beat me?"

"Because I *tattled* on you!" she shot back in a recess-time sing-song. Anna opened her mouth to speak, thought better of it *(you don't know where she has that amulet stashed—it could be within her reach)*, and started to let herself out the door. But before Anna could lock it behind her, she heard the old lady's familiar ar farewell, "And don't forget the signal!"

Anna slammed the door on the old woman's last word,cutting *signal* in half, wishing she could do likewise to the old lady herself.

FIVE—Lucy (4)

Lucy watched Anna hurry down the sidewalk outside the house, her head down, as if she was watching only her feet, but Lucy knew that she was spying on her, out of the corner of her eye. She knew all about her trick of letting her hair fall over her face so no one could see her eyes behind that curtain of hair.

Nobody but me, Lucy thought as she rubbed her upper arm through her robe, feeling the coiled warmth of the golden thing resting on top of her nightgown. Ever since that evening, out west of town, the thing refused to stay in the tiny bag, refused to curl up like a good little thing and sleep during the day.

Lucy hadn't wanted to take the chance that little Anna might see the coil bucking and butting against the pair of enclosing bags; she didn't want little Anna seeing it now—*she* knew the girl just wasn't ready for it, just didn't understand at *all*. And now, with little Anna saying that she wanted the golden creature, Lucy knew that she had to hide it *real* good, even better than by just letting it stay around her arm while it rested.

The only trouble was, Lucy wasn't sure if the thing *would* go back in its little white bag, for when she'd arrived home that night, hadn't the coiled thing bitten her, a little skin-piercing nip on the wrist as she tried to make it wind into a tiny spiral and go back to sleep?

"You never did that before," Lucy admonished. "Not even when I took you out of the tobacco can and chased that big mean dog out of the yard...not even when I put you on him and made the dog all scared," she whispered, thinking fondly of her daughter Tina's father. As if in answer—in *angry* reply—the golden beetle-and-snake-tipped amulet squeezed her arm tight, until the soft puffy flesh beneath ached, and tears trickled out of Lucy's pale ruined-doll eyes.

With scrabbling fingers, Lucy tried to pry the thing off her arm, only to feel it coil tighter, tighter. She reached inside her robe through the neckline and tried to roll it off her, but the sinuous, more-than-metal body clung tight, unyielding, bearing down so tight on her flesh that Lucy half imagined she could feel the outlines of the strange lettering on the inner surfaces of the thing imprint itself on her skin.

Lucy's left arm began to tingle, then burn dully, as her fingers went red, then whitish. And still the thing gripped, her arm, until she cried, "Uncle! *Uncle,* already! Please! I give up. Uncle uncle *uncle!!!*" her gravelly voice rising in a fingernails-on-slate screech that slowly resolved into the higher-pitched, almost ultrasonic cry of a flapping, leathery, membrane-winged bat.

SIX—Arlene (4)

"Anna Sudek, don't you have a head scarf? Shame, girl! Your poor ears must be like icicles!" Arlene Campbell warmly scolded as she poked her head out her front door. In her arms was a cat who likewise stared at Anna with almost ludicrously small green eyes set in a pinched black and white face, under the biggest pair of dark ears Anna had seen on a mammal, outside of an Indian elephant.

Dutifully, Anna stopped, remembering that Mrs. Campbell *had* invited her over a few days ago—an invitation Anna honestly couldn't recall either accepting *or* refusing outright.

"It *is* getting late," Anna tried to demur, but Mrs. Campbell already was opening the door wider, urging Anna to step in "at least long enough for me to lend you a bandana. I swear, sometimes you young ladies think you're impervious to everything but a lava flow."

Mrs. Campbell's bungalow had a homey, slightly farmlike odor—the scent of something baking (some kind of berry pie, Anna guessed), mingled not too unpleasantly with a faint, lingering wet dog and used cat litter undercurrent, overlaid with a vanilla-and-spices aroma from the small china bowl of potpourri resting on the nicked walnut end table in the cluttered living room. The animal tang in the air came from the three dogs—mutts all—jumping around, sniffing Anna's hands and boots, and the assorted sleeping and stretching cats adorning the sofa, easy chair, and ottoman.

Mrs. Campbell whacked the nearest sniffing dog with a loose-fingered hand, admonishing, "Now you *stop* that, Scruffy. Please, Anna, don't mind the boys. They're not much used to company."

Anna liked the way Mrs. Campbell unselfconsciously called her dogs "the boys." She bent down and patted a black, curly-furred mongrel on the head, saying, "I don't mind. They just smell my cats. I have this one, Bruiser, he's over eighteen pounds—"

"Goodness. I thought my babies were heavy, didn't I, Silky?" Arlene asked the cat she still cradled in her arms, an astonishingly so-ugly-he-was-cute cat who closed his eyes in ecstasy as his mistress nuzzled his huge, delicate ear with the bulbous tip of her nose.

That's me in twenty more years, with whatever cats I have after Bruiser and Mouth are dead, Anna told herself as she looked around at Arlene Campbell's living room. It reminded her so much of the living room in the house she and Ma used to share that Anna found herself unable to speak, almost unable to think.

There was the same hodge-podge of styles in the unrelated knickknacks; dented, stained, and marred end tables; curio shelves and plant stands; and ratty limp curtains that spoke of castoffs and found things, of a decorating taste formulated not in the imagination or pocketbook, but out of necessity in the garbage cans and beside-the-curb junk piles of Ewerton—the same decor Anna saw daily in her own living room. There was an air of futile, tacky salvation in Mrs. Campbell's living room, of things thoughtlessly discarded and then taken in out of a sense of duty, not out of true affection or desire. And even the older woman's animals—save for a pair of pale orange Persian cats curled up next to one of the floor registers—had that scruffy, once-abandoned look about them, like Anna's own babies at home.

Mrs. Campbell stopped blowing kisses in her cat Silky's ear long enough to say, "Would you care for a cup of coffee? Tea? I have hot cocoa." It was obvious that Arlene Campbell really *hadn't* had company for a long, long time. Her usually stem, no-nonsense eyes were hesitant and almost downcast. *She's wondering if her house offends me,* Anna surmised, remembering the times when Ma raged about nobody wanting to come over to *their* house because it was a "junkyard, a pigsty," even though no one who had ever stopped by had ever said anything negative about it. Even Terry Von Kemp had said it was nice.

"Tea would be fine...any kind." Anna placed her grocery bag on the well-worn flowered wool carpet as her hostess said, "Sit down anywhere you like—my husband used to claim that chair over there as his, but the cats use it all the time. And do you know something? If they don't use it, I *put* 'em on it. The tea will be ready in a minute. In the meantime, you can look at my rogue's gallery over there, over the sofa. My babies are there," she said as she disappeared into the kitchen.

Anna walked over to the sagging couch (the seat was covered over with a large remnant of upholstery fabric in a pattern whose colors almost matched those of the brown and orange tweed cover), to look at the twin dark wood montage frames.Both of them lacked glass; the beige-matted pictures within were protected with sheets of heavy plastic—the kind *Ewerton Herald* sometimes used for special holiday page layouts. Anna had once picked up a rolled-up sheet of

228 * *THE AMULET*, BY A. R. MORLAN

the stuff herself, to use on a glassless picture frame *she'd* once found. *We even think alike,* Anna found herself thinking as she leaned over the sofa to get a better look at the slightly faded pictures within the montages. Some of the animals Anna recognized as being the ones padding around the living room, while others were obviously long gone, but not forgotten—a German shepherd whose eyes were flashbulb-red wavering dots; a dust-mop-shaped grayish-white mutt with a gold-studded green collar (Anna suppressed a shiver upon viewing this picture); and a black and tan tortoise shell cat with heartbreakingly solemn green eyes and a sweet face.

Noticing that there were faint, silvery-gray penciled scribbbles under each of the various-shaped montage openings, Anna knelt on the couch cushions (the inner springs gave out a prolonged *twaaang* when she rested her weight on them), and peered at the words written under the oval-shaped picture of the tortoise shell cat:

> GUY-PIE, 1981-1986. I guess I was lucky to have you
> for five years, but oh, do I still miss you!

Anna didn't try to read what was written under any of the photographs; rubbing her eyes with her gloved hands until the rough knit stung her tender, moist lids, she found herself thinking about the cat she and Ma had owned during the last few years they'd spent in the old lady's home. Arthur was an orange striped cat, unneutered, so he was always getting into fights. The last one had been a doozy—he'd torn the soft skin in back of each ear. Anna had been keeping him in the house until he was healed, but she'd come home from high school one afternoon to find Arthur's blanket-lined box empty.

"Oh, he *wanted* to go out," the old lady had sputtered when questioned about Arthur's whereabouts, but the cat had had to be coaxed to use his litter pan, so Anna doubted that story. Ma hadn't been home when the cat supposedly "wanted" to go out, so neither of the Sudek women knew what had happened, but since Arthur had never really liked the old lady, Anna didn't doubt that she'd pushed the poor, sick cat outside. Whatever happened to him, he had never come home, and Anna and Tina had never found him, even as a mound of bloody fur on a roadside. But she still missed Arthur, and now she always made sure her animals were fixed and stayed indoors always, in memory of what had happened to the poor orange tom with the scab-encrusted.ears....

(And we even hurt alike—)

When Anna heard Mrs. Campbell coming back down the short hallway between her kitchen and the shabby living room, Anna sniffed back tears and phlegm, and dabbed her eyes dry.

"The water will be ready in a minute." Mrs. Campbell smiled as she walked toward Anna, then her smile wilted, and her eyes shifted toward Anna's hands as she asked, in a too-bright voice, "May I ask you something, Anna?"

Anna had just sat down on Don Campbell's ottoman when Mrs. Campbell hunkered down abruptly to get a better look at the bracelets looped around the younger woman's right wrist, adding before Anna had a chance to reply, "Are these your grandmother's?"

Anna held up her arm, saying, "Yes—she lent them to me for Halloween."

"You're a little old for trick-or-treating, aren't you?" Mrs. Campbell's voice strained to sound lighthearted and humorous, but Anna caught the tension behind her words.

Nodding, Anna said, "Oh, yes, I'm pushing thirty. These are for giving out the treats, and cadging free pop at the Rusty Hinge after that. I found one of their jackets once, so I figured I might as well get some use out of it."

Mrs. Campbell wasn't paying attention to what Anna was saying; instead, she put Silky down and then knelt to peer at the mass of bracelets, pushing them apart with a hesitant finger. When the older woman glanced down in Anna's grocery bag. Anna finally said, "Is something wrong?"

Standing up with a hollow pop in one knee, Arlene quickly said, "Oh, no, no...just looking, was all. Do you mind Lipton tea? It's either that or the IGA brand—found, not bought, so I hadn't much choice in the matter."

"Either one is fine...but are you all right? You look pale." Anna started to get up. Mrs. Campbell gently made her sit down on the ottoman again, pressing on her left shoulder with a firm, work-hardened hand, saying, "I'm fine, just fine, dear. Let me get you that tea."

When the older woman turned around, Anna got up again, asking, "But your face lost all its color. Please, is something bothering you about my jewelry? Or is it because it's my grandmother's?"

Arlene's thin shoulders rose, then stiffened under her print polyester top. She stopped midway to the kitchen before slowly pivotting on one thin-ankled leg, but whatever it was that was bothering her, she wasn't quite ready to tell Anna about it. Instead, she busied herself with making the tea, saying to Anna as she fiddled with the cups (Anna heard the familiar clacket of cheap plastic, and smiled in spite of herself), "My Don never let me have much company. He had this knack of having a flatuence attack right when I'd be bringing out the beverages. Man could stop a visit cold with one blast. And mind you, that was Don in a *congenial* mood."

Mrs. Campbell brought in the tea. Anna saw that the string on the older woman's bag was a telltale brown, and noticed that Mrs. Campbell did just what Anna did with her used bags—she ripped a notch in the little square of paper meant to dangle outside the cup for each use. The tab hanging outside Mrs. Campbell's cup was torn twice. Anna had a fresh bag; she wondered how many more like it were left in the woman's cupboard.

"He didn't want me to have company. He'd make his wishes known P.D.Q.—that's 'painfully damn quick.' Why, once, I wasn't able to go shopping for a week, and then he chewed me out for not getting in fresh groceries! And as for pets—we couldn't have any, not after what he did to poor Diablo. Imagine, a grown bull of a man going after a poor little black and white cat—a female, no less." Mrs. Campbell's eyes watered with the memory of whatever it was her bully of a mate had done to the hapless Diablo, and she lowered them.

"Oh, I suppose it was just as well—at least that little nitwit of a receptionist at the veterinary office never got her wretched paws on her. When I had Puff and Pumpkin neutered, and came in the next morning to take them home, I caught her jabbing those painted fingers of hers through the cage, like that"—Arlene splayed out her fingers and thrust them in Anna's direction—"and all she did when she finally noticed me was giggle and trot away on those spike-heeled boots of hers, wiggling her bottom at me."

Nodding, Anna said, "I've had my own experiences with little Miss Karla. When I had Bruiser fixed, she actually put a cat they'd just euthanized in the cage *next* to him. The poor thing was lying half out of the cage, tongue lolling out—"

"Did you complain?"

"Did you when you caught her?"

"I suppose the question should've been, 'Did complaining do any good?'" Arlene replied with a feathery dusting of a smile. Anna only laughed dryly; it was rumored—and not without reason—that Karla Yablinski didn't get her job by being competent, but by looking good in tight jeans and nipple-outlining sweaters. Not to mention being the daughter of a local farmer, a longstanding veterinary customer.

Coughing into her balled hand, Arlene just shook her head, then murmured again, "Poor Diablo...." Anna had closed her own eyes out of respect to both Diablo and her own Arthur, letting her gaze drift down to her wrist, where the cheap bracelets rested against her pale skin.

The silence stretched on, until Mrs. Campbell started to reach for Anna's wrist, then thought better of it, withdrawing her hand as if she expected to be stung by the touch of Anna's skin, or by what she wore on it.

"Are you *sure* you're okay? I mean...you looked scared. Does it have something to do with these?" Anna moved her wrist, letting the bracelets jangle. When the woman went white, Anna leaned forward, letting her hand drop to Mrs Campbell's knobby knee, and said, "This does have something to do with Lucy Miner, doesn't it? Because these"—she shook her arm again—"are hers?"

Pressing her weathered fingers against her thin, dry lips, Mrs. Campbell said softly, her voice muffled by her hand. "Yes, dear, it *is* because of her...because of *Lucy*," she finished in a hushed whisper.

There were a couple of beats of silence, in which Anna thought, *Her Don put her through some of the same shit the old lady put me through. If I'm ever going to tell anyone about that pet of the old lady's, it had better be Arlene—especially if she knows about what I think she does,* before asking carefully, her voice purposefully neutral, almost casual, "Were you looking in my bag for a coiled bracelet? Gold, with a green scarab on the end? A bracelet that"— and only here did Anna let caution color her voice—"that...*moves*?"

Even the dogs were quiet as the old woman nodded her head, her eyes wetly bright and fearful. Finally Arlene spoke, and when she did, it was Anna's turn to feel her eyes grow glassy with welling cold tears.

"Then she's still *using* that...*thing*?"

Anna took a deep breath before replying, "Yes. But I think it's been using her."

Mrs. Campbell stirred her cold cup of tea again before going on. "We all knew that Lucy was very devoted to her Gramma, but none of us realized *how* devoted. You already know what her father did, that night after the old woman died. My late husband's father, he was there on the scene, after the killing. He and the current coroner, August Wilkes, went looking for Lucy, thinking the worst and secretly wishing for it. Not to insult *you,* Anna, but your grandmother was a spoiled brat—a conniving *weasel* of a child—even before that October. She was always lording her fancy little clothes over us— her woolen coat with the fur collar and cuffs, and her jersey wool dresses. Her folks did without to give her nice things, just so she could flaunt them.

"It got so that we'd do *anything* to spite her, the other girls and I. The year before her grandmother died, we were all invited to her birthday party. None of us went. I know it sounds crual and petty, but when I was wearing hand-me-downs from cousins, clothes and scuffed shoes that didn't even *fit,* and my friends didn't have much better, the way Lucy used to stand in the middle of the playground, with one skinny leg tucked up like a flamingo, sashaying in those new dresses of hers really *hurt.*"

The woman began to stir her cup of tea again, while Anna remembered her grandmother's warning about how awful birthday parties were, and pity and anger warred within her—the former for little Lucy, and the latter for grown-up Lucy, who'd willingly spoil her grandchild's fun because *she missed* out on a birthday party.

"Anyway," Arlene began again, "it was a terrible shock to all of us when first Lucy's Gramma died, and then her mother. We'd all heard about her grandmother the night before—our mothers had been there helping poor Rebecca Miner.

"I don't know what your grandmother has told you about Rebecca, but she was a good woman. Very hard working, to the point of being dour, but she had reason, I suspect. Alvin, your great-grandfather, was a bit of a ne'er-do-well. Oh he *worked,* but he was too soft on Lucy, and not firm at all where it counted. His mother-in-law, for instance. That woman ended up acting as parent, grandparent, and playmate to Lucy—I remember poor Bekka complaining to my mother about it. It was her husband's idea that they take Mrs. Husa in after she lost her house."

Anna hoped that she didn't look too surprised upon hearing her great-great-grandmother's surname. No one in the family had ever referred to the old woman by name, and the last time Anna had been to the Ewerton Cemetery, where the full-sized coffin containing the old woman's severed hand and arm stub was buried, she hadn't been old enough to read the chiseled inscription.

"Odd, how her own daughter didn't want her around. Not that anyone blamed her. Mrs. Husa was an imperious old crone, all airs in that black skirt she wore. Something about that woman, the way she had of *looking* at a person, like she knew more about them than they knew of themselves. Well, never mind. It's not important.

"As I was saying before, my future father-in-law was in the house, after Alvin.... Well, as he used to tell Don, and as Don told me, it was so *eerie.* Later on, Don's father said he'd swear on a stack of Bibles that Lucy was *not* in that house while he was looking for her upstairs, yet no sooner had he gone downstairs, than the little brat showed up and walked up to August Wilkes as bold as you please, chirping, 'Hi, there,' or some such greeting.

"But the thing Don's father couldn't understand was why he didn't hear her moving around as he was going downstairs. You know how old houses creak, especially the floorboards."

"I know. When my mother used to walk in our house, you could hear the floorboards over the basement singing."

Mrs. Campbell nodded emphatically, her spoon making little clacking sounds in her stained plastic cup. "Exactly. But Don's father swore that he heard nothing until Augie Wilkes shouted for him to come back upstairs, that he'd found Lucy. My father-in-law claimed that Augie found her outside one of the bedrooms, but he did *not* hear her walk out of there, and he'd passed that very room before heading downstairs, and he did not *see* her.

"It was almost as if she'd just materialized out of nowhere after the man went down those stairs. I suppose his dislike of the girl colored his impression, but I—"

Anna set down her nearly empty cup of tea with a decisive clatter, saying, "No, your husband's dad wasn't imagining things. My grandmother *wasn't* in that room, or at least, not as herself. You saw that piece of golden jewelry she has—the one you were afraid I was wearing?"

"Yes, yes. I saw it after her Gramma died. She had it in a little Plow Boy tobacco can—the kind with the hinged lid...sort of *moved* in there, shifting and undulating with its metal-rubbing-metal noise, like an oiled machine."

Anna pressed her hands together and trapped them between her knees before telling Mrs. Campbell all she knew of the amulet— how the old lady had pressed it against her neck, what it looked like, why she suspected the old lady had been using it against people, what the book on Egyptian magic had said about the dual power of transmuted metal and the inscribed words of power. She even mentioned what Precious Isaacs had seen, ending with, "—the girl said the bird melted, then became a little girl in a long white nightgown."

"Which is what Lucy was wearing that day!" Mrs.Campbell exclaimed, setting her tea down on the coffee table with a clatter and a slosh.

"You won't believe this, but that's basically what she's worn for the past three or four years," Anna said, "ever since Ma and I walked out on her. Summer she wears a cotton gown, winter it's flannel."

"Lucy never *did* want to grow up," Arlene said succinctly. "I remember as we grew older, she still wanted to play on the swings—can you imagine—with the little children. Got to the point even *they* avoided her. But at least she didn't try to terrorize them with that amulet in the tin box. They just kept away from her on their own. I suppose it was because of what they'd heard."

"Was she retarded? From what she's told me about herself then, she seemed so backwards."

"Lucy, retarded? I wouldn't *quite* say that—not unless you count retarding oneself. She just didn't *want* to progress any further than where she was when her Gramma died. Oh I suppose all of *us* were to blame—we taunted her something terrible, asking where her Granny was. We were aping things our parents used to ask each other over the dinner table. It was the talk of many a supper around my family's table when I was growing up, let me tell you.

"It niggled at us because we just didn't know. I doubt you've ever seen a picture of her, but Mrs. Husa was a tall, big woman—a good five feet six or seven inches, which for those days was large for a woman. And she was broad, with that big black skirt swishing around her legs. I used to find her rather intimidating, terrifying, even before all those things happened.

"Think of it—aside from that hand and arm, no trace of the woman was ever found. Not in the drains, not in any trash bin or coal pile in town. Sheriff Sawyer made everyone search their yards, the alleys, just in case Alvin had distributed her, chunk by chunk... nothing. Not so much as a hair comb. They even raked out the ashes in the furnace—not a trace of her. And the blood stopped near the living room and her bedroom."

"My grandmother *sleeps* in there," Anna said. Arlene's mouth formed a dill-pickle moue before she replied, "You don't say. Ohhhh! Not in *there*."

Anna nodded, and the older woman shuddered before going on, "Well, if Lucy's hung onto that amulet of hers, that hideous thing, nothing else she does should surprise me. Goodness, Anna, it must be *terrible* for you, knowing about that thing, and not being able to do anything about it, or tell anyone."

"I've told you."

"But I've *seen* it, and I knew Lucy when all this went on. After living with someone like Don, and putting up with all that crap, nothing much fazes me anymore. I'm close to Lucy's age, but I've lived a good deal more than she has. I know I *shouldn't* believe what you've told me, but...I've seen too much. Too, *too* much lately."

Anna knew just how much the woman had seen—she'd recognized her voice from the 9-1-1 tape Bib had been puzzled over. But she didn't want to embarrass the woman by revealing what she knew about that call—it wouldn't bring that drunken Inez Hibbing back to life, and it had nothing to do with Arlene Campbell as a person who believed her.

"Once I started to hear about those people dying—those neighbors of yours, and that woman you'd worked for—I saw you in the store once, ringing things up and got to wondering, but I didn't think of Lucy's pet being connected with it, at least right off. When I thought of it, I didn't think it was her."

"You didn't see any animals, did you?" Anna blurted out before she thought better of it. Mrs. Campbell didn't seem to mind; she went on, "Yes...that night, Monday. Out in my yard. The same one I saw over at the"—She paused, stricken, until Anna said gently, "It's okay. I heard the tape they made at the station, but no one realized it was you. I figured maybe you'd headed up that way, looking for cans. They asked me if I knew the voice, and I said no. It really didn't matter."

The old woman looked down at her hands, mumbled a thank-you, then continued, "It was a cat, but it walked wrong, and it had that green spot. At first I thought it was an eye, but—it was your grandmother, wasn't it? Looking for me."

"I don't know if it was that, exactly. I think the urge to prowl sometimes hits her. Oh, geez! May I please use your phone? Not to ring through—"

"Certainly, but what—"

Anna was already up and dialing the old lady's number on Mrs. Campbell's old-fashioned black rotary dial phone, alternately putting down the receiver and redialing, until the signal was complete.

"What was that about?" her hostess asked as Anna sat down.

Resignedly, Anna explained the old lady's signaling system, adding, "If I didn't call, she'd be trying to call *me*, wanting to know where I was. I didn't want her hearing an empty line. She's always after me to call her—that's the last thing she says before I go: 'Don't forget the signal.' I think that's what got those people killed. She was reasonably sure Ma and I wouldn't be out and about. She goofed up with Inez, but maybe she had to corner the witch...Inez was like that. She'd get tanked up at one of the bars, and then forget where her car was, and wander around town all night. Used to worry Norm sick, until he wised up and dumped her. Ma had said she met Norm after he kicked Inez out, and she said...."

"Yes?"

Anna reached down and hugged her knees, saying dully, "Ma told me that Norm told *her* that Inez was bad-mouthing me all over the bars, saying that I was the reason he got tired of her, that he 'didn't want no dummy anymore.' Ma and I had a fight over it. In fact, she was worried Inez might do something weird. After all that's happened lately, I'd forgotten all about it."

It wasn't as if it was the only fight you had to keep track of before Ma left, Anna thought, as a sick certainty hit her. Ma must have told the old lady about what Norm Hibbing had said. Ma had been sitting with the old lady that afternoon, talking and having coffee. Ma had been getting chummy with the old lady, most likely at the latter's urging, and all the while the old bat had been pumping Ma for information she had no real business knowing, or acting on, yet seemed hungry to know.

Anna clearly remembered what Ma had said when she got home that Sunday afternoon, the eighteenth: "Go give the old lady the signal. I have to go to the bathroom." And Anna had dutifully dialed, hung up, redialed, and hung up only to dial; again, and with every button she pressed on that dial, she'd severed Inez Hibbing's tenuous connection to life. For all Anna knew, the old lady could have been changed and out of the house before the last ring died down in her musty, paper littered home.

And what now bothered Anna was that even though she'd detested Inez in life—as had numerous other people in Ewerton—she hated the woman all the more for being a spreading stain on her conscience. It was like that sign in glassware departments across the nation: "You Break It, It's Yours."

For now, like it or not, Inez Hibbing (as well as Irma and Elmo, and above all, Wally Inglass and his pecked prick) was *hers* to keep in the deep recesses of her mind, an unwanted acquisition. Her hand wasn't the one that did the actual damage, but it had—albeit indirectly—caused that irreparable destruction.

And Anna knew that no matter what she did, even if she *could* stop her grandmother, she would carry her broken-and-bought goods around with her forever. But she did promise herself one thing—she was never going to add another bit of human pottery to that pathetic collection stored on the shelf in her conscience.

"Anna? Anna? Are you all right? I have smelling salts."

Anna pressed her fingers against her temples and replied, "I'm fine. I have no *idea* what I can do, but I'm just fine."

Mrs. Campbell sat back for a moment, regarding Anna with concern, then leaned over to peer into her grocery bag, saying slowly, "I see you have candy. Did you get some for Lucy?"

Anna nodded, unsure what Arlene was implying, but adding, "Not that she'll give it away—she never does."

"That's typical. She told you, I presume, that her aunts wouldn't let her go out on Halloween. Oh, they were rather strict women. Older, never married, no children. They didn't approve—which drove Lucy up a *tree*. The day after Halloween, she used to try and cadge candy off of us, demanding a piece of this or that. My Lord, Anna...." Her voice trailed briefly, before her small bright eyes began to dance. "Just consider what that Isaacs girl saw. *Little* Lucy. Remember, the killing took place before Halloween, so she *couldn't* go. Now, you don't suppose she'll pass up a chance to be out *this Hallo*ween to trick-or-treat: I doubt she'll want to give up the opportunity."

Anna brightened, saying, "Of course...but would she risk it? She might just sit home and eat the candy I brought her, have it all to herself."

"But is that any fun?" Arlene teased, her mouth drawn into a thin, coy smile.

Anna smiled in reply, a slow smile and a rather uncertain one but one of hope, nonetheless.

Little Lucy would want to have her fun, now, wouldn't she? she asked herself as Mrs. Campbell began to outline a simple but devious plan—one that might work, if Lucy could be coaxed out of her house to partake in a little treating to go with her killing tricks.

CHAPTER EIGHT

TUESDAY, OCTOBER 27, 1987

ONE—The Station (4)

"Well, as long as it's not inconvenient for *you*," Ginny Yarrow told Anna, "would you mind looking after my place until Thursday morning? I should be back by then, to pick up my keys. Otherwise, I'll get them from you here at the station."

"Doesn't make any difference. One thing, are you allergic to cats? I hate to leave mine alone. They don't make a mess or anything, and I'll keep 'em locked in the bathroom."

Ginny's nose began to wrinkle, then she thought it over and said, "No problem. Uh, they don't spray or anything?"

Anna's fingers kept gliding over the keyboard as she smoothly replied, "No, not at all. I keep their nails down, so they won't claw the furniture, and I'll take all the breakables out of the bathroom before they go in. Most of the day, the'y sleep anyhow." Anna wondered if she should ask Ginny if her bathroom had wall-to-wall carpeting. Mouth had that piddle problem, but Anna figured she could bubble off any stains with vinegar and baking soda.

Ginny leaned against one of the file cabinets, cup of coffee in hand, and said, "Sounds okay. Nothing worth worrying about in my john, 'cept the stains under the rim." She dug around in her uniform pants pocket for her keys, saying, "The one for my door is gold. The big silver one's the car keys. Feel free to use the car if there's some emergency. There's almost a full tank in there. I put the number where I'll be on the fridge under a magnet, and the number of the house where Greg'll be is there, too, in case something happens. This shouldn't take more than a day and a half, but...."

Anna smiled as she pulled the paper out of the typewriter. "No problem if you can't make it back. There are enough matrons to fill in for you now with—"

"Yeah. Bib deputized Rhonda. Don't know why he didn't do it sooner, but you won't have to worry about getting a call in the middle of the night. As a matter of *fact*"—Ginny hunkered down next to Anna's desk, speaking too softly for Bib to hear from where he was sitting in his locked office—"I heard that Stu told Bib he didn't want you within a hundred yards of Precious. Something about what happened on Saturday night." Her voice trailed off in an unasked question—what did happen in that squad car?

Anna inserted another sheet of paper in the machine and let the roller bar fall forward with a muted clunk. Raising her shoulders, she said, "Stu read me the riot act after he shoved us in there, and apparently he doesn't think I was listening. He made it plain that my presence wasn't appreciated."

Ginny stood up, saying, "Don't mind *that* boob. He did the same thing when Bib hired me. Ever notice there are no full-time women employees on Stu's side of the building? If it doesn't wet the floor when it pisses, he doesn't want it working for him. Old chauvinist windbag."

"Stuart, are you fucking crazy?"

Ginny and Anna glanced at Bib's office door at the same time, then looked quizzically at each other. Behind the door, Bib was yelling, apparently into his phone, "What good is *that* gonna do...? But it's a clear case of self-def-...Stu, the bastard was *asking* for it.... I don't care if the fucking *Ripper* was the only other witness, we got two people who saw.... *Lissen*, Stuart. Both them kids have attained the age of reason. Their testimony *would* stand up.... *Stu,* for Chrissakes, how you gonna push for murder one if Wally was the one who drove out to *her* house...? She *wanted* him to come out...? Of all the asshole remarks—"

Ginny whispered, "Stu isn't going to insist it was premeditated," as Bib went on, "—since when did you pass the bar, Stuart...? Oh...? Next, I'll find out the D.A is your ninety-fifth cousin five times removed...yes, Stuart, that *was* an insult. Know what, Stu...? You're *sick.* Yes, I saw Wally's body. Yeah, it did look like he'd been trying to screw a pencil sharpener, but so *what*?"

Anna shut off her typewriter and both women quietly moved closer to Bib's closed office door.

"Stu, if his Louise had done that to him, would you be gunning for the first degree?" There was a long beat of silence, then Bib's mocking, "'It's not the same thing.' Sorry, Stu, it is the same thing.... Lissen, I been talking to some of Mayo and Precious's friends, and most of the teachers out there, too. Wally was cruisin' for a bruisin'. I have over three dozen statements from people who'll take the stand about it—yes, most of them *are* adults. Wally Inglass was losing it, Stu. Why, that very morning, he was in my office, ranting and raving like a rabid dog. As a matter of fact, there *was* a witness. I was speaking with my new clerk when he—yes, Stu, Anna. Stu...Stuart, don't hang the fuck up on me!" Bib replaced the receiver with a clack of plastic hitting plastic. Anna and Ginny scurried back to where they had been sitting and standing, where they exchanged puzzled glances and pretended to be busy typing and sipping coffee when Bib opened his door, stood in the doorway, and said, "If that don't beat all."

"What?" Ginny asked, setting her cup of coffee on top of the battered file cabinet.

Bib crossed his arms and kicked at the low nub of the carpeting as he said, "That was Stu Sawyer. Wanted to let me know that 'based on the *evidence*,' he was going to suggest to the D.A. that he should go for a murder one conviction. Murder *one,* can you *believe* it? I always said Stu's brains were in his ass, and this morning he had the turkey trots.

"All that fat jackass has got is one knife with only a couple of partial prints from Wally himself, a window that was broke in from the outside with a rock, and a few pictures of footprints in snow that melted not ten hours after the murder. And on the basis of *that,* he wants that girl sent away for life.Go figure."

"Isn't election time coming up soon?" Ginny asked.

Bib turned to her with a shrug and replied, "Either that bastard's gearing up for the campaign, or he's winding down from one. 'Fore the election, he's worried he *won't* be, and after it he's all worried again that he won't get renominated. Don't leave much time to think straight in between." Bib stared at the carpet for a few moments, then glanced up at Anna, "That thing works a whole lot faster if it's turned on." Anna lifted her hands from the keyboard as Ginny left the room to hide her giggling. Turning to Bib, Anna said, "I was rattled to hear that about Precious. I knew her when she was a little girl. This whole thing's been a shock."

Bib leaned over to Anna, whispering so that Ginny wouldn't hear him, "That reminds me...can I have a word with you? Now?"

Without a word Anna got up and followed Bib into his his office. As she sat down, Bib said, "You heard how Stu Sawyer don't want you pulling matron duty around Precious."

"Yes." Anna folded her hands in her lap and waited for him to go on, but Bib instead pulled out a little foil packet that contained a fruit roll, and after ripping it open, began unpeeling the pulpy fruit from the protective plastic. As he mashed it into an irregular ball, he said, "Now, I don't want to hear any bullshit this time. I'm going to ask you this once, and I want an answer. What did Precious Isaacs say to you in that squad car Saturday night? You said yourself she knew you."

Anna had only a few seconds to decide whether to tell Bib everything, including all she'd either observed or deduced about what the old lady had been up to, or give him just enough of Precious's statement to placate him for the time being. Finally, she pressed her hands palm to palm and said:

"I think she said she didn't do it. I'm not sure. She was shivering so much. But I heard her say 'I didn't,' and, afterward she said something about killing and Wally. I didn't tell Stu because I couldn't really understand what she was saying, and I wasn't sure if she understood her rights. If she didn't understand, and I'd told Stu anyway, the whole case would have been over."

"For someone who spent most of her time ass over knees in Dumpsters, you sure know a lot about law," Bib said without insult or animosity, even though Anna was well aware that Bib was riding her, nonetheless, as he popped the fruit pulp between his teeth and lower gum.

Anna placed her hands palms up in her lap and replied levelly, in a calm tone which belied the fact that she knew she had to go along with a loaded question regarding very common legal knowledge, both for the sake of her job and herself, period. "Not really. I watched police shows when I was a kid, and I read the papers. There's usually one or two Miranda rights violation cases in the news per year, maybe more. I just didn't want them blaming me if the case turned out to be flawed. And she was shivering so much."

Bib worked his tongue around the fruit ball in his mouth; Anna could see it moving through his cheek. The chief was staring her straight in the eye, and Anna levelly returned his gaze until he leaned forward and said, "But why didn't you want to answer me yesterday?"

"I didn't know whether I'd really heard her say anything or not. There was static on the car radio, and people talking outside. I mean, her lips were moving, but it was hard to tell if she was talking or if her teeth were chattenng. I thought I heard words, the ones I mentioned, but I'd been asleep an hour before, and I wasn't thinking clearly. I'm sorry about yesterday. But you know Stu—I was afraid he'd say I messed things up or something."

"Stu said he wanted you to tell him anything the girl said," Bib persisted, speaking with slight difficulty around the chaw of red fruit.

"Uh-huh. He did, but I'd read about cases being thrown out at a higher level, and I simply wasn't sure about her understanding her rights. You couldn't really tell if she was listening or not."

"That is true, but it was up to Stu, not you, to decide that. His jurisdiction, his case...even if he *is* a screw-up jerk with a brain smaller than the hole in a Cheerio. It was *his* case, and he wanted to know what the girl said about it. Do you understand me?"

Anna bent her head down, touched her palms together, and said contritely, "Yes."

"Now, do you want I should call Stu with this information, or do you want to go and talk to him yourself?"

Anna waited a beat, thinking fast. Then:

"I just am not *sure* what she said. Would Stu really want to hear *that*? I don't see how he could use it." She gave Bib an open, frank look that she hoped would convince him, or at least make him re-consider.

"Then you want me to talk to Stu?"

"If you think it's necessary."

"*Think* it's necessary?"

Anna took a deep breath, which in her case meant a short, rather shallow intake of air, and quickly said as she leaned forward, "Bib, I heard you talking to Stu. You yourself said Precious shouldn't get a murder one rap, yet now you're trying to put another bar on her cage. I'm *sorry* I didn't say anything about what I thought Precious said, but I just didn't know what to do. If you had been in the car with me, you wouldn't have understood her any better. The poor girl was freezing. I couldn't even drape Terry's jacket over her shoulders, not the way we were cuffed together. Stu could have found a blanket for her, something to stop her from shivering. Doesn't that matter? He didn't tend to her at all, and she was only a suspect. He didn't find her with the knife in her hand."

"But she had fled the scene."

"The kid was *scared*!" Anna said a little too loudly, and quickly leaned back in her chair, eyes downcast. But Bib didn't shout back at her; he sat there fiddling with the sheet of plastic, wadding it up and stretching it out, until he replied, "Yeah, I 'spose I'd've been scared, too, under the circumstances—*whatever* they are. I agree, Stu hasn't got a case for premeditation, but I suppose he's thinking that if he don't pursue this, they'll be kids killing their principals and teachers all over the state."

Anna crossed her arms, snorting, "That's bull. Remember that kid over in Ladysmith blew away his mom and dad? The ones who were living with a bunch of kids out in those two dilapidated shacks out in the county? People were afraid that there'd be open season on parents, and nothing happened. Heck, the whole town rallied behind the kid, got his first degree trial conviction reduced down to manslaughter. The kid never denied that he *did* it, but there were extenuating circumstances...just like there are in this case."

Gaining momentum, Anna went on, "You yourself told Stu about what Wally did that Friday morning. Now *that* I'll talk to Stu about because I remember what I heard. There isn't doubt as to what Wally was saying, and there were two of us listening. But I honestly can't recall what Precious said, or if I was imagining it or what. I *think* she said 'I didn't' followed by something that *sounded* like 'kill' and 'Wally,' but I'm just not sure. And I won't swear to what I heard on the witness stand. If I got up there and said 'I *think*' this, or 'It *sounded* like' that, I'd be thrown out of the courtroom. And if you want to fire me right now, that's fine with me. I'll understand," Anna finished softly, hoping that her words would be enough to keep her from having to face Stu Sawyer.

Anna knew that she'd crumble if she had to listen to Stu's badgering long enough. A part of her suggested, *Why don't you tell Stu and Bib everything? They might think the girl is insane. and she could get off.* But her conscience warned her, *That isn't enough. You know who's really to blame for Wally Inglass dying, and you know what you really have to do. It isn't as simple as Arlene Campbell's plan to coax the old lady out of the house come Halloween, so we can try and get that amulet away from her. It isn't that simple at all. You owe that kid something. She's taking a fall, a big, long fall, for something she didn't do. She's not going to get off, like you thought she would. Stu Sawyer's going to make every little scrap of evidence he can find count against her, and in a big way. Remember the sign, "You broke it, you bought it." I goaded the old lady into killing him—intentionally or not—and now I have to make good on the damage, and I have to catch the old lady, get that scarab thing away from her, before I can ever hope to do that.*

And in the instant before Bib opened his mouth to speak, Anna realized something else—something that had so far managed to elude her—*and I'll have to kill her to do it.*

"Now, Anna, I wasn't saying anything about firing you—I just want to get to the bottom of this Precious Isaacs business. That's all. 'Cause if she *did* kill Wally—"

"Do you honestly *believe* that? Really, Brian?"

Bib flinched when Anna said his real name, before he admitted, "No, I don't. The kid's a no-account, but I doubt she'd do *that*, even in self-defense. She didn't have any blood in her mouth—least, I didn't see any. Damn thing was so mangled who knows *what* weapon was used on it. You know, on his—"

"I saw—through the sheet," Anna said, relaxing slightly. Apparently Bib had thought better of calling Stu, which gave Anna a little more time...even though she doubted it would be enough. After hearing Precious's story, Anna doubted that fifty years would be time enough to capture and destroy that amulet. But if she was going to clear the girl's name, there was a chance that Halloween night would be too late.

TWO—The Apartment

Ginny drove Anna home after work. Anna was thankful that she didn't question her about why she had been sitting in Bib's office that morning. Anna threw a couple of changes of clothes into a mildew-stained maroon nylon roll bag she'd found dumpster diving, prior to carrying the cats out to the car. Ginny hefted Bruiser and asked, "Is he big or *what*?" before letting Anna carry him outside and driving back into town, to Ginnny's above-the-Happy-Step-Shoes apartment.

Ginny was going out of town on some sort of personal business. She hadn't mentioned any names, but Anna guessed it had something to do with the fellow she had her sights on marrying, provided he got around to popping the question. At any rate, as long as Bib had okayed Ginny's absence, it wasn't up to Anna to judge her co-worker, and Anna had no idea what raising a young child alone would be like. Ginny wasn't taking her car; her friend was driving down to pick her up.

As Ginny threw the last of her own clothes into a set of flowered burlap luggage, the kind popular when the two women had been in bigh school in the mid-seventies, Ginny said, "It's okay if you use the car to go someplace in an emergency. It's gassed up. I have food in the fridge, you might as well eat it before it goes bad. The yellow crud in the Tupperware bowl is Greg's science project, the whole class is doing 'em, so that's the only thing off limits in there. I really appreciate this, Anna, so anytime you need a favor—"

Anna understood Ginny's tacit message—I'm not paying you to apartment-sit, so let's trade favors—and replied, "I'd appreciate a lift to the vet's when I have to take Bruiser in for his shots. Last time I weighed him he was over eighteen pounds, and all I have is a carrier."

"That cat needs a stroller!" Ginny laughed, as a car horn honked down at street level. Ginny glanced out the window and waved. As she picked up her purse, she said, "Thanks again, Anna. Last time I left this place empty, I ended up losing my TV *and* the VCR. My insurance covered 'em but, *still*—so I really appreciate this."

The horn sounded again. Ginny picked up her suitcases and headed for the door, adding, "If Greg calls, tell him I'm gone and said bye-bye, and that I'll call him as soon as I get back. Now, I think I have all the phone numbers on the—"

"Go on, I'll take care of it," Anna said, giving Ginny's back a gentle nudge as she maneuvered out the door and onto the landing that jutted onto the store roof. Ginny's Prince Charming was getting out of his car, moving just slowly enough so that Ginny had to carry her bags most of the way down the narrow wooden staircase leading to the alley in back of the store. Anna waved to the couple as they drove off, muttering, "Good luck, Ginny," as she let herself back into the apartment.

Once she had the door locked, Anna let Bruiser out of the bathroom—thank goodness it had no carpeting or rugs of any kind, just an easy-to-clean vinyl floor, and no knickknacks for Mouth to tip over and break—then sat down on Ginny's recliner, with Bruiser stretched out along her torso, his paws in the middle of her breasts, and his massive head resting on his toes.

Anna rubbed the wide expanse of flesh between his tufted ears, saying, "What's Momma gonna do, huh, Brupie? I wish you could help me...I wish *I* could help me."

The cat kneaded her flesh for a few seconds, his body rumbling with a purr. Closing his eyes, he suddenly reached for Anna's face with one paw, letting his matte-finish pad glide down her cheek and jaw. Anna squeezed him against her, rubbing the top of his head with her chin tip.

"What *am* I going to do?" she asked him. "I can't let Precious go to jail for what the old lady did...for what *I* made her do. First I talk to her about Wally, and the next thing I know, he's dead. And that girl saw the old lady do it, but who'd believe *her*? That Mrs. Campbell—you'd like her, Bruiser, she's a cat person, too—she hit it right on the head. If I hadn't seen that thing years ago, even *she* wouldn't be able to believe what I told her. It's crazy—know that, Bruiser?" she asked the cat unselfconsciously, since it never felt strange to her to carry on extended one-sided conversations with the huge neutered tom, almost as if the cat were somehow her equal, if not in size, then in intellect.

"I went off to college to try to escape what my life had become...what it *always* was, but my life followed right behind me, *in* me. I couldn't escape it any more than I could escape myself. And while I was there, all it was was this or that professor telling me, 'You can't just *know,* you have to *prove*' this or that. Gut feelings were the enemy of learning. They tried to teach me that, Brupie, and I tried to listen, but they didn't warn me about the times when you can't just go look it up! They didn't say what to do when what you're facing isn't contained in some book you can pull off the shelf, page through, and then isolate the facts in." Bruiser regarded her with his wide round eyes, listening reverently to Anna's every word.

"I'm lucky I found what I did in that stupid book Professor Nuzzi made me buy...and even then, it's only the word of people who can't verify what they saw when they saw it. Nobody today would actually *believe* them. Know what, Bruisie?"

The cat draped his long, thick front legs around her neck and made a low sound, as if to say, "No, I don't...*tell* me what."

Running her hand along Bruiser's sleek, warm fur, Anna said, "I almost ended up waist deep in it, with Stu Sawyer, no less. Now *him* you wouldn't like. Him *nobody* likes...and as far as he seems to be concerned, the feeling is mutual. It's wrong, what he wants to do to that kid—only a ploy to get himself reelected. Go after the town cruds, to get the upstanding folks on his side. And Precious, she isn't exactly poster-child material. Her own family won't post bail for her. Isn't that something, Bruiser? Her own kin. And Stu only had her arraigned this morning, after he called Bib. I'm not sure if you'd like Bib. He eats a lot, like you, but sometimes I don't know about him—and guess what? The saggy-butted bastard had them go for suspicion of murder. Not manslaughter—murder.

"Can you believe it, Bru-Bru? *I* know she didn't do it, she knows she didn't do it, and that little twerp of a boyfriend of hers knows she didn't do it, but that doesn't matter—not at all," she said, tapping her finger on his flank for emphasis, "Not unless I can prove what she and I know...and I have no idea how to do that. I'll be lucky if I can flush her out of the house come Saturday. After that, who knows...who *knows*? Right, Bruiser?"

Anna's cat sighed and rested his head in the hollow under her chin. He didn't know what to do, either...but a coppery taste came and went in his mouth as he thought of what he'd *like* to do to help his Person.

THREE—Lucy (5)

Pacing back and forth before the telephone, Lucy hissed, "Ring, *ring,* RING, already!" but the black phone remained silent, mocking her. Outside the house darkness had fallen, and the grandfather clock sounded for the sixth time before lapsing into ticking quiet, yet little Anna still had not given the signal.

Lucy wandered around the living room, past the clawed, par- tially toppled, urine-splashed stacks of old newspapers, her night- gown flapping around her thin legs as she walked, just as it had done so many Octobers before: on the night she had brought her Gramma back from the dead—and before Daddy had tried to send Gramma back where she'd been.

The way he had killed Mother, when she wouldn't get out of his way...but Lucy had gotten out of the way, taking the coiled thing with her, so Daddy wouldn't try to chop *it* apart with the ax he'd gone and gotten from the woodpile out in back of the house. Lucy didn't think Gramma needed it just *then*—not while Daddy was swinging that ax, hurting her. And hadn't Gramma's eyes closed again when Lucy scooped the golden, bug-headed thing off her body and scurried out of the room on four tiny feet, her belly fur scraping the floor as she sped through between Daddy's legs, so fast he didn't see her.

Lucy had felt a *little* like an Injin-giver when she took away the slithering, writhing golden coil and held it against her body, but she knew Gramma would understand. Hadn't Gramma hidden Lucy be- hind her night skirt whenever Lucy did something Mother thought was bad, to make sure Lucy wouldn't be punished or hurt? Gramma understood how Mother and Daddy could be when they were mad at Lucy, they'd yell and spank if they could lay a hand on her, which wasn't too often once Gramma came to live with them.

Lucy was *sure* Gramma understood what little Lucy had to do that late night and early morning. Hadn't Lucy made things all better once Mother was quiet on the floor, and Daddy went running out of the house in his bare, blood-inked feet, printing a trail of long, thin five-toed tracks behind him on the street?

Lucy paused to lick her lips, torn at the memory of what Daddy had done and the way Daddy *used* to be, before the night of the night skirt and what was hidden *in* the night skirt. Part of Lucy loved Daddy, would always love her Daddy, even as the rest of her hated him—and all men, by association, for what he'd done to her and her Gramma—for oh, what a terr*ible* mess he'd left behind!

It had been *so* hard, making sure no more blood got on the floor beyond the circle of strong-smelling red tracks near Ma's bedroom—Lucy was smart enough to realize that tracks could be followed, and what was followed could be found—but she had done it, and all by herself, too. That part made Lucy proud to bursting, and the only bad thing was that she couldn't *tell* everyone how clever and strong she'd been, how she'd outfoxed that dumb old Sheriff Sawyer and all those (nasty) men who had come stomping around the house afterward. She'd even outfoxed Daddy, 'cause all Daddy had wanted to do was make sure Gramma couldn't ever be made alive again—that Gramma would be scattered all *over* the place, in so many pieces Lucy couldn't hope to push them all together so the coiled golden thing could make Gramma whole and alive again.

Not that Lucy knew about *that* part of the coiled thing's magic—at least, not that night. But later on, after her Aunt Joan and Aunt Bella came to take care of her (Lucy's age-sagging face still puckered about the mouth at the thought of mean old Aunt *Bella*), Lucy had found out about the *other magic* the golden thing could do, quite by accident.

Two years after Daddy went away, Aunt Bella's cat Mister had caught a mouse—killed it in his white and gray-furred jaws, and brought it into the house afterward. Lucy had found the mouse, with the crimson drops of blood flecking its dull, no-color fur, and just for fun, had decided to get one of the big knives out of the drawer, just to see if that nursery rhyme she'd heard was right.

Lucy had found it hard to believe that the farmer's wife only needed a *carving* knife to lop off those mouse tails; her Daddy had had a hard enough time chopping Mother up with an *ax*, and he was bigger and stronger than any old *farmer's* wife.

And although the mouse was already dead, and wasn't moving anymore, Lucy had to hack and hack at the tail, and wound up making slices in the linoleum over by the sink. Finally, she'd held on to the mouse with one hand (it sort of *squished* inside, like holding a fuzzy hot water bottle filled with jam) and pulled at the tail with the other, until the tiny spine gave way and the tail came off.

And while she'd been working, she'd rested the Plow Boy tin on the floor next to where she'd been chopping the mouse. Aunt Joan and Aunt Bella thought Lucy carried the tin around because it had been Daddy's, but it didn't matter *who* it had belonged to, as long as it wasn't alive, or something that *had* been alive, like the cotton of her nightgown, or the leather of Gramma's shoes had been...and after a while, the golden thing began jerking in the tin, making it rattle harshly.

Since Lucy never knew if someone might come up behind her unexpectedly, she tapped the tin, whispering, "Shush," but the thing grew all the more agitated in there, until Lucy sighed and whispered, "You can come out only for a *minute*," then released the lid and shook the coil out next to the dead, tailless mouse.

The golden spiral was a writhing blur as it attached itself to the mouse, wrapping itself around the dead rodent, and what happened next happened so fast that Lucy wasn't sure exactly what she'd seen. But somehow, the snake head end of the thing grabbed the severed tail and pulled it in next to the mouse. And when the golden coil released the mouse, the creature was whole and alive, and scurried around the kitchen for a few seconds before it made for a place under the sink where there was a hole leading to the basement. Lucy never saw the mouse again.

But as she quickly scooped up the sated spiral and shut the lid on the Plow Boy tin, she felt a little sad. If she had known what she knew now, she could have scooped up Gramma's hand with the stub of an arm attached, and *really* made Gramma all better.

But then again, Lucy now thought as she hovered by the silent telephone, *If I'd taken her hand, too, they might have looked for her even harder, and maybe Daddy would have told them what he saw that night. With her hand on the floor, those men couldn't help but think she was still dead. And they thought Daddy was crazy. I wish they hadn't taken him away, but they had to. He didn't understand about Gramma at all. He wanted to get rid of her, like she wasn't still family. He was just as bad as Mother—but she did try to protect Gramma from him. I have to give her that. It was too late, but Mother did come around.*

Walking away from the phone, Lucy spotted the calendar hanging on the wall near the kitchen sink—the one Tina had brought from the Savings and Loan. Lucy tried to think which day of the week it was. She knew it was a weekday, but during the seemingly unending time she'd been ridden by the coiled thing that now lay secure within its plastic-and-cloth-bag home, she'd lost track of time.

Is this the day little Anna should bring me my groceries, or is that tomorrow? It's not like her not to call. She's been strange since she took that damn police job—not paying enough attention to me at all—and I've seen her with that Arlene Weiss. Anna hasn't said so, but I know she's been with that old bitch. Arlene would do anything to get even with me, for scaring her on the playground. I know it. Just because Arlene got married, she thinks she can lord it over me. But I cooked her noodle, didn't I? She got a boyfriend, but I got myself a baby...and nobody knew how—not until I told Aunt Bella. Didn't even have to open up the tin more than a crack. Just let her have a peek, and she even believed me when I told her who had made me a mother, without me having to even show her.

That was so funny...Aunt Bella running to the bathroom and trying to shove her own head in the bowl, and Aunt Joan screaming, "What's wrong—oh, Bella, what's wrong?" I didn't say a thing, even when they came with the white wagon and the funny white jacket for Aunt Bella...just like they'd done to Daddy, only he wasn't crazy. Not at all. But if he'd told them what he'd seen, they would have thought he was.

Lucy smiled at the memory as she picked up the receiver and dialed Anna's number. But her smile curved downward into a fleshy grimace when the phone just rang and rang, unanswered.

"Damn police work...damn Arlene...," Lucy grumbled, as she pulled the thin Ewerton phone book out from under the phone and began to page through it, muttering, "Weiss, Weiss. Oh, silly, she's *married*. Don, Don something...ohhh!" until she threw the book on the floor in frustration. The name was *just* on the tip of her tongue, but not in her memory.

Lucy kicked the book across the floor. It skidded in a flutter of flimsy yellow and white pages, like a butterfly caught in a strong draft. Breathing hard, her chest rising and falling under the weight of the thing resting in the bag around her neck, Lucy picked up the receiver, dialed "0," then warbled into the mouthpiece, "May I please have Information?"

FOUR—Night Calls

"Bib, it's for you," Bib Stanley's wife Rhonda said, holding the receiver against her chest. As Bib reached for the beige receiver, she whispered, her voice barely audible over that of Pat Sajak consoling someone who'd just spun the wheel and missed the big money prize, "Sounds like Gravel Gertie. I think it's an old woman."

Bib pried the receiver out of Rhonda's hand, playfully brushing her left breast as he pulled his hand away with a wink, and said into the mouthpiece, "Police Chief Stanley."

"You get rid of that Anna Sudek." The croaking voice in Bib's ear sounded inhuman, like something raising a lipless mouth above a bubbling tar pit seconds before the black goo closed over it, silencing the quivering voice forever.

"I beg your *pardon?*" Bib motioned for Rhonda to lower the volume on the TV.

"I *said,* you get rid of that—"

"Ma'am? Ma'am, if you have a complaint to make, I'm afraid you must give me your name." That wasn't usual police procedure, but Bib knew crank calls when he heard them, and usually the callers would give if he called their bluff. But the dripping-pus voice went on, changing from guttural to shrilly grating within the syllables of a single word:

"I *said,* you better fire that Anna Sudek. Get rid of her now. Her great-grandfather, he—"

"Ma'am, I'm afraid I'm going to have to know your name before I can—"

"*You just fiiiire her!*" came the drying-cement-in-a-blender gurgle, a hoarse yet obscenely *moist* sound that made his skin feel as if it were rippling just under the dermal layer. Bib shouted into the phone, "Now, that's *enough!*" as the caller hung up. Somehow, even the dead air on the line seemed foul and as slimy as the caller's voice.

"What was *that?*" Rhonda asked, raising the volume withthe remote. Her thin face was worry-puckered under her ginger frizz of over-permed hair, her slightly flat voice suddenly resonant with worry. Bib thought her voice was the most beautiful sound in the world; it helped clean that gurgling, sputtering hiss out of his ear.

"Christ, I have no idea. Oh, geez," he said with the small pneumatic sound of a bicycle tire going flat. Bib sat down in his easy chair, absentmindedly scrubbing at his dark, stubbled cheek with his left hand. His wife sat down on the arm of his chair, taunting, "You look like Stu Sawyer when you do that, Bib! Want me to take out nomination papers for you?"

"Huh? Oh, yeah." Bib stopped scrubbing his cheek, and put both hands in his lap, in unconscious imitation of Anna Sudek. Looking up at Rhonda's overpermed mop, at the way the living room light created a ruddy nimbus around her small, rounded skull, Bib said softly, "I just remembered where I'd heard that voice before."

"That...*person* on the line?"

"Yeah...it was Anna Sudek's grandmother, old Lucy Miner."

Rhonda got up off the chair and sat down in her own, rubbing at the place on her slacks that had been in contact with Bib's chair. "*That* old shrew...I thought she'd died or something. Hoped she did," Rhonda added ambiguously letting her voice trail off.

Bib vacantly watched Vanna turning around another vowel as he said, "She wanted me to fire her granddaughter from her job at the station. Geez, if I'd only realized what the old bat was *like*. I knew she was *bad,* but cripes...she sounds like something out of the frigging *zoo*."

"The reptile house, or the aquarium?" Rhonda asked, without the least hint of a smile in her voice, or on her face.

"The place where they keep the aberrations," Bib said. before. turning his attention to the blonde-haired letter turner on the TV.

* * * * * * *

"I'm sorry, I do believe you have a wrong number, good...," Arlene Campbell began to say, but before she could slam down the receiver, the voice projected out of the phone, like hot vomit splattering her ear, "I *said,* you get *away* from her—Anna's *mine! My girl! Hear*?"

Arlene let out her breath in a shudder that left her feeling reamed out, as hollow as an empty shotgun, as she said slowly. "Lucy Miner, you are insane. You do not own *anyone,* least of all that girl. Now good—"

"—*mine!* You stay away! She's all I *got*!"

"—night," Arlene said evenly as she dropped the squawking, rumbling phone onto the receiver with a brittle click.

Arlene picked up the phone again and started to dial the police, then placed the receiver back on its cradle. No, they'd only tell her she was silly not to hang up immediately, that she'd only encouraged Lucy to keep talking. And what could they do even if they *did* follow up the call? Yell at Lucy? Tell her not to go doing things like that?

Lucy Miner never listened when the teachers hollered at her. Why should she be any different now? And she never told anyone who gave her the baby she was carrying, even after they questioned half the men in town about it, and her aunt threatened to take the baby away from her. Once her aunt went insane, the other aunt didn't seem to care if she kept the baby or not. Poor Bella, running out of that house with her hair all dripping, and the toilet tissue clinging to her braid. Good lord, to shove your own head in such a horrible place...the woman was clearly deranged. She was even kicking her cat, and Bella would never have hurt Mister like that. He was such docile, obedient animal. Lucy used to play with him like a doll, dressing him in baby clothes.

Arlene hugged Silky tighter to her thin chest, whispering out loud. "Oh she *couldn't* have...not *that.* But Bella *did* scream when the cat ran past her out in the yard, and she kicked at him, which she never would have done to her cat. Bella wasn't *like* that...but she wouldn't stop screaming and ripping out her hair until Lucy came and carried the cat into the house.

"But Lucy couldn't have...*wouldn't* have done...oh goodness, no."

Arlene dialed Anna Sudek's number, waited for twelve, then reluctantly hung up, scolding herself, "Now, that girl has enough worries on her mind...no use hurting her more. Enough that she realizes what she's up against with that thing. Besides," she whispered in Silky's huge, black-furred right ear, "there's no way the girl would *want* to believe that. Even if Lucy was depraved enough to go do something like that with her aunt's cat—not that it could've *worked,* but—"

Arlene swallowed down thick phlegm, with difficulty, before finishing her thought aloud, in the company of an uncomprehending audience, "—could Lucy have been sick enough to put that amulet on that *cat,* and then—"

No, no...no one could be that inhuman, that sick, not Lucy Miner. Oh, no, please, God, she couldn't have done that, Arlene thought as she reached for the phone again.

She wouldn't have done that—not with an animal....

CHAPTER NINE

WEDNESDAY, OCTOBER 28, 1987

ONE—The Station (5)

"Call for you on line two, Anna," Kurt the dispatcher yelled down the hallway. Anna thumbed off the typewriter, picked up the receiver, hit the flashing button located near the bottom of the phone, and said, "Ewerton Police Station. Anna Su—"

"Where *are* you?" the old lady shouted into Anna's ear.

Praying that no one was listening in on the line, Anna said as calmly as possible, "I'm at the station...you *know* that. And I can't accept personal calls like this."

"Oh, I *beg* your pardon. I *meant* to say, 'Where *were* you?'" The old lady's imperious, snotty-brat tone set Anna's nerves on edge. Feeling an incredible rush of empathy and compassion for little Lucy's hapless maiden aunts, Anna truggled to keep her voice light and even as she continued, "I was not home. I didn't think that I had to leave an itinerary with you. I'm sorry for the inconvenience."

"*Don't* you *talk* to *me* like I'm some damn *dumb* vacuum cleaner *salesman* on the—" Lucy Miner's rage was a palpable, pulsing thing; it wormed through the phone lines and crawled into Anna's ear, to squirm its way into her brain, laying eggs in its path.

"Please, would you calm down? I had to be somewhere and—"

"All *fucking night*?" The worm was screaming in Anna's brain now, dying in the throes of maddened pain. Not caring what anyone within earshot thought, Anna snapped, "I'm an *adult*. You do *not* own me, do you hear? That s*hit* may've worked on Ma, but not with *me*. Do you *understand*, old woman? I don't have to answer to you."

The old lady wailed something into the receiver, a sound that hovered between a baby's first bawl and a bull-loud bellow. Anna kept right on talking over the rising sound: "All you've done *all* your life is manipulate people, and I am sick and *tired* of it now!

THE AMULET, BY A. R. MORLAN * 255

You may've gotten away with it with Ma, but I'm *not* Ma. I don't owe you a—"

"But I'm your *Baba!*" the old woman shrieked, as if invoking a holy name from antiquity, fully expecting Anna to succumb to the word of power.

"You know what you are to me?" Anna's voice dropped several decibels, to a hissing whisper. "You are *shit.*"

All the old lady did was keen, until Anna had to hold the receiver away from her ear. The sound was worse than an oncoming tornado—all high notes with no bottoming out. "Now, don't you *ever* call me at work again like this. If you do, I'm transferring the call to the chief of police."

The old lady squalled out something about Bib "not *listening,*" but Anna overrode her with a terse, "I have to get back to work. *Good-bye,*" and broke the connection by slamming her stiffened hand down on the receiver buttons. When she got an open line, she hit the button that connected with Kurt out at the front desk.

"Hi, this is Anna. Say, Kurt, would you do me a favor? If that old woman who just called ever calls for me again, would you patch her in to Bib instead? Yeah, she *was* getting abusive. Sorry about... oh, thanks for understanding. Yeah, I think Bib will know what to do with her, too. Pardon? Oh, she's always been that way. It's a long story. You, too? She didn't do anything *serious,* did she? Uh-huh... oh, good. But listen, Kurt, if anything like that ever happens again, let me—no, no, it isn't right that she keeps getting away it...no, she *isn't* that old. Oh, okay, Kurt, talk to you."

Someone came into the station and Kurt had to hang up.

Anna turned on her typewriter again and began typing, her fingers instinctively drifting and touching down, independent of her brain.

Will I ever stop being surprised by that woman? Anna wondered, feeling as if she was drowning from within, even as she sat in a desert-dry place.

The old lady had *done* something to Kurt's little girl when the child was making the rounds selling Girl Scout cookies last year. Kurt didn't know—or claimed he didn't know—the specifics, but apparently his daughter had knocked on the door, only to be confronted by what she thought was a hideously withered crone, who said or did *something* that either the girl or her father didn't want to mention. *Well, at least it wasn't an animal. I've no idea how I could have explained that to Kurt,* Anna tried to console herself as Bib Stanley walked past her desk with a nod, then let himself into his office and quietly closed the door behind him. His passing dredged up that fragment of conversation Anna had had with the old lady—something the old bat had wailed about Bib—but Anna didn't want to approach him after what he'd said to her yesterday.

Bad enough that she had to contend with the old lady—play cat and mouse with a willful child only marginally trapped in the body of an old woman.

("But Anna, Penny said that your grandmother *was* old, really *ancient*...and she said she, well, *smelled* funny, a really weird odor, like—uh, Yes, sir, may I help you? Anna, I have to go—")

—make that a very foul-smelling old woman. Placing another sheet of paper in the machine, Anna thought, *What's the matter, Kurt, doesn't your wife serve bacon? Or did your Penny catch a whiff of the old bat's cold cream? That glop's enough to knock a person cold—*

Anna could empathize with Kurt's little girl about the age part, though; ever since Anna could remember, her grandmother had always seemed so...*constant:* the same nightgowns (albeit only worn in the evenings and on weekends), the same thinning, no-color hair, the same age-puffed face, the same bubbling-slop voice.

As if she worked very hard at being old, at being my "Baba"...come to think of it, her *Gramma was old when she knew her...my great-grandmother was fifty or so when she died, or at least that's what Ma told me once. Maybe a bit younger—no, wait, my great-grandfather was fifty. Still, they were old to have a little girl, even for those days. Didn't the old lady have dates in the 1850s written on that sheet of paper when she was figuring out that Oriental zodiac? Ye gods, Gramma must've been a crone...Arlene Campbell would know. She knew the woman's last name, and even I had no idea what it was...that's embarrassing, not knowing my own relatives' names...I suppose Ma and the old lady thought they were protecting me, but ignorance doesn't equal security, not in the least....*

TWO—The Pay Phone

"Hello, Mrs. Campbell? This is Anna Su—"

"Anna! Where have you *been*?"

Déjà-vu washed over Anna as she listened to Arlene Campbell's voice crackle over the pay phone. For some odd reason, Anna thought of that old Monty Python spoof about the "It's the Mind" show concerning *déjà-vu*. The way Michael ended up screaming when the off-camera actor placed a glass of water next to him, for the umpteenth time in the spoof, while he was sputtering about *"dé-*

dé déjà-vu-vu-vu"...the memory of that funny bit wasn't making her laugh. Anna leaned into the clear shell of the booth on Ewert Avenue, half a block away from the law enforcement building, and said over the faint sounds of traffic passing on the street behind her, "I wasn't home...I'm apartment-sitting for someone at work. Were you trying to—"

"Oh, it was nothing...I just tried to call you, that's all. Your grandmother called me last night. She was wondering where you were."

Anna ran the fingers of her free hand along the hole-dotted surface of the back of the outdoor phone, feeling the circular indentations pull at her skin, thinking, *So that's what the old lady was up to. She was playing vacuum cleaner salesman—and she didn't just call Arlene, either.*

"Anna? Are you still—"

"Yes, sorry, just woolgathering." Anna suddenly giggled into the receiver, until she had to explain to Mrs. Campbell that "woolgathering" had reminded her of her childhood nickname for the old lady. When she was finished, Mrs. Campbell said, "Well, that's a nice story, but...well, I thought of something last night about your grandmother. It...it might explain a few things, but I don't know if you want to hear them."

"That's the trouble—no one *will* tell me what's what with that woman. It's been the biggest problem of my entire life. People are always either too polite or too cowed to *do* anything about her." Anna dug her fingertips into the pierced surface of the open booth's back wall until her fingers turned brilliant fuchsia around the nails from the pressure. Anna felt the pressure welling up inside her, but she couldn't release it as easily as she could lift her fingers from the holes in the metal.

"I just don't think I should say it over the phone. You never know if someone is listening in."

Glancing at her watch, Anna said, "Listen, my time on this quarter is almost up. I get off work at three. I have to stop at the old lady's first, but afterward I—"

"Please, Anna, don't go there." Mrs. Campbell's voice was soft, pleading, coming in a gentle yet urgent rush. For once, the woman sounded as old as she really was, and Anna thought with simple wonder, *She's scared—frightened of the old lady. A tough old bird like Arlene Campbell, scared?*

"But I thought you said I should—"

"Never mind that. I realized something last night, something—"

The operator broke in, requesting another quarter for another three minutes. Anna dug around in her jeans pocket for one, and thumbed it in the vertical slot.

"Yes, Mrs. Campbell?"

"—something that may go a ways in explaining your grand-mother, and that...that thing of hers," Arlene almost whispered into the phone, as if the mention of the word *amulet* was too strong, too powerful, to repeat over a public phone line. "It has to do with when she was with child."

"My Ma?" Anna took her fingers out of the round holes and grabbed the metal-wrapped phone cord, as if trying to choke the other woman's words off in mid-utterance. The subject of Ma's father was one that was never brought up by anyone but the old lady...and then it was only referred to briefly, cryptically, with that liver-lipped smile.

"I wanted to tell you in person, but—but I think you should know *now*, before you see her. Lucy's aunt, her Aunt Bella, she had this cat, a tomcat, it was her pet, and Lucy...Lucy grew fond of the animal, and...it was around the time that most of us girls were either getting engaged or were already married, having our first babies and—"

Anna wound the short, silver-wrapped cord around her hand, her fingers and palm mottled pink-white in fury. "I don't think I want to *hear* this...," she tried to say, but Mrs. Campbell's whisper-ing tissue voice kept on and on, speaking words that were all the more awful because they made sense, despite their seeming unreal-ity.

"—and I think it was jealousy that made her do it. None of the boys wanted anything to do with her—she was too plain-looking and mean. She made Una Sawyer look good, and Una was a terribly ugly viper herself. Why, that cad Palmer Winston wouldn't touch Lucy, and he was hung like a rabbit. I think Lucy may have wrapped that amulet of hers around the neck of her Aunt Bella's...I don't *know* mind you, but when the ambulance came to take the bedeviled woman away, she kicked at the poor kitty, which she *never* would have done before."

"No...no," Anna breathed into the phone, shaking her head at the very *possibility*. "You *have* to be mistaken. I mean, it's impossi-ble, *biologically*. It can't *happen*." She realized that Arlene Camp-bell was not a woman prone to the sensational or the imaginative; she believed something because she could see *it*, or hear it, or touch it, and not otherwise. Didn't Arlene say she wouldn't have believed

Anna's tale if she hadn't already seen the coiled, oily golden amulet with her own eyes?

"I dismissed it myself, but think, Anna, it's the only way—especially when you figure what that thing of hers can do. Please, Anna, don't think it makes you—"

"Makes me *what?*" Anna found herself hyperventilating, struggled to catch her breath. "Any less than human?" she hissed into the phone as she tried to stop herself from ripping the receiver out of the booth and flinging it right into the middle of the traffic on Ewert Avenue.

Images, fragments of sound and sight, floated into her line of inner vision:.

Mouth butt-sniffing Bruiser, until Ma gave the saggy-bellied tiger a swat on her rear.

Ma, trotting confidently down a street lit by neither moonlight nor street lamps, unerring in her surefootedness.

Bruiser trying to wash his privates, bent double at the middle. but unable to reach down there because of all the muscles cording his abdomen, tiny cone-shaped member exposed and wiggling from the strain.

Ma licking the last of her ice cream out of a shallow Melmac bowl, her tongue curling delicately along the upturned rim.

Mouth, batting a fly against the window, trapping it there with her large paws, then lifting her feet just enough to let the fly buzz up, right in her open jaws, which closed as she swallowed the still-living insect.

Ma, with her large, slightly tilted green eyes, and her pale, fine hair that wouldn't grow out much below her shoulders, no matter how much she tried to cultivate a longer growth.

Bruiser, grabbing Anna's discarded socks and underwear as he rolled around on her bed at day's end. holding them in his paws and rubbing them across his broad muzzle, the top of his satiny black head.

"Oh, Anna," Mrs. Campbell was saying, "it's not your fault. Please, Anna, I'm only telling you this so you'll know...your grandmother isn't just a murderer—she's *evil*. Killing other people is one thing, but Lucy'll do *anything* to get what she wants, even if she can't get anyone to cooperate with her. She's broken taboos. You should know, so you'll be prepared when the time comes."

Ma, filing her longish nails into rounded points, long after it was fashionable to do so.

Bruiser, before he was neutered, trying to mount Mouth.

Knees buckling, Anna leaned against the narrow silvery metal shelf jutting out from under the phone as she whispered, "I really don't see how what you've told me will help me wrest that thing from her."

Her head pounded, a dull ache that encircled her entire skull, throbbing, endlessly.

"Oh, Anna. Don't you see, girl? This has turned into more than just us getting that amulet away from her and destroying it. Lucy's crossed *over*. Can't you understand? She's turned her back on what separates the human animal from the other beasts. She has to be...put *down*, Anna, as if she were a rabid beast. What Lucy did to you, your mother...it's not your fault, not at all. It's her. She's the sick, horrible one."

Bruiser, throwing up after pigging out on dinner, and Mouth pulling the wad of soiled paper towels that Anna had used to clean up the mess out of the garbage, and eating the vomit off it.

"But you're saying I'm not a human being, Mrs. Campbell," Anna began in a voice that she fought to keep from shaking. "You're saying my grandmother mated with—"

"But it must have been in human form. She had to make him human first...with her amulet. Apparently it must work an opposite way on animals. Lord only knows what the amulet did to the helpless creature to enable it to change that way, but change it must have—*completely.* That the cat was a house pet may have had something to do with it."

The way Bruiser kept stretching out across Anna, his hind paws digging for purchase on her belly and hips, his massive head framed between her breasts, as if he were—

When Anna glanced down at her booted feet, it seemed the sidewalk was rushing up at her, while she stood in place unmoving. Leaning against the glass wall of the booth, she whimpered, "But she mated with something that hadn't always been a human—"

"It's not your fault," Arlene soothed, "but you have to know that she's a danger."

Anna untangled her hand from the cord and rubbed her eyes with her tingling fingers as she slowly and quietly said in the last seconds before the operator was due to cut in again, "But *she* isn't an animal—not in the eyes of the *law!* We can't take her out in the back forty and blow her brains out, like a dog. It isn't fair that I should be charged with murder."

"Is it any more fair to that girl in jail?" Mrs. Campbell replied as the operator started to ask for another quarter, before Anna hung up the receiver.

Walking away from the pay phone, her ungloved hands jammed in the pockets of her denim jacket, Anna made herself watch the toes of her boots move forward, one at a time, in a lock-step rhythm.

"Is it any more fair to that girl in jail?" Mrs. Campbell's voice echoed in Anna's brain like Michael Palin repeating *"Dé-dé-déjà-vu-vu-vu"* in mock desperation during that "It's the Mind" spoof. And her words still weren't funny, not at all.

I owe that kid. If it wasn't for me she'd be where she should be—cutting classes at EHS and screwing her brains out with her boyfriend afterward. It was her life, and she deserved to live it her way. She wasn't bothering me. All she ever wanted from me was to know if we were moving away because I was painting the house. She just happened to be at the place where Wally was going—Wally and his unwelcome companion.

Oh, Jesus, old lady, what were you doing there? What were you doing? Trying to relive old memories? Your sick, perverted, inhuman old memories? Now I know why you always warned me about men, told me to stay away. Is it like that sick statement they make about people who have sex with people of a different color? Huh? Once you have cat you never go back? Was that what you were thinking?

And the images persisted in Anna's mind—all the dirty, offensive, animal-like things her cats had ever done, even as she tried to tell herself, *They don't know any better, they don't know.*

Anna entered the law enforcement building in a daze. She didn't dare think about what she'd just learned. She couldn't work and silently go to pieces at the same time.

THREE—The Old Lady (5)

"—so *worried* about you," the old lady gushed, setting a cup of hot water in front of Anna, who nodded numbly in acknowledgment before pushing a tea bag below the surface of the steaming water and vigorously jerking the string up and down as if it were a drowning kitten trapped in a gunny sack.

Is your Aunt Bella's cat buried out in the yard, old lady? Can't just throw someone so special into the trash, can we? What did he look like, you old witch? What did your aunt's cat look like? Were his eyes green? His fur pale? What happened to him afterward? Did he end up hating you, too, like all the boys who wouldn't service you? You must have thought you were the queen of the hill, getting yourself with child just to show you were like all your contemporaries. But you were still untouchable—all the more so for what you did. You used to ridicule Ma for getting married when she was only sixteen. No matter how bad my father was, at least he was a man.

"You hadn't called, or given the signal and after the way Ma ran off, I was so—"

Yanking the tea bag around the cup until the water was the color of old bloodstains, Anna made herself smile, nod, and casually take in the sight of the rat warren of a kitchen where the old lady was puttering around like a little girl playing chef, all the while telling herself, *No wonder Ma quit school and ran away from here when she was younger. I wish I'd had the sense to do the same thing myself, but I can't really get away from you, can I? If you had known Ma was leaving that first time, what would you have done? Turned yourself into a bird and flapped after her, riding the air currents? Or changed into something small and clinging—something that could attach itself to a departing bus?*

"Anna, that tea'll stain your stomach brown," the old lady admonished, reaching for a glass of water to dilute Anna's drink, but the girl said quickly, "No, leave it, Gramma, I want my stomach tanned. Maybe somebody'll use it for a purse after I die," Anna weakly joked. She lifted the soggy, shapeless teabag out of the water and pressed it briefly between her fingertips before placing it on the edge of her saucer. Blowing on her burned fingertips, Anna was briefly reminded of Professor Nuzzi, doing the same thing at one of St. Peter's College's annual awards banquets in the spring. She and Ma had sat with the English professor, who didn't embarrass Anna by telling Ma why he had urged his highest-ranking English major to leave the teaching department, but instead gushed on and on in his pseudo-East Coast-riche accent about how "perceptive" Anna was in his classes, how *well-prepared* she was each day, all that happy horseshit faculty members save up all year to spread on alumni parents before tuition came due the following fall.

At the time, Anna had bristled at her professor's Janus attitude toward her, but now, Anna would've given anything, even her life, just to be back at that point in time, sitting in her blue polyester and cream lace dress and uncomfortable high heels at one of the gussied-up, blue paper tablecloth-covered St. Peter's College cafeteria tables, eating spiced apple rings and cold slices of lean, dry roast beef, and watching Mr. Nuzzi strangle soggy tea bags with his pale, blunt fingers.

At least then I had some hope...I thought I knew what I was, what I still hoped I could be...I didn't have to sit there thinking about how I wasn't much better than old Gregor Samsa in Kafka's Metamorphosis, *good old Gregor, who woke up only to discover that he wasn't a human being any more...only thing is, other people saw that Gregor had changed into a gigantic vermin...I wonder what Mr. Nuzzi would think if I were to call him long-distance and tell him that I knew what it was like to be Gregor Samsa on the in-side....*

As the old lady sat down close to Anna, the motion of her robe and nightgown wafted her fulsome, hot stench in the girl's direction. What had Kurt said that morning? His Penny had smelled something she couldn't recognize or describe, and Anna had thought that Girl Scouts knew better. They trained out in the woods, didn't they? Earned merit badges for learning things? Anna supposed that identification of foul odors wasn't one of them.

As she forced herself to look the old lady's way, for the sake of appearances, Anna noticed that the cloth bag was back in place around the old woman's greasy, wattled neck. She could see the cord, weighted down with that grotesque burden. As if the pressure of Anna's sight alone was enormous, driving, the amulet shuddered under the old lady's nightgown, an almost imperceptible ripple under the dingy white fabric that Anna might have mistaken for the movement of the old woman's Adam's apple, except that it occurred at least an inch lower than where such movement ought to have. Anna realized that she wasn't simply dealing with something exotic, ancient, a relic of another time, another culture, another mind-set. The amulet itself was malign, and incredibly dangerous.

You have it hanging right there, right between your scrawny. brittle little collarbones. All I d have to do is snake my hand out fast, so fast it would be a hummingbird blur, grab that thing off your neck, snap the cord against your spine, leave a rope burn on your greasy, smelly, godforsaken flesh...but you're fast, too, old lady, thanks to that amulet. As soon as it feels the heat from my hand you'd be changed into something fast. Faster than that poor cat... you...were with. *And you've always been quick to move, even in your* human *state. You always used to surprise me when I was little, reaching out and grabbing me before I had a chance to think or re-act, grabbing me and pinching my flesh in a big twist of pulled skin...and always* under *my clothes, so Ma couldn't see. What did you think you were, a mother cat grabbing her kittens by the scruff of the neck?*

Is that why you always made yourself look and seem so old, to keep me off guard until I was smart enough to at least halfway figure you out? Was it camouflage, like a stippled beast hiding in long grass? Wear the skin of an old, old woman, to hide the tigress within?

The old lady was babbling nonsense—not her usual drivel about what Judge *Wapner* said or did yesterday, but something about when she was a child, after her daddy went away.

"—and after the *doctor* said I could come *downstairs*, Joan put some *flowers* on the *table*, a little *vase* of them, just like if *company* was coming—"

The old lady was apparently immune to the pathos of her words. Anna steeled herself from actually *feeling* for the little Lucy who once was, but she couldn't help but think, *Just like company. Didn't they pay much attention to you otherwise? Or did they resent you for what happened to the family, and for disarranging their lives? Did they blame you for the sidelong looks, the whispers behind their backs? Did they realize you were the cause of all this? I wonder if your daddy ever had a chance to say anything to anyone about what he must have seen that drove him over the edge.*

"—and they *let* me sit at the *table*, in my *nightgown*, and we all had *ice* cream in little *paper* cups, with *wooden* scoops, just like the *other* kids ate it...and there was an *actor* on the inside of my *lid*. I can't remember *who*, but he was *very handsome*."

"Too bad you didn't keep it," Anna said, simply to keep the old lady from asking her if she was, indeed; listening, the way the old lady did whenever she spoke about *People's Court*. It was yet another one of her ways of maintaining control, another childishly insidious way of making sure first Ma, then Anna, actually paid at least marginal attention to hler nonsensical blathering.

"Oh I think I *did*. I keep *everything*," the old lady bragged, rocking back and forth in her chair, making the wood protest feebly, all the while holding onto the edge of the table with her dirt-rimmed, yellow-nailed fingers.

I'll bet you do...this place is starting to smell like you've begun saving your own wastes, too, like that old eccentric in that book Mr. Nuzzi assigned us in Contemporary Novels, John Barth's The Floating Opera. *You'd have liked that character, he saved all his bodily excretions in jars in the basement, and put it in his will that they be saved—*

Anna had to force herself not to jerk in her chair as she abruptly realized what should have been plain all along, not only to her, but to everyone—the *smell.* She and Ma were used to it lately—they both thought that it was the old lady's usual scorched-meat reek, coupled with the dusty scent of crumbling newsprint and the dry, moldy odor of an old, airless house. But now Anna recognized the obvious, which had eluded her all these years *because* it was such a part of her life.

The Miner house had *always* smelled odd. True, the wood was rotten here and there, and in some rooms the wallpaper was years and layers old, and then there were the acccumulated mingled smells of cooking, dirty clothes, old shoes, kitchen trash, and all the other little living or decaying things that occur in *any* house—that special scent which signals "home" in a person's brain. But still, the Miner house smelled *funny.*

Not exactly *bad,* not *good* in the least, just...*strange.* An indistinct, redolent undercurrent that was always simply *there* to Anna, such a part of her past, her *being,* that she hadn't noticed it before she'd thought of this place in the context of that episode in *The Floating Opera.* The man in the book had been keeping his solid wastes in his basement, preserved in canning jars, but Anna didn't think that Lucy had saved anything as common as human waste, although she suspected that Lucy had, indeed, saved something human, all right.

Why the connection between the odor in the house and the old "Where's Granny" jibe hadn't occurred to Anna years ago, when she'd actually read the book and discussed it in class, wasn't clear at first, but as Anna half listened to the old lady drone, "—Aunt Joan *tried* to throw out Daddy's *Plow* Boy tin, when I was *fifteen*, but *I fooled* her, I *hid* it in my *mattress*—" It finally came to her, even as the making of one connection led to the derailing of Anna's current train of thought, onto a track heading in another, equally bizarre direction.

Back then, Anna had still been at least marginally under the old lady's dominance. She realized the old woman was dimwitted, but she still feared and half respected Lucy and her word, nonetheless. And questioning, even in the privacy of her thoughts, something as basic as the quality of the shelter the old lady provided to her and Ma, was simply unthinkable. Just as it was unthinkable for either Anna or her mother to ever ask the old lady anything about what had really happened back in October of 1931, or to ever question the old lady about the identity of Ma's father, or what had happened to Alvin Miner after he was shipped out of town clad in a white, wrap-sleeve jacket, with a restraining gag in his mouth—

("Daddy tried to bite the sheriff, so they put a rolled-up hankie in his mouth, right before they swung the van doors shut, and even then little Anna had half wondered why Baba sounded so glad about her own daddy being bound and gagged like that.)

—and vanished from Ewerton and the lives of his relatives for good. Anna doubted that the man had had a trial; apparently like his successor in rural madness, Ed Gein, Alvin had been judged unfit to stand trial. It was a shame, really. Anna didn't even know when her own great-grandfather had died, or where he was buried, yet he was her own flesh and blood.

But questions had been discouraged in Lucy Miner's household. Her word was law, and that was that, like a spoiled brat playing king of the hill, the snot-nose obnoxious one who became king and wouldn't give up that top spot on the mountain.

When I was in school, if you wanted a turn on a swing someone was using, you stood in the sand at the base of the swing and counted to ten, but some of the kids wouldn't give up the swing after you said "ten"—they'd just kick up sand at you and laugh as they swung higher and higher into the sun. All this while she was kicking sand in my face and Ma's and we never knew it...not even when our eyes were filled with grit to the point of blindness....

"—on the *radio,* on WERT, about that *girl*—the one who *killed* that *principal* of yours," the old lady was burbling smugly. Apparently she'd switched topics while Anna was lost in speculation about the almost-too-awful-to-contemplate origin of the house's strange smell.

Anna quickly sipped some of her tea, almost gagged when the too-hot liquid scalded her tongue, then said, "She's only a suspect, until she's—"

Coyly, the old lady replied, "That's not how the *sheriff* said it on the *radio.* He was live, on *Speak Your Piece,* and *he* said that the *suspect* was being *arraigned* as an *adult,* for *murder one,* and that none of them *kids* out there should try doing the same *thing* to their parents or the *other faculty* members."

Anna was dizzy. The dingy, mold-dotted pale green walls were looming in on her, while the old lady hovered over Anna like a praying mantis, goggly, colorless eyes scrutinizing her as a potential meal.

I should have spoken to Stu, should have told him what I knew, even if he thought I was insane. Dammit, I've been deputized...that makes me almost like an officer. I can arrest people...yet I blew it. Stu asked me if the kid said anything, and I denied it. Precious might have gotten off as crazy. At least they'd have shipped her out of here, for testing at one of the hospitals. Anything, to get away from Stu. Now her parents won't authorize her transfer from the jail, won't pay her bail, anything. The kid's stuck here until her trial comes up...and then she'll be tried as an adult, which means they can throw the damned book *at her...all because* I *didn't want Stu thinking I was crazy, like my great-grandfather. It wasn't a matter of them thinking the old lady was nuts, or even trying to keep what she has been doing a secret. I didn't want anyone thinking* I *was strange in the head, too....*

Dimly, Anna wondered how Precious Isaacs had been waived into adult court, since she hadn't so much as spoken yet, but this *was* Ewerton, and Dean County, and if they could ship great-grandfather downstate within hours of his crime—just pack him in the padded wagon and take him away—Anna wasn't surprised to learn about what had happened to Precious. They *have their own rules up this way—always have, always will.* she decided with sick certainty. The lawmakers down in Madison didn't have much contact with poverty- and-corruption-riddled Dean County. Perhaps they felt it best to ignore the county and its county seat as much as possible, to avoid further embarrassment. Bad enough they had to contend with the problem of all the out-of-state immigrants who were turning Wisconsin into welfare wonderland, let alone poke their citified noses into the affairs of some backwater, off-the-highway community in the north central region.

And Anna doubted that anyone would care *what* happened to Precious Isaacs. Had anyone given a damn when Inez Hibbing had been found bloody and cold in the fairgrounds woods, or Elmo and Irma were mashed into cherry-jam paste out on the old gravel road north of town? Lately, no one even mentioned *them*; nothing had changed in town after their passing. Norm Hibbing still opened his tacky novelty shop each morning, unrolling the green-and-tan-striped awning above the glass doors, and Zack Downing kept on going to work each morning, driving to his meat-cutter's job at the Red Owl. She'd seen his car in the store parking lot, on the very day of his wife and brother-in-law's double funeral. They were buried in the morning, and Zack's car was at work come the time Anna was walking home from her own job.

No, the deaths the old lady had caused hadn't caused more than a ripple in the stream of life in Ewerton. It was as if those three lives were nothing more meaningful than twigs dropped in a river that got caught on the banks and stuck there. The river flowed on, uncomprehending...and that was what was so horrible to Anna.

People had been deprived of their lives. Never mind that they were cruds—useless people nobody even missed. They had been people, and now they were something less than gaping holes in the fabric of life here. And if Wally Inglass had died alone somewhere, if his death too had seemed like an accident, things would have gone on as usual, without discernible change. As it was, Precious's plight was little more than a diversion—something to gas about over a couple of cans of squaw piss in the Rusty Hinge, or while folding dried socks and towels on the brown Formica folding tables at the Super Lunderette.

Even Stu Sawyer was using the case as a mere object lesson for Ewerton's youth, like those dramatic audiotapes the guidance counselors used to play for Anna and her classmates back in junior high about the evils of LSD, drinking, and glue and gasoline sniffing. Anna and the others listened with polite boredom, and come Saturday night the other kids would be off guzzling six-packs their older siblings had bought or snorting airplane adhesive squirted into gym socks...while Anna eternally sat home, listening to the old lady pontificate over dinner, absorbing *her* version of the past, a yesterday colored with a child's crayons and watercolors, until everything was either anger red, jealousy yellow, or envy green, with those pictures that Lucy didn't like scribbled over with thick lines of black.

"Grandmother, may I ask you something?" Anna had to fight to keep her mouth from twisting on the first word, but she managed to say it without flinching. Pretending to be interested in her cup of tea helped, but not much.

The old lady stopped in mid-blather and stared vacantly at Anna, as if the young woman was a fly that had just landed in an opened jar of jam, before collecting herself and asking in return, "Well, *that* depends on what you want to *ask*."

Don't go cutesy on me, old bat, Anna thought, as she smiled and said, "I was wondering the other day, seeing that it was the anniversary of y'know, what happened, whatever became of my great-grandfather? It's so sad to think of him dying all alone down there."

The old lady was smiling, that teeth-hidden, eyes-shifting half grin she always wore when she knew something she wasn't about to tell. Anna knew that smile from years ago, starting with the day when as a four-year-old she had written a letter to Santa (with Ma's help), and Ma *said* she had mailed it in the morning, but later in the afternoon, when Ma wasn't around, Baba told little Anna to get the long nail file out of her big leather purse. Anna had done so, but when she had opened the purse, she'd seen her letter to Santa in the rainbow-striped grosgrain-lined confines. In a sickening moment of awareness, little Anna realized she'd been duped—that Santa wasn't real, that that was why Ma hadn't mailed the letter, for the stamp Anna had laboriously licked and neatly affixed to the envelope was ripped off, presumably to be reused on a real letter.

And when little Anna had finally trudged back to her Baba, the old lady had just sat there rocking, with that tight-lipped half grin on her face, under those cold, laughing eyes. Anna realized that if she asked about the letter, and what it was doing in Baba's big black purse, Baba would never give her a straight answer.

When the old lady said nothing, Anna sipped some more hot tea and tried again, "It's just that it seems so poignant, him being down there, when he could be buried up here."

Still there was no comment from the old lady, just that incessant rocking, accompanied by the frantic mouse scree of old wood pressing against worn linoleum, and that sphinx-smug smile, until Anna made herself look into those colorless eyes that had seen much too much in Lucy Miner's sixty-some years on earth, and read something in the old woman's expression that Lucy Miner didn't *want* to say out loud.

Alvin Miner wasn't buried down in the mental hospital graveyard—if, indeed, the place had one—or *anywhere,* for that matter. Comprehension dawned on Anna. The old lady was Alvin Miner's closest living relative. She would have been notified upon his death—if he had died, which Anna now doubted. True, he had to be very old, over a century in age, but he could still be among the living.

Lucy Miner never lost that smeared-on smile, even when Anna stood up and said, "Oh, gosh, the time. I have to be going. I've still things to do," and hurried away from her half-sipped cup of tea, running out of the house before the old lady remembered to tell her to give her the signal when she arrived home—as if Anna would have given it even if the old woman *had* asked for it.

FOUR—The Hospital

Anna charged the phone calls she made from Ginny Yarrow's phone to her own number. It was time-consuming, but she couldn't stiff Ginny like that, not even for an Information call. As she dialed the various numbers, then spoke to the operators, receptionists, nurses, and finally, that overtired and loose-tongued intern on the other end of the line, Anna scribbled numbers and other data on a small pad of scratch paper Ginny had attached next to her wall-mounted phone, all the while saying, "Yes, yes, I see...." as the compressed voices whispered through the receiver.

It was almost seven o'clock by the time she hung up the phone for the last time. She ripped the top sheet of paper off the pad and took it with her to Ginny's plaid covered hide-a-bed sofa, where she stretched out on her back and pillowed her head on the lightly padded armrest. Holding the paper above her head, she read the lines she'd just penned, even though the words and numbers were branded on the soft surfaces of her mind:

> October 1931—A. Miner admitted st. ment. hsp.; diagnosed as catatonic.
> Subsequent eval. '32-'44 same diag.—patient refused to speak, eat on own.
> 1945—change after visit by L. Miner. Violent, had to be sedated, cond. lasted 6+ mo.
> '46-mid-fifties—some improv. no reason given for events of '31. Electric shock given. Later judged to be sane, but senile, unable to release.
> '50s thru '70s—physical cond. worsened, removed to nursing home, per L.M.'s instructions.

Anna had carefully written out the address and phone number of the nursing home where her great-grandfather was being kept in semi-protective custody—the one her grandmother had chosen for the incapacitated and dying Alvin Miner, back in 1979. It was in Wright County, just west of Dean County, of all places, in a hospital nursing home not one hundred yards from the fine arts center of St. Peter's College, Anna's alma mater. The same college where she'd studied the writings of Kafka, Barth and Poe, and dutifully taken notes during Mr. Nuzzi's lecture on "The Purloined Letter," Poe's detective tale of a missing letter cleverly hidden—as a *letter* in among other letters...while Anna's grandmother had played her own twisted version of the same hiding game, using her father in place of a turned-inside-out letter.

Anna had passed the Wright County Nursing Home a thousand times while going to and from classes during her three and a half years at St. Peter's, never knowing that her great-grandfather, the infamous Alvin "Where's Granny?" Miner, was strapped into a wheelchair in that very building, quietly vegetating amid the antiseptic smells of the hospital nursing home where his daughter had hidden him, not even telling her own child or grandchild where the murderer, now rendered harmless by sickness and age, was hidden.

Anna had lucked out in her timing when she called down to the state mental hospital. The intern on duty was just tired and bored and burned out enough to tell "Officer Yarrow" what Anna wanted to know, even after the on-duty nurse had hemmed and hawed, despite Anna's assurance that this was indeed official police business, and finally passed the phone to the young resident on on-call duty.

It was amazing what the mere mention of a law-enforcement title did to inspire immediate confidence and compliance. Kurt the dispatcher had told Anna and Ginny about the phone trick over lunch a few days before, explaining that prison snitches used the scam to get information about potential informant-victims over the untapped, unmonitored prison phones, or so a lawyer friend of his in the Twin Cities had told Kurt.

Anna could hear the intern puffing away on a cigarette as he spoke and shuffled through the old records. She'd probably kept him awake for a few minutes, saving him a trip to the coffee machine, or another handful of caffeine pills, or whatever the guy was using to stay on his feet. At least he'd been friendly and garrulous; he'd even read her the notation on Alvin Miner's transfer slip, about him not being allowed any visitors, adding, "Stupid, isn't it? According to this, the man's a hundred and *six* frickin' years old. What's the old fart going to do? Spit up on someone?"

Anna had forced herself to laugh, to play the part of a good policewoman whose chief wanted her to do some departmental digging, just to put a cap on an old file. Again, Anna was lucky that the intern was too bummed out to pay attention to her. Instead, he was speaking just to hear his own voice. And she'd pretended that she had to relinquish the line in the office, just to hang up before the nice young doctor thought to start asking some questions of his own.

As Anna lay there on the couch, Bruiser jumped up onto her chest and settled down along her torso, his broad black head resting in the valley between her breasts. Looking into his solemn green eyes, Anna half guiltily rubbed his back *(is this a perversion...or incest?)*, feeling the knobs of his spine deep under the sleek fur and padded flesh, and said, in a voice that stopped just short of breaking into either laughter or tears. she wasn't sure which, "Guess what, Brupie. You and I—we just might be related," until the tears won out, and she pulled the cat against her, hugging him to push away the pain and shame that warred within her.

FIVE—Lucy (6)

Lucy poured the half-full cup of tea down the kitchen sink, still wearing that silly little smile that used to drive her aunts crazy when she was a little girl. The same smile, in fact, she'd given Aunt Bella when the heavyset old woman had repeated her question, "Now tell me, Lucy, who *did* that to you? I must know," Lucy just smiled and pointed to Mister, the cat, who was curled up in the older woman's ample lap, ribs moving up and down under his soft gray and white fur as he slept.

"Lucy, don't play games, young woman. You're not a little girl anymore. Alvin may have let you get away with it. and your grand-mother as well, God rest her soul, but I'm—good heavens, what is *that*?"

And Lucy had shown Aunt Bella what *that* was, and she didn't even get a chance to take the coiled thing out and put it on Mister again, just to *show* Aunt Bella. "She was never any fun at all," Lucy said to herself, crackling-fat voice echoing in the silent, redolent house as she made her way to her bedroom and picked up the plastic bag of peaches-and-cream potpouri Tina had bought her a couple of weeks before *she* ran away.

Lucy had to rummage around in her sewing box for a few min-utes before she found the rest of the things she'd been working with, but once she found them, she spread everything out on the table next to Gramma's rocker.

As she worked, she spoke aloud, liking the way her voice re-verberated in the almost airless room's mildew-grimed walls,"I should've told Aunt Bella about *Gramma,* too. *Nobody would*'ve *believed* her. Maybe they would've *kept* her strapped up and *gagged* all day...until she *starved* to death."

Lucy rocked back and forth happily, the world's biggest and oldest baby, occasionally pausing to stroke the old nightskirt Gramma had worn so long ago, even though it didn't ripple under her touch anymore. The wool was still pleasant to feel, especially since her old hands weren't as sensitive as they used to be. She re-membered when little Anna was small, and *her* good little girl, *Baba's* girl, and they used to stroke the night skirt while singing that old rhyme, only *then* little Anna didn't mind the garbled sound of her Baba's voice—not like she claimed to hate it later.

And Lucy sang the rhyme now, her squeaking rocker keeping time with her as she warbled, "Ba-ba *black* sheep, have *you* any *wool? Yes* sir, *yes* sir, three bags *full,"* just like she and Gramma used to sing it, until Daddy came down the stairs that night, and ru-ined Lucy and Gramma's fun."Hope you're *happy* there, Daddy," Lucy said, pushing the last of the stuffing into the thumb, "'cause now *nobody knows* where *you* are...nobody *sings* at *all...*and nobody knows *where* you are, just like *Gramma.* Nobody but little Lucy."

And as the house settled softly with age, the walls rang with bubbling, merrily insane, garbled laughter.

CHAPTER TEN

THURSDAY, OCTOBER 29, 1987

<u>ONE—The Nursing Home</u>

Now I know why that jailed Nazi, Rudolf Hess, killed himself in Spandau this past August, Anna Sudek thought as she parked Ginny Yarrow's Escort in one of the Wright County Nursing Home's yellow-painted angled parking slots that early afternoon.

Not that the nursing home, situated across from the St. Peter's College's fine arts center, was a gloomy, forbidding, fortress-like structure. On the contrary, its modern pale brick and multi windowed design was surprisingly light and cheerful, the grounds as well kept as she remembered them from her years as a student.

But a prison is a prison is a prison is a prison, as Gertrude Stein might have put it—wryly, Anna remembered how Mr. Nuzzi insisted that Gertrude said the "A rose is a—" line *four* times, not three, as was commonly misquoted—and this one was, in its own, just as formidable and escape-proof as the one that had housed old Rudolf Hess in Spandau. *My great grandfather is trapped in there. For cryin' out loud, he's one hundred and six frigging years old. The doctor I spoke to this morning said the old guy isn't strong enough to lift a grapefruit spoon, let alone heft an ax, and still they're keeping him under watch. For what?*

Anna smoothed Ginny Yarrow's uniform pants over her thighs, hoping that no one would notice that they stopped a quarter of an inch short of her ankles, reluctant to leave her borrowed car, to go out into the chilly but sunny October air, and into that nursing home, to bring her charade to a conclusion. But if she were simply to walk in there as herself, there was always the possibility, however remote, that someone might tell the old lady about her visit. Her pseudo-officer status on the phone had helped her find out where Alvin Miner was, now hadn't it? If *that* worked, without any papers, uniform, or badge to back her up, why wouldn't a real uniform help?

But if they get to asking too many questions, you are in it up to your neck. I hope you realize that, she warned herself, but after having come this far, after cushioning herself in a snug blanket of lies, Anna knew that she had to get out of the Escort, walk with confidence into that nursing home, and make her pitch to whichever doctor she found.

On the passenger seat was the folder of papers she'd gathered at the station house that morning, some of which she'd typed on police stationery shortly before complaining of flu symptoms and getting Bib to let her go home for the day. ("That's what happens when you go eating that stuff out of dumpsters, next time it'll be botulism or worse and *then* you'll be sorry, kiddo....") Once she was back at Ginny's apartment, Anna had changed into one of her co-worker's uniforms. Luckily, Ginny had put on some weight since high school. Her clothes almost fit Anna—at least, as long as Anna didn't take more than a shallow breath in the safety-pin-over-the-bustline, reinforced uniform shirt. She had worn a dark pigskin pair of her own shoes, since Ginny's black uniform shoes were two sizes too small.

Looking at herself in Ginny's small bathroom mirror, Anna realized that this just might work. Once she'd rolled brown hair into a loose bun, then brushed and hairsprayed her bangs off her forehead, Anna was sure she looked enough like a busy policewoman to fool the nursing home doctors...as long as they didn't take too good a look at her feet.

She hadn't originally planned on misrepresenting herself as Ginny Yarrow to the nursing home staff, but her ruse about being part of the police department had worked so well on that resident the night before that as Anna dialed the nursing home's number before leaving for work, she simply found herself answering the receptionist's "Good morning," with a brisk, "Hello, I'm Officer Yarrow with the Ewerton Police Department," as if being Ginny Yarrow took away Anna Sudek's guilt over what she was doing.

And now she was only a few dozen yards away from the only man on earth who really knew what had gone on that horrible morning in October, over fifty years before. If *he was* still up to telling. If he was still in any semblance of a right mind.

Remember, that doctor said the old guy had had electroshock, back in the days when Sylvia Plath got her treatments, and look what happened to her. My God, the old man doesn't need to be cooped up in here, he needs to have his name read by Willard Scott on the Today *show. You went through all this trouble, told all those lies, drove over a hundred miles in a car that isn't yours, with a driver's license that expired when you were still in college...all to see some senile old relic with overcooked rice for brains. He'll probably drool all over Ginny's uniform before he tells you anything.*

But still, there was a chance that Alvin Miner might say something, *anything,* that she needed to know. Finally, Anna picked up the file of old, soon-to-be-destroyed arrest files and the few fake reports about her supposed mission to see Alvin Miner (to complete a "study" of the case Bib was ostensibly doing), tried to pull Ginny's leather uniform jacket tighter across her chest, and exited the car.

Glancing backwards at the one-story tan brick and plate glass fine arts center, framed by trees whose brilliant brown, gold, and Indian-orange leaves coruscated in the limpid white sunlight, and a gently undulating still-green lawn which sloped down to meet the highway beyond the school, and fronted with a tall stylized steel cross positioned before the double-doored main entrance—a leftover from the days when the building had housed the dormitory of a Catholic high school for boys, Anna again wished that she was back in college, safe and cocooned from a world that had, within the space of less than two weeks, grown much too confusing and hurtful for her to stand anymore.

But I have to stand it. I just can't fold myself up like an armadillo and hide. I owe too many people. I've done too much to back out. And anyhow, wouldn't giving up be playing right the old lady's hands? She gave up on life, threw herself into a hole and pulled the dirt in over herself, so she could sit around all day in a nightgown, like little Lucy coming downstairs to be treated like company *by her aunts. And the way she* does *leave the house isn't facing life either, not if she has to be something other than herself. And she wants the same thing for me, the* same damn thing. *Letting all this snow me over is* just *what she wants.*

She drove her aunt crazy, and did God knows what to make her father into a madman. She made Ma so dissatisfied with her life, herself, and the fact that she was being used *by the old lady that she ran away from home like a little kid with a bandana full of clothes slung on a stick—which is probably what the old lady wanted all along. With Ma gone, it's just Anna and her Baba again, like Lucy and Gramma...and amulet makes three.*

The images associated with that last thought did it, made Anna walk through those double glass doors and head for the blondwood receptionist's desk with a purposeful stride and a detached, professional half smile on her face. That amulet, that *thing* little Lucy had kept like a pet lizard, something to scare her classmates into submission or avoid, was Anna's real enemy. It had ruled her great-great-grandmother, as it was to rule little Lucy, and it had played a role in Tina and Anna Sudek's very existence. Without it, they wouldn't have been alive, but with it, they were still something less than truly alive, master of their own lives.

And while Anna and her mother had been helpless to stop the power of the amulet before their birth, Anna was determined to stop the cursed thing from ruining what life she did have—even if it wasn't a wholly human life. At least she had an excuse for moving, for thinking. That golden coiled monster hiding in that drawstring pouch around the old lady's neck had no such excuse, certainly not in the twentieth century, and most certainly not while it was in the hands of someone as deviant and demented as Lucy Miner—someone who hadn't the intellect or conscience to realize how incredibly dangerous the amulet *could* be.

TWO—*Alvin Miner (1)*

Crepe-soled white shoes made moist kissing sounds on the freshly washed hallway floor. As one of the pink-uniformed staff nurses and Anna made their way to the small, state-funded room where Ewerton's most notorious ax murderer—the city's *only* ax murderer, for that matter—was kept, the pink-and-white-clad woman walking beside Anna explained, "Mr. Miner hasn't had any visitors since...oh, since before *I* began work here back in 1982. The state pays for his room, of course, as it would if he were still in the *other* hospital, if they were able to take care of him. He's the oldest resident here. We have a few a couple of years younger, but they're not in his condition."

"His condition?" Anna echoed, stopping in the middle of the tangy-harsh-smelling gray-and-beige-floored hallway, trying to catch her breath, for the nursing home was seemingly comprised of an exhausting labyrinth of hallways, and she was already winded.

But judging by the nurse's tone, Anna had been right, the old man was a veggie, out of his mind insane.

The nurse stood next to Anna, hands stuffed in the pockets of her white cable-knit sweater, an apologetic smile on her slightly dry-skinned oval face. "Oh, he's not contagious, or anything to worry about. I meant to say in as good a condition as he is. Considering all he's been through, Mr. Miner is in rather good shape, physically at least. Very wiry. Mentally, though—" the nurse took one hand out of her pocket and stuck it out palm-and-fingers extended and let the hand flip back and forth, alternately exposing and downturning the palm. With a tired smile, she went on, "He sort of comes and goes. But he was alert this morning, when I looked in on him." Her voice trailed off as she started down the hallway again, gummy soles smacking against the damp tiles. Anna hurried after the older woman, bogus file tucked under her arm.

"Usually he takes a nap after lunch, so I don't know if you'll have much luck. You did say you had to be back by evening, didn't you?"

Anna nodded. Ginny had called her late the evening before, saying that she and her friend would be back by six or seven that night. From Ginny's tone, Anna had guessed that her surname wouldn't be "Yarrow" for very much longer—and she hoped her co-worker would be so happy that she wouldn't notice the extra two hundred or so miles on her odometer.

The nurse rose up on tiptoes to look through the glass and wire mesh panel set into the door of the room at the far end of the hallway. With a smile, she turned to Anna and said, "You're in luck, Officer Yarrow. Mr. Miner is awake. Would you like me to stay with you, at least until he knows who you are? I won't listen in on your conversation."

Thinking, *You don't even know who I am,* Anna replied, "Just long enough to make sure he isn't confused. If I need help, I can call for you?"

"I'll stay right outside the door."

Anna smiled. "That would be fine," she said as she edged close enough to the door to peek through the small window set into the wood. The small TV was flickering, but Anna heard nothing. The door was probably soundproof enough for her purposes, even if the nurse had her ear pressed against the wood.

The buttery-stale odor of scrambled eggs and disinfectant hit Anna's nostrils as the nurse unlocked and opened the door. Lightly touching Anna's back to guide her into the room, the woman said in a loud, cheerful voice that barely carried over the blare of the imitation wood-grain color television across from the bed, "Good afternoon, Mr. Miner. You have company." She leaned over to turn down the volume. "This nice officer would like to ask you a few questions."

Anna stood there with her right arm pressing the file tightly to her side. Her left arm was extended across her torso, the hand gripping her opposite elbow, as she slowly turned herself around to face her great-grandfather.

Alvin Miner was seated in a wheelchair, snugly strapped across his waist, the leather restraint almost hidden by a lightly pilled blue and yellow plaid lap blanket. He was a small, compact man, wiry in the way of some older Czech men, like that old Palmer Nemmitz back in Ewerton.

Andy Warhol would have looked like this eventually, if he'd lived beyond February, Anna found herself thinking as she stared at the old man's high-cheekboned and dark-eyed runneled face. Age had robbed Alvin Miner of all body fat. Waxy, translucent skin rested in wet-tissue folds and creases on his Slavic features and in-ward-clawed, horn-nailed hands. Freckle-thick age spots dotted his face, his exposed hands and forearms, the narrow triangle of wattled neck and chest flesh barely visible through his open robe and PJ top.

Most of his hair was gone, leaving just a few brittle, all-directions-flying strands to battle for dominance over his faintly scabrous, mottled scalp. No beard stubble dotted his big-pored cheeks, but Anna saw a few stray gray hairs in the wide nostrils of his age-enlarged nose, and in the openings of his huge, strangely vulnerable ears.

But his dark eyes, seemingly all pupil with little or no iris, were what made Anna's insides turn to shattered glass. Alvin Miner did not have the vacant, marble-cloudy eyes of old people—like those of his not-so-old daughter. His hearing may have been poor *(but not poor enough for a hearing aid, unless the state wouldn't spring for one),* his mind may have been fried extra crispy, hold the catsup, but his eyes were alert, and strong enough for him to seek out her eyes and lock onto them, making terrible, *knowing* contact.

"This is Officer Yarrow, from your hometown, Mr. Miner. She'd like to ask you some questions—nothing to get upset over," the nurse added with a warning tone obviously meant for Anna. Don't get him riled up, okay? came the unspoken plea. Anna broke eye contact with the old man in the wheelchair long enough to glance at the nurse with a smile and nod of her head.

Alvin Miner said nothing, but his eyes sought out Anna's the second she turned her head back in his direction. Anna thought she saw recognition dawning in those dark, dark eyes, and hoped the nurse would get her pink-uniformed rear end out of the sterile, cheerless little room before the old man said something that Anna couldn't explain away.

"—just leave you two alone. I'll be right outside the door if you need anything, Mr. Miner."

In other words, in case I set you off on a screaming shit fit, great-grandpa.

"—and remember, Officer Yarrow, Mr. Miner *does* tire easily."

"I'll only be a few minutes," Anna replied, taking her file from under her arm and opening it professionally, before taking one of Ginny's pens out of her breast pocket, in anticipation of Getting Down to Police Work. The nurse smiled, then ducked out of the room, but Anna could see the dark spot her feet made under the door, against the well-lit hallway beyond.

Anna smiled as she asked, "May I sit on your bed, Mr. Miner?"

The old man, whose eyes hadn't left Anna's since the nurse had gone, raised a semitransparent hand, the metatarsals covered with raised bluish-green ropes of veins, and let out a sound that might have been a sigh, but which Anna understood with great difficulty to be the words, "Fine with me."

Sitting down on the high hospital bed, the lowered metal sides cold through her trousered legs—Anna hadn't been able wear her long johns under the tight-waisted but big-bottomed pants—Anna gave the old man a grave look before softly asking, "Do you know who I am?"

Again the dry-skinned squiggle of a mouth opened—with a start Anna realized that the man had no teeth left, that his stumpy gums were exposed, somehow vulnerable, and noticed that there was no water glass or plastic chopper-hopper in sight—and sound drifted out, an autumn leaf rustle accompanied by the cloying redolence of old eggs and some bitter-scented medication.

"Not police...wrong *shooooes*," and Anna realized that in the second she'd looked away from Alvin Miner to glance at the nurse, he'd been scrutinizing her, looking at her feet, of all things.

"Why, you old fart, you," Anna whispered, shaking her head in wonder. Of course he'd realized her shoes weren't right—he'd had enough experience with law enforcement personnel over the years.

Looking down at her dark-cuffed boots, Anna realized that they *didn't* look right—not at all what an officer in even as casual a police department as the one in Ewerton might wear. And Alvin Miner's 106-year-old eyes were sharp enough to catch what two staff doctors and one nurse had missed.

Humbled, Anna clicked Ginny's pen, watching the blue-inked metal tip alternately retract and extend itself, as she said,"I am not a policewoman. I work in the station, but only as a clerk. But I do have some questions to ask of you...*Jeddeck*," *she* concluded, using what she hoped was the right Czech word for "Grandfather." Even the old lady had known little of her parents' native tongue, and

Anna wasn't sure if she had pronounced the word right, given it the properly harsh and guttural intonation, but it did the trick.

Alvin Miner sat up in his wheelchair, as upright as his domed back and slumped spine would allow, his dark eyes darting, eager.

"Tiiina?" came the crackling whisper, as the old man tried to shift his legs under the downy blanket, but whether he was trying to move closer to Anna or escape her was hard to tell.

Leaning forward, making sure that her back was facing the little window in the door, Anna quickly said, "No, her daughter. My name is Anna Sudek. I'm Lucy Miner's granddaughter."

There was no mistaking the old man's reaction this time. Anna guessed that the nurse wasn't watching them through the window, for if she had been, she would have been padding into the room on her squeegy white shoes in two seconds flat.

Alvin Miner's ruined face was working, twisting into new configurations of pale flesh and shifting muscle over the ridges of bone, and his dark eyes were darting around the room, unable to focus on Anna. She leaned over to place a hand over his trembling, spotted ones. The skin was slightly slippery, and too cool. Whatever blood was still circulating through his body was moving slowly, barely fast enough to sustain life.

"Please, you have to tell me. Your daughter, Lucy, she's been *doing* things, awful things. *Please,* you must tell me, *Jeddeck*...what did you see in that house? That October they...the time you left Ewerton?" Anna gently squeezed the brittle bones under the sagging, shifting flesh, her eyes focused on his ancient ones, pleading.

In the background, there were faint sounds of some soap opera—unreal people locked in unreal, highly sexy, and utterly idiotic situations, in a world that neither Anna nor her great-grandfather could ever hope to be a part of.

Anna rubbed the slippery skin, let it slide around over the raised bones and rubbery veins, asking, "Please? She's been doing things again, like when she was small."

"Small," the hollow voice echoed, as the clawed hand pulled inward toward the old man's belted lap. "Lucy...so small then. Bekka thought...Bekka thought Lucy in *trouble* downstairs, thought something...wrong...down the stairs, I heard her, and across the floor...when Bekka screamed, got out of bed...down to kitchen, for the ax...protect them, protect my girls."

The old man's eyes were focused away from Anna, at a point beyond her left shoulder, beyond this room and time, as the flaking voice droned on, "Bekka, leaning over her mother, said, 'Momma... Momma's alive. Look, Alv, look. Oh, Momma's *back*.'" The sighing voice shook, lost volume, and went on, "And she *was*. I saw her head, it was turned...eyes were *open*. Then Lucy...Lucy, holding something on her...on her body, saw it...'tween her fingers...*moved*, 'tween her fingers, it *moved*. Bekka lunged for it, but Lucy snatched it up." The knobbed, inward-twisted fingers scraped at the lap blanket, as if trying to claw up blocks of color from the plaid. "But her *head*...still *moved*."

"Whose head? Lucy's? Gramma's?"

"Gramma's," the memory of a voice echoed, then: "And Bekka's mother's *hand*, it *pointed* at me. Bekka...hugged her mother, crying, 'Momma, you aren't *dead*,' but I saw...she'd been *dead*...I saw...Lucy...was *Lucy's* doing. Took it off the body...saw it *move* in hand. Bekka grabbed for it. 'Momma, give it to Momma.' Lucy, she wouldn't. The dead hand, it froze in the air...wouldn't go down, stiff...went to *chop* it down. Bekka, she screamed. I said 'Move, *move*, woman,' but she didn't move. I chopped *Bekka*... chopped her neck...she went all *red*. Still, she hugged the body. Chopped, *chopped* to get her off it, till Bekka went for me. 'Momma, you killed *ma*.' 'But she's *dead*, Bekka. There's her hand.' But the hand was still jerking...on the floor...and Lucy, she...she—"

The old eyas focused on Anna's, and the balding head wobbled on the crepe-textured neck. "Wouldn't *believe*. No one will—"

"I do believe you...I've *seen* it. It's an—it's magical. It's evil, and your *daughter* is doing *bad things* with it! Like what she did that night, only worse."

"Thing worse," came the shuddering reply, as the old man blew egg breath into Anna's face, a thin snail trail of spittle crawling down his chin. "Lucy, she pressed it to her...saw it...*shimmy* on her skin, and then...no more Lucy. Heard a squeak...mouse on the floor, in the blood."

"That was Lucy," Anna gently explained, reaching for his hands. "It's that thing of hers, it *does* that to her...and other things— things that *kill* people."

"Bekka...Bekka stirred, reached for...mouse...bit her. Fur all wrong. Mouse but not a mouse...wrong *color*."

"It's the *amulet*. It's gold and green, and the green stays visible." Anna tried to soothe her great-grandfather, but the old man was beyond listening, beyond knowing what was *now* and what was *then*.

"Step on it, but it runs. Bekka, Bekka, wake up, wake up, Oh, no, Bekka, *noooo*. Close your eyes, bitch...close those damn eyes!"

he shouted in a hoarse, rasping bark, and Anna glanced at the door window. No face peered in, but the dark shadow of the nurse's feet was still there, waiting.

"Old witch...evil old *shrew*...close those *eyes—close 'em!* Get out, get out of there, go find Lucy. Lucy, girl, get over here. Show me that...show it to Daddy. Oh, Lucy, *no.*"

"What? What did she do?" Anna asked, but the old man was beyond questions, beyond the reality of here and now, trapped forever in that dark, blood-scented room back on Evans Street in Ewerton, so very long ago.

"Lucy, *no...horrible,* not *right*...too strange...can't *waaatch.* Run away...can't watch. That sound...the *smell.* Lucy, no...not *my* daughter, not my child. No, not Lucy anymore, not...of *earth.* Watch out, watch out for Lucy. *Watch out for LUCEEEE.*"

The old man's voice grew loud enough for even the nurse to catch; the door opened and she squeegeed into the room, frown lines splitting her forehead in two, her lips downturned.

"—must ask you to leave—"

Anna quickly picked up her file and pen, and hurried out of the room after the nurse. Behind her, Alvin Miner singsonged in that terrible, rending whisper, "Watch out for Luceeee," until the closing door muffled the sound.

Outside the room, the nurse didn't look as angry anymore, but resigned. "I'm afraid he gets like this—some mornings he used to be terrible. Least little things used to set him off—bacon for breakfast, green Jell-O, anyone's wedding ring, there's a whole *list* of no-no's attached to his file. Some of them came along with him from the other hospital, the rest we learned by trial and error. We don't dare let any new aides work with him—you just never know. I'm sorry, I should've warned you."

Anna shook her head, saying, "Not your fault. I *told* the sheriff it wouldn't do much good, but orders are orders."

The nurse nodded sympathetically, adding, "If it was up to *me,* I'd ship him back downstate in a *minute,* what with what he *did* and all. You've read the file, so you *know,*" the woman went on with a ripple of her shoulders. "I wasn't born yet, but my mother, she read about it in the papers. Terrible, wasn't it?"

They were walking down the hall now, already too far away for Alvin Miner's weak voice to carry through the thick door, but Anna thought she heard it anyway, echoing in her ears as the nurse prattled on about the case Anna was *more* than familiar with, and what shook Anna the most was the *tone* of her great-grandfather's voice.

He wasn't asking anyone to look *after* his child, or even be *looking for* her. That ruined voice was begging people to stay away from his six-year-old child, to run away for dear life and sanity.

I would if I could, old man. Too bad you only chopped up your wife while you were trying to send her mother back into the valley of shadow...too damn bad you didn't swing that ax once in Lucy's direction.

"—get the information you needed?" the nurse was asking as they neared the front desk. Anna pulled Ginny's dark blue jacket tighter across her chest and replied, "I got enough, not exactly what my chief was looking for, but it'll suffice."

"It'll have to. Mr. Miner isn't well, you know. Cancer," she said.

"Bad?"

"All over. Once it hits certain nodes—"

Anna nodded, thinking, *You won't have to keep seeing and smelling whatever it was Lucy became that morning. At least you'll be at peace, Jeddeck. At least* you'll *be free of her.*

Not that I'll ever be, Anna told herself during the ride home, driving as close to the speed limit as she dared, the wheel still unfamiliar in her hands after too many years spent away from the driver's seat. Ma had traded the old third-hand station wagon Anna had briefly owned during her college years for some repairs on the roof of the old lady's home. The old woman had been frantic to get the minor leak in the roof fixed, and her social security check wasn't due for a week, so Ma had bartered off Anna's gold LTD wagon to get the job done, and keep the old lady off her own back in the bargain.

Now Anna drove carefully, trying to balance off getting back to Ginny's apartment before five or so (time enough to change clothes, and perhaps take a stab at rolling back the odometer, if she could puzzle out how to do it), and making sure she made no driving mistakes that would call attention to her, encourage one of the state troopers to make her pull over, all the while thinking, *He didn't know what had happened to his mother-in-law...he had left while she was still in the house, still on the bed with her hand lying on the floor. The kids were right. All those children who used to ask little Lucy where her Gramma was—they were right all along. I must tell Mrs. Campbell. She needn't feel guilty for needling Lucy all those years ago....*

For as mean as the children may have seemed, and as cruel as their intentions may well have been, they alone in Ewerton were asking the right question, of the right person, about that bloody night.

THREE—*Arlene (5)*

"—would've thought the poor Alvin was *dead* after all this time," Mrs. Campbell said, her voice small and brittle over Anna's home phone. "Certainly, your grandmother never said—"

"My grandmother didn't say a lot of things," Anna replied, reluctantly stroking Bruiser's head as he curled up clumsily in her lap while she sat on the trunk next to the phone. (She'd tried to keep the huge male off her lap—especially when he kept butting his head against her lower abdomen—but every time she'd shoved him off he'd returned, eyes melting, until she'd grudgingly relented and let him stay curled on her thighs.)

Ginny and her friend had dropped Anna and the cats off only a half hour ago, both of them so lost in their lovey-dovey smooching and rump patting that Anna realized her sweating efforts to roll back the odometer had been wasted. Ginny wouldn't have cared if Anna had painted the tan Escort purple with the proverbial pink polka-dots, let alone worry about an extra two hundred-plus miles on the odometer—which, thanks to Anna's tinkering, were no longer logged on the instrument anyway.

"True, true," Mrs. Campbell replied. Anna could hear her making some sort of soft noise close to the receiver, nuzzling one of her cats, most likely. *I'm just like her,* Anna told herself, *only I don't have the luxury of being a widow. Give me another twenty or more years, and that'll be me. One thing, it does beat being like the old lady.*

"You were right, though. Lucy Miner *did—does* know what happened to her Gramma. She knew all along."

"And enjoyed every second of our wondering if she did know or not. You see what I meant yesterday, when I said she's evil."

Anna remembered the rest of what Mrs. Campbell had said,the cat part, and hugged Bruiser tight (a queasy moment of shame came and went) as she quickly replied, "I agree. No telling what she'd do...just think of what she *did.* Letting her father go down poop creek without a paddle...all because he couldn't produce the rest of the body, and wouldn't say where it was. Her own *father.*"

"Well, I wouldn't get *too* dewy-eyed about him, Anna. Remember, he *did* kill his wife, He didn't *have* to do it, you know. The man could've figured out some other option. But as for what else you said, it's like I told you, Anna...Lucy loved her Gramma. Mrs. Husa was *everything* to her, dead or alive."

"And I think Lucy had control over *that*," Anna commented bitterly, "judging from what her father told me. Think, Arlene, if I hadn't read her right when she wouldn't answer my question about where he was buried, Alvin might have died before I found him. Imagine, taking something like that to the grave. And even if he had talked, who would have believed him? Bad enough they gave him those treatments. Any more of that and he'd have been mindless."

"Wouldn't that have been a blessing?'"

"I suppose," Anna said slowly, thinking of those wildly darting dark eyes, and his somehow sad egg breath. "But it would've been a bigger blessing if he'd killed Lucy."

"Now, don't go wishing you'd never been born. It does no good, and it only makes a person think funny."

How else am I supposed to think? You *don't have a house pet on your family tree. God only knows how* they *think, or even if they do think. Bad enough that Lucy's sick little experiment* worked, *that whatever human form her amulet gave that poor cat was enough to give it human genes, even if it was only for however long it took her to* mate *with it. It was your fault, in a way. She was jealous of you,* Anna told herself, as she firmly pushed Bruiser off her lap, and crossed her legs to prevent him from gaining a comfortable spot should he try to jump up again.

"—icide never solved *anything*. You just leave your problems for the next guy."

"Maybe the next guy deserves them," Anna said dully. She was tired from the strain of driving, tired from looking madness in the wrinkled, shiny face. All the broken goods she'd inadvertently bought in the last few days were weighing heavy, *very* heavy, on the shelf of her mind.

"Now, now, Anna. That's the way your grandmother would think, no consideration. Do you want to be like *her*? Be devoid of compassion, of *humanity*? All right, your grandmother did a very wrong thing when she conceived your mother. But if you sit back and don't try to rectify things, you'll be sinking below Lucy's level. Is that what you want?"

Anna closed her eyes, until the remembered image of Bruiser trying to have his way with Mouth returned, and Anna was forced to open them again. "I don't know *what* I want anymore. I want out, but I don't—"

"—know how you can do it with a clean conscience," Arlene Campbell finished for Anna, as if she could read the younger woman's thoughts. Anna could hear her making smacking noises to one of the cats, probably the ugly-but-cute black-and-white one she called Silky, before going on, "Just don't do anything silly with Lucy before Saturday night. I've a gut feeling she'll be out, wearing little Lucy's skin again, just like that Isaacs girl saw. Don't you see, Lucy never wanted to grow up? She becomes animals because that's what's built into that amulet of hers, because they're *handy* and *useful,* but at heart she's always been little Lucy Miner, playing little-girl tricks on everyone. And for the past fifty years, she's been playing the world's longest game of hide-and-seek—with her grandmother's body as 'it.'"

Anna almost dropped the receiver when things came together in her mind with an almost audible *click.*

The drive to Wright County had forced Anna to remember that beat-up gold station wagon she'd briefly owned—the five hundred-dollar rust bucket that was good for one roofing job.The old lady had been almost *rabid* in her desire to have that roof fixed immediately. It had been the second or so week in July, a time of impending thunderstorms and possible strong winds. Ma had reasoned that they should wait with the roof until *after* the possible storm, in order to repair any wind damage along with the small leak, but the old lady was all but frothing at the mouth, insisting that the roof be fixed that day, and all they'd had in terms of ready cash was the value of the car.

Old Quinton Kelley, who used to do roof repairs on regular basis before he got to spending his days at Pearl 'n' Earl's, paying the mortgage on Earl Vincent's bar, was more than willing to take Anna's car in payment, and he'd done such a good job on the roof ("for an old lush," Anna had often told Ma bitterly) that not only didn't it leak anymore, but not so much as a shingle blew off during the storm two days later. As a matter of fact, the LTD wagon conked out before the roof did—

—but the old lady still kept worrying about the roof every time there was a storm. She'd even call up Ma or Anna at their house when a storm was coming, warbling out her fears over the crackling line.

You weren't worried about the roof, *but what would've gotten wet if it had leaked, especially into the upper stories. And then there is the smell. It's all through the house, without a definite location, but it has been there, nonetheless, ever since I can remember—that sweetish, musty, dead-insect odor, like when the June bugs pile up* next to the buildings uptown in the late spring or early summer...that dry, acidic tang that makes the inside of your mouth go dry if you bend over to pick up a can near a store and get a whiff of that dead-bug odor.

That's kind of what the smell is like, only different in a way I can't quite describe, but it's always there in the house under all the other smells, even under the old lady's greasy smell, just like her Gramma has always been there.

You hid her in the house, didn't you, Lucy? You were hiding her when Mrs. Campbell's father-in-law-to-be and Coroner Wilkes came upstairs, weren't you...or you'd already hidden her. And no matter how much the kids taunted you, you wouldn't say where she was. Whatever you did with her, you hid her well. I've been just about everywhere in that house, and I never saw her...even your aunts never found her.

Clever, Lucy, very clever. Did you ever play the game with her afterward? Did you make her alive again? If your little golden pet is anything like the ones I read about, it could do all sorts of interesting things to her body.

Anna dimly heard Mrs. Campbell waxing eloquent about how Anna was *above* all the nonsense her grandmother indulged in, all the badness she'd started up, as the young woman replayed her conversation with Kurt at the station yesterday. An old, *old* woman had answered his little girl Penny's knock. Someone so old even little Penny's dad believed what the girl said about the strange old creature.

You're still doing it, aren't you? Anna's thoughts raged. You still put that damned amulet on your Gramma, make her come to life like a big wind-up doll, and then you let her roam the house! Oh, geez, did you let her out when Ma and I were still there, when we were asleep? Was an undead thing walking through the rooms, re-living the good times with her little Lucy? Too bad you couldn't make the amulet do double duty, have it make her alive and you young again at once—or does it work that way if you hold the thing between you?

What have you been doing, old woman?

"—you listening to me?" Mrs. Campbell sounded mildly peeved, as Anna said, "Sorry, I'm awfully tired, from the drive and all. Would you mind terribly if I either call you or see you tomorrow? Thanks. And good night," she said, dropping the receiver with a muted thunk on the cradle.

Something at the back of Anna's mind warned her that she should have told Mrs. Campbell what she'd just deduced—that Lucy Miner was doing more than playing the world's most realistic game of pretend, but she didn't, out of a lingering fear that she'd eventually strain Arlene Campbell's fragile belief in her claims to the limit, and thus destroy all confidence the old widow had in her, and her theory about the amulet.

For despite the things about herself Arlene had confided to Anna, the painful spots during her life with Don Campbell, the shabbiness and pitiful economy of the woman's old age, the slavish, unconditional love she lavished on her "babies," Anna couldn't bring herself to bare herself similarly to Arlene Campbell. Anna had had so little experience with friendship, and she'd been duped by her own "Baba" too many times, that she feared that just one more revelation, just one more half-baked supposition, might ruin things completely between her and Mrs. Campbell.

And so she kept her silence.

As she got ready for bed, not even bothering to get washed or change into her PJ's, just crawling between the covers in her underpants and bra, Anna told herself, I *can't lose now. She's the only person in town I can confide in, can bounce things off. But my god, the woman has to have her limits...I can't push things,* before she drifted off to sleep, not even hearing when Bruiser began pawing at the window shade, raising it to sash level before positioning himself in front of the black window, eyes alert for whatever dangers lurked beyond the cold glass.

And not realizing just what a dangerous position she'd put her elderly friend in by keeping her self-serving silence about great-great-grandmother's possible whereabouts.

CHAPTER ELEVEN

FRIDAY, OCTOBER 30, 1987

ONE—The Miner House (1)

After leaving the Ewerton Veterinary Clinic that morning, with the just-vaccinated Persians Puff and Fluff in two wire-fronted plastic cages, one gripped in each hand, Arlene Campbell took a slightly different path home.

The two neutered males were heavy, and Arlene had to set their cages down every half block or so, where she stood rubbing her gloved hands, easing out the cramps in her palms and fingers. Arlene figured out roughly when and where she'd have to stop during her slightly-out-of-the-way walk home, so that she'd be pausing to rest right in the middle of Evans Street, which was two streets to the east of Wisconsin Street—and just happened to be the spot where Lucy Miner's lifetime home stood.

By the time Arlene reached the old prairie style white brick house, she really did need to stop and massage her aching hands. As she rested their cages on the sidewalk, she told the two orange cats, "You boys are going to have to learn how to walk on a leash. Mother can't keep this up, you know. She's getting old." Puff and Fluff regarded her through the barred cage doors with round, copper-orange eyes. As she stoodlooking down at them, they blinked kitty kisses at her, until Puff's pale pink nose began to twitch. Then both cats began hissing, the fur puffing out on their cobby bodies and their curved ivory fangs exposed against their shiny gums.

"Why couldn't you two hiss at that Karla shrew like that?"

Arlene turned around to face the Miner house, expecting to see Lucy's age-ravaged face peering out through the limp, dingy curtains, but no fabric moved behind the streaked windows. Arlene couldn't see any shadows behind them, either, and the light was hitting the house at just the right angle to make most of the curtains in the front of the house translucent enough for her to make out vague furniture shapes through them.

No Lucy—not unless she could see through the curtains from a great distance—and Arlene Weiss Campbell remembered how Lucy used to have to sit up near the front of the classroom in elementary school because of her poor vision. Not enough to need glasses for everything, but not perfect vision, of that Arlene was almost certain.

And it couldn't have improved with age. Nothing *about that woman improved over the years. She may have eagle eyes when she's wearing that* amulet *of hers, but if her voice over the phone the other night is any indication, the human Lucy hasn't aged very well at all.*

Down on the sidewalk, the cats were still sputtering and hissing. Fluff was jammed so tight against the back of the plastic and metal enclosure he almost knocked his cage over from within. Arlene glanced at the house again; no movement whatsoever. Even the brown-petaled hydrangea bushes that flanked either side of the sidewalk leading up to the house were still, unmoving in the slight, chilly breeze.

Bending over to pick up her cats, Arlene asked them,"What's wrong, babies? What is it?" even though she had a good idea as to what was bothering them. Trotting briskly down the remainder of the street, Arlene did turn around once to look at the left side of the house. Again, no curtains shifted back into place, and no shadows were visible through the backlit windows.

"Old shrew must be sleeping in," Mrs. Campbell mumbled, then added with a private chuckle, "Certainly needs her beauty sleep, Lucy does," as a curtain behind the one window in the Miner house that Arlene never would have considered looking at shifted silently back into place behind a pane of age-clouded glass.

TWO—Bib (5)

Through his closed office door, Ewerton Chief of Police Bib Stanley could still hear Anna Sudek and Ginny Yarrow chattering next to Anna's desk. He considered telling them to keep the noise down out there, but then decided to just sit back and listen to them. He figured it would help him when he called Anna into his office later on in the day. By eavesdropping on her conversation now, he might get an idea of exactly what she'd been up to yesterday, when he'd seen her driving back into Dean County in Ginny Yarrow's car, wearing Ginny's uniform jacket.

Not that Bib expected the woman to blurt out to Ginny, "Oh, and by the way, I borrowed your car and uniform for a little jaunt yesterday, when I was supposed to be sick in bed with some sort of intestinal flu. At least, that's what I think I told Bib it was." Bib Stanley's nasal whine may have sounded a little namby-pamby when he spoke, and he knew that his slightly sunken cheeks didn't really make him look all that clean-cut and officer-like, but the man was not stupid. A bit slow to make connections sometimes, and certainly too trusting for his own good many other times, but no matter what names Sheriff Sawyer called him both to his face and behind his back, Bib Stanley wasn't the totally ineffectual law enforcement officer many people in Ewerton thought he was.

And he certainly wasn't a Keystone Kop, regardless of Stu Sawyer's opinion.

Bib had been driving his wife Rhonda's car to Ewert Park (his was in the shop, getting new brake pads), for a little chow down and serious thinking session on his favorite bench before supper at seven that night, when he saw Ginny Yarrow's tan Escort crawling over the hospital bridge, the driver signaling well in advance of the shallow left turn onto Church Road—a turn so slight few drivers, Bib included, even bothered to signal. After all, only one road fed the bridge. Bib had put his jug of milk down on the frost-swirled painted tabletop and watched the car roll cautiously past, slavishly observing the "Slow When Children Present" sign where Church Road intersected with Lumbermill Drive, even though the many children who usually were at play on that street were all home watching television or eating supper.

Bib recognized Ginny's car, but not the style of driving. Ginny Yarrow was notorious for her heavy foot while behind the wheel. Then he saw Anna Sudek's strong-jawed profile, caught a glimpse of a blue police uniform jacket. And as she slowly drove the Escort into town, stopping dutifully at the red-and-white sign posted at each intersection Bib could see from his vantage point in the park, he had slurped down his milk, thinking, *Anna doesn't have a license, but even if she did, what the heck is she wearing Ginny's jacket for? And she has her hair up. I've never seen her wear it any other way than how she usually wears it, hanging down with bangs in front. Besides, she's supposed to be sick.*

And as he finished up the last of his Little Debbie brownie, Bib had kicked himself for not asking Anna about that call her grandmother had made to his house on Tuesday night. The girl was obviously up to *something,* and for all he knew, Lucy Miner's call might have been a part of it.

Damn hinky bunch of women, he'd thought, shoving his jug and wrapper into the metal Dumpster before getting behind the wheel of Rhonda's Rabbit and heading home. *Crazy, every last one of them. Tina was boy crazy, Anna's sneaky, and Lucy...Lucy's something else—what, I don't know.*

But this early afternoon, as Bib listened to Anna as she chatted with Ginny, the chief couldn't tell that Anna was lying as she assured Ginny that everything had gone fine while she had been out of town, and that no, she hadn't had to use the car, but thanks anyway, and so on. Her voice didn't rise like most voices were wont to do, and she didn't compulsively pile on the words or the pauses between them. She just gave a smooth, convincing account of a couple of days spent quietly in a friend's apartment, resting on the daybed, nursing a bout of stomach flu.

The part about not using the car gave Bib a start, until he realized she must have turned back the odometer. Anna was certainly bright enough to do that—and sly enough. If she'd only been confident enough to drive a little faster, he might not even have noticed her crossing the bridge, but he realized that getting pulled over for something as basic as not having her lights on was out of the question.

And while Anna gushed over Ginny's engagement ring, loudly admiring it over the steady hum of her IBM, Bib wondered, *What were you pulling, hmm? You're so good at sneaking around the alleys and poking in Dumpsters at three in the morning, I wouldn't put anything past you. But what did you need the uniform for? And the new hairdo? Who'd you want thinking you were an officer? Who had to think you were with the department? You've been acting weird ever since Wally Inglass got his old peeker just about pecked off. You were strange before that, actually, but you've been really mysterious since old Wally's bullet got bit.*

"—have a bite to eat uptown? My treat?" Ginny was asking Anna outside Bib's office. The clerk replied, "Sure, I'd love to, but you don't have to—"

"No, you saved me from getting ripped off again by apartment sitting. It's the least I can do." Ginny's voice trailed off; Bib guessed she was going to get her jacket from her locker. Anna followed her, saying something Bib couldn't hear plainly, then both women's voices grew louder, with Ginny saying, "—damn fuzz. That's the trouble with this jacket. I just *look* at something that sheds and it's all over the cuffs. *Sheesh.* You got any tape in your drawer? I'm going to have to get this stuff off before I go uptown."

Instinctively, Bib got up and hurried to his door, opening it with a casual, "Now, don't you girls go flirting with that cute kid who works the lunch shift at the 'Dairy Queen,'" as he surreptitiously glanced at Ginny Yarrow's sticky-tape-wrapped hand. She was trying to brush clinging yellow and blue fibers off the right ribbed cuff of her jacket. Something about her motions bothered Bib, until he remembered that Ginny was a lefty, which meant she'd be more likely to brush against something with that arm, not her right.

Anna Sudek was standing next to Ginny, her face in profile to Bib, holding the roll of tape in case Ginny needed a fresh handful of it to brush off her sleeve. Anna's strong jaw and the little rounded tip of her nose were unmistakable, and nothing like Ginny's weak-chinned profile.

Bib was about to ask Anna to stop by his office after lunch, but kept his mouth shut. He didn't need to give her any more advance warning than necessary. As it was, she thought faster than he did, and he didn't want the odds tilted anymore in her favor than necessary.

* * * * * * *

Anna was smiling and still chattering with Ginny when the two young women returned to the station, cardboard French fry liners in hand, and she wasn't suspicious when Bib poked his head out of his doorway and said, "Anna? May I have those reports you've been working on? Thanks," then retreated into office and half shut the door.

"Here are the reports," she said a couple of minutes later, leaning over his desk to place them in the "In" section of his tiered black plastic and chrome desk rack. Before she stood up, Bib casually remarked, "You know, most people don't signalwhen they come into town off the hospital bridge. You needn't have bothered."

Geez, doesn't that woman ever give an inch? Bib thought with dismay after Anna replied, "I know, but I always figure it doesn't hurt to do it. It's a good habit to get into."

Recovering somewhat, Bib said, "Yeah, that it is...driving with a license is an even better habit."

Anna shrugged, with an apologetic smile, saying, "It was a bit of an emergency. A friend of mine was ill in Wright County, and I wanted to drop in to see the family. I figured it was worth the fine if one of the troopers pulled me over. If I was sick I'd want someone to do the same for me."

"Must be a really good friend," Bib remarked as he reached in his drawer for a mashed fruit roll-up and slowly opened the foil packet, thinking, *Friend, my ass...you aren't the friend-making type.*

"One of my old professors from college. He was a very special teacher."

"Not like old Wally, eh?" Bib popped the wad of gummy fruit mash into his mouth.

Anna's eyes grew opaque at the mention of Inglass; all flat and reflective, like seeing one's own blurry image on the back of a spoon. Wondering how Anna did that with her eyes, Bib said, "You read in the paper about the whole school turning out for his funeral on Tuesday?"

Anna shook her head, and her light brownish hair rippled over her shoulders. "I don't read the *Herald*—it costs too much. Fifty cents a pop for it is ridiculous."

"Too bad, they had a picture of Wally in there and everything—taken *before* Saturday, of course," Bib said around his mouthful of fruit pulp. Anna smiled, saying, "Too bad. I might've paid fifty cents to see Wally covered with that sheet again. Just hard to believe he's really gone."

"Rode your ass pretty good when you were in school, didn't he?" Bib leaned back in his chair, chewing and watching Anna, but she didn't go into the diatribe he had been hoping for. Instead, she uncrossed her arms and said, "You saw how he was last Friday... imagine that every school day," before leaving his office with a smile.

Before she sat down at her typewriter, Bib yelled, "Say, Anna?"

When she reappeared in the doorway, he asked, "This professor of yours, he very sick?"

"Heart attack. Nothing major, but he'll be in the hospital for observation for a while," she said glibly before turning and going back to her desk.

Bib mulled that over for a few moments. She was coming from the west...only one big county hospital out that way. And it was next to the college, which made it plausible that one of her old professors might be there. *She must figure I could check it out, find out if she was in the vicinity. Too bad you didn't think it through better, Anna,* Bib thought, as he reached across his desk for his Rolodex.

"I was *waiting* for you."

Anna almost hung up the phone when her grandmother's bleat crackled over the line, but remembering what Arlene Campbell had suggested to her about tomorrow night, Anna decided to play devoted granddaughter for as long as she could stomach it.

"Oh, I'm sorry. I thought I told you I wouldn't be able to come by every day. Is there anything you need—food, candy for tomorrow night?"

"Tomorrow *night*?" the old lady started to warble. Anna gripped the thin part of the receiver, wishing it was the old lady's greasy neck, as she replied patiently, "Halloween. I gave you a bag of mixed candy for the children."

"That was for the *children*?" Anna smiled to herself; Arlene Campbell *did* know the old lady as well—or better—than Anna did. While Anna had sat in Mrs. Campbell's American hodgepodge living room, sipping Lipton tea, the the elderly widow had said, "That grandmother of yours was always pinching candy from the rest of us, especially after Halloween. Her aunts didn't dare let her out of the house on that night—she was such a holy terror they didn't trust her. But they couldn't buy any candy to give away, either—she'd make pig of herself on it. So any child who ventured up to the Miner house come All Hallows' Eve received a nickel wrapped in a little piece of colored tissue, which was really better than candy, even if most of us were too scared to set foot on that porch! Pathetic when you think about it. Once, Vernilla Nemmitz dared me to go up and knock on their door, and when I did, poor Bella answered the door and handed me a twist of tissue with a coin inside. Just inside the door, I could see Lucy. She was dressed up in a costume made from a nightgown, with little pasteboard wings and a halo of sparkly wire suspended above her hair. But the look she gave me wasn't at angelic."

"—ate the *last* of it *yesterday. Now* what do I hand out?"

Anna was tempted to snap, "Nickels in colored tissue," but instead asked, "Well, do you really get that many kids, anyhow?"

"*You* were the *one* who was worried about the *windows*." *Damn*, Anna thought. She'd forgotten that she'd insisted the old lady hand out something tomorrow night. That didn't jibe well with Mrs. Campbell's plan to get her out of the house.

"That was before I talked to Bib about it. He said a lot of the parents would be keeping the smaller kids at home, and he was going to be keeping an eye on the older ones himself because of what happened to Wally Inglass," she added nonchalantly.

There was a pause on the other end of the line, then the old lady warbled, "Well I'd just as soon call it a *night* tomorrow. *I* don't like those little *brats*."

"Then you don't want any candy, anything like that. Just turn your porch light off and—"

"How can I turn it *off* when I don't put it *on*?" Anna could almost imagine little Lucy Miner standing there flouncing her nightgown skirts as she said that, in a little-girl singsong that contrasted bizarrely with her age-garbled voice.

"Whatever. Now I've got the day off tomorrow, so don't try calling the station if you need anything. I'll be home all day, but I want to sleep in late, so if the phone rings more than a couple of times don't get worried, okay?"

"I don't *think* I'll need anything," the old lady began, and at that point Anna decided it was time to spring the rest of Mrs. Campbell's plan—the part Anna considered the riskiest, but the old widow considered the most necessary.

("We can't *count* on her going trick or treating. Oh, I know she'll probably *want* to, but we can't be positive. But if she has a reason to be out that night *anyhow,* what better way to go about her business than by blending in with the other children? With that many people out and about, someone might remember a green-spotted animal running about, or a bird or bat flying around. And once she's out of the house, more vulnerable out in the streets, with that amulet of hers in plain sight on her, then it should be easier to get it away from her, especially with the two of us distracting her.")

At the time, Anna had had her doubts about this part: she'd argued that *they* might think a little Lucy disguise was the most logical, but would *Lucy* think that way? Yet Mrs. Campbell had been adamant, claiming that the look on Lucy's face that Halloween years before was assurance enough for her that Lucy would, indeed, want to go trick-or-treating before making yet another kill.

"That's good, because I'm *really* beat today. Y'know when you get so frustrated mentally that your body gets tired, too?"

"Frustrated?" the old lady began, and Anna could imagine the old woman's thick lips turning vulpine, as the saliva flowed over a furred jaw. Anna wondered if the old lady was holding that little cloth bag in her hand, stroking her quicksilver-fluid green-and-golden pet as she went on, "Oh, at the veterinary office. I went in to

get some eye drops for Mouth, and the little twit of a receptionist, Karla Yablinski's her name, she was about three classes behind me at EHS but to look at her you'd think she was a teenager, she wears her hair, oh, y'know, sort of up and out, like those girls in the hair mousse commercials—"

"I *know,* all the girls on TV look *alike*—" the old lady gurgled in rapt agreement.

"—and she dresses kiddish, skimpy sweaters and acid-wash jeans, well, anyhow, she wouldn't come to the desk to wait on me. Just teetered out on those hooker-style boots she wears, saw that it was me waiting, and toddled back to the rear of the clinic, where Dr. Mertz was working. All I could hear was her tittering and him laughing at *something,* so I went and opened the door to activate the buzzer, and wouldn't you know it, Karla minced out to see who was there, saw me, and went into the back again! Finally the doc poked his head around the door and saw me, so I got the medicine, but I suppose I should've told him to shove it once he came to the desk."

While Anna told the old lady about an incident which, while true, had actually happened last summer, she was careful to toss in abundant clues for the old lady, down to the houndstooth coat Karla wore to work, the color of her teased and moussed brown hair, and the bumper stickers adorning the trampy woman's small blue car, the one she drove to and from work. The dark blue Ford car Karla had, up to a few months ago, driven home to a house not too far away from the Sudek house.

But Karla had surrendered the house to the FmHA; Tina Sudek had seen the paperwork on the case resting on one of the desks in the FmHA office, along with a dozen or more other such notices of abandonment.

And once Anna had walked past Karla's former house out at the end of Railway Drive, close to the pine-tree-hidden sewer plant by the river, during a beautiful September afternoon when it was just too nice outside to stay indoors watching CNN with Ma. The FmHA had to contend with so many abandoned homes, they hadn't even gotten around to putting the Yablinski house on the market. The curtains were still up and drawn, and with no "For Sale" sign on the lawn, it was impossible to tell that the little green frame house was even empty. Anna had figured that the FmHA was going to wait until the snow came to actually put the house on the market; that trick was common out by the sewer plant, when the summer sun wasn't beating down on the plant, and the strong breezes didn't blow the stink out across the immediate neighborhood. Sometimes the air got a *little* whiffy as far west as Anna's house (which she and Ma had bought in the early spring, naturally), but houses as close to the plant as the deserted Yablinski one were almost impossible to sell, even in the winter.

Anna had again walked down to the Yablinksi house before coming home that afternoon, just to be sure—no realtor's sign yet, no telltale soggy yellow newspapers cluttering the front stoop, and no one in that part of town was very zealous about raking up the leaves off their sidewalks or lawns.

"You *complained* about it, to the vet?" the old lady was asking, and Anna truthfully replied, "Of course I did...not that it'll do much good," remembering how she *had* complained about the dimwitted receptionist to the other, female veterinarian at the clinic, but Dr. Mertz refused to listen to Anna's complaint, or the other vet's account of it; instead, he actually called Anna up to bawl her out for daring to complain about his "good little bookkeeper." While Anna didn't doubt that Karla was *good*, she doubted that bookkeeping had anything to do with it.

"Isn't that the way it *is?* All they hire are *dummies*. Like that Irma *Downing*," the old lady chirped, pronouncing the dead woman's name with careful glee. Feeling cold moth wings fluttering in her guts, even though that tramp Karla Yablinski was in absolutely no danger whatsoever (*unfortunately,* Anna thought), she weakly replied, "Yeah. I think being a moron is one of Dr. Mertz's job requirements. Karla was the same way at EHS," she went on, stressing the "EHS" part, until the old lady grabbed the bait and sunk the hook into her fleshy lips:

"Then you *knew* her and she still *did* that? Was she in your *class*?"

Crossing the fingers of her right hand, Anna said, "Three years behind me—class of seventy-nine. The old yearbook is probably there. She had some kids, but never got married."

And as she went on, Anna could hear the old lady riffling through a book of some sort, and guessed that it was the yellow-covered Ewerton white pages.

FOUR—*Afternoon Calls*

"—not even checked in a few days ago? Oh...well, thank you for the information. Pardon? No, I didn't. I thought they only took elderly people. Oh, I see...uh-hm. No, no, I'll call over there myself. I have a WATS line. Could I please have the number? Thank you, ma'am, you've been a big help."

Bib Stanley hit the buttons on his phone, listened for the dial tone, then dialed another long-distance number in the 532 exchange. He heard the phone ringing, then said to the Wright County Nursing Home receptionist, "Oh, yes, you can help. I'm Brian Stanley, the chief of police in Ewerton, over in Dean County, and I believe that one of my officers may have—"

"A young woman? I believe I spoke to her yesterday. She was asking about our patient Mr. Miner. Something about putting a cap on some old files associated with his case. She mentioned your name."

Bib silently mouthed his wife's favorite word come Saturday afternoons—"Bingo!"—before quickly telling the woman on the line, "Just making sure she followed proper procedure. She's, uh, a new officer"—*(you don't know how new, lady!)*—"and I wanted to make sure she handled the situation properly."

"Oh, she was very nice, very professional. You'd have been quite proud of the way she handled herself, especially when Mr. Miner threw one of his tantrums...although there *was* one thing." The receptionist seemed reluctant to continue, so Bib said, "Any problem?"

"Oh, *no,* not with *her.* But if I could make a slight suggestion, Chief Stanley."

If Anna did anything stupid out there I'll wring her neck, Bib began to think, as he urged, "Certainly, ma'am."

"Well, it had nothing to do with her performance, but it would be nice if you could issue Officer Yarrow a uniform that fit a little better. She was having an awful time getting her jacket to stay closed."

"I'll get right on it," Bib quickly said, before something else came to him—something he'd seen earlier that day.

Officer Yarrow, brushing fuzzy fibers off her cuff—tiny crinkly bits of color, like the downy surface of a blanket.

"Excuse me, but is Alvin Miner bedridden? Officer...*Yarrow* didn't mention it in her report."

"Not all the time. Mostly he's strapped in his wheelchair, and bundled in blankets against any chill. We take *excellent* care of—"

"Thanks, ma'am, you've been a big help. Good day," he said, hanging up on the woman.

As soon as he had an open line again, Bib dialed Anna Sudek's home phone, and grimaced when he got a busy signal. Reluctantly putting down the receiver, he said softly, "So Alvin Miner's back up north now. Did Lucy Miner arrange it? No wonder Anna pulled that stunt. I don't suppose they'd let just any cluck off the street in to see him, for fear some yo-yo'd blow his brains out just for ruining tourism up here, or some such nonsense. Too bad Lucy didn't see fit to notify any of us where her daddy was, although I don't 'spose she's all that anxious to work hand in glove with the law around here."

Bib tried dialing Anna's number again, and was rewarded with a buzzing line. "Oh, quit yakking already!" he said to the squawking receiver before slamming it down with a brittle clack. On impulse, he looked up Lucy Miner's number, and dialed that. He only needed to listen to a second of the busy signal before hanging up, putting the receiver down gently this time, as if he feared that the hissing, stinking old woman might be able to feel his unwanted presence on the line; would know if he were to drop the receiver back on the cradle, and come attack him if he did so.

FIVE—The Miner House (2)

Arlene Campbell, her hands free of the cats in their carrying cages, and now jammed in the deep pockets of Don's old peacoat, approached the Miner house from the south, wishing that section of Evans Street was bisected with an alley leading from Share Avenue to the east. She wanted to approach the house from the back, but there was no way to do so—the Miner backyard abutted the fenced backyard of one of the houses on west side of Share Avenue, which meant that if she wanted go into Lucy Miner's backyard, she'd have to cross the slightly overgrown, unraked lawn and circle around the house while actually on the old woman's property.

And Arlene Campbell didn't want to risk doing that, even if Lucy Miner and Anna Sudek's lines were both busy, which indicated that Anna was busy feeding the old woman the bait for tomorrow night. For there was no reason why Lucy couldn't speak on the phone and look out the window at the same time, and for all Arlene knew, the old woman could have one of those extra long curly cords on her phone, allowing her to move freely about the house as she talked.

Wish I'd asked Anna about that, Mrs. Campbell thought as she stood on the sidewalk, the cold from the concrete leaching up through her shoe soles into her hard-skinned old feet, and peered up at the attic of the Miner house. Before Puff and Fluff had started that growling and hissing business that morning, Anna thought that they were looking up, at something *past* her, perhaps on the roof of the old weathered house.

Silly kitties probably saw a bird up there, or a squirrel. They got all worked up. and then you got all worked up. All for nothing. But my boys don't usually act like that. Took me hours to calm them down when I got them home. Even after getting their shots they don't behave that way. No. they sensed something here. I'm sure of it. Lucy must have been playing with that thing *again, changing over into something Puff and Fluff could smell—some horrid beast.*

No curtains shifted behind the old-style storm windows. No old flickers of light or dark showed to suggest that anyone was moving within, so Arlene stepped onto the leaf-matted grass, her too-smooth soles slipping a little on the wet mosaic of brown, orange, and faded yellow that covered the dead brownish-gray lawn. Holding her hands away from her sides for balance, hoping that no one was watching her from within the houses on either side of the quiet street, Arlene Campbell walked parallel to the south side of the house until she reached a spot on the lawn opposite the corner of the house.

Still there was no movement of the curtains, no feral face or knobby claw hand to be seen through the mottled glass. Arlene now walked along the greenish-gray unvarnished wood fence that marked the property line of the sprawling ranch house on Share Avenue, all the while looking up at Lucy's house about a hundred feet away from her.

Even though she'd lived all her life in Ewerton, Arlene Weiss Campbell had never seen the Miner house from this angle before, not up close like this. The grass was more overgrown here, lying down in one direction like shower-rinsed hair, all damp and faintly glistening in the weak sunlight. Some of the leaves from the locust, elm, and sugar maple trees had been raked up and heaped against the back wall of the house itself; a rake whose wooden handle was blue-whorled with traces of old paint rested against the flaking siding.

Arlene recognized the underlying color the house had been when Lucy and her aunts lived there—a vaguely cloudy shade of gray. Anna and her mother had painted the bricks off-white, but the memory of the stormy hue remained, working its way to the surface, in some places obscuring the more cheerful white.

The only thing about the house that looked really well cared for was the roof. Arlene remembered seeing the truck from Everett Roofing in Lumbe parked alongside the house two months ago, even though that old drunk Quinton Kelley had put a new roof on not five or six years ago.

You never get the same people to work for you twice, do you, Lucy? Arlene thought, remembering the succession of young boys and men Lucy had hired to cut her lawn and tend to her fall leaves each year after Tina and Anna moved out. Every time Arlene happened to walk down this way for some reason or other, there was always someone different working here, while old Lucy watched from the porch, giving orders and commands in that quivering blubber voice of hers. Even loony Vinnie and Leo Larson, who liked to sit around in the Wooden Keg all day with those drunken Yingleys, slopping down can after can of Diet Pepsi, couldn't stand working for Lucy Miner, and Vinnie and Leo liked *everybody*—even that bear Stu Sawyer.

Coming a little closer to the silent, looming house, Arlene thought, *You can't even buy companionship. When your Gramma died, you lost everything, didn't you? She was the only person who truly loved you...and you lost her. Trying to mold Anna into a new Gramma's girl? Or are you hoping she'll be a Gramma to you?*

Suddenly Arlene paused, uncertain if the shifting patch of lightness she'd seen in the rear attic dormer was just the reflection of the clouds scudding above, or something actually moving within. She drew herself deeper into Don's old jacket, until her arms were digging into her heaving ribs, as she watched the uncertain grayish whiteness flicker in the distant window.

If only I was on higher ground. The angle is too steep for me to see clearly. But why would Lucy sit up there? I don't think the attic is even finished, Don's father said it wasn't, that it was all boards and two-by-fours up there, not even habitable. Alvin and Rebecca didn't need the room—they had plenty below.

Then Arlene remembered her late father-in-law's words, the ones he'd repeat whenever anyone was willing to listen to the old man tell of the most exciting day in his life:

"Walking was a bitch up there...step in the wrong place and your foot'd be wiggling on the ceiling of the room below. Only a little light comin' from them little dormers set up above our heads. Me and Auggie, we didn't hang around too long in there, on account of Auggie was scared shitless about fallin' through the ceilings. Heard tell *he* claims we didn't even go up, on account of *me,* but I think it was because he didn't want no one knowing how frightened he was in that house.

"But what spooked me up there was the way them dormers were set up so high, so's you couldn't even see ground through 'em. From the outside, you'd think you could stand belly-level with 'em, but they was *high.* I remember Auggie balancing on one of the exposed floor joists, to take a gander out the window, hopin' to see the old woman's body out in the yard or in the trees, some asshole place, and he almost fell off and through the floor. And Auggie would've made a damn good missile, at that."

Arlene remembered how tubby and short Auggie Wilkes was; he stood perhaps five seven or so, and was roughly that much around. Her father-in-law was likewise a short man, albeit wiry and lean.

Whatever Lucy's become, it must be tall enough to reach those windows—or hover before them, she thought, the increasing chill in the air filtering through the loose weave of her plaid head scarf, making her ears ache so much she had to rub them gently through her scarf. And just as she moved her hand, something *definitely* moved behind the attic window.

Something small and brownish, as near as Arlene could tell; something that passed by the bottom of the window, until the light curtains within rippled. And then she saw the face, just the forehead and eyes part, peering out at her. The age-clouded glass made it hard to discern the features of the face, but it was a face nonetheless. The dark eye openings were unmistakable, as was the broad expanse of forehead under a thin cap of hair, whitish hair.

Lucy. She'd climbed up to the part of the house with the best vantage point, and now she'd seen Arlene trespassing on her land, no doubt up to no good.

Not knowing what else to do to minimize the situation, Arlene smiled and waved, then continued walking along the wooden stake and plank fence until she reached the corner of it, then kept moving along the rest of it, until she found herself on Share Avenue, all the while telling herself, *There's no sign posted. I've seen kids cutting around yards like this all the time. She can't have me hauled in for walking along a fence. Why, those people who put it up might have set it farther in, so as not to have it touching her property line. People do that all the* time, *so she can't do anything to me at all.*

And it wasn't until Arlene was within sight of her own house, and could see her cat Silky's big-eared black-and-white head peeping through the bottom of one of the high-set living room windows that flanked her front door that Arlene realized something. Lucy Miner was only about five foot one or two when she was a young woman, before age had had a chance to compress her spine, shave inches off her already short height. Unless she'd dragged a chair up to that attic, or had the floor finished—both dubious options—there wasn't any way she could have poked so much as the top of her head into that window.

Looking at Silky proved that. He was a long, lean cat, easily two feet stretched out, yet his head barely showed through a window set two feet off the ground. And Arlene was sure she'd seen the head and hand of an old woman, not a monkey-nimble child.

Letting herself into her house, and pausing to pet all her cats and dogs before taking off her scarf and coat, Arlene realized something as she first pulled off her gloves. Mrs. Husa, Lucy's grandmother, was at least five-six or taller, espeially in those medium-heeled black leather shoes she used to wear.

Arlene actually had the receiver in her hand, and was halfway through dialing Anna Sudek's number, when she thought, *No, don't rattle the girl over something* you *can handle. Anna never saw Lucy's Gramma. She doesn't realize how* formidable *a woman she was. Worse than Lucy, even. But she shouldn't be hard to handle, not if I can get to her while Lucy's out of the house tomorrow. Unless Lucy can split that amulet into two, which I doubt, she can't use it on her Gramma and herself in the same night.*

Putting down her receiver, Arlene said aloud, "I'll just let the poor girl rest up for tomorrow. I don't think her Gramma should be much trouble, not in the shape she must be in after all these years, amulet or *no* amulet," before she got ready to make an early night of it herself, once she fed her pets and gave each one a goodnight hug and kiss on his or her furry domed head—

—for the next-to-last time in her life.

CHAPTER TWELVE

SATURDAY, OCTOBER 31, 1987
HALLOWEEN

ONE—Anna (3)

The tip of the black EI Marko pen made little *squeeging* noise, as Anna Sudek drew the rounded front of a capital "P" on the back of a square of cardboard cut from an empty box of Friskies dry cat food. The sound reminded her of that nurse's shoes in the nursing home, but the smell of the ink in the pen was totally inhospitable—a harsh, chemical-inky odor that Anna found both unpleasant and vaguely stimulating this early in the morning.

As Anna finished writing the rest of the word "Please," she found herself thinking of Alvin Miner, of those dark darting eyes undulled after years of institutional life and countless shock treatments, and of his sour breakfast breath. *Poached eggs, most likely,* she thought, as she drew two parallel vertical lines and joined them with a short horizontal dash in the middle. *He hadn't any teeth. Did he lose them because of poor diet or neglect?*

Anna found it best to think of her great-grandfather in simple, common terms, reducing him to a series of isolated observations. His eyes. His breath. The liver dots on his dripping-wax hands. The way his remaining hair looked crumpled, each strand kinked in impossible configurations. The leather strap belting him into his wheelchair.

Should've brushed off Ginny's jacket cuff. Should've noticed the blanket fuzz. Good thing love makes Ginny unobservamt.

For a moment Anna wished that she wasn't so observant herself; it was so tiring, this business of having to file away every little detail, of needing to always think, If I do *this,* later on I'll have to do *that* to cover my tracks.

For the past few days, Anna felt as if her intestines were being wound on a stick, a massive fork of pulpy pinkish spaghetti, until she found herself unable to eat, almost unable to eliminate. She'd lost three pounds in just two days, or so the ancient bathroom scale she'd bought for fifty cents at a garage sale told her. The scale wasn't the most accurate, but she did notice that her pants were loose enough for her to fit two fingers and a thumb easily into the waistband and wiggle them around, and not even touch the skin of her waist.

As Anna wrote the small letters "e-l-p" after the big "H," she noticed that the ink smell was starting to give her a slight headache over her right eye. She recapped the El Marko, put it next to the sign she was working on, and walked into the kitchen for a glass of water. In there, a stale, musty odor hit her nostrils—the catsup lettering on the cabinet doors was fuzzy gray, a caterpillar marching band doing the "I fucking quit" goose-step.

As she sipped her water, Anna considered scraping the mess off the wooden doors, then decided against it. All her life she'd had to pick up after both the old lady and her mother, a dirty ankle sock here, a dropped gray-coated hairpin, or else face the consequences.

"Anna, don't just step over that, pick it *up*."

"Are we too *good* to pick up dirty *clothes*?"

"Don't be a slob like that father of yours. Bad enough you look like him."

They didn't want a daughter or granddaughter, they wanted a new parent, someone to look after them.

Anna finished her water, saying to the mute, moldy cabinet as she put the glass down on the counter, "You're not the only one who wants to quit, Ma...but some of us have obligations we didn't agree to take on in the first place."

Quickly, before her cat Mouth woke up and tried to "help" her, Anna finished lettering her gray cardboard sign, not really caring if the neighborhood kids obeyed her request to "Please Help Yourselves—One Piece Each, Okay?" or not. If Anna hadn't already put up the orange-and-black cardboard decorations (scrounged out of the IGA and Red Owl Dumpsters each November) in the front windows and on the glass storm door, she wouldn't have even bothered with buying candy to give out, but she felt obliged. *If you advertise, you have to deliver,* she thought as she taped the sign to the front of the big plastic mixing bowl she used for candy each year, wrapping a long strip of cellophane tape around the sign and the bowl itself. She then placed the unopened bag of candy she'd bought earlier in the week in the bowl and set it aside on the dining room table. If she dumped the loose candy in there now, Mouth would carry it off piece by piece and hide it under the stairs in the basement.

That obligation fulfilled, Anna glanced at her watch, wondering if Mrs. Campbell was awake. The old woman hadn't been out Dumpster diving lately; Arlene confided to Anna that she had reached the point where the sight of a stray cat's tail rounding the corner of a building was enough to give her the willies if she was out alone in the dark. Anna herself had intended to sleep in late, but she'd had a bad dream:

(Gordy Grey had been waiting for her at the door of the Super Suds, arms crossed, face grim, saying, "They've done it again...the pigs have been here," before pointing to the open driers, the over-flowing rubber trash bins, the red-splattered washers, and she had to get all the mess out of those places, every last slippery scrap, and as she worked, her clothes became soaked, the fabric smelling of old iron.

(Her hands so slick they could barely hold onto their burdens, Anna worked quietly, frantically, trying not to attract the attention of the magazine-reading customers over by the folding counters. And as she worked, she realized just what *she was digging out of round dark places, and began to assemble what she could, into* what *she could, until the bodies of all the old lady's victims were pieced together into hideous, slippery, barn-animal-sized red-pink-ghastly bone-white configurations on the grimy floor and folding counters of the Super Suds Launderette, only fragments of their new bodies recognizable for what they had been. And the fetid air was pinkish-steamy, clinging to her exposed skin, the indoor/outdoor carpet spongy soggy underfoot, with watery blood, squishing with a ham fat sound. Faceless customers ran gasping and screaming away from the butchery, making vague, frantic motions toward the car-nage as they passed Anna. And as she moved closer, reluctantly ever closer, Anna saw the mottled gray rinsing hose rise, bobbing and weaving, out of the small single-tub sink near the back of the laun-derette, while the chunks of melded, bleeding flesh quivered, giving off gurgling, muffled sounds as the rinsing hose snaked out past the sink, toward Anna. And the front of the big black rubber head was sliced or bitten off, revealing a molded-in pattern of a face embed-ded in the rubber, a face with wide, flattened lips and canted, no-color, vacant eyes—eyes that slowly, evenly blinked.)*

—and awoke to find Bruiser's face jammed into her own, wide-set tan-flecked green eyes less than an inch from hers, his stiff whiskers grazing her lips and chin. For a seemingly endless instant,

Bruiser's face merged with the face of the drain hose in her dream, and she started to screech, a thin, mewling wail, but Bruiser reached out his right paw and ran it down her face, his slightly rough pad moving along her skin gently, tenderly. After forcing herself to overcome the twin revulsion she felt over the dream and her... kinship to Bruiser, she finally pulled her hand out from under her quilts and stroked Bruiser's lustrous fur, feeling the strong musculature under his skin.

Then her cat did such an unusual, *human* thing Anna was immediately torn between wanting to hold him all day, and needing to get out of that bed immediately—for Bruiser had draped both his paws around her neck, as if hugging her, and carefully pressed his gleaming black-lipped mouth against her cheek, his short whiskers tickling her skin, before letting out a fish-food-scented sigh and fitting his immense head in the of flesh and bone under her chin.

After a few seconds Anna had said, "Sorry, I have to get up," and shifted the cat off her body, before getting up and putting on her jeans and sweatshirt. But what broke Anna's heart was how Bruiser just sat there on her unmade bed, staring at her with those melting, luminous eyes, as if saying, I understand...I'm always here if you need me.

Bruiser now padded around the house with Anna (she found herself torn between wanting to lock both her cats away in the bedroom, just so they wouldn't keep reminding her of what the old lady had done with that other cat and needing their company), as she prepared what she could for tonight, putting a small flashlight and square of aluminum foil in the pocket of her denim jacket (she'd toyed with the idea of wearing her Rusty Hinge stadium jacket because its silver satinette surface was safer for night walking, but Anna didn't think it wise to be *too* memorable, too identifiable, in case things went wrong outside the abandoned Yablinski house, and someone driving past saw her), and digging out the dark woolen stocking cap and knit gloves scrounged from the Dumpster outside the Dean County Clothing Exchange. The cap and gloves had holes in them that Ma hadn't gotten around to knitting patches for (Anna never had learned how to knit), but the holes didn't matter tonight. Just the dark color did.

The moon was a couple of days into the first quarter, and what with the forecast for clearing skies tonight, Anna was going to be all too visible the way it was. She didn't know if Mrs. Campbell was going to wear a different head scarf (her plaid one had many white and pale yellow patches), but her pea coat was regulation blue-black, so she'd blend into the darkness between the street lamps fairly well.

Anna didn't have any dark jeans, only that pair of black elastic-waist cotton dress pants she'd found at the launderette, but those reminded her too much of her nightmare *(wetly gleaming masses of pieced together flesh, with bits of their faces showing, the eyes looking at me)* for her to wear them for a *long* time, let alone a few hours from now.

Then she remembered—Ma had left most of her *clothing* behind. Many were baggy-legged elastic-waisted polyblend slacks, but Anna did find a pair of men's dark blue corduroy jeans Ma sometimes wore in the winter. They were loose-waisted, but Anna took up the slack using a couple of big safety pins.

By the time she was done rummaging through Ma's clothes, it was almost nine o'clock. She walked back into the dining room, just in time to see Mouth rip apart the piece of foil she'd placed in her jacket. The heavy foil had been scrounged from the IGA Dumpster, and must still have smelled of deli food, even after Anna had washed it.

"Bad *girl*," she yelled, running over to give the huge spotted tiger cat a swat on her rump, but Mouth ran for the basement before Anna could reach her. After balling up the torn pieces of foil in one hand, Anna went back into the kitchen and stood on tiptoes to peer into the high cabinet over the stove, where she and Ma stored their Corningware and washed and folded sheets of used aluminum foil. Anna selected another small sheet, folded it into a two-by-two square again, but placed it in the pocket of the corduroy pants this time.

That piece of foil was the most important thing Anna planned to carry out of the house that evening. If Mrs. Campbell's story about the Plow Boy tobacco tin, and her own childhood observation that the old lady had had the amulet in a small plastic bag *inside* the cloth drawstring bag were both correct, Anna would need something nonorganic, *nonliving* (or previously living) to place the amulet in once she got it away from the old lady.

Before she had gone to bed last night, Anna had reread that book of Egyptian magic—especially the passage about the magician from Zurarah, in the Kufa district of Babylon, who'd turned himself into a camel and killed and decapitated a man...only to reunite the head with the body, and make the man whole and alive again. The book didn't make it clear exactly *how* the magician of Zurarah had channeled his powers of working magic, but he had supposedly performed these feats in front of respected witnesses. And Anna guessed that whatever he'd used, it probably was golden, coiled, and decorated on one end with a beetle of pale green. Anna had also found herself wondering what the *hekau* inscribed in her grandmother's amulet actually said—just what unimaginable secrets were contained in those words of power.

And she'd remembered Alvin Miner's whispered tale of a moving, staring corpse, of the wife who couldn't bear to leave the side of her resurrected mother, and wondered if the man had ever really been insane at all, or if he'd been *too* sane all those years. Somehow, the latter seemed all the more awful. Anna found herself wishing that the old, old man she'd so briefly seen, so briefly touched in reassurance, had been a little quicker, a little freer as he swung his ax in that copper-smelling house, and killed Lucy before she had a chance to continue with her childish, conscienceless, petty games of discovery and death, before the amulet allowed her to escape that red-sheened swinging blade.

What makes you think you can catch her? Old Alvin Miner was armed, all pumped up with fear and anger. And he couldn't chop her down. Do you really think you can get that amulet away from her, without it changing her into something that will kill you before you even get a chance to try? That thing needs her as much as she needs it. She doesn't just use it, it uses her. It isn't the instrument of a simple Babylonian or Egyptian magician or holy man anymore, the tool of a person who understands it, and is using it for whatever purpose it was designed for—a child *has it now.*

A sixty-three-year-old child who has a lot of getting-even to do, for herself and her kin...just like her Gramma, only she was *a little more selective, a bit more careful when she did her thing. Lucy's Gramma never killed in front of witnesses, like a little girl showing off.*

Anna felt rather like a small child herself, a Brownie or Camp Fire Girl, perhaps, as she went about getting everything laid out in preparation for tonight. Her jacket and knitted things rested on top of the bookcase by the front door, the flashlight tucked in the pocket. She brought up an old TV table with a rusted top from the basement, for the sign-fronted bowl of candy. And the square of foil felt slightly cold through the thin cotton pocket of Ma's pants and Anna's long johns, a small metallic presence pressing slightly against her upper thigh, her own protective amulet.

"—once you have the amulet, wrap it up in the foil right away, before it makes you change, too. Judging from what that Isaacs girl said to you, this thing works *instantly*," Mrs. Campbell had said, adding, "Does it respond to *thoughts,* I wonder? Perhaps that's why it allows Lucy to do such nasty things...because *she's* such a horrid person, like that Mrs. Husa was. Not to hear her talk, or anything like *that,* but that woman had such cruel eyes...almost colorless, like your grandmother's."

("That reminds me—what did Lucy look like when she was small? If she ever had any pictures of herself, she got rid of them before I was born."

("What did she *look* like? A very plain little thing, lank brownish hair in braids, usually, thin lips—nondescript, really—dishwater drab. And when she tried to act cute, or coquettish, when she was older, it only came across pathetic, made her plainness all the more apparent.")

"You're *still* pathetic, old lady," Anna said aloud as she paced back and forth in the living room, trying to decide whether to call Mrs. Campbell or just walk over to her house. They hadn't actually planned on meeting during the day; Arlene had said she'd give Anna a ring in the early evening, as soon as the children started coming around trick-or-treating. Then Anna was to call the old lady's house, give the signal, as if she wanted the old lady to call her back for some reason. If she *did* get an answer, Anna would know that the plan was off for tonight—either the old lady was suspicious, or she'd tried visiting the Yablinski house the night before.

("That's another thing, Arlene. Suppose she goes off to kill the Yablinski *that* night, instead of waiting?" Anna had asked Mrs. Campbell, to which the elderly widow had replied with an emphatic shake of her gray hair, "That doesn't matter. Look what happened with that awful Mr. Inglass. She couldn't find him Friday night, so she followed him on Saturday. Lucy isn't bright enough to be all that adaptable. If you could have seen her trying to go up that down stairway in school, day after day...oh, Lucy'll be there all right. Think, Anna, she'll have to assume that the Yablinskis will be home—it'll be Hallo*ween.* People usually give out candy, don't they? She'll think they were just out Friday night. You see, she'll be there.")

Anna wished she could share Mrs. Campbell's confidence. It was true that Arlene Weiss had known Lucy Miner ever since both women were small children, which gave Arlene the advantage when it came to knowing what the *young* Lucy Miner was like, but Anna had spent most of her life in day-to-day, *hour-to-hour* contact with the *old lady*...and that Lucy was an entirely different kind of animal.

Anna's leg muscles were tense from pacing in tight patterns on the living room carpet. As she leaned over to rub them, her stomach began to growl. Not that she felt hungry, but Anna figured that she should force down something, even if it was just a cup of hot cocoa. Anything to keep her energy level up, to keep her from knotting up inside from pure tension when when she followed little Lucy—or *whatever* the old lady decided to become that night—to the Yablinski house. For she couldn't depend on Mrs. Campbell being able to chase and run down Lucy, even if she was planning to bring along her late husband's pellet gun—the one he'd used to shoot birds and squirrels off telephone wires for fun while he and the rest of the city crew repaired the roads leading out of town.

"Only in *case*," Mrs. Campbell had said, showing the long-barreled pistol-like weapon to Anna that Monday night. "Just in case...I won't even carry it loaded because she's your grand-mother—not because I care about *her*."

Now, as Anna stirred the packet of cocoa powder and hot tap water around in her beige plastic mug, she hoped that above all, Mrs. Campbell was serious about carrying that pellet gun unloaded—but not because Anna was worried about the old lady getting hurt. Anna didn't have any real friends, let alone close ac-quaintances, in Ewerton, but she hated to lose Arlene Campbell, the woman she'd once cursed on her morning Dumpster runs, and now feared losing more than she'd ever dreaded losing anything, even her own life.

TWO—Arlene (6)

Not only was it true that Arlene Campbell knew the young Lucy Miner much better than the woman's own grandchild, but Arlene had another advantage over Anna Sudek that Halloween morning—she had known Lucy's Gramma, the imposing, intimidating, *vile* Mrs. Husa. As Arlene briskly walked toward Evans Street, her arms pumping by her sides, she wondered why Alvin Miner hadn't taken an ax to the old woman long before he lopped off her hand and a portion of arm as easily as a woodcutter chops down a gnarled branch.

Arlene remembered how Lucy and her precious Gramma used to sit on the Miners' front porch, whispering to each other, giving dirty looks to the people passing the brick house, before dissolving into conspiratorial giggles. They did that to Arlene a few times, and Arlene's ears felt so hot with embarrassment she was half afraid her hair would catch fire and burn to a brittle charred stubble on her scalp, until the day she told herself, *They're the ones acting silly...* *grown-ups should know better,* and skipped down the street, making sure that she was out of sight before impulsively sticking out her tongue at the house and the sniggering pair seated on the porch.

To her surprise, Arlene felt her tongue starting to poke out of her mouth and bit down on it, scolding herself, *Now who's the one acting silly? You're getting as bad as Lucy and that crone of a Gramma of hers.*

Thinking of the face she'd seen behind that attic window so-bered Arlene up, made her remember why she'd come out here. No matter what happened tonight, whether Lucy Miner lived through the night or not (and right now, Arlene Campbell had no qualms about helping make sure the second option became a reality), sooner or later, someone was going to have to contend with what Arlene had seen peeking out the bottom of that age-distorted window.

She doubted that Anna would be able to handle it. The girl hadn't *seen* old Mrs. Husa, hadn't looked into those imperious, oddly glinting eyes. And Arlene didn't want to take the chance of Anna coming into the house afterward, with the amulet still on her person, and getting anywhere near the body of Lucy's Gramma.

Lucy's been putting that amulet on the old woman's body, I'm certain of it. Anna mentioned that sometimes Lucy hasn't had the little bag around her neck, but I know where it was when Lucy wasn't wearing it. Anna doesn't realize how much those two meant to each other. She wasn't that close to Lucy, so she can't under-stand.

Arlene was within sight of the Miner house now, standing in the long, cruelly defined blue-gray shadow it cast. All the shades were down between the curtains and the window glass; there was no movement anywhere. No decorative fringes rippled, no lines of black appeared alongside pulled-back shades. The house was quiet. No radio or television sounds drifted out to the sidewalk where Ar-lene stood, hands in her pockets, the fingers of her right hand grip-ping the little gun Don used to keep in the bottom drawer of his nightstand.

Not the long-barreled pellet gun she was going to carry with her tonight, but a real pistol, with copper-jacketed bullets—a whole chamber full of them.

Carefully, Arlene made her way along the side of the house, then walked parallel to the Share Avenue neighbor's fence, staring up at the house all the while. The rising sun, weak but still bright behind a gauze-filmy cover of clouds, shone on the attic window, turning the glass into a mirror of the morning sky—a translucent mirror; Arlene could still see the faint folds of the thin curtains behind the glass.

Arlene wasn't worried about anyone reporting a gunshot; when she and Don were only middle-aged, they used to go to the gravel pit outside of Lumbe to target shoot (only nonreturnable glass bottles, or old steel pop cans, not Don's favorite—live targets—at Arlene's insistence), and Arlene knew that the noise this pistol made wasn't too much louder than a firecracker, or a good quality child's cap pistol. And with the weather being this chilly, nobody was likely to have their windows open. Even the neighborhood kids weren't playing outside. And Lucy herself might not know, unless she was sitting up there with the body, commiserating.

She didn't even think that she'd actually be shooting off his old pistol. She knew that she might have to stand out in this backyard all day before (or even *if*) the curiously animate corpse of Mrs. Husa decided to take another peek out of the high-set window.

But it must be awfully boring, just sitting *up there in that attic, isn't it, old girl? That's where Lucy hid you, isn't it? Probably shoved you in among the floor joists, over in the shadows. As long as you weren't moving around, you wouldn't be likely to crash through the ceiling—not if your weight was evenly distributed. How Lucy got you up there is a mystery, but Lucy always was good at keeping certain things to herself. Like what she did with poor Bella's cat. Just kept it to herself, until the old woman couldn't do anything about it.*

Did Lucy giggle, I wonder, when she told her aunt? Damn fool creature was always giggling...giggling or hissing like a venom-toothed snake, either one extreme or the other. The child or the devil, with not much in between.

Nothing moved behind that sun-streaked glass, and after a few minutes, Arlene began to feel as foolish as she no doubt looked. *Really, what do you hope to accomplish by taking potshots at a corpse?* Shaking her head, she muttered, "All you'd do is drive Lucy out of there much too early, ruin the plan. Have to get Lucy out in the open."

Which would be the perfect time to go destroy Mrs. Husa's corpse, make sure nothing could reanimate it, Mrs. Campbell thought with excitement. She had planned to call Anna as soon as she spotted little Lucy that evening *(If you do go trick-or-treating, I don't think you could resist stopping by my house, just to rub it in, show off...and I'd know that angel outfit anywhere. I'm positive you'd have kept it after all these years. I doubt you'd throw out your own excrement if you didn't have to),* then leave her own house and follow Lucy or what*ever* she might become at a safe distance, until she met up with Anna, who would already be waiting at the Yablinski house.

After that, the plan grew vague; somehow, they'd catch Lucy, locate the green spot on whatever her body had become, and try to remove it...*and if worse comes to worst, I shoot at her, stun her, or kill her if I dare.*

Even though she didn't realize it, Mrs. Campbell had a little girl inside of her, too, just as Lucy Miner did. While Arlene Weiss hadn't been as stupid or sneaky as Lucy Miner, she hadn't been above sticking her tongue out at people, or just plain wishing that terrible things would happen to people she hated, either. She hadn't had a special golden thing trapped in an old tobacco tin, nor had little Arlene been really serious when she dreamed her tiny dreams of revenge, if she *had posse*ssed such a magical metallic pet. Arlene Weiss had been brought up a little differently from Lucy Miner.

Her upbringing wouldn't have allowed her to *keep* such a momento of a dead relative's special brand of love and revenge...but that had been Arlene *Weiss,* before she married Don Campbell, and learned a little bit about how rotten the world can be, and what a cruel place it really was, especially for animals and weak-bodied women. And after Don had gone to his deserved reward—whenever Arlene thought of him she found herself looking down past the floorboards, where she prayed he was burning for all eternity— Arlene only allowed her heart to grow soft and open when she was with her animals, never with people. Not after Don.

But when she was with Anna Sudek, she became sorry she hadn't had any children (hadn't let herself *remain* with child, that is, and Don never did suspect a thing), who, in turn, would have given her a granddaughter like Anna. The girl was a lot like her—tough because the world was a hard place, yet soft inside because she was *humane,* regardless of whatever awful thing Lucy Miner had done with that sweet little cat her Aunt Bella owned.

Her head facing down to make sure she didn't slip and fall on the frost-slick grass and leaves, Arlene Campbell began to walk away from the Miner house, not bothering to glance at the shaded window, even as she stepped back onto the sidewalk and headed back to her home on Polk Street...so she didn't see one of the ground-floor shades pull ever so slightly away from the window, until just a thin line of blackness, broken only by a yellow-nailed thumb holding the shade taut, briefly appeared behind the glass.

Then the thumb vanished, and the shade settled back against the cloudy glass.

THREE—Lucy (7)

Lucy watched Arlene Campbell trot briskly down the sidewalk. her thin ankles scissoring under her too-short pants legs, until the woman looked to be the size of a little girl. Only then did Lucy release the shade and shuffle over to the peach-scented object resting on her dresser, next to which was a tiny cotton gown, with rounded wings attached to the back with rusted safety pins, and a greenish-gray encrusted rough oval soldered to the top of a foot of wire whose bottom end was attached to a knotted, graying ribbon headband.

Lucy ran one finger along the halo, and came away with a verdigris-powdered fingertip.

"This won't do...not at all," she said aloud, her gravelly voice echoing slightly in the silent room. Petulantly she crushed the greenish halo, until it was a free-form mass of twisted, crumbling metal. She threw the halo onto the floor *(little Anna can pick it up later on...when she comes back home),* then stepped over it as she walked to the sewing basket that rested on her bedside table, and found a spool of white thread wound round with several needles Tina had threaded for her, because she couldn't see the eyes of the needles anymore, and glasses—being *completely* inorganic—were simply out of the question.

Lucy wouldn't let Tina buy anything but pure cotton thread, either, even when it became hard to find in the department stores uptown. But polyester wouldn't *work,* wouldn't *change,* so using cotton thread was utterly necessary, even if Tina thought her mother was just being persnickety, just exercising her control again.

"Tina just didn't *understand,*" Lucy said out loud, as if Gramma could hear her now. "I didn't know *myself* until they came out with all those *dang fool synthetics...*clothes just *stayed* there, sometimes they got *ripped,* and then *Tina* got mad, said *I* was *doing* it *myself,* on *purpose...*and then she'd *yell* like *Mother* used to do."

Lucy frowned at the memory while she turned up the hem of the tiny nightgown. Her aunts would never let her wear it short enough.

Frowning in earnest now, Lucy gave the little nightgown a shake, thinking, *Bad enough I can't have my halo*—and tears welled in her eyes at the memory of the gold-painted shiny halo wrapped in blue tissue, the one she'd saved all these years, in the hope that someday, some Halloween, she'd have a little girl who would wear it, and then later *give* her a granddaughter who would continue to wear the dainty costume. But Tina simply wasn't the *angel* type, and by the time little Anna was big enough to wear the costume, the girl's mind was poisoned against her Baba, so Lucy wouldn't *let* little Anna wear the angel gown and halo.

But when little Anna called yesterday, it just *came* to Lucy, this clever, wonderful, *delicious* idea...only now her costume didn't have a halo, and at the very least it *had* to have a halo.

Lucy looked at the little wind-up alarm clock on her bedside table—already half past ten. Less than seven hours until darkness, when all the *other* kids would be out trick-or-treating, getting all that candy.

Lucy threw the mended gown on the bed in disgust, and let out a squeal of anguish as the makeshift costume hit the bed and partially disintegrated.

"Oh, *noooo,*" she wailed. "Noooooo. *Now* how can I go?" and began clawing at her sagging face, her yellowed fingernails digging in her ears, punishing her withered flesh.

FOUR—The Wall

Blank, its pebbly surface unadorned and naked, the pale-painted wall beckoned, waiting for embellishment.

Alvin Miner's tired, weak body shuddered with the effort needed to push the old man over the high steel rail on the left side of his bed. Judging by the faint sounds of activity beyond his closed door, Alvin realized that he had so little, *little* time.

"Warn...." He breathed softly. "Warn...her...Anna...got to... doesn't know...didn't *see*—"

Miner fell on the floor from a height of over two feet, enough to both knock the wind out of his chest and break two fragile ribs. But he hardly felt the pain, hardly felt anything at all anymore as he slowly inched along the floor, hitching forward with feeble motions of his bony, almost fleshless elbows.

*Got to show them, so they'll know. Wouldn't listen before, didn't believe...them and their shots and jackets and bolts of juice through my brain...stirred my brain like a pitcher of icy lemonade, but...but she'll know...the girlie with the wrong shoes...Anna. Called me Jeddeck. Knows me. Not like Lucy...won't come, least not in per-*son...*but I seen, I seen her...flapping outside my window, caw open wide, shitting on the sill. Others, they don't know, but the girl...got* *to prove...got to* show *her...not crazy...never was...just too* sane, *is all.*

Nostrils quivering, Alvin Miner sniffed the noxious air, as dim realization sunk in—he'd done a number in his own pants, and hadn't felt it, hadn't realized, just like a diaper-bottom baby.

Or like someone dead from the ass up, he thought wryly, with the last vestiges of humor he possessed.

The wall was looming before him now, yard after yard of pale emptiness, waiting, waiting.

Hurry, got to...be coming, soon....

Got to warn her....

FIVE—The Old Lady (7)

"'lo?" Anna pulled long hairs out of her mouth. She'd been curled up on the couch, trying to rest up for tonight, and she'd drifted off to sleep when the phone began ringing. Her left ear was still tender from the way she had slept on the arm of the couch, and she kept the receiver a short distance from her head.

"Anna?" came the old lady's jiggly gurgle, and for a second the face in the hose-head hovered before Anna's eyes, and she phantom-smelled coppery steam.

"Yes...Grandmother. Is something wrong?"

"Yes and *no.* I *need* something." The old lady's coquettish tone made Anna bite down hard on her bottom lip to keep dry heaving into the mouthpiece, before composing herself enough to ask, "What?"

"Cardboard—two pieces," she sputtered so explosively Anna reflexively wiped imagined spittle off her cheek.

"What kind of cardboard?" Anna asked, thinking, *What in hell are you up to now?* before going on, "The corrugated brown kind, or lightweight? And how big?"

"Big *enough,"* the old lady said with emphatic evasiveness.

Anna wanted to tell the old lady that she was in *no* mood for games, when the old woman quickly amended herself, "Like from a *cat* food box. The *big* sides—"

"Oh...okay. Yeah, I have an empty box in the trash."

"It *has* to be *clean,"* the old lady insisted, and in Anna's mind, an image formed. The old lady was taking her up on her suggestion about putting out a sign saying that the kids should pick out their own candy tonight. For all Anna knew, the old bat might not have eaten all the candy, or any of it. She was that, playing little games all the time...and a bowl of candy sitting on the porch could be construed to mean that someone *might* be home, sleeping, not wishing to be disturbed. *Even when no one suspects you, you cover your tracks, Anna* thought as she assured the old lady that the cardboard was perfectly clean.

"And could you bring something *else?*"

"What?" Anna suddenly had a vision of the old lady asking her to buy another bag of candy, anything to control her, make sure she knew where she was at any minute.

"*Scissors*...the *big* ones. For *cutting*," she added, as if Anna was unfamiliar with their function.

"*Yes*, Grandmother, I know. I'll be right over. G'bye."

Anna didn't hang up in time to miss the old lady's warbled, "*Good-bye*," but she was out the door, a paper bag containing an empty dry cat food box and a pair of scissors in hand, and a quarter of the way down the block, before her phone began to ring again.

SIX—The Nursing Home (2)

After listening to Anna's phone ring a dozen times, Bib Stanley sheepishly handed the desk phone back to the receptionist at the Wright County Nursing Home and said, "Must be out...she has to do the running for her grandmother."

"I have Mr. Miner's daughter's number right here. I could—"

"No, no...she's an old woman, she should hear it firsthand from either her granddaughter or from me. It might come as a shock."

"Of course." The receptionist smiled apologetically, the movement of her cheeks making her oversized glasses ride up on her face. Bib was struck by how much the woman reminded him of old Palmer Nemmitz's bespectacled wife Bitsy back in Ewerton, and was tempted to ask her if she was somehow related to Mrs. Nemmitz, but decided this wasn't really the time for such a trivial question.

Instead, he asked, "Can I talk to whoever found him this morning? I have to know a few things."

"Certainly." The receptionist lifted the receiver and hit a certain raised button on the switchboard, saying as she covered the mouthpiece with her shoulder, "One of our day shift nurses was in to change his bedding, and—hello, could you send Clarissa up to the front desk? There's a gentleman here to talk to her. Yes, uh-huh... send her up, will you, Doris? Thanks."

Bib had been in law enforcement long enough to know what "*uh-huh*" meant. What still amazed him was how *other* people didn't think he knew what they were talking about. *And that buffoon Stu Sawyer thinks I'm stupid,* he thought with a slight shake of his head as the elevator door down the hallway opened, and a pale, pudgy blonde nurse tiptoed out, then headed for the desk.

"Clarissa, this is Chief of Police Stanley, from over in Ewerton. Chief Stanley, Clarissa Hood.

"She's the one who...."

"*Thank* you," Bib said quickly before addressing the whey-faced young nurse with a calm, "I just need to know what you found in there this morning. Is there someplace we can speak in private?"

The receptionist butted in, "There's a lounge, right down hallway to your left," and Bib merely nodded a curt thank-you before ushering the terrified young nurse away from front desk, reassuring her, "Don't worry, I don't bite...although receptionists are another matter," until the girl's white uniformed shoulders relaxed, and she began to giggle a little.

That made Bib think of Anna Sudek, and how she had giggled the night Wally Inglass was found—last week, in fact—only now, he was beginning to understand why Anna had been able to stand there giggling helplessly.... *It was probably either that or scream her head off, if just half of what I've heard so far is true. and she was thinking what I think she thinking.*

SEVEN—The Weapon

"Is this all right?" Anna held up the empty Friskies box so that the old lady could see the front of it. The old lady measured the box with her eyes, then finally nodded and said, "I *think so*...but I have to measure"—then snatched the box from Anna's hands and hurried back into her bedroom, almost slipping on the carpetless floor before she reached the closed door. When the old lady opened it, Anna caught a brief glimpse of something whitish lying on the comforter-covered bed, and smelled that peach-sweet odor.

While her grandmother was busy measuring the box in her bedroom, Anna happened to notice that the phone book was folded under the black phone, so that the white pages were showing. Leaning over just far enough to make out some of the writing on the top page—in case the old lady popped out of her room unexpectedly—Anna saw the names:

Yates, James—
Young, P—

before the bedroom door opened again and the old lady stepped out, shutting the door so fast she caught the hem of her nightgown between the door and the jamb. The old lady was wearing that loopy, half-assed grin she always wore when she thought she was putting one over on someone.

"It's perfect. Now, could you leave the scissors here? Or do you need them?"

"No problem," Anna said, eager to get out of the house, yet also itching to reach out and pull open the old woman's closed robe, aching to ask, "Are you wearing that thing, or is it Gramma's turn?"— until she heard the knocking at the front door.

"Who is it?" the old lady singsonged, and a male voice replied, "Everett Roofing...about that leak."

Anna had never seen the old lady take off so fast, even when she was younger. She moved so quickly, in fact, that the door opened when her nightgown pulled free as she hurried for the front door. For a second, Anna was torn—stay where she was, or try and duck in the room, see if she could find anything important?

Two sidesteps took her about a foot into the room. She half listened to the old lady jabbering with the roofer as she glanced around the bedroom (wrinkled comforter on the lumpy bed, tiny wallet-sized school photo of Anna, taken in the first grade, tucked in the frame of the over-the-dresser mirror). Her eyes came to rest on something small and shining. The old lady's sewing scissors, with the tiny blades, not much bigger than a bird's beak—

—and about the same shape as the wounds on Wally Inglass's body. The tiny paired punctures Bib had noted in his report—

—and, the handkerchief from her stadium jacket pocket in hand, Anna reached into the room and lifted the scissors off the end of the bed, using the white cloth to shield the silvery metal from her own fingerprints, before stuffing the cloth-covered scissors into her jacket pocket.

"—Monday will be *fine*," the old lady was telling the man, before warbling, *"Good-bye"* and shutting the door. By then Anna was back where she was standing before, saying, "I'll be by on Monday to pick up the scissors...," as she pressed the stolen pair against her side, her fingers crossed inside her pocket.

EIGHT—Alvin Miner (2)

"—was half out of the bed when I came in. He was cyanotic and hyperventilating, so I called for help, and while I was waiting, he told me, 'Tell Anna...tell Anna,' over and over, and as I was getting him back onto the bed, I noticed what he'd done on the walls, and so I didn't hear all of what he said next, but I think it was something like, '—out for *Lucy, out* for *Lucy,*' only his voice was going already, and it was hard hearing him."

The blonde nurse looked expectantly at Bib over her foam cup of coffee, as if seeking approval for what she'd done for the dying old man in the small private room. Bib knew nothing of hospital procedure, but nodded anyway, saying, "You're doing just fine," as she swallowed and went on, "But before the doctors came, he pulled my head down with his hand, grabbing me by the hair," a light note of disdain crept into Clarissa Hood's voice as she fingered a recently washed section of hair. Bib had seen the old man before they moved the body. Alvin Miner's right fingertips were stained brown with excrement, like a child who had been using fingerpaints.

"And then I heard him say real plain, '*Tell* her, watch out for the golden *snake!*' and I guess he meant *that* thing, on the wall."

Bib only half listened to the rest of the plump nurse's story. He'd only wanted to know for *sure* that that was what the old man had drawn on the pale walls of his room, using his own body wastes for paint. "*That* thing" Nurse Hood had referred to, the huge representation of something coiled like a snake, a spiral composed of wide loops that tapered down to a snake head on one end, but started at the top with a stylized bug, with a tiny oval dot of a head and a vaguely rectangular body divided into three sections—one horizontal across the top, surmounting two smaller vertically divided portions—plus six mismatched legs.

Bib hadn't been very good in biology when he attended EHS years before, but he knew a beetle when he saw one. And so did that professor from the college across the parking lot from the nursing home—that short, dark-haired fellow with the glasses and East Coast accent, who'd showed up after the Wright County sheriff had to leave the nursing home to attend to another call. The professor whose Italian name Bib immediately forgot, even though he wouldn't so easily forget what the animated middle-aged man in the fussy tweed sports jacket and dark blue plaid shirt had to say:

"Considering the *circumstances*, that's one of the best renderings of a scarab I've ever seen. This man was insane, you say? Oh, such a *waste*. This is an excellent representation. Apt choice of medium, considering that the Egyptians worshiped a dung beetle—ah, yes, about the *drawing*.

"I've never seen anything *quite* like this, but I believe it's supposed to represent an amulet of some type, although the addition of the snake at the bottom is quite unusual. I wonder, did he draw this from memory? Seems almost...*alive.* Notice how it looms down, glaring at us? Marvelous forced perspective. Pity the man wasn't trained, he had talent—or else his memory was exceptionally vivid, either way. A genuine amulet of this type would be quite rare and valuable."

Bib had had to interrupt the professor at that point, asking what such an amulet might be used *for*...and when that professor (Nunzi? Nuzzi?) told Bib, the chief had thanked him profusely, then hurried downstairs to phone Anna Sudek, again kicking himself for not telling her what Lenny Wilkes had told him about Auggie seeing Lucy Miner wearing a spiral "slave bracelet" with a "lizard" and a "bug" on the free ends—

—even though he'd suspected that Anna Sudek knew all about the amulet, and was fully aware of what it could do to the human being who wore it.

And I'll bet I know why you've been keeping that lip of yours zipped about what Precious Isaacs said to you, Bib thought as the wet-haired nurse dutifully explained how she and the doctors had tried to save the 106-year-old man now lying in the morgue of the adjoining hospital building. As he nodded every few seconds and sipped his own cup of tepid coffee, he promised himself that he'd stop over at Anna's house as soon as he could shake himself loose from the nursing home and drive back to Ewerton. *After* the young mustached college staff photographer whom that professor had dragged along with him developed the dozens of photographs he'd snapped of the brown-smeared drawing—photos Bib intended show to Anna.

This time, he *had* to see the look on her face when she saw what her great-grandfather had smeared on those pale pastel walls...for Bib doubted that even a cool kitty like Anna Sudek could maintain her composure under *all* circumstances, in the face of the revelations he was prepared to make.

NINE—*The Miner House (3)*

Arlene Campbell was just emptying a bag of fun-size candy bars into a plastic ice cream bucket when the phone rang. But before she had a chance to say "Hello?" an out-of-breath voice on the other end gushed, "What would Lucy need two pieces of cardboard for?"

"Anna?"

"The old lady...she had me bring over an empty cat food box. She said she had to measure it, and then she said it was just perfect and sent me home."

"When was this?"

"Oh, about forty-five minutes, maybe an hour ago. I tried knocking at your door on the way home, but there was no answer—"

"I must've been in the bathroom—"

"Oh. I thought maybe you might be out, and would be home later. *Anyhow.* She kept my scissors, but I—"

Arlene didn't hear the rest of Anna's breathy words; her mind was whirring.

Cardboard from a box of cat food. That's about a foot by eight or so inches, give or take...two big pieces...a pair—

"Anna, she's getting ready for tonight. Her costume had wings on it, out of cardboard. They wouldn't have held up after all these years. See, I was right, she *is* going to come out as—"

On the other end of the line, all Arlene could hear was wheezing, and asked, "Anna, is something wrong?"

A pause, then, "No, I had bronchitis when I was a kid...diminished lung capacity. I was running to get back here and I overdid it. I'll be fine in a minute."

"Well, go lie down. Sit with your head between your knees."

"No, no...I'm *fine*, really. Just winded. Be...better in a minute."

"But how will you manage tonight?"

Anna coughed for a few seconds, then replied, "As long as I don't run full tilt I'm okay. I should've known better today, but I was curious."

Arlene was about to say, "And that's how the cat was killed, too," but luckily she caught herself before she *really* went and upset the poor girl. Instead, she said, "When did you have this bronchitis?"

"Years ago...second grade. I was out of school for a month... expanded my rib cage. Ever notice?"

Arlene had thought that Anna was simply a bit stocky about the chest and waist, but now she realized that the young woman's rib cage *was* rather large...and then another thought came to the woman: *There's no way Anna can possibly hunt Lucy down tonight...I'd thought the girl was a tad on the lazy side, never moving all that fast, but if she's winded like this after a five-block run, what will happen if Lucy decides to give chase? I can't catch her. I was counting on the girl.*

"Anna, dear, why don't you go take a nap, rest those lungs."

"No, Arlene, really, *I'm fine.*"

"Now, you just go curl up on the sofa with those cats of yours and catch twenty winks. I'll give you a call around four. How's that sound?"

There was a pause, then Anna said, "If that's an order."

Arlene smiled at the receiver as she said firmly, "Yes, it is. Now you just take that nap."

"*Yes,* Mother," Anna said with mock seriousness, then, warmly, "Thanks for your concern. *I'm fine,* but...thanks anyway. Talk to you at four, then?"

"At four. Now sleep tight, and good-bye," Arlene said, after Anna repeated "Good-bye," the line went dead, but she stood there listening to the phone anyway, as if she still heard the young woman's warm voice breaking through the static coming through her earpiece.

And even after she hung up, Arlene felt a glow inside. After all these years alone, someone other than her four-legged babies was counting on her, and appreciated the concern Arlene felt for her. It was a strange feeling, both liberating *and* confining. For the first time in years, she felt free of the niggling doubt that *she* had been the one who had brought out the bad in her late husband, brought out the *mean,* yet she also knew that this new concern she felt carried with it responsibilities.

As she arranged the tiny bars of brightly wrapped candy in her bucket, placing them all logo-side up, Arlene spoke to her babies, her voice filled with new concern.

"Can't let that girl go running around tonight—not the way she sounded just now...if something happened to her, I'd never forgive myself.... What should Momma do, hmm, Silky?" she asked the mottled white-and-black cat as he climbed onto her lap and kneaded her thighs. "What's Momma to do? Last thing I need tonight is for Anna to collapse out in the street. Poor child sounds almost tubercular. Thought she'd cough her lungs out there and then. This wild goose chase *was* my idea."

Silky looked up at Arlene, his small green eyes bright and pleading. Rubbing the narrow patch of furry skin between his enormous ears, Arlene said, "Momma should just take care of this herself, shouldn't she, Silky? She knows what to do...and Lucy should be busy, getting her little costume ready. Bet a dollar to a doughnut she won't be wearing that amulet."

Silky just kept looking up at his mistress, kneading paws working steadily against her polyester-covered thighs, small pointed upturned face poignant with love and adoration.

Stroking his soft-furred back, the old woman said, "After all, Momma can't guarantee that Lucy *will* stop over here tonight. She might go straight to that Yablinski house, before the moon gets too bright."

Arlene's hand stopped in mid-stroke on the cat's back, as she sucked in her breath. The *moon.* It was two days into the first quarter, and the weatherman on WERT said that the skies should be clear tonight, which meant the moon would be nice and bright—almost as bright as a full moon. *And Anna said that that Deputy Von Kemp saw the white dog when it was too dark out to make it out clearly. You like darkness, don't you, Lucy? You only went after Wally when you did because you got over-anxious, couldn't find him the night before...but the longer you wait tonight, the more likely you'll be seen. Why not strike early, perhaps before the other kiddies come out. Go up to the Yablinskis' door, hoping you can wheedle your way in. Ask to use the bathroom, or some such excuse. You were always a wheedler, Lucy, I remember. A whining, tattling, lick-spittle little brat...and you never did change, never did grow. I wonder, Lucy, which is the real you, the old lady or the little girl who's coming out tonight?*

Arlene suddenly got up, hugging Silky tight before gently placing him on the floor, then went to each of her babies in turn, hugging furry bodies and kissing warm-skinned heads and muzzles, before pulling on Don's old pea coat and putting on her head scarf. For a second, she hesitated about bringing the gun along, wondering if it would *really* be of any help if things went wrong in the Miner house. But the thought that Lucy had a weapon of her own, a golden fluid bauble of unimaginable, unholy power, made Arlene leave the tiny pistol right where it was in her pocket.

Before she left her home, Arlene scanned the faces of her babies as they sat or rested curled in warm balls by the registers around the room, looking into their shiny brown, green, and amber-orange eyes, fixing their expressions in her mind, even as another face fixed itself firmly in her brain—that of a young woman.

"Be good babies, Momma loves you," she said before taking one last glance around the living room at those sweet, furry faces, and then exited her house, locking the door—and all the love of her babies—behind her. It may only have been her imagination, but the October wind had never felt so cold before as it whistled through her head scarf, numbing her ears and exposed cheeks, almost freezing the single line of moisture running from her right eye.

It was only around quarter to two by the time Mrs. Campbell reached the Miner house, but the sky was already that ashy blue-gray color Arlene associated with a much later time of day, and a slightly later time of year—mid-December, perhaps. The ragged clouds were feathering away at the edges, leaving larger and larger patches of clear sky, in anticipation of the cold, cold night to come. And Arlene's breath was a puffy plume before her face, gently obscuring her vision with each exhalation.

When seen through her billowing breath, the Miner house seemed to be floating in a fine cloud, hovering slightly above the leaf-scaled grayish-green lawn. A few of the shades had been raised, but only in the front of the house. Those in the back remained drawn, turning the windows into blank eyes set in a chapped, peeling face.

As Arlene walked along the backyard, keeping close to the wooden fence, she wondered if she should just go up to the front door and knock, then try to get into the house on some pretext, or attempt to break in somehow. *But that's no good. She'd hear me, call the police, or do something worse.*

Arlene paused in mid-thought when she saw movement in the attic window—a brief flash of brown along the bottom of the glass, followed by the unmistakable ripple of the curtains. *She's gone upstairs to be with her Gramma. Lucy's put the amulet on the body. Perhaps she's up there right now with her, playing with Gramma before going out to kill. They always discussed things, heads touching as they whispered, always that infernal whispering.*

The brown forehead and eyes appeared at the window again, until the head jerked out of sight, quickly, as if someone had pulled the brown figure, and Arlene saw the top of another head slowly rise from the bottom of the window, as if someone was giving a small child a boost up—someone with tired old joints who couldn't move up fast under a heavy, moving burden. Arlene ran for the house before that *other* head could clear the windowsill, her feet slipping on the scattered leaves and lank grass, until Arlene felt her left knee pull in a painful direction, but she kept on running until she reached the front of the house, her breath billowing before her like the steamy exhaust from a clothes dryer.

Lucy was up in the attic, and her Gramma was holding her up to look out the window, like a parent might hold a child up so that she can see above people's heads at a parade.

That's...that's obscene! Arlene thought, stepping onto the porch where she paused, panting, by the front storm door, before trying to open it. The storm door was unlocked, but the inner door wasn't. Rattling the knob for a few seconds, Arlene thought, *What do they do on the TV? All those policemen and private eyes?* as she reached for Don's pistol.

Pressing the end of the barrel just under the place where the knob met the door, Arlene mouthed a silent prayer that the whole shebang wouldn't explode in her hands, then pulled the trigger, jerking her hand away the second her finger twitched inward.

The noise seemed tremendous, numbing, at such close range. Her hand stung from the heat and the powder bums, but the door opened when she pushed forward on the wood, so she didn't take the time to analyze the situation, or wait and see if anyone was coming outside to investigate the gunshot. Shoving the gun into her pocket, she just stepped into the musty smelling dark house and hurried for the staircase at the far end of the room, her footfalls sharp and ringing across the bare wood floor, her breath loud and dissonant in the silent room.

Anna never could have done this, Arlene told herself as she climbed the steps two at a time, propelling herself up the smoothly worn wooden treads, her gloved hand picking up splinters as she ran it the wrong way up the banister. *The poor girl would still be gasping on the landing.*

Arlene had heard her late father-in-law talking about the Miner house so often that she almost knew the floor plan of the place; the stairs leading to the attic were the kind you pulled down from the ceiling, using a pole with a hook on the end to snag the little ring set into the door set into the ceiling. Then the stairway came down to the floor, wooden risers set into the rectangular door, which led to the unfinished attic beyond. And this opening in the ceiling was located to the rear the house, at the end of the central hallway.

Arlene suddenly stopped, breathing hard but steady, as she saw that the trapdoor leading to the attic was already back in place, the pole with the hook on the end rehung on the nearby wall, the wood swinging slightly in place on the nail...and realized that even if Lucy had pulled up the stairs after her, so she could hide in the attic with Gramma, she couldn't have hung the long pole back up on the wall,

Heart jumping in her narrow chest, Arlene looked at the doorways that lined the hallway on both sides. Every door was shut, and the narrow space where each hung just above the bottom of the jamb revealed nothing but darkness within. The hall itself was faintly lit by a window set in the end of the wall, a window that lacked curtains in front of the yellowing canvas shade—a window that emitted just enough light to reveal that hallway was perfectly empty. No mouse-sized Lucy scurried along the baseboards; no bird-small Lucy flew around the ceiling. Just Arlene stood there in the gloom, facing a hallway of empty rooms, save for the unknown one that was sheltering a being whose present form Arlene could only guess at.

Lucy's listening to me breathing, ear or what-have-you pressed to the door, as she gloats. "Olly-olly-oxen, home, home free...." only none of us would play with you, would we? You'd never abide by the rules, never play fair...but I'm game, Lucy. Oh, am I game now.

Slowly, Arlene advanced down the hallway, moving closer to the glowing yellow window at the end...and the long-handled hook still vaguely swinging nearby, saying aloud as she walked, "Come out, come out, wherever you are. I've counted to ten, Lucy, I'm coming for you," but didn't bother looking under any of the darkened doors, or try rattling any of the dull brass knobs. Arlene didn't have the extra strength to waste by going through each of the rooms, only to have a mouse-sized Lucy dart out between her feet and hide in the next room down the line. Such a search was useless—her late father-in-law and Auggie Wilkes had found *that* out over fifty years ago.

Arlene continued down the echoing hall, her calling voice so amplified and distorted that it might have been coming from *any* direction, until she reached the now-still hook hanging from the bent nail on the wall. The wood was still faintly warm around the smoothest, most worn part of the handle; Arlene almost recoiled when she touched it. And as the last of the faint echoes died down behind her, she quickly lifted the hook off the wall and tiptoed below the trapdoor, looking for the hanging metal ring.

On her second try she snagged the ring. When pulled, the door-stairway came down effortlessly, almost noiseless from frequent use. Standing at the bottom of the risers, Arlene peered up into the murky brown-orange gloom above, the unfinished interior faintly illuminated by the light filtering through those high windows. Then the smell reached her—a dry, decaying, yet sweetish odor, harsh and cloying at once...and for a second, Arlene wanted to *run*, just get out of the house and let Anna take care of her vile monster of a grandmother, but the memory of Anna's wracking cough and wheezing voice telling her that everything was "just fine" gave her the strength to mount those rough wooden treads, pole in hand, until she was in the attic itself. And as she pulled the door up after her, she fought the urge to shout, "I'm with *Gramma*, Lucy...*your* precious *Gramma*...come out, come out, *whatever* you are"—for the reeking darkness was all around her, turning the attic into a rough, alien landscape populated by a sometimes living corpse.

THE AMULET, BY A. R. MORLAN * 331

But as her eyes grew accustomed to the murk, she could see how different the attic had become since Don Campbell's father and Auggie Wilkes were up here. Then another, marginally more pleasant odor hit her nostrils, as Arlene heard a warbling, singsong voice sputter, "I thought you'd never come up here, little Anna."

My god. She thinks I'm the girl! Arlene remembered how marginal Lucy's eyesight was. Surely, in the gloom, Lucy must have mistaken her for her granddaughter, until another thought hit her, *And just what does she have planned for Anna?*

Lucy was babbling, "I *knew* you'd have to come *see*. We've been waiting for so long, getting everything ready. Look, little Anna, isn't it beautiful—" until she took a couple of steps closer, moving with difficulty over the raised joists covering the ceiling of the rooms below, and Arlene knew that she should move, *now,* get herself down those fold-up stairs and out of the house, but what she saw held her transfixed, stunned into inaction like a deer impaled by a flashlight's beam.

For even in the dusky, filtered light, what she saw was grotesque and strangely poignant. And then she shifted her eyes to the right, and saw—

And then Arlene found herself unconsciously averting her eyes when she saw the oily glimmer of the amulet's aureate coiled body, topped with the sheen of the stylized scarab, for to gaze upon what was holding the amulet was madness, total, evil *lunacy.*

"Where's little Anna?" Lucy hissed, as Arlene noticed the snake head's sliver of a tongue flickering, lashing *outside* the golden jaws, "Supposed to be little Anna." Arlene began to back away from Lucy at last, muttering, "No...no, Lucy, she can't—she *shouldn't* see this. I couldn't let her."

"Noooooo!" Lucy screeched, her wattled hand reaching, reaching backwards for the amulet. Her knobby fingers wrapping around the scarab-adorned end, Lucy sputtered, "She's mine, *my* little Anna. She *belongs* here. You have no *right. My* Anna, all *miiine.*"

"I have to protect my *friend*," Arlene shot back, as the cloying reek of the attic stung her nose and made her eyes tear, until she felt the rush of Lucy's warm breath as she hooted, *"Nooooo."*

"You are *insane,"* Arlene whispered, her voice softer than the shifting of crisped leaves on wind-teased branches, as she edged closer, closer to the trapdoor, hand clutching the bulletless gun in her pocket, averting her eyes from what stood before her in the horribly changed attic. But Lucy didn't want Arlene to look away, oh, no, not at all, and when she rushed forward, talons spread, there was a strange rending sound in the air, the metallic recoil of something malleable yet rigid stretching, and then giving way.

TEN—Trick or Treat

Anna Sudek woke to a muffled pounding of fists on wood, and the whispers and giggles of children. Rubbing her eyes, she glanced at her watch and jumped to her feet, her head swimming from the effort as she hurned to go get the bowl of candy, ripping open the bag as she walked back to the front door, flicking on the porch light before she unlocked the door. It was past five o'clock, close to five-thirty.

"Trick or treats!" shrill voices shouted in near-unison, as five or six plastic pumpkins and crinkly shopping-type bags were thrust forward, each already containing several pieces of candy. Anna mechanically dropped a couple of pieces of candy in each child's bag, and flashed a weak smile at the pair of mothers who stood partly obscured in the shadows beyond the porch light.

"Thanks...thanks, lady...t'ank—ooo...thank you," then the children were gone in a scramble of crackling vinyl costumes and swinging bags of candy, the mothers following them at a distance. When Anna glanced down the street, she saw that her neighbors had their porch lights on, as well as a few flashlight-illuminated pumpkins sitting out next to their front doors, or behind front windows, and there were other packs of children running farther down the street, some of them heading this way.

But Arlene was going to call me at four. She isn't the type to forget something like that, Anna thought as she set the bowl of candy on the little TV table and placed it on the porch between the door and one of the living room windows, then hurried back in the house. As the next group of children bounded onto the porch and began jabbering as they picked out candy, their voices indistinct through the closed doors, Anna dialed Mrs. Campbell's number, hanging up after a dozen rings.

"Where *is* she?" Anna asked the cats as she pulled on her denim jacket and knit hat. "Where in the hell *is* she? Oh, *shiiit!* I should've stayed *up*," then hurried to the door, opening it in time to see the kids run off the porch and head down the street. Anna glanced at the bowl on the table as she shut the door behind her, saw that there was still some candy left, then let the storm door slam behind her as she ran down the middle of the street, heading for Polk Avenue, steering clear of the clumps of children hurrying from lighted house to lighted porch.

Her side was aching before she made it to the intersection. She stopped for a second, arms wrapped around her middle, her eyes closed, shutting out the ever-darkening neighborhood around her, trying to get her wind back, when the sharp pain in the backs of her legs made her cry out, a strangled, airless keening sound that was quickly drowned out by a hoarse, familiar cry.

"Bruiser, how did *you* get out?" Anna turned around and scooped up the heavy animal, carrying him on her shoulder as she crossed over to Polk Avenue and hurried down that street, all the while whispering to the ebony animal who resembled a slice of the surrounding darkness, with luminescent, oddly glowing eyes, "Oh, god, Bru, you think something bad happened, too? C'mon, Bruisie, almost there. Oh, *nooooo*."

Arlene Campbell's house was dark, unlit by either a porch light or interior lights. Not so much as a bowl of candy sat on front porch.

Bruiser hugged Anna's neck, his claws digging in through her jacket and sweatshirt, his breath coming in noisy little hitches, moist snorts against her exposed neck. She saw his hackles rise, a thick fur Mohawk bristling across his shoulders and back, and hurried down the street until she reached Lumberrnill Drive, then continued down that street for a block and a half, until she came to Evans Street, Bruiser now growling in earnest, his whole body vibrating in her arms.

In the street lamp's glow, Anna's breath was a fine golden mist, surging away from her nostrils and half-opened lips in billowing waves. Her chest felt like she'd just inhaled crushed glass, all sharp points of tumbling pain going up and down her air-starved lungs.

She got worried when I called...should've waited, shouldn't have gotten her all worked up. She went there—she went to take care of the old lady by herself. But when? Anna trudged on, wheezing and sending forth great clouds of pale mist from her tortured, ruined lungs, Bruiser growing heavier in her arms with each step, his claws seeming to grow longer and more dagger-tipped as she moved closer to Lucy Miner's fortress and foul barn.

Above Anna, the clouds were almost all gone, save for a few wispy umber-tinged fringes still masking the quarter moon's white-toothed smile, a leering grin set in a depthless blue-black face. Its eerie whitish illumination turned the denuded trees pale grayish-white, their branches contrasting sharply with the dark horizon beyond, making the neighborhood a reversed negative of its usual self. And at her feet, the streetlamp's feeble golden glow made the fallen leaves seem alive again, still tree-attached, as if the sky and the ground had somehow reversed themselves, turning Anna's universe topsy-turvy, so that she felt like she was walking through the sky, stepping into the topmost branches of a tree as she shuffled through the wind-blown mounds of warm-hued leaves, and snagged her boots on some fallen branches.

Beyond her, the Miner house was silent, unlit, but that meant nothing; the old lady often sat in silent darkness, rocking and re-membering. But when Anna stepped onto the porch, smelled the harsh odor of gunpowder, and almost lost her grip on Bruiser as the huge tom hissed and struggled in her arms, she doubted that she'd find a placidly rocking old woman sitting in that house.

The storm door was closed, but Anna saw that the inner door was wide open, revealing the black maw of the living room within... and when she elbowed open the screen door, Bruiser was out of her arms and sucked into the surrounding blackness within a second. Anna was too out of breath to yell for him to come back; instead, she leaned against the open door frame, sucking in lungfuls of chilly air until she began coughing again, her diaphragm hitching and ach-ing from the effort. Finally, she reached over and felt for the main light switch that controlled the two table lamps in the living room.

Nothing *seemed* to be amiss, aside from the front lock being shot apart. No furniture was turned over, no knickknacks were out of place, and what she could see of the dining room was likewise undisturbed. Bruiser was nowhere in sight, though. Hugging her throbbing rib cage with both arms, Anna quitted the living room, moving on to the dining room and then the kitchen. No Bruiser, and nothing out of the ordinary. She backtracked to the old lady's bed-room, and cautiously pushed the door open with one hand.

Right away, Anna noticed that the room smelled different, within the space of a few short hours *(Oh, Arlene, how long have you been here?)* The peach potpourri odor was gone, only a faint memory in the musty, spoiled-meat-tinged air. Anna merely glanced around the room, at the weeping brown stains on the wallpaper, and the clutter of doodads on the dusty dresser scarf *(Pictures of little Anna in the mirror. Wasn't I ever supposed to grow up?),* then hur-ried away from the room. Whatever it was in there that the old lady didn't want seen, it had been removed, that much Anna sensed as she hurried to the stairs, calling weakly, "Bruiser? Bru-Bru? Where *are* you?"

The stairway was dark, the outlines of the treads murky, until blackness obscured even those nebulous traces. And the switch that controlled the stairway light was located at the *top* of the staircase.

Her hand on the smooth wood railing, Anna called up the stairs, "Arlene? Bruiser? *Grandma?* Anyone?"

Faintly, very faintly, she heard Bruiser's rough pads hitting the bare floorboards, a rain-steady pit-pat that echoed slightly in the silence. The hallway was like that, so empty and elastic-floored that sounds bounced in weird ways, until a person's own footfalls sounded like they were coming from in front of them. That hallway had terrified Anna when she was small; every little sound was magnified, distorted, until she was pee-in-her-pants terrified.

C'mon, Bruiser, get down here...or reach up and get the lights. Even a flashlight isn't illumination enough to make me go up there.

The hollow padding sounds continued, amplified by the floorboards...and then Anna heard something that made her reflexively wet her pants, until the corduroy was hot and damp between her thighs.

When she realized what the sound *had* to be, Anna pulled the flashlight out of her pocket and hurried up the stairs, following the imperfect golden circle of light until she reached the landing and snapped on the hall light. The bedrooms were yawning open, all five of them, the doors swinging slightly on their hinges, and the hallway still rang with the thunderous noise of what Anna now realized had been wooden doors slamming hard enough to mimic the sound of gunfire, for no gunpowder stench hung in the air, only the stale scent of old damp wallpaper paste and unvarnished wooden flooring.

"Where did you *go?*" Anna shouted in the empty hallway, and her scream echoed back at her, mocking her even as the sound diminished into near silence...*near* silence because of the faint, rain-delicate *plashing* sound coming from the far end of the hallway, near the shaded window—the sound that was drowned out a second time when Bruiser leaped onto Anna's shoulders and she screamed as she went down on one knee from the sudden weight on her back.

Anna hadn't heard him come up behind her, but she'd heard *something* padding around up there, something moving on rough-soled feet...or paws.

"Bruiser, you *idiot,* where *were* you?" she asked the cat as she pulled him off her back and cradled him in her arms. Bruiser pushed his muzzle into the crook of her right ann, hiding his face, and Anna thought, *He's scared...but of what?* as the *plashing* noise filtered back into her consciousness. And looking at the end of the hallway, Anna found the source of the sound—the trapdoor to the attic was leaking; drops of water were falling through the crack, to hit the wood below.

Only the "water" wasn't *water,* not unless water was red, and glittered richly in the light from the distant bulb set in the ceiling.

Slinging the cat under her arm, Anna raced to the end of the hall, almost slipping and falling when her foot hit the fist-sized puddle of crimson on the floor directly beneath the little ring set into the trapdoor. But when she went to reach for the pole with the hook on it, the thing was gone, the rusted nail bent and empty.

"Noooo...*noooo,*" she keened in frustration, slapping at the papered walls with the flat of her free hand, until she heard movement up in the attic...a lurching step *clump,* as if someone was walking across an uncertain surface, and had to feel out each step before putting down the full weight of his or her foot.

"Arlene?" Anna cried, as the plaster ceiling above creaked close to the trapdopr, and dark spiderwebbing cracks formed in an ever-widening circle. And then the door began to move, shifting down toward Anna, until the blood-runneled steps were extending in front of her, mutely waiting for her to step upwards, into the black attic.

Shifting the flashlight's beam upward, her aim unsteady because she was holding Bruiser with that arm, Anna saw a flash of something that jerked out of her line of vision too quickly for her to make out exactly what it was.

"Arlene...you up there?" Anna prayed that the old woman would show herself again, or at least *say* something.

"A...ah...ahnna?" A rasp unsupported by breath, a sound as weak as a sigh, yet oddly *strong,* too.

"Arlene, hang in there, I'm coming," Anna said, mounting the slippery steps, her flashlight trained upward, and then outward when she was actually in the attic...until the jaundiced beam played over the still form of Arlene Campbell, which was lying just to the side of the now-opened trapdoor, her mouth sagging open, her eyes staring up at Anna, past torn tatters of eyelids.

"Ohjeezusohmigodno!" Anna screamed, almost dropping the flashlight, as the old woman shifted ever so slightly at Anna's feet, and the blood-streaked mouth formed words:

"Anna, you *came.*"

Careful not to fall down through the open trapdoor, Anna hunkered down in the acrid-musty attic and whispered, "Yes, Arlene, I'm here.... Oh, *Arlene,* why? *Why?* We were going to go together."

Down by the open doorway, the old woman weakly shook her head and tried to hold up a worn, wrinkled hand, saying softly,

"You...didn't know. Thought...thought *I did*, but...wrong. Worse, worse than...we thought. Anna...the amulet...it's *two* now."

Still holding Bruiser, Anna got down on one knee, her other leg hanging out into space, as she soothed, "Shhh...you need help. I'll go call—"

The old woman reached up and grabbed Anna's arm with surprising strength. With ebbing strength that seemed to leech from her body into Anna's with each word, she said:

"No...time. Lucy...*split* it. Was angry. I wouldn't *look*, so she ran forward while...holding one end...it broke, so now Lucy has the... bee...tle...left the...rest...with...*her*." Then, as if sensing that she only had seconds left to say an hour's worth of farewells, Arlene said, "Babies. Take my babies, take care...Anna." The staring eyes under the ruined lids, the fragile flaps of crepey flesh that Lucy— either as herself, or as something sharp-clawed and furious—had raked in rage, turned whitely inwards, and just before Arlene Campbell's hand relaxed, lifeless, and let go of Anna's forearm, the young woman felt the older one give her arm an affectionate squeeze.

"A...ah...ahn-na?"

Bruiser started to growl again. As Anna felt his body stiffen through her jacket and sweatshirt sleeve, she told herself, *It's an echo. This attic echoes,* until she heard the awkward shuffling and the voice wholly unsupported by breath again said her name.

Moving cat-quick, Anna whipped the flashlight's beam in the direction of the sound and the voice...and wanted to gasp but didn't have the breath for it when she saw what was pinned in the yellow beam of cruel, defining light. What was standing there in the attic, *smiling* at her.

ELEVEN—*Gramma Husa*

Anna had to grab onto the edge of the trapdoor hole with her free hand to keep from falling through the opening when Lucy Miner's beloved Gramma smiled at her. Breathing hard through her mouth, unable to speak for a few seconds, Anna could only stare at the figure standing a few feet away from her, that dark figure with skin the color and texture of June bug wings, topped by a head of almost cobwebby softness and color. That heretofore undefinable insect-dry-rot-spoiling preserves odor was strong now, even overpowering...but not altogether *unpleasant,* for there was a new scent in the dank air that almost obscured the odor of mummification and long-ago decay. The delicate bouquet of peaches....

"Ahn...*na*," the voice said again, and as the dried husk of a woman spoke, Anna could see that her face skin actually *cracked* with the effort. Tiny flakes of withered flesh scattered like winter ashes on snow across her dusty white gown, shifting down her bosom.

"You killed her," Anna hissed softly, anger rising in her like bile. "You killed my *friend.*"

The brown stick woman shook her head; creases in the chitinous flesh broke with a fingernails-flicking sound. "Nuhohhh..."

Swallowing down sour spittle, Anna tightened her grip on the struggling, hissing cat and said, "*Lucy* did this then? *Your* Lucy?" her voice rising, growing thin with anger.

Lucy's gramma moved closer; Anna could hear the mummy's unlubricated joints *scree* with the effort. And as the mummified body inched closer, Anna saw something in the flashlight's circle of light that stunned her, even more so than the actual corpse. Attached to the right arm was a lacy glove, stuffed with something peach-colored and prickly, adorned with ribbons, bows, and little embroidered roses, and secured to the sleeve of the dingy nightgown with ribbons and dark-headed baby's safety pins.

Lucy's gramma held out her potpourri-smelling "hand" and said, "Muh-my *Looo-cee,* moo-made it fuh-for her g*ramma.*"

And most awful of all, the old woman, the old *corpse*, was smiling, proud of her new hand. All Anna wanted to do was crawl off somewhere and *cry...*both for herself and the pitiful *being* that stood there beaming down at Anna, and for her own grandmother, too. Lucy *had* loved her Gramma, in a twisted way no one had ever really understood, in an evil-wonderful-*pure* way no one could *ever* comprehend.

Unable to look at the withered husk in the dusty, mildew-dotted gown, Anna panned the flashlight across the attic, even as the thing kept on speaking to her, anxious to explain.

There were dolls nestled in the floor joists, a dozen or more, holding tiny bouquets, and an old comforter, brown-dotted with bloodstains.

"*Ahn-na...Looo-ceee* left...buh-but be-forr you go...must tuh-tell yooou—"

—and next to that, little Lucy's robe, balanced on one of the joists, along with the child's tea set, the three cups waiting be filled with tea, and a pretend wedding cake topped with two tiny figures, all in readiness for a macabre feast—

"—nuh-not long...not long to...*live*"—even in breathless un-death, the woman's voice was ironic, *comprehending*—"the *braaacelet, Looo-ceee* broke it, took thu-the rest of it...luh-less *puh-power*...for my *half*—"

—and three little chairs from the years when Lucy was small, dragged up through the trapdoor and arranged up here, in this awful playroom. And on one of the tiny pink enameled chairs rested the sunken, dusty-furred bow-necked stretched-out body of a white cat with irregular gray splotches, the extended paws withered, with fac-eted nubs of faded pink and black pads, the eyelids mere sunken squiggles, the moistureless mummified gums pulled back from curv-ing yellow-ivory incisors—while on the other chair rested an old wedding gown and veil.

(Good lord, that's Aunt Bella's cat—my grandfather. She kept him.)

"Ahn-na...puh-leeease...*lisss-en-*"

Anna returned the flashlight's beam to the face of the brown be-ing. The pupils of the shriveled eyes were past contracting, past di-lating, only hard, dry marbles set in that multifaceted counte-nance...and Anna realized that even as the thing spoke, it was weak-ening, losing little flakes and dustings of husklike flesh.

"Where did you get that amulet Lucy has?" Anna asked, her voice quiet but forceful as she knelt next to Mrs. Campbell, feeling the warmth seep out of Arlene's body as the dusty-gowned entity spoke:

"Thuh...*old* cuh-country...Prauuuge. Puh-paaarlor maaaid tuh-to a guh-glass muh-manufaaacturer, muh-Missster *Nezvaaal.* Hisss fruh-friend was...archaeolllogist, suh-sent it thu-to hiiim. Eeeevil maaan, Muh-Missster Nezvaaal. At-at-attacked meee...haaad hisss *waaay.* Guh-get *eeeven*...tuh-took suh-somethiiing fruh-from out of wuh-wooden buh-box on thuh taaable—gold and greeen braaa-celet... pretty. Un-untiiil I *heh-held* it...claaawed hiiim...to *death.* Run...run awaaay...huh-hid it in muh-my skiiirt...buh-black skiiirt...in hem...on buh-boat...tuh-to thisss coun-treee...skiiirt gruh-grew *powerfuuul*... fruh-from the braaa-celet. Wuh-words *in* the braaa-celet. Ah-and *Looo-ceee,* she haaas it nuh-now...baaad *guh-girrrl.*"

"Why did Lucy kill my friend?" Anna asked through tears; but the withered husk remained silent. The story the dried shadow of a woman had told Anna rang true in its simplicity, and Anna's imagi-nation quickly filled in the details the withered, helpless woman could not:

She had been a maid in the household of a Mr. Nezval, a man probably rich enough to think he could get away with anything. But he didn't count on the victim of his desire stealing something to settle the score. And Mr. Nezval, in all likelihood, probably didn't realize what sort of an amulet he'd been sent from what was most likely his friend's latest dig in Egypt or a surrounding land. If he'd had an inkling, Nezval had been stupid enough to leave the amulet lying around where a despoiled and angry servant could grab it. And Anna couldn't blame the woman for wanting to steal something, probably to hock—nor did Anna blame her great-great-grandmother for what happened afterward, certainly not under the circumstances.

But with the explanation came other questions—far too many for this disintegrating creature to answer—so Anna hugged Bruiser close and chose her words carefully.

"Have you been...*this* way ever since that night...when Alvin Miner did that"—she aimed the beam at that exquisite, grotesque prosthesis—"to you?"

"Yesss," came the sad, defeated reply, the "ssses" reverberating in the dank attic. "Up heeere...*Looo-ceee caarrried* meee in her *teeth*...luh-like a kiiitten in a caat's muh-mouth...ooohnly, sheee was a luh-lion." And as if suspecting that Anna might fmd her words incredible, Gramma Husa shifted slightly, to reveal a jagged arc of tooth holes in her gown, before going on, "Sheee *plaaayed* with-meee, puh-put braaa-celet on meee and weee'd plaaay...buh-but *Looo-ceee* never gruh-grew, uuh-pah-up."

"*Why?* Why...did she kill my friend?"

Marble eyes rolled as the flaking lips moved, like the rusted mechanism of an antique metal doll. "Whu-waitingfuh-for *yooou...Looo-ceee* thu-thought it waaasss yooou, puh-playing huh-hide ah-and go *seeek. Looo-ceee* thuh-thoughtyooou cuh-came up thuh traaapduh-door...thu-then she saw it waaasssn't yooou thuh wuh-wuhmaaanwuh-whouldn't luh-loook at meee...duh-didn't luh-like what sheee saaaw. The wuh-wuhmaaan tried to leave, waaarn yoo-outuh staaay awaaay. *Loooceee* ra-raaan forwaaard, buh-but sheee waaas huh-holding thuh braaace-let...I duh-didn't let *guhh-go...*it stretched...buh-broke. Looo*ceee* duh-didn't kun-caaare, fuh-for Looooceee guh-got so juh-jealouss...wuh-wuhmaaan suh-said *your* nuh-name, and Looooceee wuh-wanted her luh-little guh-girl all tooo her*self wuh-wanted* to be a gruh-gruuureat-gruh-maaa, luh-like meee...wuh-wanted yuh to...to...," and the tall flaking creature only briefly glanced toward the small mumfied cat before going on sadly, "Wuh-wanted yuh to bee haapy-luh-like *weee* were...."

Anna hung her head, resting her chin on Bruiser's hackles, letting the raised fur brush her mouth as she whispered, "And the others? She killed them...to make me *happy*?"

"Tuh-tooo luv-fff her...to muh-make you luv-fff her luh-like she luv-fffed meee...." The memory of a voice was regretful, the syllables trailing off in sorrowful static.

Even you realize it...dead over fifty years and you know you can't make anyone love you...but little girls don't know things like that, do they? Little girls like Lucy with no friends, and parents who don't seem to care.

"—and grandchildren who don't care either," she mouthed into Bruiser's fur. Never mind that the old lady was intrinsically unlovable, unlikable...*she* didn't understand that about herself. All Lucy had known was that she wanted love, wanted to keep hold of the only love she'd known.

Suddenly Anna's thoughts were interrupted when something glinting and gold caught her eye—something that was shifting on the brown woman's real hand.

It was the snake head end of the amulet, and a bit of the coiled body—just enough to fit around a withered parody of a little finger... but the golden stub of a body was undulating now, dropping off the flesh to land with a most unmetallic thud on one of the joists. And in the second before it fell, Anna flashed the golden cone of light onto Lucy's Gramma, where she saw not panic over impending dissolution, but a relaxed expression of eternal peace before the body in the flowing gown crumpled, crunching inward until it could stand no more and collapsed, to nearly vanish in a cloud of thick dust and swirling, floating strands of kinked hair among the raised floor joists.

And Bruiser was out of Anna's arms, jumping for the wiggling stubby end of the broken amulet, his strong black body arcing and diving among the joists, until he bounded back to Anna, golden wormlike object jerking in his jaws.

Anna pulled the sheet of foil out of her pants pocket, and shielding her fingers with it, she grabbed Bruiser by the scruff of the neck with her free hand, then yanked the golden tail of the amulet out of his mouth with her foil-protected hand. The snake head was *warm* through the foil, throwing off heat like the coil of an electric stove, but *moving,* too. She could feel the minuscule jaws open and close, snapping, snapping....

Panting, Anna twisted the foil around the hitching quicksilver-fluid segment, then shoved the bundle in the tiny zippered pocket above her left breast, where it flopped weakly for a few seconds, then rolled up and grew still and cold.

What had Lucy's Gramma said? That the "braaa-celet" wasn't as strong, as powerful, now that it was broken in two? *What was it, old woman? Didn't you enjoy seeing your precious Lucy in action? Did it finally dawn on you...did you finally* realize *what a* "baaad guh-girl" *Lucy was all along?* thought Anna, as she walked down the blood-splattered risers, Bruiser squirming under her arm, and hurried along the hallway and down the stairs, regretful over leaving Arlene's body *(Oh, Jesus, Arlene's eyelids were tattered! I know you wanted love, old lady, but her eyelids were shredded!),* yet anxious to get herself to the Yablinski house a quarter of a mile away from here. For if Great-great-gramma Husa was right, little Lucy was going to be in for a nasty surprise soon. And Anna wanted to make sure she was around when little Lucy's fun came to an abrupt, writhing end.

TWELVE—The Sewer Plant

When Anna left the blighted Miner house, the wind had picked up a brisk, yet capricious breeze not strong enough to move in more warming cloud cover, but enough to make the leaves scuttle down the street, the oak leaves tumbling end-over-end, stiff—clawed and clutching, the smaller, oval elm leaves skittering flat and mouselike along the pavement, their surfaces mottled gold-brown-red in the distant street lamp's glow.

Hugging the growling Bruiser against her, Anna walked into the wind, head bent, in a southerly direction, only looking up to see if she was nearing an intersection before bending her face again. She was almost at the end of Evans Street, getting ready to cross the intersection and head for Lumbermill Drive, when she saw her grandmother...or what Lucy Miner had once *rightfully* been, the little girl who loved her Gramma so much she wanted people to *appreciate* her revived Gramma, enough to risk breaking apart her most precious posession, just so Gramma could see little Lucy as she used to be...not even realizing the consequences of her actions.

You were right, Arlene...she wanted her wings, Anna thought as she watched the little girl in the tentlike white gown and the fluttering gray cardboard wings walk down Lumbermill Drive, her long hair flowing behind her, almost covering the place where the paper wings were attached to her nightgown. When Lucy moved, Anna could just make out dark printing on the undersides of the wings—

the pattern on the other side of the cat food box. Lucy had left the two rounded "wings" attached to the narrow spine that formed one of the sides of the box, so that they seemed to flutter as she walked barefoot down the street, her soles making faint *slapping* noises as she moved forward, her back to Anna, an old pillowcase full of candy slapping against her bare legs. Faintly, her rotted odor wafted in Anna's direction.

No children walked with little Lucy Miner; some passed her, a few paused to stare at her odd homemade costume and bare feet, but none of them would fall into step with her—none wanted to linger near the smelly little girl with the Friskies cat food wings.

Lucy was only fifteen feet from Anna now, near enough to hear her granddaughter's booted footfalls and hitching, chuffing breath, but she seemed oblivious to Anna, unmindful that she was being tailed.

Bruiser's growl resolved into a snarl so strident that a group of children half a block away stopped, turned around, listened, then ran off, screaming and shouting. Little Lucy Miner froze. Turning around, looking into the darkness at the face of her grown grand-daughter, Lucy started to give Anna that familiar old half-assed smile—and then she saw Bruiser, struggling to jump out of Anna's arms and rip apart the little girl in the ersatz angel costume.

Lunging forward so quickly she felt some muscles strain pain-fully in her shoulder and arm, Anna grabbed Bruiser by his scruff just before he vaulted out of reach. In the half second before Lucy dropped her bag of candy and ran into a pool of darkness between the reach of the street lamps, Anna saw the liquid glint of gold and cats-eye green around the girl's upper arm, and felt the remaining third of the amulet wiggling in her jacket pocket.

Anna ran forward, into the wind and scudding leaves, past the dropped pillowcase full of treats, and into the dark stretch of Lum-bermill Drive, where no porch lights gleamed, and little light fell, save for cloud-hazed moonlight. A sudden gust picked up a loose guttered mound of leaves and blew them into her face, their cold, brittle surfaces briefly catching on her knit cap before drifting away with a dry, scuttering sound. But just as the wind started to die down, a clawed maple leaf, its surface richly veined in gold with a trace of green, came flying for her face, and scratched her cheek with its passing, its surface heavy and warm, like a misshapen, with-ered hand.

"Damn you, Lucy!" Anna screamed after the wickedly sharp points of the heavy leaf dug into her skin, leaving five aching bloody lines on her left cheek, before it blew past her head and van-

ished in the darkness behind her, one of half a million similar wind-blown leaves...until Lucy decided what *else* to become.

"Who *could* love you, you *witch*?" she screamed, not caring if any children heard her, or if any doors were opened in puzzled curiosity and people stuck their heads outside, listening and watching. Tucking Bruiser under her arm like a squirming football, and squeezing him tightly, Anna cut across Lumbermill Drive until she hit the residential remains of Ewert Avenue, and kept running until the pain in her lungs would let her run no more, and she doubled over, her lungs straining for air, wheezing and sobbing in the cold darkness, "You didn't have to *kill* her. You *didn't*. How *can* I love you? You're *evil*." As she neared the abandoned Yablinski house, and the sewer plant beyond, Anna could hardly walk, could hardly take a breath deep enough to let her know how close to the sewer plant she really was.

Feeling like a deflating rubber ball, the breath hissing out of her mouth in a trailing plume of steamy white, Anna wound up walking almost on all fours, her back bent over so far her knuckles touched the ground with each step. She couldn't remember when she'd let go of Bruiser, and she wasn't aware that the foil-wrapped remains of the amulet had dropped from the pocket she'd forgotten to zip closed until she saw her cat streak past her, something glinting and wiggling in his strong ivory teeth.

"No...*no*. *Bru-Bru*—" Anna wailed, as she painfully straightened up and tried to see where the black animal had gone, but this section of town was thinly inhabited, and only a couple of houses on the block had even so much as interior lights on, let alone bright porch lights.

To her right was the Yablinski house, dark and empty. Anna wished that there had been snow *tonight*, so she could clearly see if there were any tiny footprints leading up to the door...but then the flash of white caught her eye, just a bit of lightness darting out of the drooping hydrangea bush near the corner of the house closest to the line of trees that camouflaged the sewer plant by the river. On aching legs, Anna stumbled over to get a better look. In the moonlight she saw something small and white-furred being chased by something bigger, a patch of moving blackness against the slightly lighter, frost-specked ground.

Bruiser. He was chasing Lucy toward the river, toward the large round white structure surmounted by a smaller, square-shaped gray stucco building—the sewer plant—the remainder of the amulet in his mouth, wiggling like golden bait in the murky moonlight, as if in anticipation of being reunited with its missing section.

Panting deeply as she trotted behind Bruiser, Anna crossed the dirt road that bisected the line of pines hiding the sewer plant from the street beyond. A faint waste odor washed over her, until she felt almost too dizzy to keep walking, and spots of squiggling blackness chased each other across her line of sight.

In the distance, across an uneven landscape of bare ground, irregular patches of scrubby grass, lopsided towers of used truck tires, mounds of broken asphalt from the street repair project this past summer, and a few broken-down gas pumps for fueling the city trucks, Anna could just make out the dark shape pursuing the smaller, lighter one, and once, when the clouds drifted off the moon's face, she saw *three* flashes of green on the body of the feline thing Lucy had become—two for eyes, and one green blotch close to its shoulder, up near the neck—before Bruiser chased Lucy behind a jagged mound of stacked asphalt chunks. Anna followed, her boots slipping on patches of frost. She didn't dare lose her footing, for fear she wouldn't have the strength to get up again.

The sewer plant made a subtle *whoosh-swoosh* sound, not much louder than the sluggish-running river one hundred yards to the west. As Anna kept moving in the direction she'd last seen Bruiser and the transformed old lady running, something came back to her, as she panted and huffed out under the moon's colorless idiot grin, in this blasted, lonesome, stinking place—*The scarab is a dung beetle. They roll balls of it from east to west,* and then she caught sight of Bruiser, but he wasn't chasing the white cat-thing anymore, he was trying to jump up, extended, as something flew above his head, just out of reach.

Anna had to move so that Bruiser was positioned between her line of sight and the ghostly stucco surface of the sewer plant beyond before she could make out what the cat was looking at—a huge dark bird, as big or bigger than a ringed pheasant, but black, all black, save for the glistening of pale green on one of its wings. The talons on the thing were massive and cruel; they shone in the moonlight as Lucy toyed with the leaping cat, letting those enormous talons skim the top of the cat's broad head, until Bruiser made a mouth-closed, strangled sound, and Anna saw something dark and moist shining between his small tufted ears.

"Don't you *touch* him!" Anna screamed, running forward on rubbery legs to grab for the bird, but her grandmother was loosely flapping her wings so that she was just out of Anna's reach, excreting watery pale blobs of guano that splatted noisily on the hard-packed dirt below, *teasing* Anna and her cat. The bird then took off toward the river, and in frustration Anna screamed, "I hope you fall in and fucking *drown* before you reach the other side!"

The bird heard her; lazily it flapped back to Anna, swooping and diving for her hat, pulling it off with a motion that left Anna's scalp bleeding. As the blood dripped down her forehead, into her eyes, Anna lifted Bruiser up and held the cat in the air, the stub of the amulet still quivering between his black-tipped jaws, screaming, "It's no damn *good* anymore! You *ruined* it! It fell *off* her! She's *dust*—nothing but June bug wings in the attic! You weakened your little *pet* when you split it! You stupid old *bat*."

Anna saw the bird pull *into* itself in midflight; first there was a long stretch of wings over a huge dark body, then the lines of the creature grew wavery and indistinct against the moonlit scud of clouds, almost graying in color, like old melted tallow, before it regained definition and swooped down at her, a tiny thing with wide, leathery, membraned wings, and minute pointed ears above a squeaking sharp-toothed mouth, with a rough oval of green below.

Instinctively, Anna bent down, covering her exposed tangle of hair with her arms, but instead of feeling the bat feet raking her scalp—

(But Mama, I saw her: she was a bat, a bat flying out of the bedroom. Why won't you believe me, Mama?)

—she heard a hoarse, choked snarl, followed by a futile, leathery flutter of wings, strangely close to the ground. Uncovering her head, Anna followed the sound until she discovered its source. A horrible fight was taking place over by the sewer plant's main rounded building—two dark shapes were jerking and rolling in sharp relief against the pale stucco.

Bruiser pinned the bat against the wall, until it bit him and he let it go long enough for it to melt into a smaller, lighter shape—a rat. The thing tried to dart away from the cat, but Bruiser pounced on it, powerful front paws wrapped around the pale hairy body, his hind legs digging at the exposed belly, while he bit down on the rat's spine, close to the neck. The rat screamed—not with a rodent's shrill screech, but with an almost *human* wail—and Anna ran forward, shrieking, "Bruiser, enough! Bruiser, get *off* her! Get away from Lucy!"

Bruiser looked Anna's way; it was too dark to read his expression, but Anna could sense his puzzlement. He was *saving* her, yet she wanted him to stop. But Anna couldn't let him kill Lucy, not while she was in *that* form.

Taking advantage of Bruiser's momentary pause in the fight, Anna shouted, "Baba! I want you, Baba. Please, Baba, *come back.*"

The shape in Bruiser's grasp melted, flowing outward, growing larger than the cat, larger than a dog, and Bruiser backed away, hackles rising, as the pulsing grayish blob of matter resolved itself into the old lady, her body barely covered by the torn child's nightgown she wore, the cardboard wings, crushed under her back.

The old lady's limbs jerked strangely, spasmodically, as Anna knelt beside her. Quickly Anna yanked off the amulet coiled around the old woman's arm with her gloved hand, hoping that the knitted covering would protect her from her *own* anger. She grasped the warm, undulating amulet and started to shove it in her pocket when she saw the brilliant yellow headlights and flashing red and white lights arc around from the east to illuminate the nearby towers of tires, the jagged clusters of broken asphalt, and the far side of the building, close to where she was crouched down, and heard Bib Stanley's amplified voice bleat, *"Anna—if Lucy Miner is here, stay away from her. Anna, come out, now."* She felt the scarab-mounted coil ooze through her grasping fingers, to drop to the ground. Seconds later, Bruiser leaped forward to pounce the limply flapping thing, then ran off to Anna's left, heading homeward, both pieces of the squirming amulet dangling from his jaws.

Behind her to the right, Anna heard Bib saying, *"It's just me, Anna. And I know. Your great-granddad, he warned me."*

"Daddy?" came the gurgling burble from the old lady, and Bib, homing in on the sound, hurried over to stand next to Anna, staring down in stunned muteness at the broken old body clad in the pathetic remains of an angel costume lying close to the sewer plant, until he found his voice.

"Yes, Lucy...*your* daddy...only daddy's dead, Lucy."

"Noooo!" the old lady cried, her limbs jerking of their own volition, resembling those of a beetle lying helpless on its back—*like Gregor Samsa, in Kafka's story...he wound up dying too,* Anna found herself thinking, as the old lady's lips went blue in the cold moonlight. Beside Anna, Bib asked in a hushed whisper, "You okay, kiddo?"

Anna nodded her bleeding head, blurting out, "Fine," before remembering that that very word had led to the death of a person she loved not an hour ago. Turning her head away from the old lady, she whispered to Bib, "Lucy...tried to kill me. She killed—killed Arlene Campbell. She's...Arlene's in the attic...with Mrs. Husa's—"

The old lady gave them that vacant smile at the sound of her gramma's name before mouthing it silently. Bib said, "She's in shock. I'll call an—"

"No, Bib," Anna said, leaning over the old lady. "Bruiser did a number on her, a good one—didn't he, Baba?" The old lady nodded, her scalp streaming with tiny ribbons of blood, as Anna coaxed, "Can you tell the nice man what you did for me? To those mean people who were hurting me? About what you did to them because...." Anna's voice quivered, but she got the last out, in a faint whisper, "because you wanted Anna to love her Baba?"

"Well...*do* you?" came the weak singsong. Bib winced and turned his head away, reflexively rubbing his palm against his stubble-covered cheek. The rasping carried far in the chilly darkness, a lonely, small sound.

Anna nodded, thinking, *All this bloodshed, in the name of love. And what Arlene Campbell did, because she didn't think I could handle the old lady alone, that was a form of love, too.*

The weight of her head was bigger than the world, bigger than the mass of all the bought bodies resting inside, and she cried silently as Lucy Miner gurgled out a boastful confession for the nice man standing next to her little Anna before her eyes closed one last time, and she joined her gramma in a place where they could sit on the front porch all day long, whispering, giggling and telling each other all sorts of secret things known only to grammas and the little girls who loved them.

THIRTEEN—Bruiser (2)

Bruiser curled as best he could behind the bushes near the far corner of the house when the car with the revolving many-colored lights parked in front of his Person's house, hiding his aching, scratched and bitten body in the shadows, until he heard his Person's voice: "Oh, and Bib? Before she...Arlene asked me to take care of her ba—pets. Should I go there now or—"

Then the voice of a male Person Bruiser didn't know: "I'll have someone from the department stay in her house tonight. You can pick up the animals come morning...that okay?"

Bruiser's Person said something too soft for Bruiser to hear (ever since the funny-tasting things had wiggled into his mouth and slid down his throat as he ran home, his hearing was *different,* not as sharp as before), and then Bruiser heard the sound of feet impacting on the curb, followed by a muted rubbery crunch on asphalt and a low engine roar, fading quickly.

His Person turned on her flashlight with a tiny *click.* Soon the grass was sparkling before her as she stepped up to the porch and shone the small yellow light all across the front of the house, softly calling: "Bru-Bru, come out...Momma won't burt you. It's all right, Bruiser, you were a *good* boy. Everything's gonna be all right. Precious won't have to go to jail. Bib is gonna take the pair of the old lady's scissors I found and claim that Wally was killed with those. Bruisie, c'mon out. It's okay, baby, it's all over now. Momma's home, Brupie, and it's all right. *C'mon,* Bru-Bru, I see your eyes, you can—"

Timidly, Bruiser quit the bushes, letting his torn head and still-bloody mouth come into view, as his Person reflexively took a step backwards and lowered the beam of her light away from his face. It was hard for Bruiser to see his Person's face in the darkness. Even his eyesight was changed, now that the hard yet strangely soft thing was within him, nestled just under his neck, resting between the wings of his collarbone. With a rustle of dried brown branches and leaves, Bruiser tried to come forward through the bushes, but each movement was painful. The dead branches and stiff leaves hurt his tender flesh. He let out a small cry of anguish over his aching skin, his ruined eyesight and hearing, and when she heard him. His Person trained the beam on him again, letting the light play over his face, his chest.

"Oh my god. Oh, *Bruiser,* you *didn't...*no, no, wait, baby, c'mon back here, don't run off."

Bruiser hunkered down, chest and belly to the ground, head turned away in shame. His Person's voice was anguished, and he felt shame for having done something to displease her, to displease the only Person he loved.

Then his Person was saying softly, gently, "Oh Bru-Bru, what *happened?* Did you swallow it, baby? Or did it do this to you?" Her fingers touching the slightly raised bump where the thing rested just under his flesh, she said: "C'mon, Bruisie, have to get into the house. No, Bru-Bru, Momma *can't* carry you. C'mon, follow me... no, no, Bruiser, don't walk like *that,* you can't...*do* that anymore. C'mon, Momma'll tend to those scratches. Yes, you were a good boy. C'mon now, *yes,* that's it. C'mon, we go inside now."

And when Bruiser followed his Person inside, he realized how beautiful she was in his eyes, how it had been worth it to lose all the things that he had been, out of love for his Person. For when he looked at her face she said softly: "You did good, Bru-Bru...you made Momma proud," her fingers moving past the place where the gold-green thing shone through his skin with a faint illumination all its own, and kissing the top of his scratched head, whispered, "Bruiser, I thought it all ended back there, near the river...but it won't ever end for us, will it? Perhaps it was meant to be this way."

Bruiser didn't understand everything she said, but he understood her tone and her meaning.

He wouldn't have to leave this house, like he'd had to leave his first home because he was no longer small and cuddly anymore. His Person still loved him, regardless of the way he looked now. That was compensation for all the familiar things he'd lost, and for all the unknown things he'd gained.

EPILOGUE

Walking carefully between the precariously stacked rows of full shopping bags, and piled books that comprised all she'd wanted to take away from the house of her grandmother—all that she could bear to take with her—Anna Sudek carried the bundle of letters the postman had just left in her mailbox into the dining room. One of Arlene Campbell's cats was rattling the bathroom doorknob, and a fuzzy orange paw snaked out through the narrow space between the bathroom and the floor. Over her shoulder, Anna warned, "You be good in there," glad that Arlene's dogs did little more than sleep away the day, as she made her way to the cluttered dining room table, near where Bruiser was sitting on a big box of books. He silently watched her open and set aside the letter from the realtor handling the sale of the old lady's house, the sympathy card signed by her co-workers in the station, the "In Your Time of Sorrow" card from Terry Von Kemp (inside Terry had scribbled, "Sorry to hear about what happened, and just plain sorry"), a bill for the autopsy, along with a photocopy of the death certificate Anna had requested, just to remind herself that the old lady *was,* indeed, dead and gone. (Death due to shock, exposure, severing of the lower spinal cord, as well as blood loss," according to doddering Doc Calder.) Plus a letter to Anna, written in a handwriting she knew quite well.

Anna turned Tina's letter over and over in her hands for a minute or so, looking at the Eau Claire return address written in her mother's handwriting in the upper left-hand corner, and at her own name written across the front of the pink envelope, and the cute stylized cartoon of a kitten adorning the back flap, before she took the letter into the kitchen and, as she leaned on the counter under the mossy remains of her mother's previous correspondence, carefully wrote, "Addressee Moved—Return to Sender" across the front of the envelope, then scribbled out her own address.

Anna knew that what she was doing was cruel—unnecessarily so, since her mother had also gone through hell at Lucy Miner's hands—but considering what Anna knew (what Anna could never, *ever* forget), there was simply no way Anna could tell a little of what had happened in the past two weeks without telling her mother *everything*—and Anna doubted that her mother could stand that knowledge.

She probably remembers that cat her poor aunt owned—the one I buried in the backyard of the old lady's house. I could barely stand finding out. I have no idea what it would be like to actually have known the animal.

With a sigh, Anna placed the unopened letter on the counter, facedown, thinking, *What she's probably read in the papers is enough. I know the news was in the Eau Claire papers—I saw the headline about it the other day. It would only be a greater cruelty to fill her in on the details*—as she picked up another envelope off the counter, this one unstamped.

The same one Bib had handed Anna as she cleaned out her locker at the station yesterday, the one containing the letter of recommendation for that clerk-matron's job downstate.

"Anna, I know you don't want to talk about...uh, what happened down by the sewer plant, so I won't go into that, but I wish you'd tell me what happened to that thing of your grandmother's."

"Do you really want to know about it?" she'd asked, not looking at Bib, who started to say something about "this professor guy" he'd met in Wright County, who claimed that the amulet could fetch a pretty penny, until Bib cleared his throat and mumbled, "Just as long as that thing won't be causing no more harm."

"It's harmless now. Trust me, okay? It'll never...do anything again. No more deaths. Just don't ask me where it is. You wouldn't like the answer."

"That bad?" Bib hunkered down next to where Anna stood, so she couldn't help but see his worried face. And she'd taken her sweet time before replying, "Not bad...just something you'd have a hell of a time rationalizing. But I can handle it."

"Don't doubt *that*," Bib had snorted, with a wry smile.

"You're one tough little cookie, know that? But you aren't bad—not like that grandmother of yours. I 'spose I should ask you where that thing is, but you aren't Lucy Miner, so...it's forgotten, okay? History."

History. *Yeah, it is at that,* Anna thought, as she looked up from Bib's letter, past the kitchen into the dining room, where Bruiser was still perched on one of the packing boxes, while Mouth sat on the floor at his feet, growling softly, her dark striped tail thumping against the carpeting with a muted *whump,* and said, "Sometimes it isn't worth it, reopening the old wounds, is it, Bru? Not if the infection is preferable to the cure. Sometimes...it's best to just cut ties and go."

* * * * * * *

The confession and death of Lucy Miner had been the talk of the Rusty Hinge for six days running now. Coroner Lenny Wilkes patiently endured the comments of his drinking buddies ("Couldn't you've worn a different shirt, Len? Yellow's not your color either.") when his red-cheeked face appeared on the six o'clock news on Channel Thirteen *and* Channel Eighteen; Palmer Winston loudly proclaimed that Lucy Miner had been "no damn good from the second she first drew breath. Only girl in town I wouldn't have thought of...*you* know."

Palmer Nemmitz claimed that his wife Bitsy's cousin, Sheriff Stu Sawyer, insisted that Chief of Police Bib Stanley couldn't have possibly just been lucky enough to figure out exactly where Lucy Miner was skulking around on Halloween night, let alone had the time to read the old shrew her rights before she croaked, no matter what that granddaughter of hers claimed, and Wayne Mesabi just kept on urging everyone to buy his Old Dutch chips, and never mind *how* Bib Stanley got the confession out of Lucy Miner.

"A confession's a confession," Wayne began to say late that afternoon, as he popped a fried corn curl in his mouth, but ex-English teacher Palmer Winston finished the thought for him—"is a confession is a confession. I don't care how Bib got it, just as long as all this hoo-hah is over with. Waste of my tax money, all this investigating and interviewing."

Lenny Wilkes sighed. "But you guys didn't see them *bodies.* I mean I ain't *never* seen noth—"

"What burns me is how that old nut case Alv Miner was sittin' in that private nursing home on *our dime*," Mesabi mumbled around a mouthful of half-chewed blaze orange cheese curls, "'stead of being where he *ought* to be."

"Oh, let it rest, Wayne. What's done is done. Who knew *what* Lucy Miner was thinking when she did...*that* to Arlene Campbell?" Nemmitz asked before taking a noisy, slurping pull on his can of Leinenkugel's, then wiping dribbles of pale beer off his thin lips and gray-stubbled chin, and setting the red and white can down on the imitation wood table with a sloshing *thunk.*

Nemmitz's lifetime buddy Palmer Winston started to say, "Oh, did Lucy really *think?* I always assumed she acted on instinct, like an ani—" until Nemmitz kicked Winston under the table and whispered, "Shut up...her grandchild's coming in here."

All four men stopped drinking and eating, and even Arnie the bartender stopped watching "Win, Lose, or Draw," turning around to stare when Anna Sudek and her companion walked through the door. Anna was dangling a set of car keys from the fingers of her left hand, and was holding an envelope in the other.

Palmer Winston was the only one of the four men sitting around the table who was close enough to her to actually read the embossed return address on the envelope, and later on, he said over a third can of squaw piss, "It was Bib Stanley's official Chief of Police stationery, and there wasn't a stamp on it, either—just 'Chief something-or-other, Milwaukee Police Department' on the front, as if she was going to *hand* it to someone, like a résumé."

And standing just a foot or so behind Anna was a young man in his mid-thirties or so, not exceptionally tall, but powerfully built, with big shoulders and a thick, pale neck under a head of slightly wavy, glossy black hair. But his tan-flecked green eyes were shy, slightly downcast, as he stood near Anna. He was wearing Anna's silvery Rusty Hinge stadium jacket, a pair of dark blue corduroy jeans, and a soft pair of moccasin-like shoes (later on, Lenny Wilkes insisted that just this past Monday he'd thrown out a pair of slippers just *like* 'em, until Palmer Winston told Len to put a lid on it), and a slightly vacuous, if polite, toothy smile.

As she jingled the car keys, Anna said, "I just wanted to drop by and say good-bye to you fellows. I've put the houses on the market."

The two Palmers exchanged a wink, knowing full well that she was abandoning her little frame house to the FHA.

"—be leaving tomorrow morning—"

"Not on account of...*you* know," Wayne Mesabi began, until Palmer Nemmitz whispered, "You frigging *geek*," then turned halfway around in his scarred captain's chair to ask Anna, "You driving? Couldn't help but notice the keys."

Anna nodded, fingering the silvery keys as she replied, "Got my license yesterday afternoon. I've rented a van, but once I get downstate and work a while, I'll be buying my own. I...inherited Mrs. Campbell's pets. We're taking them along with us."

Palmer Winston winked and, indicating Anna's silent companion with his half-smoked Lucky Strike, asked, "You and your friend here? I don't think we've had the pleasure."

Anna's cheeks colored deeply, as she quickly said, "Mr. Winston, Mr. Nemmitz, Mr. Wilkes, Mr. Mesabi, this is...Bru. Bru, this is Palmer Winston, Palmer *Nemmitz*—"

"They only look like twins," Wayne Mesabi cut in, until two gray-haired Palmers each shot him a moue and a sour look.

"—and Lenny Wilkes." Behind Anna, the surnameless "Bru" nodded shyly and then began fingering the silver buttons on his satinette jacket, until Anna reached over and held his hand still, while she went on, "I just wanted to see all of you before we took off. I don't think we'll be coming up here to visit for quite a while, and...." She let her voice trail off; all the men in the bar knew what she meant.

Thanks to Bib and Anna Sudek finding Lucy Miner out by the sewer plant on Halloween night (the article in the *Herald clai*med that Anna Sudek had trailed Lucy there, following her discovery of Arlene Campbell's body and that *other* badly decayed corpse in the Miner house, and that Bib—who was en route to Anna's house to tell her of Alvin Miner's death—saw her heading for the sewer plant, even if Stu Sawyer *didn't* believe a word of the story), and Lucy's subsequent complete confession to Wally Inglass's murder while she lay dying of injuries sustained when she was attacked by an "unknown animal, large type," as the autopsy report stated, Precious Isaacs was now free in the custody of foster parents over in Lumbe. Lucy Miner's motives were supposedly a longstanding dislike of Wally Inglass, exacerbated by "recent developments" left unspecified in the *Herald.*

And while Anna Sudek wasn't blamed in *print,* or facing any charges, it was no secret that Stu Sawyer was itching to bring *some* sort of charges against her, or so Terry Von Kemp hinted to Lenny Wilkes after Lucy Miner's burial next to the last remaining fragment of her dear, long-dead gramma: "Stu's still fumin' 'bout him not bein' there when they found old Lucy. My Millie swears Stu thinks it would've helped him win bigger come election time."

So none of the men in the Rusty Hinge challenged Anna or protested when she said, "It's best I leave town. A lot of people'll be happy to see me go, and I hate to make them happy in that way, but it was making me too unhappy just to make sure they weren't. Am I making sense?" she asked, with a candor that took ten years off her, making her seem almost childlike, new again.

Palmer Winston spoke for his companions when he replied, "Just perfect, Anna. Sure there isn't some room for me in that van? I know a lot of people who'd be dancing in the streets if I were to quit this place."

From behind the bar came the sound of Arnie doing a Fred Astaire soft-shoe on the linoleum, and Mr. Winston shouted. "All right, Fred, hold your horses until Ginger shows up," then turned his attention back to Anna, teasing as he took a deep draw on his smoke, his blue eyes hooded. "If you go, we won't know what really happened out there. Bib's got his mouth shut so tight about it lately he can't even slip a straw 'tween his lips."

Anna smiled, and leaned back slightly against the solid and unspeaking Bru, saying, "Oh, there's been enough talk about this already. I think Bib just wants the matter to rest—I know *I* do. Oh geez, is it five-thirty already? Good to see you fellows, but we have to be running. Finish packing up the van, all that."

Anna and the men at the table said a round of good-byes, the silver-jacketed Bru remained silent, save for a smile and a closed-mouthed, surprisingly high-pitched grunt that might or might not have been a good-bye, and then the pair were gone from the bar, Bru following close at Anna's heels, once ducking his head to lightly butt her shoulder from behind, leaving the four men to their beer, their snacks, and their gossip.

Watching through the grime-whorled bar window as Anna and her friend got into the dark brown van, Palmer Winston tapped his smoke into the full black plastic ashtray near his can of beer, and mused expansively, "Never would've thought I'd live to see the day when Anna Sudek was making lovey eyes with some fellow."

"Looks more like a side of beef with hair," Mesabi groused around another mouthful of cheese curls, but Nemmitz snapped, "I'm *looking* at worse. At least he seems clean-cut."

"That's only 'cause you and him got green eyes," Mesabi grumped, while Lenny Wilkes began, "I don't understand how she got a license this fast."

"Bib probably *gave* her one, for helpin' catch old Lucy-goosie," Winston said, taking a deep puff of his smoke before adding, "You boys see that tattoo, near that Bru's throat, 'bout *here*?" The old man indicated the spot where the wings of his collarbone met, using the tip of his Lucky Strike as a pointer.

"Nope. You sure, or is that the squaw piss talking?" Mesabi asked, spraying the table with moist orange crumbs, but Winston insisted, "Yes, I am sure. It was a new one, still all puffed up. Looked kinda like a bug, in green."

Lenny Wilkes shook his head, saying, "Awful weird place to get tattooed. Downright painful. Say, any of you fellas *know* that guy?"

"Never seen him before," both Palmers said at once, but Wayne Mesabi, ever the wag, quipped, "Maybe Anna scavenged him out of some Dumpster."

"Get outta here," Nemmitz said, taking a look out the window at the van as it pulled away from the curb (clouds of dust billowed, luminous, in the street lamp light), into the cold November darkness, the deep blue sky just showing the first hint of the new moon. "Soft-hearted girl like Anna, she probably took some hitchhiker or home-less guy in, like a stray puppy."

"Kitten," Palmer Winston amended, almond-shaped eyes hooded under slightly jaundiced lids as he blew smoke at the window and the diminishing van beyond. "Fellow reminds me of...a *cat*. Don't know why. Deballed one, at that. See how he stood back there, quiet and obedient, behind her?"

"Don't matter where or how Anna found him...least she has *someone*," Lenny Wilkes said with a nod of his crew cut head toward the window, as he filched one of Mesabi's cheese curls and shoved it in his mouth. "Life's awful lonely without someone being there for you...no matter *where* he comes from."

"Or what he *is*," Winston added, too softly for the others to hear, pushing his unfinished can of Leinenkugel's away from him *(not only is this stuff pickling my liver, now it's playing tricks on my eyes)*, as he remembered how the quiet young man's tattoo had seemed to *move*, just a little, under his milk-pale skin, almost like it had a life of its own, he thought with just a hint of a shudder, before Anna's rented Ford van rounded the corner and the twin red tail-lights winked out of sight.

ABOUT THE AUTHOR

A. R. MORLAN published her first piece, a quiz, in *The Twilight Zone Magazine* in 1983, and her first story, the novelette "Four Days Before the Snow" (the first tale set in her fictional Wisconsin town of Ewerton) in 1985 in *Night Cry*. Since then she has penned many more short stories, quizzes, novelettes, and novellas in more than 100 different magazines, anthologies, and webzines, as well as erotica written under two different pennames (one male and one female). Most recently, she has focused primarily on science fiction, culminating in an appearance in the thirtieth anniversary issue of *Isaac Asimov's Science Fiction Magazine* in 2007. She is single and childless, although she is "owned" by many cats, with whom she shares her life in the upper Midwest.